The son of Galloway parents, James Barke moved to Glasgow in his teens, where he worked in the shipyards and participated actively in the local political and cultural life. His first play – *Gregarach* – was produced by the Scottish National Players in Glasgow when he was eighteen years of age, but the failure of the National Drama movement caused him to turn to novel-writing. His first novel – *The World His Pillow* – was published in 1933, and was followed by *The Wild Macraes* (1934), *The End of the High Bridge* (1935), *Major Operation* (1936) and *The Land of the Leal* (1939). The recurrent theme that pervades these stories of the Highlands and Islands is the sadness and bitterness of the empty valleys and glens, and of the men and women who had left – some moving to the cities of the south, some emigrating overseas.

All this was a prelude to the ambitious task that Barke resolutely set himself in re-creating the life of Robert Burns in a series of five novels. A lifetime of arduous research, combined with a novelist's rich talent, ensured that *The Wind that Shakes the Barley*, *The Song in the Green Thorn Tree*, *The Wonder of All the Gay World*, *The Crest of the Broken Wave* and *The Well of the Silent Harp* have deservedly been bestsellers and attained worldwide success.

James Barke died in 1958.

THE
WIND THAT SHAKES
THE BARLEY

·

A NOVEL
of the
LIFE & LOVES
of
ROBERT BURNS
·
by
JAMES BARKE

THE
BLACKSTAFF PRESS
BELFAST

First published in hardback in 1946 by
William Collins Sons and Company Limited, Glasgow
This Blackstaff Press edition is a photolithographic facsimile of the 1986
edition printed by William Collins Sons and Company Limited, Glasgow

This paperback edition published in 1992 by
The Blackstaff Press Limited
3 Galway Park, Dundonald, Belfast BT16 0AN, Northern Ireland
with the assistance of
The Arts Council of Northern Ireland

Printed by The Guernsey Press Company Limited

British Library Cataloguing in Publication Data
Wind That Shakes the Barley: Novel of the
Life and Loves of Robert Burns. – New ed
I. Title
823.914 [F]

ISBN 0-85640-488-8

TO

WIFE AND WEANS

without whose heroic
patience the book could
not have been written

NOTE

THIS is a novel; and since a novel is devised for entertainment it should be read for pleasure: or not at all.

It may be objected that since this novel deals with the life and loves of Robert Burns it is not in the strictest sense a work of fiction.

Maybe; but it is not biography. Good biography keeps to historical facts and draws its own conclusions. Fiction is not concerned with conclusions; but in so far as it can claim to be historical it must rear its creative edifice on solid factual foundation.

Here the reader may care to know how far this fictional life of Burns adheres to historical fact.

It does so much more firmly than the biographies.

This adherence to truth has cost me many pains and confronted me with many difficulties. It would have been simple to have invented pleasing fictions. But facts are chiels that winna ding. The historical novelist must be historically accurate. The creative artist who cannot thus discipline himself rules himself out of court.

Here and there (in the relation of the needle to the haystack) I have taken some liberty with the minor facts of history in order to achieve a profounder spiritual and artistic truth. Otherwise I have let the facts speak for themselves. If certain facts seem startling, or even alarming, I am not to blame that, hitherto, the biographers have found it more convenient to ignore them.

Not that I wish to minimise my debt to the Burns historians: my debt to them is incalculable.

Perhaps my debt to James C. Dick for his monumental work, *The Songs of Robert Burns*, is greatest. To the nineteenth century biographers and editors I owe great debt—especially to that grand old Tory, William Scott Douglas. Debts must also be acknowledged to William Wallace for his scholarly re-editing and re-writing of Robert Chambers's *Life and Works*; to T. F.

Henderson (despite his snobbish affectations) for his work on *The Centenary Edition*; and to Duncan MacNaught whose long editorship of *The Burns Chronicle* can never be forgotten. In acknowledging my debt to the diverse labours of men like Mr. J. C. Ewing and William Jolly, I acknowledge the labours of all such from Robert Heron to Mr. John S. Clarke and Mr. J. R. Campbell.

To modern American scholarship I owe a debt of incalculable magnitude. To Professors John DeLancey Ferguson, Franklyn Bliss Snyder and Robert T. Fitzhugh the non-academic Scot bows his thanks with humble deference.

But though academic mountains and a waste of years may divide the old Scots editors from the new American scholars, they are brothers under the skin.

It fell to Mr. William Stewart, the Grand Old Man of Scottish Reform, to write the greatest book on Robert Burns: greatest because it is still the simplest and the most profound; and I am glad of this opportunity of saluting him while we are both this side of the grave.

There are other debts of a more personal nature I wish to acknowledge. To Mr. John Dunlop of the Mitchell Library, Glasgow, for an invaluable family memoir (in manuscript) of the Poet; to Miss C. S. Ferguson of Whiteinch Public Library, Glasgow, for her unfailing courtesy and kindness in meeting my plaguing requests; and to Mr. William Young of Mount Blow, whose tempestuous zeal for the Poet is matched only by his insight into and understanding of the heart and soul of the essential Burns problem.

To those who may be unaware of the international aspect of the cult of Burns, the burden of this note may seem superfluous to the introduction of a novel. Here I restrict myself to the observation that since Robert Burns is the world's greatest poet of common humanity it is incumbent upon those who would lay hands on his memory to ensure that their hands are clean.

J. B.,
Bearsden, December 19th, 1945.

CONTENTS

Part One

WHEN THE OLD CLAY COTTAGE WAS NEW

Part Two

UPON THE CARRICK BORDER

Part Three

THE SAFFRON PLAID

Part Four

Part Five

CHARACTERS

in their order of appearance

(Fictional characters are printed in *Italics*)

JAMES YOUNG, blacksmith in Alloway.

JOHN TENNANT, crofter in Alloway.

WILLIAM BURNS, peasant-farmer.

AGNES BROUN (MRS. BURNS), Kirkoswald dairy-maid.

JEAN YOUNG, blacksmith's wife.

AGNES MacLURE TENNANT, crofter's wife.

REVEREND WILLIAM DARLYMPLE, Minister in Ayr.

ROBERT BURNS.

GILBERT BURNS, second son to William Burns.

JOHN MURDOCH, a school teacher.

ANDREW GRAY, a school teacher.

PROVOST WILLIAM FERGUSSON, of Ayr.

MR. & MRS. ANDRA KERR, out-going tenants of Mount Oliphant.

NANCY BURNS, first daughter to William Burns.

ANNABELLA BURNS, second daughter to William Burns.

BETTY DAVIDSON, Aunt to Agnes Broun.

WILLIE BURNS, third son to William Burns.

EBENEZER ELPHINSTONE, lawyer.

JOHN BURNS, fourth son to William Burns.

ISABELLA BURNS, third daughter to William Burns.

JAMES MacCANDLISH, Dalrymple blacksmith's son.

NELLY KILPATRICK, Perclewen blacksmith's daughter.

SAMUEL BROUN, peasant-farmer-smuggler.

DAVID MacLURE, merchant in Ayr.

JEAN KENNEDY, of the Kirkton Inn, Kirkoswald.

DUGAL GRAHAM, of Shanter Farm, Kirkoswald.

JOCK CAMPBELL, peasant-farmer-smuggler.

A SMUGGLER'S AGENT.

BESSIE RICHMOND, Kirkoswald light-o'-skirts.

ANNE KENNEDY, of the Kirkton Inn, Kirkoswald.

JOHN RANKINE, farmer of Adamhill.

ANNIE RANKINE, housekeeper at Adamhill.

SAUNDERS TAIT, Tarbolton tailor and rhymster.

WILLIAM RONALD, farmer of the Bennals.

JEAN RONALD, daughter of William Ronald.

ANNE RONALD, daughter of William Ronald.

DAVID SILLAR, Tarbolton farmer's son.

WILLIAM MacGAVIN, Tarbolton lad.

ALEXANDER BROWN, Tarbolton lad.

WALTER MITCHELL, Tarbolton lad.

ANRA MacAUSLAN, Machlin dancing-master.

PEGGY DUNLOP, Tarbolton lass.

MYSIE GRAHAM, Tarbolton lass.

ALISON BEGBIE, Tarbolton housekeeper.

PATRICK SILLAR, farmer of Spittleside.

HUGH REID, Tarbolton lad.

THOMAS WRIGHT, Tarbolton lad.

JOCK RICHARDS, Tarbolton publican.

PROVOST CHARLES HAMILTON, of Irvine.

REVEREND JAMES RICHMOND, Minister in Irvine.

ALEXANDER PEACOCK, heckler-smuggler, Irvine.

SARAH PEACOCK, wife to Peacock.

JOHN HAMILTON, medical student.

MAGGIE LAPPER, Irvine ale-wife.

MRS. MacCUTCHIN, Irvine widow-woman.

CAPTAIN RICHARD BROWN, Irvine sailor.

JEAN GLOVER, a strolling player.

JEAN GARDNER, an Irvine lass.

MR. & MRS. WILLIAM GARDNER, fleshers in Irvine.

MR. STEIN, a ship's mate.

MR. & MRS. WILLIAM MUIR, The Mill, Tarbolton.

ROBERT AIKEN, writer in Ayr.

JAMES GRIEVE, farmer, Tarbolton.

GEORGE MacCREE, merchant, Ayr.

JOHN CAMPBELL, merchant, Ayr.

JOHN HAMILTON, Laird of Sundrum.

JOHN BALLANTINE, Dean of Guild, Ayr.

JAMES GORDON, Sheriff's Officer, Ayr.

ROBERT DOAK, Messenger-at-arms.

JOCK LEES, shoemaker, Tarbolton.

DR. JOHN MacKENZIE, physician, Machlin.

GAVIN HAMILTON, writer, Machlin.

JOHN RICHMOND, clerk to Gavin Hamilton.

JAMES SMITH, haberdasher, Machlin.

ELIZABETH PATON, farm servant, of Largieside.

JOHN DOW, host of The Whitefoord Arms, Machlin.

REVEREND JOHN MacMATH, Doctor Woodrow's assistant, Tarbolton.

JAMES TENNANT, farmer, Glenconnar.

CHARLES NORVELL, gardener, Coilsfield.

DR. WILLIAM MacGILL, Minister in Ayr.

WILLIAM PATON, crofter in Largieside.

' He'll hae misfortunes great an' sma',
But aey a heart aboon them a'.
He'll be a credit till us a' :
We'll a' be proud o' Robin! '

From: "There was a Lad was born in Kyle"
By: Robert Burns

Part One

WHEN THE OLD CLAY COTTAGE WAS NEW

LIFE WITHOUT LAUGHTER

THE VILLAGE of Alloway straggled back from the banks of the river Doon to where the ground was firmer and drier; and here William Burns decided to make his home. He had acquired the right to labour some seven acres of rough ground lying back from the main road that meandered out of Ayr town on its winding way to Kirkoswald, Maybole and the South. Here he pegged out a small rectangle, brought boulders and clay and began bigging himself a shelter from the elements.

The Alloway folks had kindly dispositions for they were not given to overwork. They helped William in odd lethargic moments since it amused them to see a man so tireless and energetic. But of course: the man was a stranger and not in his right mind.

"Damned," said John Tennant, the village blacksmith, to James Young, his horse-dealing neighbour, "it's no' canny to see a man working himself harder nor a dumb brute."

"Aye, you're right there, Jock: it makes the sweat break on you to watch him."

"Ah weel, Jamie, he'll no' break sweat; for bedamned! if he hasna sweated away every ounce o' flesh under his hide till there's nothing left but the bones and the muscle-strings to work them. But dinna tire yourself watching him; for it's a sair sicht."

When the puddled clay had been well packed into the rough stones; when the roof tree had been set in place and the thatch well roped against the west wind (forever soughing with its slobber of grey rain), William Burns brought his lass to inspect his work.

"It's not a bad house, Agnes. There's not another like it this side o' Ayr. It will need a week's firing before we think of moving in. But . . . you like it?"

"It's more nor I bargained on, William. It's a better house nor I was brocht up in at Kirkoswald. It's a palace of a place set by the cot-houses of the farms here. . . And the ingle-neuk! That's a fireside ony woman in Ayrshire would be proud of. You've made a real snod job o' it, William." Then she added shyly: "Were you ettlin' for us to be settled in afore the New Year?"

"I was, Agnes. We'll be married and settled in by the middle of December. Aye: we'll be tight and cosy here, Agnes. I hope your brothers will like my house. . ."

They hadn't many words for each other. They were past the daffing days of youth. Indeed there had been no daffing in William's days. The chill of penury had more than damped his youthful ardour. He had been reared to poverty and hardship, to the endless moil and toil in the rachle of clay and stone on the bare braes of his native Clochnahill, swept by the haars from the North Sea and chilled by the blasts from the bleak North.

His young years had been bleak with the aftermath of the '45. The hope of the Stewarts had almost bled to death on Drummossie Moor. The remnants of that hope and the greater hope of Scotland's independence had been butchered by the soul-calloused Cumberland, hard tempered in the art of human butchery.

The Earl Marischal had backed the Stewarts and lost. The Burns folk had been cast adrift from his feudal mercies and ever since had fought a losing battle to grub their bite of thin nourishment from the soured north-east clay.

In the end there had been no alternative: William and his brother had packed a farrel or two of bannocks in a cloth and with a few precious bits of small silver and a scatter of groats had gone trudging down the Howe of the Mearns to seek a crust of barley bread in the kindlier South.

They had tramped down through Perth and crossed the Tay and trudged on through the bare patches of Fife till they had stood on the shore of the gloomy Forth and had seen the reek of the Capital hang like a black cloud above the ridge of its rock even as royal Jamie the Saxth had seen it before he had gone slobbering South glad to be free of the stink and stench of its narrow wynds and closes.

But William Burns had seen the reek-cloud as a pillar of smoke guiding the destiny of his steps towards employment.

There he felt that the green finger of his gardening knack would enable him to find a buyer. Auld Reekie was throwing her legs from under her lousy blanket. Her family was growing and a few of them were reaping the rewards of the Union with England. New houses were going up: a new town for the rich merchants; and there was a general laying-out of gardens and open spaces.

So William Burns sold his labour in Edinburgh and tasted the first fruits of wage-slavery. But he was a peasant brought up to the land and calling no man master save in the way of feudal right. He soured at the meanness of his petty slavery and hankered after a plot of land somewhere where he could work as he pleased, work for his own economic salvation and sustain the pride of his manhood.

So he scraped and hoarded his groats together; and eventually, without a backward glance at the Sodom of Scotia's darling seat, turned his dour Presbyterian face towards the West country.

And by and by he met with one, William Fergusson of Doonholm, Provost of Ayr in the Baillery of Kyle; and from him he rented a few acres and set to gardening on a market basis.

But as always when Adam delves Eve must spin and William needed a wife that he might settle and prosper now that he had fulfilled his ambition and won free from the haggle of day labour.

William Burns was dour but his heart was not unkindly. The spine of his East-coast manhood was strutted with an independent integrity that would not allow him to deviate from the path of his self-hewn righteousness.

He was of the race that had stood against the drilled legions of Rome when race after race had bowed to their yoke; he was of the race that had knelt in the ring after Falkirk, that had died at Flodden and that had marched to Derby—and been butchered and sold for their pains.

He was of the race that turned from Scotland, trudged to the ends of the earth whether with Park and Livingstone in the heat and treachery of Africa, Murray in Australia, MacKenzie in America or Learmonth in the vast Muscovite plains. . .

He was of the handful of continuing Scots, enduring against all hardship and circumstance, enduring best when enduring alone, sheet anchored in the tradition of their race and the fear of the Lord. Looking for no reward this side of the grave and looking indifferently enough on that; grimly fortified in the knowledge that though they had lost their nationhood they would, in the end of all earthly things, come to a Kingdom where only the upright could enter and only the pure in heart see God.

He, like the intrepid sons of his race, neither knew nor sought any other reward. Neither sought he any approbation other than the silent deep-hidden approbation of his conscience.

William Burns was not to know he was to father into the world the greatest of his nation's great sons. Yet could he have known, had he lived to know, this knowledge would not have caused him to deviate from his course.

There was no meanness or hypocrisy about him and nothing of the canting moral humbuggery of the Presbyterian bigots. Yet he was essentially and fundamentally Protestant. He stood alone before his God, inexorable and unbending even as his God was. Justice measured all his actions as he hoped for mercy. But laughter never broke the line of his drawn purposeful lips. He had never—and with some reason—known anything in life to arouse laughter. And having no sense of humour saved him many a subtle heartache.

In the grey poverty and the grey labour of his days the sunshine of laughter had no place. Not only was life grim and earnest: it was an unending struggle against a flint-hearted nature and the greedy exploitation of rent and capital. Here there was but one justice: to him that had would be given and to him that had not even what he had would be taken away.

Out of the hardship of their days and the lonely misery of their nights, Scots like William Burns had created a God of their own image.

That they could endure through hellish physical torture even unto violent and agonising death was a tribute to their devotion to a purpose and an ideal beyond the hunger of their lean bellies and the clamour of their flesh and blood. . .

So William Burns stood on the beaten floor of his first dwelling raised by his own hands and looked towards his bride. He had chosen with particular care the partner who would share the burden of his future days. He might hope, reckoning by the psalmist's span, for another thirty odd years of life.

It cannot be said he loved her. Love in the sense of romantic or physical avowal of the physical attributes of the mate was something William Burns did not know and, had he known, would have rejected as a sinful blasphemy.

But his attachment to Agnes Broun was deep and affectionate. If he experienced no desire for daffing in the lea of a thorn bush or beside a rig in a field of barley, it was very much to his mind that he should provide his bride with a good home— together with the means of maintaining it. Though they both accepted the poverty of their lot and knew that hardship would in all probability companion them to the grave, yet William had faith that his skill and industry would win for him (and the family he hoped for) a measure of independence—and perhaps comfort.

Agnes began to labour with her first child on the 24th of the second January of her marriage and the twenty-seventh year of her age. William was anxious: maybe for the first time in his life he experienced a tremor of fear; but the only outward manifestation he showed was in his quickened speech and movement. He called for his neighbours, Mrs. Tennant and

Mrs. Young. But Jean Young, who had known many sore and difficult labours herself, had no stomach left for midwifery. She would come if Mr. Burns couldn't get anyone else; but, well, let him try Aggie MacLure—Mrs. Tennant—who had a steady nerve and a deft hand.

By morning the worst was over and a male child was born to Agnes and William. William was relieved and happy beyond the reach of prayer. Having seen that Agnes was comfortable, he remembered his duty to God and his newly-born son and heir. He saddled the pony and splashing through dub and mire battered his way into Ayr town to the manse of his parish minister, William Dalrymple, and brought the good-natured man cantering through the dubs, with a good wind in his broad back, to christen the child Robert after his own father at Clochnahill.

William took his vows solemnly and with great sincerity. Never happy unless he was undertaking great moral obligations, he found that the obligation of undertaking to bring up his new-born son in the way of the Lord lay prouder to his heart than any other that could have been imposed on him.

Here, if ever, his word was his bond, so that there was no need other than the formal one to have his neighbours, John Tennant and James Young, to witness.

The birth of Robert had passed off without any alarms or excursions and the event had disturbed the dull tenor of Alloway's lethargic ways even less than any other birth might have; for nobody got drunk and not even William or his intimate neighbours as much as wet their dry Presbyterian whistles with a drop of whisky, nor did they slocken their honest drouth with a draught of tippenny—the common ale of the day.

But a few days after the baptismal service when Agnes was beginning to move shakily about the house a great blustering gale came tearing in from the sea and raged and ravaged

through Carrick, Kyle and Cunninghame, bowing down the
stunted trees and tearing away thatched roofs whose unfortunate moorings had gone rotten with age and the all-
prevalent dampness.

Maybe William (who was, after all, but a skilly amateur)
had not been over-knacky with the setting of his fire jambs or
the balancing of his stone lintel. Under the strains and stresses
of the storm his gable wall collapsed and the entire structure
was like to tumble about his ears.

William would not have minded that, so great was his
mortification and wounded pride. But he could not have the
house falling about the ears of his wife and infant son.

He rose and proofed himself against the lashing rain,
wrapped Agnes in his own warm plaiding and, happing the
wailing infant under his cloak with an armful of blanket,
ventured into the storm to seek safety and shelter with the
good neighbourly Young.

Folks were superstitious, always looking to either hand and
over their shoulders for signs and omens and ever reading
sinister meanings into ordinary happenings.

Many an auld tongue wagged knowingly, telling Agnes
how her first-born had had a stormy entry into the hard and
stormy world and that for a surety he would have a stormy
out-going with a stormy passage in between : as if the wild
west wind had never blown in the gable of a clay biggin in
Cunninghame, Kyle or Carrick in all its endless centuries of
blowing.

William muttered darkly against the bletherin' auld wives
of the West country with their all-but-pagan conception of the
ways of the Almighty.

But even as he muttered he doubted. There was a thousand
years of Scottish blood in his veins and much of it Gaelic
blood. Maybe there was something at the back of all their
blethers.

Whatever lay behind the inscrutability of the dark universe,
he set to with determination and made good and doubly siccar

the damage to his clay cottage—even as the gale blew out its last breath in gusty sobs.

Never again would a child of his lie at the mercy of weak and faulty workmanship.

There were folks in Alloway who hoped William Burns had been taught a much-needed lesson and that the fall to his pride would do him good.   There were many folks who found the dour taciturn superiority of William Burns hard to thole. Damned, they thought in their soft lazy way, why did a man need to have such a stubborn pride in him merely because he came from Aberdeen-way and was well thought of by the dirt of gentry? A man who couldn't unbend and take a drink and lift a lawless leg on occasion was a poor creature for all his hard-won and harder kept seven acres and his grand job with the Provost of Ayr.   Damned, they finally concluded, life had no savour or salt to it that way at all: a man might as well be dead with his bones rotting in Alloway Kirkyard and his soul burning in hell—where doubtless it would burn any the ways of it.

In his evenings, when all labour had been cast aside and everything that could be accomplished by way of work had been done; when Agnes, tired and worn out, had gone to bed to snuggle her first-born and give him his supper suck, William carefully placed a sheet of rough paper on the end of the table, put a point to his goose quill and laboriously and awkwardly set down the first question and the first answer in his manu- script on which he had already scrawled the title—*Manual of Religious Belief.*

He was determined above all else that not only would he implement his parental vows to the letter but that, in the essential spirit of Protestantism, this child Robert and such brothers or sisters as he might yet have, would grow up blade true to the faith of the covenant between God and man and spotlessly free from the bawdy heresies of the ignorant and licentious damned who, in their silly ignorance, thought that the paths of glory led but to the grave, instead of through the grave, the grave of all worldly things and the more worldly flesh.

The child Robin was perhaps a trifle more delicate than either his father or mother would have liked. But his mother hadn't long to nurse him. Not that she had much time on her hands; for the market garden was but a poor crofting and she had to attend to the cows and the pony and the chickens and work about the seven acres carrying manure and labouring generally to her husband in the spring evenings when he came home from his gardening at Provost Fergusson's estate along the banks of the river Doon.

Not only had she little time to nurse her precious first-born. Before he was a year old she had again conceived.

A large family was an economic necessity if a man wanted to eke out a living on the land and could not afford to hire labour. William Burns was not the man to bring children into the world for the sensual pleasure they might bring him: he was much too hard-bitten a Puritan to indulge in wanton conjugal hedonism. He undertook their begetting, as he undertook everything to which he set his mind, with a high and premeditated seriousness.

But if there was no song in his throat at the pleasures of parenthood there was a deep and enduring pride.

He had a horror of the poverty that had dragged down his father and broken up his family. He was determined he would never drag his own family down into the morass of poverty and suffering. Yet the fear that he might somehow fail in this gnawed at his vitals like a fatal cancer.

Education was the one certain specific against poverty as sure as the fear of the Lord was the certain specific against sin. His family might be poor; but if only he could provide them with education, they would be equipped to battle with life above the level of the clay from which they delved their bread.

Had he not had the truth of this seared into his flesh and

burned into the very marrow of his bones? Had he not suffered from his boyhood even as his father had suffered from the want of that education that would have given their labour a value beyond the pittance of unskilled day-wage drudgery?

At whatever cost then he would provide his children with the best education he could afford. Nor would he spare himself any pains in bestowing on them his own hard-won knowledge.

So as his family grew and Robert and Gilbert—more like twins than brothers—began to scamper about and wear out the patched and re-patched seats of their duds, William decided it was time a proper school was set up in Alloway.

He went round his neighbours and spoke solemnly and with the air of unchallengeable authority on the benefits of education second only to the benefits of religion. Nay, was not religion itself and the revealed word of God little better than the darkness of superstition without the light of education to reveal the just proportions of its truth and beauty?

The neighbours who were now familiar with William's inner worth were won over to his scheme. First they must agree among themselves to make good a dominie's annual fee of five pounds. They must agree to provide him with the shelter of four walls and a roof wherein he might hold his school. Lastly, they must undertake to see that the good man did not starve in any literal sense since this would bring their project to ruin.

A few of them demurred at the expense of the project. Times were so bad that no one indeed remembered when they had ever been good; and the ways of nature and God were as uncertain as they were inscrutable.

But William's thin dun face, like a slab of his famous North-country granite, was set against any defeatism. A sufficiency of neighbours consented as would guarantee the minimum requirements of the scheme. William thanked them solemnly and undertook to find a suitable dominie.

He had some trouble finding such a man. Dominies were hard-pressed, ill-paid devils and most of them had a failing for the bottle and were not over-fastidious about the moral code; and William was adamant about both.

He wanted a dominie out of the ordinary run. He wanted a young man who would see life and the significance of education as he saw them: a man after his own heart.

After much cautious enquiry (and some assistance from John Tennant) he heard of a young man of the town of Ayr who seemed to have all the essential qualifications. He made the necessary appointment and rode into Ayr to keep it.

William eyed the prospective dominie keenly across the tavern table. He plied him question after question.

John Murdoch was nervous but he did not betray himself. This quaint swarthy-skinned man with his slow deliberate and formal English was no rustic Ayrshire clod-hopper native to the Ayrshire clods. This man was something of a genius in his stern almost forbidding way. He knew what he was talking about. He knew the value of good teaching: it would be half the battle to have his keen interest and support.

So John Murdoch, coming into his nineteenth year, keen, ambitious and born to pedagogy, shook William Burns warmly by the hand as they clasped to close the deal.

There remained the final test. William's eyes screwed up from their recessed sockets and went out through the back of Murdoch's skull. He wavered for a moment, fearing the worst.

"You will join me in a drink, Mr. Murdoch, so that the bargain may be sealed in our Scots fashion?"

Murdoch coughed to gain time. There was a trap here—or was there? Best to temporise—and in his best pedagogic manner.

"My thanks to you, sir, for the honour you pay me. It is an honour that I may not lightly disregard. Nevertheless I make bold, my dear sir, to convey to you the intelligence that I do not normally indulge in any form of stimulating beverages. Pray, sir, that you do not misunderstand me. I am not, I hope, a bigot; nor would I have you think that I am so dull of wit, or lacking in a proper experience of the world, as to draw no fine line of discrimination betwixt abstention and a proper abstemiousness. And so, if I will be pardoned for any seeming discourtesy—which, did it arise, I hasten to assure you would be accidental—I will join you in sealing our bargain—which as you rightly say is our Scots fashion—in a small ale or tippenny."

William was fairly staggered by this speech and Murdoch panted for shortness of breath. But he showed no sign of wonder or surprise. He ordered the tippenny in a casual off-hand manner. He resumed conversation in a more friendly and less formal manner.

"I have two sons, Mr. Murdoch: Robert aged six and Gilbert aged five. It is customary, perhaps, that a parent should have a favourite—we have the authority of The Book itself on that point. But I have no favourites."

"A good principle, Mr. Burns. . ."

"Nor do I want you to have any favourites. Judge them by the book. I am not a harsh man, Mr. Murdoch. I am not a bigot in matters of religion, though I am none the less strict in my precept and example for all that. So do not you be wrongfully sparing of the rod; neither be you given over to brutality out of the evil of ungovernable temper."

"You wrong me——"

"No: I don't wrong you, Mr. Murdoch; but you are a young man; and, if I have not misjudged you, an ambitious one. I've lived much longer than you have and seen much callousness and suffering. Now I'm depending a lot on you. My boys are good boys and I have done what I could to bring them up in the fear of the Lord. I do not doubt but they have something of the grace of God about them. I have prepared a manual for them by way of helping them—and myself for that matter—in questions of a religious nature. Maybe, Mr. Murdoch, I could depend on your scholarship in assisting me to cast the book in more polished and grammatical form?"

"Most certainly, Mr. Burns. Indeed, sir, you place my talents in very great obligation to you for the honour you pay them. I shall be only too happy to assist you to the limit of my powers. Although perhaps I ought to point out that, though my devotion to religion comes before my devotion to English grammar as the basis of all real eloquence in forming an English style, yet my religious convictions lean rather to the New Light doctrine."

"Well . . . I don't think we will quarrel much over that, Mr. Murdoch, though, for myself, I think it is the Light that matters not so much its Oldness or its Newness."

"Very neatly expressed, sir. As neat an epigram, sir, as I can recollect having been turned in Ayrshire."

"I don't think we'll fash ourselves overmuch with epigrams, Mr. Murdoch, though I am not insensible to your compliment. Now let's get down to some practical business details for I have not much time on my hands."

So they discussed the books they would need. It seemed they wouldn't need many; but nothing but the best and most reliable would serve. *The Spelling Book*, of course; the Old and the New Testament; Mason's *Collection of Prose and Verse* and Fisher's *English Grammar*.

William was impressed. This youth took his pedagogy with a high and proper seriousness. He took his leave of him and rode back to Alloway feeling pleased with himself.

Murdoch watched William go down the narrow cobbled street and then returned to Simson's Inn. In a short time his colleague in pedagogy arrived to hear his news. He was older than John and much less pedantic; but for all that he, like his comrade, had sedulously sloughed his tongue of the Ayrshire idiom and dialect and tried to emulate the formal methods of the new breed of polite Anglicisers.

Andrew Gray liked his drink. Instead of ale he brought to the table where Murdoch sat a drop of spirit.

"Good morning, my fine friend: I trust your intelligence is of an encouraging complexion?"

"It could not be better, Andrew. . . Andrew: I have just said good-day to the most remarkable man in Ayrshire—

perhaps in Scotland—William Burns, a peasant of sorts in Alloway."

"A rustic?"

"Yes and no. He is from the North-east coast—somewhere about Aberdeen I gather. But a rustic, Andrew, of the most remarkable accomplishments. Self-taught, of course; but not to be despised on that account. His mode of speech and command of the English language is truly phenomenal. And he has intelligence. I tell you, Andrew, I never suffered such an ordeal. Questions—and always more questions. He will be satisfied with nothing but the best. He wants me to go down to Alloway and teach his two boys, together with the children of such neighbours as have agreed among themselves to stand good for the expense of the business."

"And can you trust his word for the expense?"

"Implicitly, my dear Andrew: implicitly. His word is his bond, and his word is irreproachable, quite beyond suspicion. I shall be on tip-toe all the time, for I can see that he will not be deceived with slipshod work of any kind. Indeed, if I can pass muster for a year or two at Alloway I shall have no fear in passing muster anywhere—I mean London or even Paris. This is all very different from what I expected."

"You expected a clod-hopping rustic who wanted his brats and his neighbours' brats to be drilled in their A.B.Cs. and their tables? Wait till you've seen the place, John, before you allow your enthusiasm rein. There must be something amiss with your learned rustic—or he wouldn't be a rustic."

"But he isn't just a rustic—and I am certain he will not always remain one. I suspect he is of good family and may have suffered from the effects of the late rebellion."

"Ho! A Jacobite?"

"No, no, my dear Andrew. Not a Jacobite. As sound a Hanoverian as you could wish. Sounder than most, I'll wager. You must promise me to come down to Alloway when I am settled and I shall introduce you to him."

Andrew Gray signalled for another drink.

"I can only congratulate you, John, on your appointment. I hope you prosper—as indeed I know you will—and I hope your learned rustic maintains your elevated opinion of him. In the meantime what say you to some mutton broth?"

"Capital! A moment ago I felt my appetite had completely left me. Now I am most sharply aware of a prodigious craving for sustenance."

WHEN TREES DID BUD

The dark eyes that now watched John Murdoch writing his thin spidery letters on the blackboard betrayed no emotion, gave no sign how much Robin disliked and feared him.

He disliked him for his prim pedantic way of speaking, disliked him for his thin angular jerky motions. And he feared him for the knowledge that was stored in his long knobbly head.

And John Murdoch, as he surveyed his dozen pupils in the bright light of that first May morning, did not warm towards the pupil to whom, for his father's sake, he would have to direct special care and attention. He knew at once that he would have to thrash this boy for his smouldering dourness and he knew that thrashing would do little good.

So different was his younger brother, Gilbert. Ah! here was a pupil who would well repay attention—a bright amenable boy who would mould and enjoy the moulding.

At the end of the week, what night he was lodging again with William Burns, he had to admit he did not know what to make of Robin.

Strolling down to the Brig of Alloway in the lengthening dusk of the May evening, he delivered himself of cautious and yet encouraging sentiments.

"It is, you will understand, my dear sir, premature to give an exact opinion. I am much encouraged with Gilbert who has all the potentialities for a superior scholar."

"And Robin?"

"Now there, sir, I am just a point perplexed. Oh, he is a fine boy, and I do not for a moment doubt but that he will turn out well. But there is at present an element of opposition in him that somewhat eludes my comprehension."

Seeing the cloud that gathered on William's brow, the young dominie stroked his long nose.

"Not, sir, that it is more than a trifle. I am persuaded that the mood is of the moment and will pass over when he has settled into my routine."

"What you have to say, Mr. Murdoch, does not surprise me. Robin is given to strange unaccountable moods. He has never been as robust as I would have wished him. But I find he reads very well."

"Excellently well, sir: excellently well."

"But we must have no moods and sulks, Mr. Murdoch. The remedy for that is in your hands and I will not gainsay you. There must be respect for your authority—as there is for mine."

Murdoch felt very uncomfortable even though he felt relieved. He had been afraid that William might have been asking questions and he was by no means certain of the answers Robin might have made.

"And you think you will take to our school, Mr. Murdoch?"

"Indeed, sir, I find my attachment to it growing in strength and affection with each passing hour. But for the transient shadow of Robin's mood I should not be guilty of the hyperbolic case, sir, were I to affirm that I am exceeding content."

They leaned on the arch of the bridge for a few moments and Murdoch noted the first of the skimming swallows.

But Murdoch's contentment was superficial. Like the swallows, he wanted to stretch his wings and discover the contours of a larger world. Ambition buoyed him up and beckoned him on. Like the swallows too, he would be but a bird of passage. But first he must test himself here in Alloway and measure his ability, which he was incapable of doubting, against the approval of William Burns.

As they turned from the bridge James Young met up with them. They saluted him gravely. But James was an Ayrshire man and not given to coffee-house conversation.

"Aye . . . a grand nicht. . . You're having a sair strissle wi' thae callants at the scule, Mr. Murdoch. How d'you find thae thick-skulled laddies o' mine?"

"Your sons, Mr. Young, are showing a commendable attitude of diligence."

"Ah well, Mr. Murdoch, just belt into them if they tak' the gee in the shafts o' learning. What do you say, William?"

"There's nothing wrong with your advice, James. I was just giving Mr. Murdoch the same. But Rome wasn't built in a day: we must give Mr. Murdoch time to settle down."

"Aye . . . it'll tak' a day or twa. Still, education's a grand thing to have by you so that you can lay hands on it when you feel the need for it."

"If I am not overbold, sir, may I take you up on that observation and add that without education we are as the beasts in the field or as the savage in his untutored blindness."

"Aye . . . they're fell unchancy brutes the savages by all accounts, Mr. Murdoch. And yet, man, I've kenned savages in Carrick that could neither read nor write and yet they left a hantle o' the yellow Geordies an' a weel stockit mailen gin the clods were happered down on them. Aye, man, I've kenned mony a creashy Carrick farmer . . ."

James habbered and havered on and neither Burns nor Murdoch sought to interrupt him. He was but scantily lettered and though he saw the need for learning in his sons he resented, without there being any bitterness in his resentment, the implication of John Murdoch that mere book-learning was an end to life in itself.

The gloaming gathered over the burgeoning rigs. Peesweeps tossed and flapped and cried as they passed the fields by the roadside; and an early bat struggled blindly in the web of the spinning dusk.

Robin, who had been roving along the banks of the river Doon in search of birds' nests and who had sat down on a grassy bank to watch the skimming of the swallows as they flashed across the clear rippling waters, found that the words of a song his mother would be singing came unbidden to his lips:

"When trees did bud, and fields were green,
  And broom bloom'd fair to see ...
  Gang doun the burn, Davie, love,
  And I shall follow thee."

But even as the words formed on his childish lips he became conscious of the gloaming gathering beneath the river's banks; so he rose up and, barefoot, scudded home through the dewy grass.

Though Robin did not make the progress with John Murdoch that was expected of him he was nevertheless making progress.

The world was opening up to him; the world of Ayrshire lying beyond Alloway and the world of Scotland lying beyond Ayrshire.

He listened to his mother singing. Agnes Broun sang not only because she liked to sing and had a fine voice for the songs and ballads of the Scots people. She sang as a bird in captivity will sing. Her life was hard; the conditions of her labour were inexorable. She sang as most of the Scots peasants did: to remind herself that life should not be a treadmill of toil.

And Robin drank in the lilt of her singing though his outward ear was apparently dull to melody. John Murdoch thought so: he could get little response from Robin in his efforts to inculcate the elements of church music.

But not only did the melody permeate the fibre of Robin's consciousness: the words burned themselves into his memory so that he was never to forget them.

Not that he listened to his mother as he listened to Murdoch. He heard his mother as he heard the sough of the west wind sighing in the wet trees and sobbing aslant the grassy knowes; he heard his mother as he heard the lintwhite, the mavis and the gowdspink: against the background of peesweep and plover and moorland whaup. He heard his mother singing as part of his natural environment.

But Murdoch, speaking a strange tongue and possessed of

an unfamiliar and unprepossessing presence, caused Robin to withdraw within himself, withhold the delicate antennae of his consciousness, so that he appeared dumb and unresponsive and intractable.

Inwardly he was not unresponsive. Inwardly he was noting everything Murdoch said. But, unlike Gilbert, he was unable to reflect brightly and sharply, with an almost spontaneous reflection, the drum rolling dicta of the young dominie.

Still panting from his running, he slipped into the cottage and by the light of the fire-glow saw the dominie seated at the ingle with his father.

His mother, dishing a bowl of brose at the table, looked up quickly and said: "Losh, Robin, where hae you been till this time o' nicht?"

Robin heaved on an intake of breath and replied: "No-where."

His father's head turned slowly and his eyes said: That is no answer. So Robin gulped and said quickly, but with a touch of defiance: "I was doon the burn watching the swallows——"

William Burns averted his eyes. "Will we read a chapter while the brose cools, Mr. Murdoch?"

"Nothing, sir, could be more fitting."

William Burns took down the Book and, tilting its pages to the glow of the peats, read slowly from the Old Testament.

And when the chapter was finished, Robin and Gilbert kneeled down on the earthen floor and added their fluting accents to the bass droning of the Lord's prayer.

Then the lads sought their coggie of brose and clasping their horn spoons retired to their chaff bed in the far corner.

After the first ravenous mouthful, Gilbert said: "You werena watching the swallows . . . were you, Robin?"

"I found a shelfie's nest——"

"Where?"

"You've no' to tell Davie Young or Willie Cowan?"

Gilbert drew the nail of his forefinger across his throat and made the motion of spitting.

"I'll show you to-morrow," said Robin, simply.

"Do I know the place?"

But Robin, his mouth full of the warm brose, shook his head so that his black locks fell over his brow.

When they had scraped their coggies clean they curled under the clothes of the chaff bed and were soon asleep.

Later on John Murdoch came tip-toeing ben and stretched himself out beside them, drawing the patchwork quilt of cloth cuttings over him.

THE BOOK AND THE BRAE

For two years Murdoch taught the Alloway bairns the rudiments of elementary education. He came and went among the Alloway cotters, sleeping here and taking his bite there; but always it was his greatest pleasure to come back to William Burns.

The more he saw of William, the more he respected and admired him. The respect was mutual. The Burns family held education in a sacred esteem. The others treated him with a slightly off-hand deference, never warming to him as did the Burns family.

Robin and Gilbert were not only his favourite pupils: they were his brightest. Gilbert was a model boy: from him he expected great things. Robin still remained a problem. He moved slowly in fits and starts, always grave and mostly moody. Yet when he did move, he moved in a way that startled the dominie. But Murdoch was no more than startled. There was something irrational about Robin and, with the irrational, Murdoch was out of his depth.

The young teacher was happy at his work. He was a success as he always knew he would be. But there was discontent in his happiness for he was ambitious and eager to conquer the world that lay outside the boundaries of Ayrshire parishes. He dreamed much of Paris. . .

Robin also dreamed; but his dreams were of a different kind. He dreamed of the world of the old Scottish songs and lived again in his childish way the battles fought and won and lost by the heroes of Scotland; and above and beyond all those heroes towered the epic figure of William Wallace.

Once upon a time Blind Harry, the minstrel, had toured the Scottish land reciting from his ageless memory tales of the deeds and valour of Scotland's liberator. But that was long ago.

Then came Hamilton of Gilbertfield and put the minstrel's now archaic Scots into the language of his day; and now in the footsteps of the minstrel came the chapmen selling their penny chaps both sacred and profane. The sacred were very sacred: the profane very profane. Between the extremes came such a series as the life and deeds of William Wallace.

To Robin, as to his family, the printed word had about it the sanctity only good black print could bestow. Nothing was too dull or too learned to remain unread. Even though Robin's mind might stammer and halt in the maze of a dull Latinity, his whole body glowed when he came to read in more simple and poetic language of the deeds of his country's saviour.

Thus throughout his young life the great and heroic Wallace who had tasted victory and drunk the dregs of the most bitter and humiliating defeat, who had trod a calvary of his own choosing, appeared before him as no other hero was ever to appear.

Between spells of reading and dreaming there was work to be done. No hands could be idle in so poor a household where so many tasks lay to hand.

But there was time for playing. Time for running about the braes, for paddling in the burn and for pulling the gowans fine. Time for roving about the banks of the bonnie Doon, for bird-nesting in the green shaws and along the bosky linns. Time for watching the long-eared hares leaping on the grassy knowe. Time to lie and watch the hawk hover and drop to death. Time to linger in John Tennant's smiddy and hear strange tales and wonder at the busy life of the adult world that passed by on the highway from Ayr to Maybole.

And time, and more than time, in the long winter nights, with the door barred against the sobbing sough of the west wind, to gather round the blazing ingle and hear tales of a far-off country away to the North-east where life was strange and hard and wild: the land of his fathers.

Slowly, in vivid patches, he began to piece together the life his father had lived—and his father before him. How once the life had been fine and gay and meal had been cheap and plentiful; how the Burnses of the immediate past had gone out in the Rising following their feudal lord, the Earl Marischal; how defeat had come to those who had fought, not so much for Charlie as for the continuity of their half-Celtic, half-feudal and wholly Scottish way of life; how on the heels of bitter defeat had come poverty and hardship to the men of the North-east coast; how starvation and privation and the grim skeleton of naked want had stalked the land.

Till the end of his days Robin was to remember that terrible moment about which his father never spoke without betraying signs of a terrible inner anguish: that day he had stood with his brother on the brae of a hill and looked back over the bare rising ground to the bare steading of Clochnahill that despite all its bleak poverty had been all the warmth of a home he had ever known; where he was leaving an ailing father with his younger brothers and sisters to face the losing battle against hunger and want; the home he was never to see again in his earthly life but the home that was never absent from his inner eye; the home caught in that backward glance in a morning of anguished parting . . .

But there were nights when the frost crackled in a shower of stars, and Hawkie hoasted in the byre through the partition, when his father would be busy at the mending of a brogue and his mother at the patching of a garment. Then she would be telling of happier times: of the great ploys at Hallowe'en, of the dancing and merriment at the harvest kirns, and tales of adventure and smuggling along her native Kirkoswald coast.

Young though he was, Robin noticed the difference when Murdoch occupied the seat of honour by the ingle. Then the sad happy stories of the old life gave way to a learned jaw about affairs of state. It was clear to Robin that his father had some-how managed to put behind him the old Scotland that had given him birth, that he had made his peace with the Union. Clear too that his mind thrust deeply into the contemporary jungle of events; that he enjoyed with a keen relish his comparing of notes with the pedagogue who carried such a wise and learned head on such young and narrow shoulders.

But, summer or winter, in the byre or on the braes, in the schoolroom or lying on his chaff bed listening to the seeping rain, Robin was learning: storing his mind in every neuk and crannie with a queer interpenetrating mixty-maxty of life and letters.

And his learning was the deeper and his knowledge the greater because the most vital and vivid part of it was being absorbed unconsciously.

THE BARREN MOOR

Provost William Fergusson of Doonholm knew that in William Burns he had a good man. But now that his gardens had been laid out around his new house and everything under the guidance and hard labour of William Burns had been put in order, he knew that he would be unable to keep him much longer in his service.

He looked at him across the table, saw that he was greying and ageing, and looked from him out at the window where grey autumnal rain wept from grey skies.

"And what have you in mind, Burns?"

"Well, Mr. Fergusson, your policies are in good order now. There is nothing that a good handyman cannot keep in order. Besides, things are getting a bit tight for me in Alloway. My family is growing: I could well do with a bigger place. I was wondering, Mr. Fergusson, if you would care to give me any advice about the possibility of settling into a small farm?"

"Farms are not so easy come by, Burns; but I agree you couldn't do better. You will appreciate that the stocking of a farm requires a bit of capital. You have thought of that?"

"Yes. . . If I could get rid of my holding at Alloway I would have some ready money at my disposal. But before I could do that I would need to see my way about another place."

Fergusson looked from the gaunt face to the weeping rain outside. There was Mount Oliphant, an unprofitable moor of a place. The lease would be vacant come Martinmas and it might be a while before he got a suitable tenant. It would be a difficult place for Burns to make good in, but on the other hand he had his own interests to think of and the place would soon be a wilderness without a tenant.

"You know Mount Oliphant, Burns? It's a good farm: a man like you would have no difficulty in turning good siller on it. There's a rough seventy acres of ground there; and it's good ground for the money."

"And what money would Mr. Fergusson be thinking of?"

"Oh, we winna quarrel about the money, Burns—a matter maybe of £50 per annum—or maybe £45. From an outsider I'd be asking £10 more."

Fifty pounds was a lot of money. Every week, before they tasted a bowl of brose, he would need to find twenty shillings to pay away in bare rent. Twenty shillings was a lot of money.

"It's rather more nor I bargained on, Mr. Fergusson; and there will be the stocking of the farm and maybe I won't win free of my garden in time."

"Well . . . think it over, Burns. There's no need to rush a thing like this, though I must warn you there is no time to lose either. There have been Carrick men after me already, and scarce a market day passes in Ayr but I have enquiries for just such a place. The lease becomes vacant on the eleventh of November. As for stocking the place: well, I wouldna see an industrious man like you, Burns, handicapped at the onset. I think that the loan, say, of £100 might be arranged."

William Burns rose to his feet.

"You have been a kind master to me, Mr. Fergusson; and I promise you that if you can see your way to do me this favour I will not disappoint you as a tenant."

"I hae little fear of that, Burns. You are a man who deserves to get on. I've nae doubt that your industry and application will repay itself. Take a look at the ground and let me have your mind on it. If we can come to terms I'll give you a twelve years lease, with a break at the first six should you rue your bargam."

William Burns thanked his employer and went out into the rain. Unmindful of it he strode home with a strange triumphal light in his sunken eyes.

At long last he was winning free from the thraldom of service. At long last, and in the forty-fourth year of his life.

he was about to fulfil the ambition he had seen dwindling on his father's hands. He was about to become a farmer in his own undisputed right.

He discussed the matter with Agnes and she too was delighted for Alloway had become a bourach of a place. She would be glad of a house with its barn and outhouse where there would be room to move about and not be eternally cluttered up within the confines of the cottage.

So William despite the rain threw the saddle on the pony and plodded up the hill to Mount Oliphant lying on the rising moors two miles to the south-east.

But he had already made up his mind, standing at the end of Provost Fergusson's table, his feet uncomfortable on the luxury of a carpet strip, that Mount Oliphant must be his.

No other way would he come into possession of a farm. The Provost though a worthy man drove a hard bargain. William knew that he would not advance him the fortune of a hundred pounds to stock another man's land.

Even when he rode into the quagmire of a court with the water running in brown rivulets from the dung midden; and the rotting barn door swinging on its twisted hinges: even as he surveyed the poor rachle of buildings he knew no misgiving.

Andra Kerr the outgoing tenant was bent and twisted with toil and the spirit to live was low within him. He had given the best of his blood and bone to the seventy wet sour acres of Mount Oliphant. He had torn the moss from the clay and turned it over into fallow rigs. He had laboured early and late and withal he was going out a poorer man than when he came in.

He had no interest in William Burns and William had little in him.

"You can see all there is to see, Mr. Burns. You canna hide anything on a bare place like this."

Beyond that he would say little.

Mrs. Kerr, heating her worn-out frame at the ingle, did not rise from her chair to greet him. Slowly she turned her head on her scrawny neck and looked at him. The embers of life had long died in her eyes. She had not enough interest left in her to feel pity for William Burns; but in a dull disinterested way she felt he was a poor man to be taking up the burden they were letting drop from their hands.

William saw little of this and guessed less. He noted that the house was stone-built; that the thatch was in good repair and the floor reasonably free from dampness. There was altogether more room about the place and already in his mind he had changed the atmosphere of death and decay into one of life and hope.

The grey rain swept in from the sea and came sweeping up the moors in endless drifts. He could not see the grey surging of waters along the Ayrshire coast and the hills of Arran were hidden far in the grey mist.

He thanked Andra Kerr solemnly, mounted the steaming pony and slipped and slithered his way down the long slow hill to Alloway.

Nothing mattered but that he would soon take possession of seventy acres and that they would be his to plough and sow and reap as, with the blessing of God, he willed.

Part Two

UPON THE CARRICK BORDER

MOUNT OLIPHANT

IN THE following summer when they took possession of Mount Oliphant Robin saw it for the first time.

It had been a good May with plenty of grand growing weather; with showers and sunshine and fresh breezes blowing in from the sea.

As the flitting pulled up the slow hill from Alloway, the backward view gradually extended, sweeping out towards the sea, where to the north-west were the smoke-blue ridges of the Arran peaks.

Robin began to exult and feel that his inner world was developing with subtle harmony. He felt too that he was entering into a world that would become a splendid and unique adventure.

Gilbert, always more restrained and sober in his enthusiasms, felt much like Robin but was unable to give expression to his boyish rhapsodies.

For the moment neither of them knew any regret at leaving the warmth and shelter, the stir and bustle of Alloway. The road that twisted upwards and away from the clay cottage led towards a new world.

And for a while the sun shone on Mount Oliphant. The farm prospered and the Lord blessed the unceasing husbandry of William Burns.

Robin and Gilbert skelped down the hill to Murdoch to be drilled in their fundamentals, but lingered on the road in the evening, tired and hungry: heavy with their day's load of learning. But they were happy during those long summer days when everything was young and fresh and fair.

Even the first winter was mild and only the wettest days held them from school. And on a winter's night Murdoch would sometimes trudge home with them, taking them in their grammar as they walked, for nothing seemed to damp Murdoch's pedagogic ardour and there was no point in wasting the journey in idle conversation.

Robin noted how his father's face lit up when Murdoch appeared and how eagerly he plied him with questions once they were seated comfortably round the ingle. At such times it seemed that William Burns grew in stature; his voice in firmness and authority; that the beasts and the crops of Mount Oliphant mattered nothing to the moves on the political chessboard of Europe.

Robin listened with unobtrusive attention to those intellectual discussions, admiring the weighty polemic his father developed against the more nimble thrust and parry of the dominie's metaphysic.

He liked the grave utterance of his father even when he could not help admiring the wit with which Murdoch garnished his rejoinders.

Lord knows but William Burns had need of John Murdoch's company. His labours were hard and lonely. He saw little or nothing of the life around him: in very truth he was a lone hand ploughing and sowing in the wilderness.

Gone were his talks with Provost William Fergusson at Doonholm and gone too were his conversations with his Alloway neighbours. True, there was still John Tennant (cousin of the Alloway blacksmith) in the nearby farm of Laigh Corton with whom he could exchange words and enjoy friendship. But John Tennant was as poor as himself and burdened with a large family.

Above all William needed Murdoch to sustain his belief in his own wisdom and essential virtue. He needed—though he would never have admitted this need—the flattery Murdoch subtly heaped on him.

Maybe they needed each other. Murdoch was not insincere in his flattery. He needed no proof now to support him in his view that William Burns was perhaps the most remarkable man in Ayrshire. Not only had William an upright heart, the quality of his mind provided a rare whetstone against which Murdoch could sharpen his wit and his intellect. No other man to whom he had the access of friendship could have done so much for him.

But Alloway could not hold him for ever. By the second winter he came to bid the family at Mount Oliphant a sad farewell.

Murdoch, pedagogue to the last, thought that the most appropriate way he could celebrate his farewell was to read to the assembled family the play of *Titus Andronicus* by William Shakespeare.

The family gathered round the ingle. William Burns especially desired that this reading should be marked with due solemnity: there were few households in Ayrshire where the dominie could drop in and read Shakespeare to the family.

It was a sad blow to all of them this leaving of Murdoch's: particularly sad to William Burns. But however this might be, William was not the man to show emotion on such an occasion.

Murdoch's emotions were of a very different character. He was leaving to better himself and he was buoyed with ambition about to be fulfilled. He could not resist the unconscious temptation to show off.

When Murdoch came to the scene where the ravished and mutilated Lavinia is brutally taunted, the three children could stand no more. Robert, Gilbert and Agnes shrieked their protest and wakened Annabella, the bairn, much to their mother's annoyance.

William was aghast at this display of bad-mannered hysteria: this was a scandalous way to show their gratitude to Murdoch.

"Enough!" he cried sternly: "enough I say! If this is the gratitude you are prepared to show Mr. Murdoch then he will take away his play."

Robin's big black eyes were wet with tears. He clenched his fists in the tension of his outraged emotion.

"Aye!" he cried. "Let Mr. Murdoch take it away; for if he doesna then I'll burn it in the fire."

"Robin!" cried his father, feeling a wave of choleric anger rise in him at the audacity of his son's impertinence, "Robin——"

But Murdoch closed the book and rose with a laugh.

"Indeed, Mr. Burns, the fault is mine. I should have brought something of Shakespeare that would have been more to the minds of the children. I beg of you, sir, that no more be made of the incident. I would not have my last memory of Mount Oliphant and the happy nights I have spent under its roof-tree marred by any displeasure. Indeed, my good friend Robin shows the excellence of his sentiments; and we would do well to acknowledge them!"

Not for the first time Agnes felt that Robin had shown sound common sense in telling Mr. Murdoch he would burn the play: to her private mind the rubbish was fit for no higher end.

But then, in her heart of hearts, Agnes had never really liked Murdoch and had never warmed to his pedagogic poses. She was glad he had the education of her sons. But she could not see that reading such blood-thirsty nonsense was in any way part of their education.

As he walked down the road with Murdoch, William again apologised for Robin's behaviour. "I am worried at times about him," he confessed.

"There is really little cause to be worried, Mr. Burns. I admit that Robin is in some small parts peculiar; but his peculiarity is that of a very sensitive boy. Indeed, Mr. Burns, I would make bold to say that there is an element of the precocious in our Robin. Yes, I think I may be so bold as to state that belief."

"Precocious, Mr. Murdoch?"

"I mean—in parts—a more than usual ability. His retention of memory is of quite surpassing excellence. His understanding of our English authors is of the very first order. I confess that the dullness of his ear in the simple harmony of music is something that puzzles me."

"No, Mr. Murdoch: Robin is no songster. But I don't think that that will be any great drawback in his education."

"Oh no, I don't think it will be. Nevertheless, sir, I have striven to give the boys the very best education and I merely point this out to show you what I mean by his precocity."

"But what am I to do, Mr. Murdoch, about their education now? That is what worries me."

"Mr. Burns, sir: there is nothing that has given me more thought than leaving your boys without the proper means of education. Yet they have a good grounding in the essentials. I am certain that with your aid they can very profitably continue in their studies. At least they can continue with you until you can come to some suitable arrangement."

"I am worried, Mr. Murdoch. More and more I am needing Robin's help in the fields. Until I find my feet on the farm and manage to put a little capital by me, I don't see that I could afford to send them into Ayr. It is a grave handicap being so far out of the way here in Mount Oliphant."

But Murdoch didn't comment on this. The gloom that seemed to gather round his friend's mind was something that blended ill with his own happy thoughts.

They said good-bye at the turn of the road. Only when Murdoch had bidden farewell did he begin to feel he had parted from a very worthy friend and that he might not meet with such a man again.

THE NEW TEACHER

Robin and Gilbert were sorry that Murdoch was gone: it meant their schooldays were over. It had been a pleasant and often exciting change going down to Alloway, mixing and playing with all their old schoolmates.

But another teacher soon came to see them—Betty Davidson.

She came from beyond Kirkoswald near the coast and tramped up through Maybole and Dalrymple and over the hill track to Mount Oliphant.

Once she had been a fresh bonnie girl, once the sonsy mother of a young family; but her husband had died and her family had married and left her and now she had no home of her own. So she wandered about amongst her family and friends. She was getting old was Betty Davidson, bent and grey haired. But she still had her health and could still cover in a day twenty miles of rough roads on her bare feet.

She came to Mount Oliphant because she knew that Agnes Broun would be good to her as she had always been; kinder to her than any of her good-sons allowed her daughters to be . . .

Betty was physically hard as flint, thin as bare bones and string muscles can be thin. In her sharp-featured weather-roughened face flashed pale eyes keen as a hawk's. But though the world had treated her harshly, Betty remained kindly. Bairns loved her; and bairns love only the kind of heart.

Betty's culture was a peasant culture. Like Agnes she had no book knowledge—nor had she need for any. Her peasant directness (and cunning) together with her forthright natural-ness were all the aids she needed in her journey through life.

So the songs she sang (and she was always singing) were as natural and direct as the love-making of the Scottish peasant. And Agnes for all her Puritan streak found no offence in them since much of her own singing belonged to the same order.

Robin was enchanted with them; and he accepted their sexual bluntness without unease or self-consciousness.

Betty's mind was stored with all the things Murdoch would have described as superstitious nonsense and William Burns would have dismissed as auld wives' clash—much the same kind of clash as had so annoyed him when his gable-end had collapsed when Robin was born.

But William was glad to put up with Betty's blethers. She was a great help to them, not only at the rock and the wheel, carding and spinning, but with much-needed help about the house. William's humanity would not have turned her away; but he was more than glad she earned her keep.

When their father was busy, the children gathered round the fire and listened to Betty as they had never listened to Murdoch. Her hands deft and nimble with her wheel, she set to her tasks and let her tongue wag at her tales of the supernatural—that rich inexhaustible peasant literature concerning the nature and habits of devils, ghosts, fairies, brownies, witches, warlocks, spunkies, kelpies, elf-candles, dead-lights, wraiths, apparitions, cantraips, giants, enchanted towers, dragons and other trumpery. And above all with the fell and unchancy doings of the Devil who, as Auld Hornie, Satan, Nick or Clootie kept up a familiar intercourse with the Scottish peasantry and was not averse on occasion to a visitation upon the gentry themselves.

Robin's great black eyes danced and glowed with excitement and wild pleasure: sometimes they grew bigger with fear and terror. He didn't know that Betty was completing the circle of his knowledge, filling in the gaps left by the rationalism of Murdoch. Though Murdoch had not scamped his work Betty built on a much sounder foundation. This foundation was nothing less than the day-to-day life that lay around him—the environmental world whose savour seeped into the very marrow of his bones. . .

". . . oh aye: there were wraiths."

"Did ye ever see one, auntie?"

"I did that, Robin. I can mind the day as if it were yesterday. My Uncle Patie was drowned off the Kirkoswald shore in a big storm and his body was never found: it must have been washed out to sea. Aye, he was a good man, my Uncle Patie; and his eldest son, my cousin Jock, was gey upset, the puir laddie."

"Why was he so upset?"

"Because he hadna been able to give his father a decent Christian burial. That's a gey important thing for a son to see done to his own father. . . Ah weel, it must have preyed on my Uncle Patie's mind. . .

"Some o' us lassies were coming up from the shore where we had been gathering seaweed for the rigs when I spied my uncle coming over the brae to meet us. Weel, it wasna exactly my Uncle Patie since he was drowned; but you couldna have told the difference. . .

"Oh, we got a gey fricht. I dropped my creel and ran away into the moss with the other lassies hard on my heels squealing and yelling.

"We didna say anything that nicht: we were that frichtened. But the next nicht the same thing happened at the same time and at the same spot. I tell ye, we never stopped till we were hame and had blurted out the whole story.

"My cousin Jock was sent for and he questioned me back and forward till he got every detail out of me. He said he would come with us on the following nicht and see what happened, for a wraith seldom gives more nor a third appearance.

"And sure enough he came with us the next nicht and sure enough there was his father's wraith for him to see as plain and as natural as if he had been in the living flesh.

"He bade us go on as if nothing had happened and he would stay behind and talk to him.

"But what they said to each other and what passed atween them is something that will never be kenned.

"But it must have been something terrible, something that he couldna put tongue to.

"My poor cousin Jock went hame to his bed and his hair turned white and by the third day he was dead."

"Why did he die, auntie?"

"Ah, but that's what I couldna tell you, Robin: that's something is buried wi' him in the grave."

With this explanation the children had to be content. But Robin's mind kept on thinking about such things long after Betty had stopped talking.

Not only did he think of the tales Betty told him: he pondered long on the strange words she used—words that seemed older and broader than those used by his mother. The lilt and rhythm of her couthy dialect was music to his ears.

Betty was a born story-teller. She used all the shades and colour of intonation; and across her careworn weather-beaten face every shade of emotion passed in some subtle and expressive way. Robin noticed every feature, watched how the pale eyes flickered and dimmed, sparkled with merriment or softened and dissolved on a salt tear.

And sometimes Betty would sing to them and Gilbert and Nancy would laugh; for she had a quaint croon to her voice and most of her songs were merry ones.

But Robin seldom laughed: his interest was much too deep for outward laughter; but within himself he would bubble with merriment.

And the words and their meaning and the lilt and rhythm that linked them in song embedded themselves in his mind even as they wrought deep emotions in his heart—emotions beyond the plumbing or probing of his intellect.

Sometimes when the children were out working or playing, Betty and Agnes would sit down and have an intimate talk concerning the heart of their problems and difficulties. Betty knew just how much Agnes was devoted to William. He was more than the head of the house; he was more than husband: he was something in the nature of lord and master. Betty was no farmer; but she was peasant enough to see that the Mount would never be a paying proposition—not with William working it himself.

More often they discussed the children. Somehow Betty sensed Robin was not his mother's favourite. She was surprised at this for to her Robin was by far the most lovable and gifted boy she had ever known. So she was always putting in a word on his behalf.

"Na, na, lass: Gibbie's a grand laddie and he'll be a fine son to you. But Robin's the laddie will surprise you all."

"Maybe he will, Betty. But if he sticks in and helps his father that will be a' the surprise any of us want. Don't think, Betty, that the one means more to me nor the other. They're both my bairns. But there's a dour stubborn streak in Robin that's no' in Gilbert. Maybe he takes it from his father's side for he doesna take it from me nor mine."

"It's just that the laddie's deep thinking, Agnes. There's more in him than in Gilbert; and because it's deeper in him it'll maybe take longer to come out. But when it does you'll see what I mean—or my name's not Betty Davidson."

"Weel, I suppose we'll just need to wait and see, Betty; and them that lives longest will see most."

"Aye . . . but be good to him, Agnes. For if ever a laddie needed kindness that laddie is Robin.

"But for guidsake, Agnes, ye maun get away frae here. I dinna ken what William Burns is thinking on. It's a dirty bog o' a hole this: ye'll never get out o' the bit."

"William kens best, Betty; you mauna question that."

"Oh, he's a guid man is William: I'll no' dispute that. But he's made a bad choice o' a farm: couldna hae picked waur."

"Our luck'll maybe change yet."

"Luck'll never grow crops on thae spritty knowes; an' there's mair sap o' life in my auld paps than there is in thae bog-sodden rigs—and ye ken that as weel as me, Aggie, for ye're neither blate nor glaikit."

"Dinna let William hear you talk that way, Betty. Guid

kens but his temper's brittle enough wi' a' his cares and worries."

"Aye: he's a worrying man William. And an honest upricht man. Aye; but ye can be ower honest, Aggie. And folk that are ower honest never live tae claw an auld pow. Ye ken as weel as I dae how folks live about Kirkoswald. . . I hae nocht against William Burns; but ye can be ower independent, mind: ye could smuggle a gey pickle o' stuff awa' here an' naebody would ken. . ."

"Oh, for guidsake dinna talk like that, woman. Gin William heard a breath o' that he would put you tae the door."

"Weel maybe; but I'm only saying what ye ken yersel' . . . An' I dinna like to see that laddie Robin hashin' out his young guts for nae end or purpose."

Workaday life on Mount Oliphant was brutal. Had the brutality been their father's then Robin and Gilbert could have eased themselves in hatred of him. But it came from the soil, from the weather, from poor seed, from inadequate fertilising and lack of gear and labour. Above all from the lack of money that would have provided for their wants and necessities.

From the first William did everything he could to ease the burden on his family; but month by month and as year ran into year he was compelled to call on their immature strength for help.

Robin gave his help willingly and without reserve; and on him the burden fell harder than on the younger Gilbert.

Yet through it all William never relaxed his effort to afford them some measure of education. In the winter nights by the light of the dip candle he would take them in arithmetic and grammar and explain a passage from his *Manual*. And he never failed to read his Bible chapter and to say his prayer.

Every Sabbath the family trudged into Ayr to the morning service of William Dalrymple. William Burns liked his sermons since they were of a milder temper than the sermons of the stricter Old Light Calvinists.

William Burns's natural humanism (albeit it was still a humanism rooted in Calvin and the Old Testament) was drawn to the New Light theology. But the bastions of the Scottish Kirk (compounded of the fundamentalism of Calvin with its battle cry: All Power to the Presbytery) were not to be breached by the polemics of liberally-minded pastors whose thoughts were but timidly reflecting the issues of a deeper struggle—a struggle that had not yet come fully into the open.

Robin had heard Murdoch and his father debate the fundamental issue between the Old Light and the New Light theology; and the essential outlines of the controversy were firmly fixed in his young mind.

He could recognise, in his own way, the arbitrary God of the Old Lights sending some to heaven and many more to hell, not for any good or ill they might have occasioned, but purely (and hence arbitrarily) for His own glory.

Robin did not warm to this cruel, arbitrary and capricious God. He warmed more to the God of the New Lights who recognised man's strengths and weaknesses and weighed in the balance of their sins their faith and their good works.

He was always overawed when he entered the crowded kirk in Ayr and found himself crushed in the narrow wooden boxes. Sometimes the kirk was warm and stuffy—especially when there were many standing. Bodies stank and sweated and the air was rank with the smell of the human herd. Sometimes it was cold and draughty and the herd crouched in upon itself and coughed and hoasted and was ill at ease.

But no matter what the conditions were Robin's dark eyes burned with observing interest under their drawn brows.

Here and there a prosperous merchant, a rich farmer or a well-to-do laird was dressed in good broad cloth; but mostly the congregation was clad in sober homespun, the hoddin grey of the peasant and the artisan.

Here and there a woman might drape herself in the generous if severely elegant folds of a silken shawl—here a mulberry, there a russet brown, betimes a flaming scarlet, but more often a glistening black. As a rule, however, the shawls were of good plain Kilmarnock plaiding.

Some had bonnets trimmed with lace and some had plain bonnets set squarely upon their heads. But most had mutches with a frill or a facing and tied under their chins with a bow of ribbon.

Robin noted all this going to or coming from the kirk for no detail escaped him. But he commented to no one and kept his thoughts to himself.

Not that Robin's interest was solely taken up with the surface appearance of things. From the bleak poverty of Mount Oliphant and from the unique angle of its comfortless isolation he noted much in the morals and manners of the parish of Ayr. The gulf between the mass of the poor peasantry and the more prosperous land owners, lairds, tradesfolk and petty burghers yawned deep and wide before him.

And he never failed to feel ill at ease when some young lass was on the cutty stool exposing her sin of fornication. It is true that William Dalrymple dealt less harshly with this sin than a stricter Calvinist would have done. But, Old or New Light, fornication was fornication and the guilty (unless they were of the gentry and in a position to bribe the Session) had to exhibit themselves on the stool of repentance for at least three Sundays and hang their heads in shame while the nature (and details) of their offence was recited from the pulpit and they were exhorted in the paths of virtue.

No soul in Scotland was too innocent and no mind too tender to go in ignorance of the sins of the flesh however vicious or unnatural such sins might be. No young mind was shielded from the shame of sodomy; nor was there any protection against the lurid details of incestuous practices. And since the stool was seldom free of a penitent fornicator, youth could hardly escape the conclusion that the pleasures of the flesh must be more powerfully potent than the virtues of the spirit.

Indeed Robin and Gilbert in their moments alone were wont to discuss the more curious aspects of the cutty stool offences, so that long before they themselves reached adolescence they possessed a complete if grim theological picture of the physical aspects of sexual morality.

But if Robin felt shame for the moral offenders he often writhed at the exhibition of petty and callous class snobberies within the walls of the parish church, as when a young lout in broad cloth would order a serving lass from his bench so that he might be seen to worship without the contamination of the lower orders.

But the mass of parish humanity he saw only in its Sabbath mood of kirk-going. By the afternoon the Burns family were trudging back to Mount Oliphant where isolation enveloped them for another six days.

MORTGAGED MANHOOD

The first six years of the lease of Mount Oliphant wore in and Robin reached his thirteenth year. He had long been doing a man's work and mortgaging a man's strength in the process.

He was weary with hard back-breaking toil: already his thin growing body was warping itself to the labour of the plough-stilts. He was overworked and under-nourished. His step was slow. For too long had he dragged himself up and down the wet heavy rigs. Even the straw rope with which he bound his legs did little to protect him from the seeping dampness. The ill-tanned porous leather of his cheap brogans soon became spongy and his feet were never dry. The loosely woven hoddin grey, the work of old Betty or his mother, hung about his shoulders; and for the most part it hung damp on his bones unless the wind blew it dry.

His face was gaunt and pale. His black hair was lank and lustreless. It was a face pinched with poverty, tensed with strain and drawn with the draining of adolescent upsurging. Puberty had assaulted him with unusual violence. Adolescence battled in his blood with all the ardour of a battle of attrition.

But in that pale face were eyes that glowed and smouldered; eyes that fascinated and repelled; eyes that exposed a quivering sensitivity to a brutal world; eyes shielded with a smoke-film of suffering; eyes into which no mother could look without being seared with sorrow. . . .

His mother did not look into his eyes: she lacked that nerve-tautened courage; and his father had looked too long into the eyes of pitiless pain to know any quickening response.

Sometimes William held the plough-stilts, sometimes Robin. They took turns in leading the team of four hardy ponies. Gilbert, with a long pointed stick, acted as gaudsman, prodding the beasts to even and steady effort.

The plough was heavy and cumbersome yet it cut but a shallow furrow in the thin stony soil.

Opening up and ploughing a new rig was strenuous labour. Leading the team, Robin watched for the bigger boulders. When he saw one in the plough's path he halted the ponies, took the spade from his shoulder, dug out the obstruction and rolled it to the edge of the adjoining bawk.

Sometimes he would need the assistance of his father and Gilbert to wrestle and lever the boulder out of the clay. Sometimes the water would lie in great puddles and he would have to squelch through it up past his ankles or endeavour, if the lie of the ground permitted, to dig a trench so that it might drain away.

It was slow work, laboriously heavy, and they were always late with their ploughing, always trying to catch up on bad weather and work that had fallen behind.

Cold, wet and hungry, with strained muscles and over-taxed heart, Robin would trail himself home in the evenings, sup a thin watery gruel, munch a dry bannock and then crawl up to his bed, worn out and exhausted.

If he sat by the ingle his head would nod and he would drop off to sleep, only to waken stiff and sore.

And like as not he would start up in the night with a pain at his heart, a throbbing in his head and an ache in every joint.

Then his heart would flutter and palpitate and miss an odd beat. Cold sweat would break on his brow and fear would clutch at his heart.

He would crawl out of bed, taking care not to disturb Gilbert, and grope for the edge of the water tub. He would plunge his head into the icy water, gasping and spluttering.

This cold water cure had been recommended by John Tennant in Laigh Corton; and though he admitted it was an old cure he assured them it was effective for a wide variety of complaints and a certain remedy for heart flutterings and dizziness.

When he had rubbed his head dry, Robin would crawl under

the blanket again; but fearful of lying down in case the palpitations resumed, he would fall asleep with his head and shoulders resting against the bed board.

And always the cold dawn came too soon, long before his overstrained body was rested; and he would have to drag himself on to the floor, sleep still heavy in his eyes.

Long before the break in his lease William Burns realised that his rachle of seventy stony acres was a ruinous bargain and that he would be better quit of it.

But he realised that without capital it was impossible to quit. He had come to the Mount with three children, Robin, Gilbert and Agnes. Now he had to provide for the additional wants of Annabella and William. To make matters more difficult, Agnes was again pregnant.

Seventy bare acres could not sustain his family. To have any success with farming he would require as many acres again. Burdened with debt how was he to succeed? And how was he to come by the lease of a larger place? There was only one possible remedy: to find someone who would sub-let the Mount from him. But though he made many inquiries he found nobody foolish enough to make him an offer.

The alternative remained. He could get rid of Mount Oliphant, realise what money he could, send Robin and Gilbert out to service and then sell his labour to some wealthy farmer who might be induced to pay him a shilling or two above the six or seven pounds of a land worker's yearly wage.

But he had been determined ever since he left his father's house that he would never subject his own family to such an ordeal. If he sent Robin and Gilbert out to service that would be the end of their prospects for education and advancement. He would endure much before he would break up his family.

He discussed the matter with Agnes.

"That is the position, Agnes. I have weighed it up from every angle and I can see no hope other than to renew the lease."

"But surely, William, there must be some other road for us. You ken fine if you continue working so hard you'll kill yourself."

"The place could hardly be worse. . . And yet Robin is growing up a strong boy and every year is making him stronger: he is a willing lad and a clever lad and together we might just manage. Gilbert's coming on behind him. . ."

Agnes was bitterly disappointed. She knew what farms like Mount Oliphant could yield ; knew something of the slavery that poor soil demanded ; knew her husband was not of the strongest and that Robin was no substitute for a grown man. In her heart she feared the worst. But experience had taught her that William was an extraordinary man who could do things ordinary men could not do. There was just the chance he might yet make something out of the ruin of Mount Oliphant.

Robin and Gilbert discussed the matter between themselves and came to the conclusion that their father was right. Neither of them wanted to be thrown out into the world. However bad Mount Oliphant might be it could not be worse than service.

Robin was deeply hurt to see how much his father suffered and how much anxiety he was given over the business. So bitter did he become that he overflowed with bitterness against all those who were comfortable and well-off. He knew of no one who worked so hard and diligently as his father: he knew of no one so harshly ground between the millstones of poverty and want. In his bitterness he watched the beggars going from door to door with their meal pokes. The beggars and their lean weather-beaten women were doubtless poor; but they didn't seem to be weighed down with the cares of the world. Their ragged brats seemed happy enough to be sometimes whistling as they scampered down the dusty loaning. . .

Often he envied the beggars their freedom from want and their freedom from the brutality of toil. . .

THE PROMISE

The sultry autumn afternoon became oppressive. The sky dulled to darkness and the sun was blotted out. There was a sudden brilliant flash of lightning. Great blobs of rain spattered down on the barley. As if the earth was being torn apart, the thunder came tearing out of the west and crashed down upon Mount Oliphant with colossal reverberations.

William hunched his shoulders against the expected deluge. But it didn't come. He looked over to the house, huddled below the leaden sky, and thought of Nancy who had such a fear of thunder. He let his gaze wander over the barley rigs, still thick with the thistles he had been thinning. Indeed there were more thistles than barley.

There was another flash of lightning. William trudged along the rig-end using the reversed thistle cutter as a staff.

When he came into the house he found Agnes nursing the baby and Nancy clutching her skirt in terror. William lifted her in his arms and went over to his seat and placed her on his knee.

"Now, now: what has my pet lamb to be afeared of? There is nothing but noise in the thunder: nothing but noise. And a noise cannot hurt anybody. Nothing but noise and a bright light; and the bright light's far, far away even though it looks so near. Far, far away, my pet, and nothing can touch you when you're sitting on my knee. . . And Robin and Gilbert are away down to get the pony shod at the smiddy; and they'll be safe down there. . . There's your mother there; and see! William's not afeared the least bit. . ."

His tone was so soft and gentle that Agnes stopped her low crooning and watched him with strange fascination.

Nancy had her head pressed against his breast. She quivered with spasmodic sobs. Soon all her terror was gone. Despite the rolling and crashing of the thunder she went to sleep in her father's arms.

When the storm had broken and passed over and the sun began to shine in the little window, William wakened her gently and took her by the hand and went out to the end of the barn. There behind them, towards Balsarroch, stood a rainbow in all its unique and harsh splendour.

"There," said William, "is the promise of Almighty God that never again will He destroy the world."

As he looked at the rainbow William made up his mind. He went in to Agnes.

"There is nothing else for it, Agnes: I will go down to Mr. Fergusson and tell him that I will be keeping on Mount Oliphant for another six years."

But William did not see Fergusson. The Laird of Doonholm and ex-provost of the town of Ayr was too ill to see anybody.

William put off the matter of renewing the lease, hoping that his old master would soon be well enough to give the business his attention.

But Fergusson died; and soon thereafter William was summoned to Doonholm to meet a very different person in the shape of one Mr. Ebenezer Elphinstone, an Edinburgh lawyer, who had been appointed to administer the Fergusson estate.

Ebenezer was lanky, wolf-faced and yellow of tooth and complexion. He was brusque and businesslike.

William disliked him intensely. He came back to Mount Oliphant fuming with impotent rage. Agnes never remembered seeing him so ungovernably angry.

He told her how he had been treated. Not as man to man, but as servile debtor to lordly creditor. Mr. Elphinstone had been looking through the late Mr. Fergusson's books: in future there would be no days of grace either for payment of rent or repayment of loan. All monies would have to be paid on the due dates. If not . . .

William did not like this "if not."

"You would think I was some beggar off the roads, the

way he talked to me. But I'll show him. A grasping ignorant man with the mind and manners of a scrivener. Clever enough maybe at hounding the law on to a poor broken man. But I am not a broken man—and with the help of God never will be. I will wear out the rest of the lease here; but I'll show him—and all who are like him. Threatened me too! Aye . . . threatened me. Said I had a very bad record with regard to my payments. And when I told him I had an arrangement with Mr. Fergusson he had the shame to say that the law took no notice of a dead man's word unless it was set out in due legal form. . . But I haven't been broken yet. . . I'll go into Ayr and consult a lawyer. . ."

But for all his irascible fuming and raging, William feared that the jaws of circumstance were closing in on him.

In anguish of heart and mind and body, Agnes took to her bed and gave birth to her last child.

In the evening William Burns took down the Book and inscribed below the name of John: Had a daughter, Isabella, 27th June, 1771.

THE HEART OF STORM

The years dragged in a grey monotony of labour and semi-starvation. The sour wet soil of the Mount held the seeping rains. The crops thrived but poorly along the stony rigs. Many of the cattle beasts, unable to survive the long winter on the miserable fodder salvaged from the blighted harvests, hoasted out their tubercular lungs and died.

Robin toiled late and early, trachling in the glaur and gitter and chafing under the enforced idleness when wind and rain outside made labour an impossibility and there was little else to do but water the beasts from the well and grind a ration of grey oats on the knocking stone.

Sometimes he would turn his back on the Mount and upon Alloway and Ayr, trudge to the brow of the brae towards Balsarroch and look down into the lisk of the land falling gently away towards Dalrymple and Maybole.

Sometimes there would be a lift in the storm. The sun would come out and the seeping mists would vanish. His eye would trace the horizon from the shoulder of the Craigs of Kyle round by Dunston Hill, Gartskeoch, Farden William and Pinmerry; across the Maybole Fault till the ground swelled and rose again to come full circle from Glenalmond along the gentle slope of the Carrick Hill to the clenched fist of the Heads of Ayr. . .

His heart would beat and throb and swell in his breast. Tears would well in his great eyes. The world of nature was vast and heart-scalding in its timeless beauty; and the world of men was harsh and heart-searing in its remorseless indifference and remorseless cruelty, grinding down against the galled flesh of poverty the hapless sons of toil who had nothing but their bare hands and their poor tools with which to wrest a living from a cold and unresponsive soil.

The strings of his emotion were tuned to the harsher elements. Let the wind blow the salt tang of the sea up the slow slope of the brae from the mouth of the Doon. He would turn his face on the valley of the Doon as the black clouds came down and the slow soft-swelling ground was blotted out; turn his face towards the sea, hidden in the driving rain, the incessant rain, driven from that cold distant unknown and unknowable Arran Isle, land of fantastic peaks seen (when seen) in the dizzy blue of peat-reek intangibility; the incomprehensible outpost of the Gaelic land; the fantastic *terra firma* of the margin of the ocean, of the land of mists and an unknown tongue, forbidding as only the mind's eye can forbid and restrain. . .

On such solitary walks, taken often in the heart of storm, Robin found ease for his troubled spirit and a harmony for the riot of his thoughts and emotions. Over and over in his heart and mind he pondered the question: **Why was man made to mourn?**

COMPASSION

John Tennant had moved from Laigh Corton into the parish of Ochiltree—nearer Machlin than the town of Ayr.

Their friendship was sadly missed at Mount Oliphant. Robin missed the company of the Tennant boys—especially during the long summer nights when the crops were ripening and there was little to do in the evenings apart from herding the cattle beasts—a task that could well be left to Nancy and Willie.

It was during the summer evenings Gilbert and he would go walking across the rising hill ground, explore the banks of the Doon or maybe loiter for an hour at the smiddy of John Tennant in Alloway and hear the crack of the older men.

The Alloway smith was something of a reader (it was he who had first given Robin the chaps of Blind Harry's *Wallace* to read); and he had a soft side to the sons of William Burns. It worried him to see Robin looking so poorly.

"What in God's name's cam' ower you, Robin?" he said to him one night. "Are you no' getting your bite up at the Mount? To hell, laddie, you'll need to be guid to yoursel' or you'll never mak' a pleughman."

Seeing how Robin blushed, seeing how his great eyes filmed with pain, the smith felt he could have bitten out his tongue.

He put his hand on his stooping shoulder and he grued to feel how the bones were sharp beneath the hoddin grey and the skin.

"I didna mean to hurt you, laddie. I ken fine how things are wi' your faither. Aye: it's a sair fecht trying to grub a living out o' a bog like the Mount; but that's a grand drying win' that's shaking the barley. . . Aye: I think we'll hae a guid hairst the year. We've never died a winter yet, Robin; and I hae nae doubt that you'll prosper gin the hairst were by."

Robin slunk away in an agony of shame. Had the smith spoken harshly he could have retaliated; but he had spoken with kindness and from the depths of a sympathetic heart. His gently-spoken words cut deeper than any insult.

When James Young came into the smiddy later in the evening the smith said:

"Hae you seen young Rab Burns lately? God, Jamie, but that laddie's starved. He's just mouth and een and a rachle o' banes."

"It's a bluidy shame!" agreed Jamie. "They're in beggary up there. William Burns's dying on his feet: nothing but that damned independent pride o' his keeping him abune the ground."

"He's a guid laddie that Robin. He doesna say much; but you can see he's a great thinker."

"He's a great reader tae, they tell me. You've lent him a wheen books yoursel', Jock?"

"No' this while back. . . 'Coorse, things canna be the same for William Burns since the auld provost died: I think the provost helped them noo and again."

"Oh, Fergusson wasna the worst, though Burns made a bad bargain wi' him ower the Mount. But this Elphinstone's my darlin'. An Embro lawyer: a heartless bluidy skinflint. . ."

"And tae think o' the money was spent makin' that estate o' Doonholm. It's well seen auld Fergusson made his siller in India—damned, Jamie, wi' the wealth he had he was nigh comin' on for a Nabob. He didna need to wring the last bawbee out o' Burns."

"Especially when you think on the way he laboured on that estate when he first cam' hereabouts. God, but he was a worker —nicht and morning, wet and dry."

"Ah, weel, Jamie, I carena what William Burns does wi' himsel'; but I'm damned if I like to see thae laddies o' his suffering. Man, I just canna get ower the look in Robin's face. Without thinking I asked him if he wasna gettin' his bite and sup. . . I could hae bitten oot my tongue. Man, Jamie, he

blushed like a young lass and a look cam' intae his een I canna
describe: I couldna hae hurt him worse had I hit him a clour
wi' that chappin' hammer. . ."

So deeply was Robin mortified that he decided to shun
company for the future. It was bad enough to know he was
under-nourished, that the whole family were under-nourished;
but it was humiliating to think that he carried the visible
evidence of poverty and starvation stamped on his face for all
to see.

He did not know that his white face (despite the natural
swarthiness of his skin) was no more pinched than Gilbert's;
he did not realise that the great luminous eyes set deeply in
his head accentuated the pallor of poverty and underscored the
state of his starvation more eloquently than any words.

To make good the loss of human companionship—especially
the adult conversation of kindly men—he took every opportunity to bury himself in books.

It is true that books were few and far between at Mount
Oliphant. *The Four Fold State* of Thomas Boston and Harvey's
Meditations Among the Tombs could not for ever hold his interest.
But William, noticing how Robin was avid for good black
print, made a point of borrowing a few volumes from a friend
in Ayr. If he could not get food enough for his growing body,
he would feed his questing brain with the sacred sustenance of
learning.

SUMMERS OF LEARNING

The summer following the birth of Isabella, William realised that his boys were sadly in need of contact with the more civilised world. So he arranged with the dominie in Dalrymple village to take Robin and Gilbert week about with the ostensible object of improving their handwriting.

In Dalrymple (lying a rough mile away, beyond Balsarroch hill) Robin met the smith's son, James MacCandlish, a lad his own age and with much similar tastes in the way of learning.

If his handwriting did not greatly improve at Dalrymple, the whole tenor of his being was considerably toned up. Indeed he brightened in a day and his great eyes that had smouldered so long flashed with new fire and fresh interest.

"I'm more nor glad I fell in with you, Jamie," said Robin one night as they roved the banks of the river Doon. "Your ideas are much the same as my own."

"But where did you get your education, Robin?"

"Oh, I'm no' educated the way you are. I had a good teacher when I was a bit laddie—a grand teacher—he's been away in Paris; but I hear word of him coming back to Ayr. . . My father took Gilbert and me in grammar and arithmetic, aye, and anything that lay to hand in the way of learning."

"Your father maun be a gey clever man?"

"Aye . . . William Burns is learned above the lave, Jamie. But self-taught for a' that. Still, I've read what I could myself —it's a wonderful education reading . . . if I could only get the right books."

"An' what kind o' books are you after?"

"Any kind of books as long as they can teach me. Religion, geography, natural science, philosophy, history . . . a man

canna know too much; and there's so much to be known. I
carena what I learn, Jamie, as long as I'm learning."

"Aye, that's just the way I feel about things, Robin. An'
languages: we've got to master foreign tongues—especially
the Latin. There's nae learning without Latin. I'll need to
master Latin if I've got to go to the university. . . It's a pity
you couldna come."

"Aye . . . it's a pity. But you see, Jamie, I had the misfortune
to be born into poverty. Hard work will need to be my university. But I'm not grumbling: as long as I keep my health
and strength I'll manage . . . someway. We'll no' aey be poor."

"It's a pity though: you've a grand head on your shoulders:
I wish I had its neighbour."

"We're quits then, Jamie, for I envy yours. There's method
in all your learning—seeing you have a goal at the end
o't. But I've just got to store my head wi' whatever comes my
way."

"But d'you no' think you read poetry ower meikle? You've
mair ballads off by heart than I ever kenned existed."

"Poetry fires the mind, Jamie: you can feel your blood
tinglin' to it: it sets your thoughts singing. I would rather
have the name o' writing a guid sang than preaching a grand
sermon."

But here the smith's son could not follow him. Though
neither indifferent to beauty nor unresponsive to the clamour
of humanity his mind had a hard rational bent; and he was
much too honest to give himself airs about things he could
not comprehend.

But in those few summer weeks in Dalrymple, walking and
talking with James MacCandlish, Robin felt that he had
accomplished more than he had done in the past few years.

He forgot his poverty and trembled no longer for his lean
jaws. His mind was agog with ideas and his imagination
flamed. He was beginning to have faith in himself; beginning
to find his own foot-hold along the dizzy crags of human
thought and speculation.

And he had talked so much that when he returned home his ears rang with the unaccustomed conversational silence.

William Burns noted with secret pride how much Robin had improved. So when summer came round again and he could spare him after the bog hay had been cut and dried, he arranged for him to go into Ayr for a week or two to lodge with John Murdoch and come under his tutoring.

It had been a proud day for William when Murdoch rode into the court-yard of Mount Oliphant on a borrowed pony to renew the old acquaintanceship.

Murdoch readily consented to take Robin under his wing for a few weeks on the payment of a small cheese and a couple of fowls past laying—and the promise of more to follow.

For all his travels, Murdoch was impecunious as ever and any foodstuff that would eke out his table in Ayr was as welcome as coin of the realm.

Robin plunged into his studies with tremendous zest. His keenness pleased Murdoch; but the progress he made astounded him. It was difficult indeed to realise that this was the same Robin who had sat under him at Alloway some seven years ago, shy, diffident and often dour. Verily they had not been lean years in the growth of his mental faculties.

So great indeed was Robin's enthusiasm that Murdoch, grown somewhat cynical with the harsh realities of the world, was touched; and being touched he was moved to respond with genuine concern and application.

Towards the end of his stay in Ayr, Robin, flushed with the pride of his new learning, took a sheet of paper and jotted down some notes by way of a first draft of a letter to his good friend James MacCandlish:

My dear friend,
            I now write to inform you of my latest progress. Mr. John Murdoch, concerning whom I have spoken much, returned to the school here some little time ago; and

my father, thinking to improve me further in grammar, arranged with my old master to have me boarded with him for some three weeks so that I might attend his classes in the daytime while having the benefit of his individual tuition in the evenings.

As I am now about to finish here it occurred to me that some account of my studies would not come amiss. . .

My grammar and composition needed no more than a brush though I must own to making progress in syntax and construction. . .

You know how often I have expressed the desire to have some acquaintance with the French language. No sooner had I expressed my sentiments to Mr. Murdoch than he immediately plunged me into the grammar of that language.

We applied ourselves without stint. When we walked, or had a meal, Mr. Murdoch lost no opportunity of adding to my vocabulary by naming as many objects as possible in the French. . .

My progress has been rapid. I am now reading the Adventures of Telemachus in Fenelon's own words. . .

The students here have been helpful to me. My young superiors never insulted the clouterly appearance of my plough-boy carcass, the two extremes of which have too often been exposed to the inclemencies of all the seasons. . .

Nevertheless, my dear James, despite the success I have made in my studies I cannot but admit that I have been much embittered by the inequalities. . . The veriest blockheads have nothing to do but waste the time of their masters. But because their fathers have money they may do so with impunity for as long as need be, while I must hurry hence and return to the Mount where harvest awaits me. Had I but more time. . .

I shall take my French books with me and shall apply myself to their further study with diligence. . . I have also made some little acquaintance with the Latin tongue and have secured a copy of Ruddiman's grammar. As you know there is no difficulty in the pronunciation of this language; so with application . . .

As soon as harvest may be safely gathered I hope to see you at Dalrymple, or you may find your way over to the Mount. . .

Let me hear from you, my ever dear friend, and inform me of the progress of your own studies. . . And believe me to be ever your sincere friend. . .

FIRST LOVE

It was autumn again, he was fourteen years old and just back from his schooling with Murdoch. There was an exhilarating feeling about harvest time: the reaping and bringing into the barn of the fruit of a hard year's work.

The weather held good. Day after day the sun shone round and warm with a lazy ripening heat. It warmed his bones—and they needed warming. It thawed out his incipient rheumatism and set the blood coursing in his body, dispelling the too early accumulation of toxins and the poisons of frequent fevers.

But his blood was hot from the sun of lusty manhood beginning to stir within him. Stir and disrupt and exult, ebbing and flowing in great red waves of passionate emotion, bringing the old coarse songs to his lips with new meaning and new urgency, giving life a new and secret awareness, a new pulse and throb.

But not only the pulse and throb of the flesh, clamorous as that was.

The brain too was afire, questing and thrusting and probing; turning over and dreaming; revolving with such speed and ease that it seemed to be storing energy against a day of need.

His whole being was active, flux-like in its activity, ever breaking down and re-forming, grouping and regrouping; but building all the time, growing in awareness and quickening in sensitivity : efflorescent. . .

He took his heuk to the harvest field, eager to test its new-whetted blade in the yellow grain.

But here was his binding help: a bouncing bright-eyed lass much his own age and already ripening into the thumping quean who would dance the *Reel of Stumpie* with the best. She was neat and clean, her bare legs shining from the wash in the burn; her toes pink with their cleansing in the dew-drenched grass.

The blood hammered in his head even as he eyed her. The last time he had seen her she was but a slip of a lass; before puberty had plumped her for maidenhood and lit the radiance of sex in her.

It was this radiance that drew response as he watched her making circles with her heel in the dust of the court. Immediately he knew shame and fear for the sound of his father's voice in conversation with Gilbert came to his ears.

He moved forward.

"Well, Nelly? It's a fine morning."

"Aye, Rab. I saw Mr. Burns—he said I was to wait for you . . ."

"Right then, Nelly: we'll get down to the rigs."

He was conscious of her radiance as they strode down the brae to where the grain waved bravely if thinly, burnished against the slant of the morning sun. He talked in jerky formal sentences in an attempt to hide the emotional reflexes of his spurting blood.

"Grand weather for the hairst, the year?"

"Aye . . . it's fine. It makes you want to sing."

"You like to sing?"

"Aye: when I feel like it."

"And what . . . do you like to sing about?"

"Och, anything that comes into my head."

"Or your heart?"

"Och, dinna be daft, Rab."

Daft? Maybe he was daft. There was something daft about the singing at *his* heart. Maybe that was why, when he read a glorious line in a length of poems, his heart throbbed in emulation.

His hand trembled as he re-whetted the sickle. Then he brought the shining blade neatly and deftly through the grain stalks close to the earth, saving the blade from blunting on the stones by his deftness.

Work had to be done. The good weather was a miracle not to be flaunted. It might rain any day now and keep on raining

for weeks. And if Robin hadn't the self-knowledge how much
depended on the success of his labour there was the twisted
shadow of his father lying across the harvest field to remind
him.

There he stooped to the hand-scything of their thin grain:
a tumult and riot of emotions with the new awareness of sex
stirring and erupting in his blood; and his young soul sending
out shoots through the dank mould of the Presbyterian faith:
his idiot piety being overcome from within. He swept the
stalks to the ground unheeding the strength of his right arm,
unmindful of the energy that flowed from him.

Nelly applied herself with vigour. The daughter of the
merry gow of Perclewan, whose smiddy rang to his lusty
hammer blows and echoed to his equally lusty laughter, she
had inherited physical vigour and good nature. She could not
know if Robin was in love with her: such knowledge was
beyond her immature years. But she knew in her blood he was
attracted to her, that he vibrated to her sex.

He was not the first who had done so this year back, since
ever the bloom of her blossoming maidenhood had flushed
her cheek and set the lights dancing a merry jig in her blue
eyes.

Gourlay of Whauphill farm had a son back from the school
in Ayr, and he had written a verse or two to her beauty—and
Willie Gourlay was not half the lad Rab Burns was—though
his folk were as bien as the Burns were bare.

Meantime here was the dark, disturbing puzzle of Rab
Burns. . .

She was working well, keeping her end up with him; but
her mind was day-dreaming with Willie Gourlay and the
golden days that lay ahead. . .

Unwatchful, her hand closed tight on a great jagged leaf
of thistle.

She yelped a little for the thistle pricks dug deeply into her
soft flesh.

Rab flung down his heuk.

"Let me see?"

He took her hand in his roughened paw. The paw was delicate and tender in its deftness.

"Aye. . . You'll need to watch, Nelly. This damned rachle o' stanes grows more thistles than it does barley."

But the roughness of his tongue was only simulated. He put the palm of her hand to his mouth and drew out the pricks with his teeth.

The odour of body sweat went to his head. . . The nearness of her flesh, pulsing and throbbing in its virginity, played on his senses with a pain so intense and exquisite it seemed as if his sensory nerves had been exposed from their sheaths. . .

William Burns straightened his bowed and aching back from his labours and cast a cold censorious eye on them from across an acre and a half of stubble. Yet he might have stood by their side.

Robin dropped her hand and went back to his heuk.

Some day he would battle his way out of this dreary hell of unending drudgery; some day he would win clear of the shadow and the substance of his father's silent disapproval— aye, and Gilbert's accursed meal-mouthed meekness.

And he thought what a relief it would be if only he could bring himself to hate his father, or his father would put in words the measure of his disapproval. But he could not know hatred for his father: only the anguish of pity for a man who had placed himself in the yoke of thraldom that he and Gilbert and Nancy and the other children might be rescued from any corresponding servitude; that they might have some measure of education and enlightenment; that they might in the end win free from the plough-handle and the cow's tail and know something of a life more full and free than ever slavery to the soil could bring them.

He remembered his father's words when he had gone into John Murdoch's at Ayr.

"Apply yourself to your lessons, Robert, and let nothing distract you. You know it's no' easy for me to spare you. But

I'm anxious that you should get every chance to add to your learning. You may not see the wisdom in that just now, Robert—but if you apply yourself you'll thank me in later years."

And he remembered how he had looked momentarily into his father's tired and sunken eyes and looked away again, swallowing hard on the rising lump of emotion in his throat. Some day he would take his vengeance on a heartless world that treated honest poverty with such callous cruelty.

He would master the world of knowledge; he would plumb the depths of the world's poetry and scale the heights of its thought. He would master French and force the treasure from the classics with the key of his Latin. . .

He would defy the world despite his clouterly appearance and the hoddin grey of his poverty. His stomach might be empty but his head would be full; his body might be covered in rags but he would clothe his mind with the purple of poesy and the fine linen of philosophy.

He had crawled up and down the stony slopes of Mount Oliphant: some day he would stride in independent manhood the rich slopes of Mount Olympus. . .

His dreaming was gone. He looked up; for now he realised that the bubbling jet of the lark's song had wavered and trickled back to earth.

He ran his hand over his black hair and the sun was warm on the nape of his neck.

Then his blood leapt. Here was Nelly Kilpatrick taking up from the lark, warbling her virgin-clear notes. . .

"What's that you're singing, Nell?"

"You don't know? I Am A Man Unmarried—my favourite reel."

"No: I haven't heard it."

"I thought you would have known that."

"Keep on wi' it, Nell, till I get the line o't richt."

"You never heard the words afore?"

"Never mind the words."

"You dinna ken wha wrote them?"

"Do you?"

"They were wrote for me by a poet—a real poet."

He dropped his heuk.

"A poet?"

"He had a notion of me."

"Oh?"

"Aye. . . Do you know Willie Gourlay?"

"No, no, Nell. Willie might have a notion o' you—and I wouldna blame him for that. But dinna confuse him wi' a poet. He wouldna know a poem from a paitrik."

"I think they're gey and bonnie—and I think you're only jealous."

"Do you now? Well . . . sing on wi' your reel—and gin the horse be to the fore and the branks bide hale I'll let you have a verse for your song that'll show you the measure o' Willie Gourlay. Aye . . . and give you a taste o' the sweetness o' a song."

"I didna ken you could write verses, Rab?"

He took a quick impulsive step towards her. Then he halted and let the arms he would have embraced her with drop helplessly to his side.

"Sing, Nell, for godsake. There's a shadow on the stubble no sun can dispel. But your singing helps me to forget it."

Nelly thought how queer and lovable a lad was Rab Burns with his black hair and swarthy skin—and his eyes. How they had lit up a moment ago. And how the light had died in them and how sad and strange he had become, speaking strangely and without sense—or with a sense beyond her knowing.

With queer heartache she felt she might be in love with him. But such love as she knew was the faint blush of virginal emotion.

For Robin the emotion was virginal enough. Yet his emotion went deeper, for his consciousness, his apprehension, his knowledge, his awareness, his sensitivity went deeper.

He saw Nelly Kilpatrick even as his father or Gilbert saw;

but he noted every detail of her lineaments to a degree to which neither his father nor Gilbert were capable.

He saw Nelly as the ideal woman. He added, in the final alchemy of summation, the quality of objectivity. Nelly became invested with all the qualities of vestal girlhood related to the Parish of Dalrymple—and to the eternal feminine.

It was too early yet to ask if this was the face that launched a thousand ships; but it was time to recognise in the lass evidence that her sex constituted Dame Nature's greatest work.

Over the supper brose he was distant and abstracted; but no one paid much attention for every one was dog-tired with the day's darg in the harvest field. Physically he was as tired as the others: mentally he was very much alert and active. He had much to think about. His thoughts were wonderfully lucid and luminous. He was inwardly exalted and nervously tensed.

His thoughts revolved round Nelly Kilpatrick. He saw her in every state of dress and undress; he saw her at every conceivable task; he saw her at her humble social round at kirk and market. And the more he saw her the more she became the embodiment of the ideal without ever losing her essential and distinctive personality.

He was moving towards creation though he did not know it. He had told Nelly he would show her what a song should be. He had spoken without thinking. Now he realised that he had put tongue on an ambition he had long cherished in his inmost mind. It needed but Nelly to sing her favourite reel and to add words written by Willie Gourlay for him to pick up the gauntlet and make his boast. He knew Nelly and he knew Willie. He was contemptuous of Willie Gourlay as a man: much more contemptuous of him as a poet—if he could call a mere scribbler of doggerel rhymes a poet. Nelly poured wine into his blood. And suddenly, without knowing how or why, all his reading and dreaming and seeing and thinking fused in the flash of inspiration. The flywheel of his will turned the gears of his mind; thought fashioned itself into rhyme and metre; neatly to the music's measure the words flowed to his tongue.

> She dresses aey sae clean and neat,
>   Both decent and genteel;
> And then there's something in her gait,
>   Gars ony dress look weel.

A shard of the harvest moon was showing above the mist bank of the western horizon. He walked down the hill aslant the day-old stubble, singing in his heart.

Every doubt and fear was cast off, all the poverty and hardship of his days was forgotten, the deep sorrowed lines of his father's face did not haunt him. Nothing out of the past could discourage him now.

For now he was entering into his kingdom, the gates of bardship swung open against his coming.

There was a touch of mist among the banks and along the braes: a risping of early frost whetted the air.

Good to be alive! Good to know the goodness of the Creator! Good to know that the future was there to be lived through and experienced!

RETROSPECT

Ploughing and sowing, harrowing and harvesting came and went and three rounds of the seasons found Robin still slaving to the Mount Oliphant soil.

Then came the great adventure when he was sent to Kirkoswald, in the care of his uncle Samuel Broun, to sit under the far-famed dominie there. For three summer months he enjoyed a freedom such as he had never imagined could fall to his lot.

And when he came home, buoyant in spirit and nourished in body, he found that his father had made a bargain with David MacLure, the Ayr merchant, and was about to become tenant in the farm of Lochlea that lay in the low hills some ten miles to the west between the townships of Machlin and Tarbolton.

Eleven years they had laboured on Mount Oliphant: eleven of the best years of his boyhood and youth. It was hard to believe that at long, long last he was winning free, that they were all winning free. They were going up out of the wilderness into the promised land. . .

The exaltation was almost overbearing. There would be no more factor's snash to thole; no more bitter weeping when rent day came round again leaving them bare of all comfort and hope. . .

And God grant there might be human company about Lochlea for the awful loneliness about the Mount had been a terrible price to pay for the seclusion of poverty.

There was but another winter to wear in and that could be borne gladly; for the spring would come and the grass would be green to welcome them to a new home and a fresh hope.

Elated and buoyed on a great wave of expectancy, Robin

found the hunger to write gnawing incessantly; and he was fired to emulate the poets he read and studied. Sometimes he reviewed the lines on Nelly Kilpatrick and thought they were as good of their kind as any he had read. How often during those past years, when dull toil and monotonous food had almost corroded his will to live, had he been sustained by that achievement and the greater promise that lay there. . .

Up in the attic he went through his bundle of papers, weeding out what he didn't need in preparation for the flitting to Lochlea; looking over half-forgotten efforts and mulling over old memories.

He had made attempts before now to keep some sort of record of his life, sometimes by way of an elaborate diary, sometimes by keeping copies of his letters with James MacCandlish and the friends he had made at Kirkoswald. . . Once he had attempted a play in stodgy and grandiloquent blank verse. . . .

He sat up in the half-boarded loft with his copybook resting on the wooden chest that served for a table. He cast a critical eye over an early attempt at autobiography.

"I remember coming to Mount Oliphant at the age of seven. Nature wore a very pleasant aspect as the weather was good and the time was early summer. I remember thinking in my childish way that the farm buildings were much more substantial than those we had left behind at Alloway; but that by virtue of the secluded and generally retired position of the farm it was lonelier and in every way devoid of human company. This was to some extent set off by the general air of freedom that was all around the place."

But Robin did not think as he wrote for he did not think in English; and he was never, to the end of his days, able to do so. He wrote English as he wrote French—only the degree differed. He had learned it from Murdoch who rightly, if unconsciously, treated it as a foreign tongue.

He thought, in so far as his thought process had relation to verbal images, in his native Ayrshire dialect, a strong heady dialect of the Scots language. More: the mood and tense, the contour and colour of all his thinking was Scottish. He could write poetry of a kind in the Scots language, reflecting his national characteristics. But he could only imitate the English poets in his conventional English rhymes.

So between his translated paragraphs, of which he was so inordinately proud, his mind spun a gorgeous web of imagery. But so far as his literary work of the moment was concerned, his mind worked in vain. How could it be otherwise when he had no literary model of native Scots to guide him?

He would picture clearly those far-off days when he had come first to the Mount. Glorious days there had been that summer, running about the braes of the Oliphant burn, paddling there with Gilbert and lying on the grassy banks pulling the gowans. . .

A year after that William had been born. That was the first time poor old Betty Davidson had come to the Mount. Poor Betty, God bless her! She had been kind to him, kind to all of them and especially to his mother. But for Betty how would his mother have fared? And the tales she used to tell them when they were children! She had died by the roadside coming to see them the summer before last. She had died alone with nobody about her and only a weasel maybe popping its head out of a hole in the turf dykes. . .

The summer months had been a great time for births. The summer after Murdoch had left Alloway, John had been born. Two summers after came Isabella. That had been a bitter year: the year Fergusson of Doonholm had died and that damned rascal of a factor had taken over.

He flushed and burned as he thought of the insolent threatening letters Elphinstone had written to his father; how his mother had wept. . .

And all for a paltry matter of a few pounds of ready cash run past the rent day! How they had toiled and sweated and starved themselves to pay that money.

He would not spoil his new Journal by writing about

Elphinstone: he would settle accounts with him some other day and in some other way. . .

Dalrymple and James MacCandlish. . . Robin cut a fresh point on his goose quill. Ah, Dalrymple had been but a preparation for John Murdoch and Ayr; yet what did either mean when set beside Kirkoswald?

He must put down some record of that glorious time. The quill scratched rapidly on the rough grey paper. . .

"Another circumstance in my life which made very considerable alterations on my mind and manners was—I spent my seventeenth summer a good distance from home, at a noted school on a smuggling coast, to learn mensuration, surveying, dialling, etc. in which I made a pretty good progress. But I made a greater progress in the knowledge of mankind. The contraband trade was very successful: scenes of swaggering riot and roaring dissipation were as yet new to me, and I was no enemy to social life. Here, though I learnt to look unconcernedly on a large tavern-bill, and mix without fear in a drunken squabble, yet I went on with a high hand in my geometry. Then a charming girl who lived next door to the school overset my trigonometry, and set me off in a tangent from the spheres of my studies.

"It was vain to think of doing any more good at school. The remaining week I stayed I did nothing but craze the faculties of my soul about her, or steal out to meet with her; and the two last nights of my stay in the country, had sleep been a mortal sin, I was innocent.

"I returned home very considerably improved. My reading was enlarged with the very important addition of Thomson's and Shenstone's Works: I had seen mankind in a new phasis; and I engaged several of my schoolfellows to keep up a literary correspondence with me. I had met with a collection of letters by the Wits of Queen Anne's reign, and I pored over them most devoutly. I kept copies of any of my own letters that pleased me, and a comparison of any of them and the composition of most of my correspondents flattered my vanity."

No: that was too bald, conveyed little of what Kirkoswald had meant to him. He couldn't put down all the details on paper. It would never do to breathe a word, now or ever, as to how he had helped his uncle with the smuggling trade; of the silver coins he had got for carrying the bundles of silk to the agent. His father would never forgive him if he knew.

Aye: Kirkoswald had been an adventure. And the drinking and singing and ribald laughter in Kirkton Jean's public-house! Before going to Kirkoswald he wouldn't have dreamed of spending twopence on a measure of ale. But there, with the clink of good money in his pocket, he had let the bill mount up. . .

And what talk there had been to listen to. Ah! the Kirkoswald men knew how to live. They knew how to jink the law, dodge the excisemen and escape the iniquitous imposts of the English parliament. They were the lads with a bold levelling creed who were not going to allow a parcel of rogues in a nation to do them out of their rights and their living.

If they did drink too much, were they to be blamed for that? Theirs was a hard and dangerous calling. And when a successful cargo had been run and the contraband disposed of at good prices, were they not entitled to have a night or two's fun and merriment?

Maybe it was wrong. But if so, they had not started the wrong; and they would have been fools to have let themselves be singled out for poverty and hardship.

But there had been other sides to the Kirkoswald sojourn.

He had applied himself to his studies under Hugh Rodger. Dominie Hugh had seen to that. Rodger was not the man to be trifled with. If his pupils didn't acquire knowledge by virtue of their native wit and industry he was not above lambasting it into them.

And there too he had made friends with Willie Niven, a fine lad not unlike James MacCandlish, but maybe not so fine in the grain, not so sensitive.

Willie and he had been boon companions, sharing not only

their smuggling secrets but also the secrets of their hearts and minds. Great times they had had debating with each other, taking the pros and cons of their argument with formal seriousness, addressing each other as they imagined a public audience might be addressed.

Honest good-natured Willie Niven and Thomas Orr were his correspondents now: they would always engage in an epistolary commerce.

As he thought, his mind, brooding and drifting quietly and imperceptibly, stopped thinking; the boarded confines of the loft dissolved and vanished. He was back again in Kirkoswald. Against the inner eye the miraculous camera of his mind projected the scene.

The fug of the lunting pipes was thick in the air for it was a windless night and there was no draught blowing between the roof joists. There was a strong smell of spirits and a heavy odour of ale. A broad wooden seat ran round three sides of the room. The men sat there for it was much too warm to sit round the long table by the wide open fire. The sun had set beyond the stack of Ailsa so the lantern, swinging from its long chain hooked to the rafters, was lit; and there the great tallow candle burned with a bright and steady flame. A cargo of wine and spirit had been successfully run and disposed of: the men were happy and in a mood for relaxation.

Willie Robb, the mason, was singing *Green Grow the Rashes*. It wasn't the first time Robin had heard the song; but he had never heard it sung in company and never with such open and unashamed gusto. Nearly every man joined in the chorus. Willie didn't stop when the landlady came in and one of the men gave her a hearty smack across her broad buttocks and said:

"You'll be glad you are no' a widow, Jean?"

And Kirkton Jean laughed merrily and said that as far as she was concerned she was as tight a lass as they could find in the parish—and that was how she intended to remain.

Robin took a gulp at his caup of ale. God, but the folk here

were different and didn't stink with the sour smell of Auld
Licht sanctimoniousness. Here were honest hearty men who
knew life was not meant to be spent wearing long faces.

"By the Lord, Robin," said his uncle, "if your father knew
what was going on he would tan the hide off you—by God, he
would ride post-haste down here and try tanning my own.
But for all that, your father's a grand man, Robin, even if he
is a bit strict—a real God-fearing man; but a fool for himself.
Na, na, Robin: he'll never make a living in a damp dirty hole
o' a place like Mount Oliphant. I couldna make a living myself
here if it wasna for a brig coming in now and again. But mind:
never a word. There are men here would cut your throat
without looking over their shoulders."

But while he was listening to his uncle, burly Dugald
Graham of Shanter farm called to Jean for the fiddle. When it
was brought to him he screwed the pegs and rubbed rosin along
the bow. He scraped the bow across the gut and finished his
tuning.

"Come on, Shanter, and give us the Reel o' Stumpie,"
roared Jock Campbell, who was his neighbour in farming and
in smuggling.

But the Shanter had been inspired by the singing of *Green
Grow the Rashes*: it was this tune he now transformed into a
wild strathspey. His great coarse fingers nipped down on the
cat-gut with amazing dexterity. His bow swept about the
fiddle bridge with ease and grace.

The Kirkton Inn went mad at his playing. Some of the
sailor lads brought in their lasses and began to dance. A
stranger who was representing one of the Glasgow smuggling
agents came in with Bessie Richmond, the finest dancer and
most desirable light o' skirts in the parish. The stranger had
plenty of money and he was something of a dandy. He sported
a fine bottle-green coat with brass buttons and his breeches
were of the best plush.

He stared round the room and his glance was supercilious.
He ordered wine for himself and Bessie and, while Jean was

bringing the drink, turned to the Shanter who had laid aside the fiddle.

He tossed a silver coin at the Shanter's feet.

"Music, fiddler! Let's see what you can do by way of a French measure!"

The Shanter did not appear to hear him. He quietly and unhurriedly finished his ale.

The room was silent. Robin sensed in the silence how the stranger had committed grave offence.

The Shanter rose unsteadily to his feet and grasped the fiddle. He faced the stranger.

"D'you think I'm some damned tinkler to be thrown money at?"

Without a word of warning he raised the fiddle, brought it down on the stranger's head and hung the wreck of it round his neck.

Bessie screamed. Kirkton Jean gave a scraich that would have fleyed the Dutch. Someone doused the lantern.

In a split second the place was in an uproar. The sounds of blows, yells, curses and breaking glass filled the room.

Sam'l Broun gripped Robin's arm.

"Don't move, for Godsake, or you'll get your brains knocked out. The Shanter's raised and he'll redd the place or tear the tripes out o' that daft beggar o' an agent."

Then Jean appeared brandishing a great fiery faggot above her head.

"Out into the road, the lot of you. Out into the road! D'you want the excise on us?"

A sailor had his arms round Bessie. Someone drew a measure across the back of his head that felled him where he stood. The Shanter was worrying and guzzling the stranger on the floor. Jean's sister, Anne, came in and started laying about the pair of them with a besom handle. . .

"Come on," said Sam'l. "Let's get to hell out o' here afore somebody's murdered."

That had been a night . . . standing with his uncle across

the street in the soft gloaming watching the folk being hustled out of the Inn door by Jean and Anne, who finally dragged out the stranger, his green coat torn to shreds and his plush breeks ripped to tatters and hanging round his ankles. . .

Oh, Kirkoswald had been the place for life and fun. Would he ever enjoy a time like it again?

The camera of his memory changed its focus.

Peggy Thomson, dear charming Peggy! She had done more than upset his trigonometry. She had upset him more than ever Nelly Kilpatrick had done. Those autumn nights in the deeper shade of the lea rigs and the wind sighing across the burnished barley! Oh, damn the world and all its mean money-grubbing ways! What signified the life of man and it werena for the lasses? Women were made for love and men were made for women. This was the solid sense and true purpose of life. All else was but sham and illusion. Peggy had been as sweet a lass as he had ever known—maybe he would never know a sweeter. . .

His mind gyrated, spun in dizzy exaltation. . . Peggy dear, the evening's clear: thick flies the skimming swallow.

Damn all books and all learning. Three months at Kirkoswald had taught him more than all the books he had ever read. He would write a book some day that would show what life really meant; what the joy and purpose and significance of it all meant.

Not a prose book. Prose would never capture, and set for all the world to see, the gay exaltation of the heart and mind.

He would sing as the lark sang. Sing as the wind sings when it shakes the barley and caresses the yellow corn. Sing as the lintwhite, the gowdspink and the mavis sing—without thought of fame or money or the cent per cent of the business world. . .

Some day he would gather his forces . . . find an aim and a purpose in words and in music, and linking and blending the twain, climb to the crest of the world and chant to all the downtrodden suffering sons of toil what life really meant and what God's will, translated to earth, really signified.

Oh Peggy dear . . .

How was it that women moved him so; played on his heart-strings as the zephyrs drew sweet harmonies from the aeolian harp?

How was it that some of them could make him quiver and tremble like a spray on the thorn? How was it that they could send his blood leaping along his veins and set fire to his imagination so that his thoughts crackled . . . ?

What words had come unbidden to his lips as he had held Peggy in his arms in the deep shade of the lea rig while the sun had been going down in a great blaze of glory in the waters of the west; and the crows had wheeled and counter-wheeled, swelled on the perimeter by the tenor-billed jackdaws, while the swallow and the swift had lanced athwart the ripening grain?

What words? The why and wherefore of them? Words flashing across the contact of flesh and flesh. . .

Peggy dear. . . But he would never be Peggy's. For many heart-throbbing nights there had been that possibility. But now he knew that Peggy was but another love, another experience, another enriching of the heart. . . .

How was he, a poor clod-hopping rustic with no prospects and no money, ever to emerge by way of love into the state of married bliss?

Maybe at Lochlea . . . maybe there he would find the new prosperity and the new affluence.

Maybe he would do well to give up his books and his reading and apply himself to agricultural studies and pursuits; learn about flax and flax-dressing and how to grow crops of potatoes and turnips. He had heard that some of the wealthier farmers were feeding turnips to their cattle beasts in the hard months of winter; and there was talk of a new grass seed that gave an excellent hay for fodder. . .

He gathered his papers together and locked them away in

his chest. He could not see clearly the road ahead. There were too many turns and dips and twists. Forward he could not see. Backwards he could look over prospects of dreariness and toil, lit with occasional patches of sunshine and laughter. Out of the past a great hand held him to the plough-stilts and the threshing flail. The present claimed him for its daily toil. . .

That would be Gilbert's foot on the wooden stair. He would continue his writing some other night. He reached for his bonnet. He did not want to talk to Gilbert now. He wouldn't understand: maybe he would never understand. . .

That was another tragedy against the bog of Oliphant. It had sucked out the song that had once welled in Gilbert's heart. Something of the sour Presbyterian bog-water had got into his blood. . .

When they first came to the Mount, Gilbert's eyes had danced with childish glee and innocent wonder. His head was bowed to the yoke now and his spirit drooped.

Robin squeezed past his brother at the head of the stair: neither of them spoke a word.

But that last winter exacted its toll from Robin. The spring found his body a battlefield of conflicting pains.

One night towards the end, William stood in his night shirt at the foot of the loft stair. Many a night he had stood there, fear and anguish and pity in his heart for his eldest son who cried out in the night.

What could he do? There did not seem to be anything organically wrong with Robin. There was nothing to show where the pains might have their seat. Maybe they were growing pains. But surely they had lasted over too many years and were much too severe to be growing pains?

Maybe he had worked the boy too hard. At the thought William groaned and Agnes stirred in her bed.

"Is that Robin again?"

"Aye: it's him. I would go up to him, Agnes; but it only agitates him the worse. I'm wondering if maybe I've worked him too hard and him growing?"

"We've a' worked ower sair, William: there's been nothing else for it but hard work—but nobody's worked harder nor you. Come to your bed and lie down now: there's little you can do."

"Let me be, woman. I couldna lie down and him up there moaning that way. Sometimes I'm feared for that boy, Agnes: sometimes I'm feared that the Lord may have laid His hand on me through him."

Agnes did not reply. He wondered at her indifference. Had Gilbert called out she would have been up the stair to his side in an instant. But there had grown of late a queer coldness between Robin and his mother. Nothing that could be pointed to, nothing that obtruded, nothing that had been put in words; but a coldness that could be felt when both words and action were suspended and only the intangibility of mood endured.

William heard the water splashing. He gripped the wooden rail and ascended the stair.

There was Robin kneeling beside the wooden tub plunging his head into the cold water.

"Are you worse the night, Robin?"

Robin spluttered and gasped.

"I—I thought I was dying, father. I thought I was dying. Father, why have I to suffer like this?"

William put his arm round his shoulders and dried his head with the coarse linen towel.

"If there was anything I could do, Robin. . . But the Lord's will must be done. Pray to Him and tell Him of your sins and temptations—ask Him to guide you and comfort you, for it is only the Lord who can. We all pray for you, Robin; and the Lord won't turn a deaf ear."

Robin freed himself gently from his father's arm.

"I'm all right now."

"Where do you feel the pain?"

But he shook his head slowly.

"It's not a pain like any other kind of pain—it's a feeling more than a pain. Sometimes I feel my heart will stop beating. Sometimes it does stop—and then starts again."

"Aye. . . You're shivering now. Cuddle down beside Gilbert there and I'll hap you up."

Gilbert slept quietly and peacefully and did not waken. William tucked the bedclothes round the shivering Robin. He allowed his thin bony hand to caress gently the thick damp hair. Robin closed his eyes.

William withdrew his hand and as he did so he thought of Abraham raising the sacrificial knife. . .

He knelt down by the bed in silent prayer.

He was cold and stiff when he got back to his own bed. After all, he was past his fifty-fifth year now and he stiffened easily. He sighed deeply as he got into bed. Agnes was sleeping soundly.

Maybe the Lord was leading him out of the wilderness of Mount Oliphant into the Caanan of Lochlea.   God in His infinite mercy grant that it might be so.

Part Three

THE SAFFRON PLAID

THE FARMER AND THE TAILOR

WHEN JOHN RANKINE, farmer of Adamhill that lay on the rising ground above Lochlea, stepped into his kitchen for his midday bite, he found Saunders Tait, the travelling tailor from Tarbolton, sitting at his ingle supping a bowl of brose.

"Damn me if it's no' Saunders himself!" he roared. "And how are you, man? Still the same auld prick the louse, eh? Aye: and what's your latest in crack the day?"

"Oh, I'm no' so bad, Mr. Rankine. It's getting a sore trachle up thae bits o' braes you have about Craigie. I'm no' so young as I used to be."

"Get another bowl o' that brose into your auld wame and I'll lash you down a gill o' whisky that'll put smeddum into your auld heart. Any fresh fillies couped the cran on your travels?"

"Aye: houghmagandie's the national sport nowadays, Mr. Rankine."

"And aey was. Man, Saunders, it'll be a bad day for the country when the lads start courting the lassies wi' a bunch o' flowers. I see you smirking there, Annie. Lay down the dinner, lass. Nobody'll court you with a bunch o' flowers. Maybe a docken leaf——"

Rankine roared with laughter: he was essentially good natured. He was a coarse raw man with a tremendous vitality and appetite for life. But he was no clod. He had wit and a lively imagination. He liked to bait the unco guid and he loved a scandalous well-told anecdote almost as much as he liked a dram of good whisky.

His daughter, Annie, was a great sonsy good-looking lass inheriting much of her father's robust sense of life. She would have taken houghmagandie in her stride had there been anybody to stride with her. But most of the lads were rather put out by her overpowering vitality or were afraid of offending her father. Annie was still in her teens: she knew her day was coming.

By the time Rankine had finished his meal, the whisky had warmed up old Saunders' heart and his tongue was ready to wag.

Rankine poured himself a drink and drew his chair over to the fire.

"See and make a job o' thae breeks, Saunders, or by God it's the last pair you'll make. Double thread them. I don't want my hurdies laughing through the seams the first time I stoop to tie my shoon."

"Oho! You'll have your joke, Mr. Rankine. You never found ony seams o' mine giving way—as long as the cloth holds——"

"Hae you no fresh verses, man? Damnit, Saunders, your muse's drying up on you."

"Well, I haven't been scribbling much of late, Mr. Rankine."

"You're no' getting enough to drink, Saunders—and you're too stiff getting in the joints for the houghmagandie. But I'll warrant you, Saunders, you've seen the day—what? Hold up your bowl, man, till I fill you a dram. . . Aye. . . what kind o' folks have moved into Lochlea?"

"Queer folk, Mr. Rankine. Damn queer and damn kittle folk."

"Aye, man. Burns they call them?"

"William Burns—or Burnes I sometimes hear them called. It seems they came from the other side o' Ayr. Mount Oliphant was the name o' the place. I ken the district—a wild un-improved place: hardly civilised."

"It's a' that. And what have you against the Burns folk?"

"Oh, nothing against them as it were. I got no order when I called in at Lochlea. Make all their own stuff. They're gey near the bone if you ask me. I don't know what David MacLure was thinking about renting Lochlea to siccan like folk."

"I don't know, Saunders. MacLure told me he was getting

a pound the acre. And that's a hell o' a money to pay for a damned bog like Lochlea."

"I wouldn't say now it was a bog, Mr. Rankine. It's maybe a wee wat——"

"Wat? Aye, and sour. You could wring it out like a dish clout. A wat glaury hole."

"Oh, but MacLure's giving them lime to sweeten it up—and that comes off the pound o' the acre."

"Damnit, they could hurl lime from the Machlin kilns from now till doomsday and they'd never sweeten yon clay. But that's atween them and MacLure. What kind o' folk are they?"

"Oh, a proud stuck-up lot. This William Burns is too stuck up to speak to a travelling tailor like me. And he's a big dour lump o' a laddie, maybe about twenty, with black brows hanging down on him like the gable end o' a thatch: Robin they call him. Then there's a prim sour-plumed brother maybe a year or twa younger: Gilbert they call him. A bad beggar yon if you got the wrong side o' him."

"Damn: there's nothing like the thing there for Annie at all. So they're a coarse set o' tinks, Saunders?"

"Oh, they're no' tinks. They've seen better days, yon lot. Speak like the book, Mr. Rankine. Most proper and polite. I don't know where they originally hailed from; but they're no' Ayrshire. And then there's a daughter or twa and twa-three bits o' boys."

"They sound interesting, Saunders. But they havena goaded you on till a poem?"

"No; but from what I hear tell of, the Robin lad tries his hand on a set of verses back and forwards like. But—it'll be mostly book-learned stuff for they tell me if you go near the place at meal times you'll see him and his brother—and their father—with their eyes in a book, and their mouths in the brose bowl, never speaking a word the one till the other, but tearing on at the readin' as if you could grow a crop of barley on a rig or twa o' black print."

"The devil you say, Saunders. Damnit, they must be

scholars. Maybe they're thinking o' coming out ministers?"

"No, no: I wouldna say that. Fegs no: the other way round if you ask me."

"What's that? Does the Reverend Paddy know about this?"

"Oh, Patie Woodrow'll hear about them afore long—or I'm gravely mistaken. There's more nor a touch o' the New Licht heresy about them."

"Aye: they would get that from Willie Dalrymple in Ayr: they tell me he's been shapin' New Licht this while back."

"Rank heresy, Mr. Rankine: rank heresy. . . No' that Doctor Patrick Woodrow is as strict a man on the Westminster Catechism as I would like—seeing that his reverend father wrote The Sufferings of the Kirk of Scotland."

"If he'd wrote about the sufferings o' the farmers o' Scotland it would have been a damned sight more to the point, Saunders. The Kirk has aey had a long black sour face till it. I'm all for a touch o' good goin' heresy, Saunders: it puts a bit o' wit into the discourse. Aye, man; but you interest me about the Burns folk. I'll need to call in there in the by-going some day and pay my respects—and size them up. But have another dram, Saunders, for I'll need to be on my way. I've never kenned you so empty o' a good goin' scandal——"

"Well—you'll ken Lizzie Dodds——"

"Damnit, Saunders, you'll have fathered one or two on her yourself—or helped! How often has she been on the cutty stool?"

"This'll be her seventh!"

"Aye . . . poor Lizzie. It's a damned shame that anybody should be responsible for her condition."

"Nobody ever confesses; and Lizzie has never been able to name ony less than three or four at a time. Aye . . . there's a sorry bit about Lizzie, Mr. Rankine. It's the lass that has to bear the brunt while the men go scot free. And that's no' the way it should be, Mr. Rankine."

"Damn you, Saunders, you're going doited. Your sins are beginning to worry you. You see Auld Nick's horns peeping out ablow the bed at night. Pour that whisky ower your auld craig and ply your needle. Time enough for a man to start sermonising when he's lying in the kirk yard."

With that John Rankine rose from his seat and went out to work.

When Annie came in she found Saunders making a wild attempt to thread his needle.

"Here, auld man: let me see your needle. Has my father filled you fu'?"

"Na: I'm no' just fu', Miss Annie—but I'm a wee canty-like."

"You men are a' the same: you'll drink and blether till the kye come hame. Now get on wi' you. If thae breeks are no' finished when John Rankine comes back you'll maybe get the other side o' his tongue: the one side's as rough as the other's smooth."

"I've a wee bit poem I could recite to you, Miss Annie?"

"No: I've heard some o' the poems you recite to the lassies when you get them by their lane. There's nothing wrong wi' my imagination."

And with that Annie Rankine swept the coggies off the table into the tub.

Saunders watched her from under his purposely lowered eyebrows. God! he thought: what a lass. The muscles on the balls of her legs and the scrieve of her houghs made his ancient heart pumping its mixture of thin blood and neat spirit fade and flutter in his breast.

He wished he could hit Annie off in a verse or two—if John Rankine didn't get to hear about them. For though he made the most outrageous remarks concerning his own daughter, he didn't allow anyone else to do so in his hearing.

Saunders had always admired strong women, women who accentuated the female anatomy in clearly defined muscles: women who worked hard and never ailed. Weak sickly nervous women he abhorred.

But in all his long years of travel round the farmhouses of

many parishes, Saunders Tait, self-taught rhymster of the village of Tarbolton, had never met with a woman who measured up to the attractive Amazonian qualities of the young daughter of Adamhill.

Nor, for that matter, in all his wide experience had he ever met any family that in any way resembled the Burns family.

But while Annie Rankine roused his thoughts to idiotic maudling, the Burns family caused him to be afraid. They were strange, alien, outside his experience—and they were scholars of some sort or other.

He feared this learning they had from books. Saunders also read books. But he had read enough to know the shallowness of his own learning. Maybe the Burns folk were wiser. Maybe they would scorn him and ridicule his poetry and his songs.

Let them dare! He hadn't been cobbling verses and sticking patches of songs together for thirty years not to know a trick or two. And he had some barbed shafts lying waiting in his quiver against the day when some enemy, thinking to have him cheaply, crossed his path.

THE REJECTED SUITOR

Mr. William Ronald of the Bennals was in way of being a gentleman farmer. Actually he was a bonnet laird, since he owned as well as occupied his own two hundred acre farm. Saunders Tait reckoned he was worth a good £300 per annum and Tait was seldom out in a calculation of the kind.

Mr. Ronald was very proud of himself and he was not without pride in his two daughters, Jean and Anne. The girls were good-looking and their personalities were attractive. But had they possessed neither looks nor charm, their prospect of dowry would have provided them with attraction enough in the way of suitors.

Their father was in no mood to have either of them married off his hands to the first suitor that happened along. Their future husbands would have to be chosen with care and with a view to future business.

But while they waited, he saw no reason why they should not be indulged a little. He even allowed them to indulge themselves to the extent of a birthday party—a new-fangled notion that had the blessing of the gentry.

Among the pick of the young people who had been invited to this party were Robert and Gilbert Burns.

Jean, the elder, whose birthday was being celebrated, had chosen Gilbert.

"He is verra refined," said Jean to her sister. "He must have had a good education."

Anne then insisted that Robert be invited.

"He is the most handsome young man in the Parish—and the only one to have his hair tied. I think it is verra becoming."

"I think you are in love with him," said Jean.

"I ken he's in love with me," said Anne.

And she spoke the truth.

The party was both a novelty and a success. The Bennals spence was crowded with young folks, laughing and chattering. Gilbert Burns was very quiet and looked at Jean with the eyes of a whipped cur.

Robert seemed to be in his element. His conversation was bright and lively and he made everybody laugh.

At the break up of the party he found the opportunity to clutch Anne's hand in the dark and lead her to the lea of the kail-yard dyke and bestow on her an urgent, searing kiss.

But when she met Robert the following Sunday she averted her eyes—and blushed. Her father gave him a nod, the curtness of which would not have been lost on a blind man.

William Ronald had spoken to his daughters; and he had not minced his words.

"Such trash are no' company for my daughters. Anne: I forbid you to cast a glance at this Robert Burns again. Perhaps you think because he ties his hair in a ribbon and sports a saffron plaid that he is some kind of a dandy. But it's the beggar's fidge he's gotten. They're beggars every one of them and will never be ony better. Had I kenned you were inviting such tinkers to my house I would have forbidden it. They are totally without money and without pedigree. Now let that be an end to it. The Ronalds of the Bennals will have no truck wi' cadger's brocks."

There was no arguing with William Ronald; and his daughters knew better than disobey him in any particular. Once before he had shut them in the attic and fed them on bannocks and cold water for a week for the sin of disobedience. They had no desire to incur his wrath again.

They were good-natured girls; but they were immature and without experience. They were too young to know that a man must not be judged by his appearance but by the infallibility of his pedigree and the worth of his possessions.

Robin had no such handicap of immaturity. All his life he had known what it was to suffer from a ragged coat and a clouterly appearance. He knew there was a dividing line separating those who had from those who had not.

When he had come to Lochlea he had thought he might pass himself off as a farmer's son. But he lacked the pedigree to sustain him in the role.

Saunders Tait and his like were not long in nosing out his past history and blackguarding his antecedents.

Besides, his father was but a poor tenant farmer in bondage to another man's capital. It was difficult to play an independent role with debt and loans hanging like a beggar's badge round your neck.

And yet for all his knowledge of this, Robert found it difficult to believe that such things could count behind the laughing eyes of a young and pretty girl.

This cut from the Ronald girls cut down into the quick. The cut from their father he could understand even while he could not forgive. But that a girl who had but lately yielded in his arms and had parted her red lips to the touch of his own could cut him at their next meeting was a wound of deepest offence.

Ah well: if that was to be the way of it, he would show them. He would see day about with the proud Tibbies of the Bennals. He would sharpen a goose quill and paint them in their true colours.

For some days Robert was moody and spoke little to anyone. When Gilbert asked him what he was writing (when they went to bed in the loft) he said it was nothing.

It wasn't until he had finished his poetical account with the Ronalds of the Bennals that the black mood passed from him.

They were digging their supply of winter fuel in the peat bog below Lochlea when he first gave intimation of the poem.

They had been cutting the long turves in the heat of the June morning, lifting them up to the girls who stacked them together on their ends to dry.

They had worked hard. Then came the noon-day break and

they sat up on the sunny knowe to eat their cheese and bannocks.

Many workers from neighbouring farms were gathered there together with a sprinkling of folks from the village of Tarbolton.

Some of the lads and lassies who were friendly with Robert and Gilbert gathered round them. Even Saunders Tait was there, chewing a grass stalk with his rotten yellow teeth and slavering into his yellow-white beard. Saunders always liked to be where the young lassies were. . .

David Sillar, the farmer's son from Spittleside, was sitting beside Robert. Already there had grown up a close bond between the pair. Sometimes David tried his hand on a set of verses too—much to the chagrin of the ancient Saunders.

The company was relaxed, jesting and laughing through each other, when the burly figure of John Rankine came over the knowe.

He greeted them with a roar.

"Aye: so you're a' here that's ony worth? What the devil are you doing up here, Saunders, you auld faggot! Stealing your peats off the lassies, eh? Aye: well, I was wondering if I might not lift a load or twa o' turfs out o' this bog. The bog o' Craigie's no' just as sappy the year as I would like to see it. What d'you think, Davie lad? Sit over, damn you, till I ease the weight off my shanks. There now! And how are you, Mr. Burns?"

"I'm fine, Mr. Rankine. It's not often we have the pleasure of your company down this way."

"Well, there's an auld farrant remedy for that, Mr. Burns —you'll just need to make your road oftener to Adamhill."

"Thanks, Mr. Rankine: I'll take that as an invitation. I'm told you have an uncommon good-looking daughter?"

"Oh, the hell you have, have you? She'll fix you, Mr. Burns. She's maybe no' the kind you'd get about the Bennals —but she'd make twa o' yon head-in-the-air hizzies wi' enough left over to serve a gaudsman. Aye: news travels, Mr. Burns: news travels."

"Aye: and there doesn't seem to be any premium on the direction, Mr. Rankine."

"What! Has auld Ronald cut you off by the pouches? Man, if it was a poet he wanted in the family he would have nabbed Saunders here long ago."

Saunders drew the grass from his mouth.

"Ah, but Mr. Rankine kens that Saunders Tait never went snooking where he wasna wanted."

"To say nothing of where he wasn't invited," cut in Robert.

"There's one thing about my Annie. She never needs to send out ony invitations. Wha catches her eyes in the right glint's got all the invitation that's needed. It's you kens that —eh, Davie?"

"Oh, she's a fine lass Annie, Mr. Rankine. And I reckon if Robert here goes up to Adamhill he'll no' be disappointed."

"I can't say that I've had to rack my memory recalling any verses you made on her, Davie. As for Saunders here, his whistle's as dry as a back-end kale runt."

"So you've a notion of poetry, Mr. Rankine?"

"Man, Mr. Burns, I'm surprised at you. Man: the place was rotten with poets until you came. Now they're frightened to let a cheep out o' them. But I'm still waiting the pleasure o' hearing your top notes, Mr. Burns. I'll no' deny I've heard rumours——"

"——rumours about the Ronalds?"

"No: that was no rumour. I had that straight from William Ronald himself at Machlin mart. He was inquiring after you—no' just about your health either. Well: I was as honest wi' him as I am wi' a' bodies. I told him I had passed the time o' day wi' you: but that I had heard tell you were something o' a poet and that poets and placks never went thegither. And since I had no doubt it was the placks he was after——"

Here Rankine stopped to roar with laughter.

"By God! He didn't like that. That let the pride out o' him like the stink out o' the belly o' a bogged braxie."

In that moment Robert warmed to John Rankine of Adamhill as he had seldom warmed to any man. In the flush of his warmth he reached into his pocket and drew out the manuscript of his poem on the Ronalds of the Bennals.

"There's a poem you might like to read, Mr. Rankine?"

"Who? Me? No, no: Mr. Burns. I'm no hand at reading verses. If you're going to be a songster in Tarbolton you'll need to be like the mavis: get on to the topmost twig and sing so that everybody'll hear you."

There was a chorus of approval at this. Robert flushed. But Davie Sillar nudged him and said:

"You can't go back now, Robin. Let's have it."

So Robert raised his head and looked away over the shimmering heath for he had the verses running sweetly in his mind.

"In Tarbolton, ye ken, there are proper young men, and proper young lasses and a', man: but ken ye the Ronalds that live in the Bennals? They carry the gree frae them a', man.

"Their father's a laird, and weel he can spare't: braid money to tocher them a', man; to proper young men, he'll clink in the hand gowd guineas a hunder or twa, man.

"There's ane they ca' Jean, I'll warrant ye've seen as bonie a lass or as braw, man; but for sense and guid taste she'll vie wi' the best, and a conduct that beautifies a', man.

"The charms o' the min', the langer they shine the mair admiration they draw, man; while peaches and cherries, and roses and lilies, they fade and they wither awa, man.

"If ye be for Miss Jean, tak this frae a frien', a hint o' a rival or twa, man: the Laird o' Blackbyre wad gang through the fire, if that wad entice her awa, man.

"The Laird o' Braehead has been on his speed for mair than a towmond or twa, man; the Laird o' the Ford will straught on a board, if he canna get her at a', man.

"Then Anna comes in, the pride o' her kin, the boast of our bachelors a', man: sae sonsy and sweet, sae fully complete, she steals our affections awa, man.

"If I should detail the pick and the wale o' lasses that live here awa, man, the faut wad be mine, if they didna shine the sweetest and best o' them a', man.

"I lo'e her mysel, but darena weel tell, my poverty keeps me in awe, man; for making o' rhymes, and working at times, does little or naething at a', man.

"Yet I wadna choose to let her refuse nor hae't in her power to say na, man: for though I be poor, unnoticed, obscure, my stomach's as proud as them a', man.

"Thou I canna ride in well-booted pride, and flee o'er the hills like a craw, man, I can haud up my head wi' the best o' the breed, though fluttering ever so braw, man.

"My coat and my vest, they are Scotch o' the best; o pairs o' guid breeks I hae twa, man, and stockings and pumps to put on my stumps, and ne'er a wrang steek in them a', man.

"My sarks they are few, but five o' them new—twal' hundred, as white as the snaw, man! A ten-shillings hat, a Holland cravat—there are no monie Poets sae braw, man!

"I never had frien's weel stockit in means, to leave me a hundred or twa, man; nae weel-tocher'd aunts, to wait on their drants and wish them in hell for it a', man.

"I never was cannie for hoarding o' money, or claughtin't together at a', man; I've little to spend and naething to lend, but devil a shilling I awe, man."

When he finished there was a moment's silence. The company was impressed. Saunders Tait had spat viciously several times. Not a muscle moved on Rankine's strong lined face, though the narrowed glint in his eyes betrayed his deep concentrated interest. Gilbert felt very proud of his brother.

"Mr. Burns," roared Rankine, "here's my hand to you. In token o' friendship if you'll have it that way: in token o' admiration whether you will or no'. By God, sir, and that's a poem. If you'll honour me wi' a copy I'll see that it gets the honours at the Machlin mart. Saunders! that gimmelled a hole in your chanter you'll never cover wi' your thumb—

barring you grow one like a pig's clit. And you, Davock?
What think you o' that?"

"I never heard better, Mr. Rankine. Robin's got more nor
a gift there."

"Weel, Robin: I'll need to be pushing on over the hill.
But listen, lad: gin it's a lass you want, and a tight clean
hizzy wi' the pith of honest pride in her, make your way to
Adamhill. But make your way to Adamhill ony the ways o't
—for John Rankine will be honoured to give you the best seat
at his spence-ingle ony night—and a gill o' the best malt or a
caup o' ale this side o' Kilmarnock. Is that a promise now?"

"That's a promise, Mr. Rankine."

With that John Rankine gave him a slap on the back and
with a wave to the others went up over the knowe ridge.

The sun seemed to stand still in the blue-white heavens
and bake a heat into the very bowels of the earth. But Robert
bathed in its heat for it seemed to bake out of his bones all the
vapours and distempers of long bleak rheumaticky years.

But he also glowed from a warmth that was not of the sun.
He glowed from the warmth of achievement, from the warmth
of praise and pleasure given and taken, from the wiping out
of the insult he had received from the Ronalds of the Bennals.
And this was dear to him. He had laboured long and often in
the dark, hiding his efforts from all eyes—sometimes indeed
not trusting his own. Now this was all changed. He did not
need to hear the chorus of praise and approbation from all
sides. He had known, even before he had finished the first
verse, that he held his audience. . .

The mood of their responsive appreciation had flowed into
him as he read, had given him confidence and added zest to
his reading.

Years ago, when he had told Nelly Kilpatrick of his song,
he had become conscious that the gates of bardship were open
against his coming. . . He had had a vision then that only
now was beginning to transform itself into reality, beginning
to take shape.

Long after the others had gone back to the cutting of the peats he lay on the baking knowe in the full glare of the sun, his bonnet pulled down over his eyes, thinking and dreaming.

His pride was stirred and his vanity was given a lift. Despite wealth and honours and fertile well-stocked mailens he was a better man than any of them. Aye: the whole parish of Tarbolton hadn't his equal: he would make them accept this some day.

It was time to assert himself. He was coming twenty. Soon he would be all the man he would ever be. Already he had tied his hair—on dress occasions—as a symbol of his independence— as a distinguishing badge of his bardry. And if he wore a saffron plaid it was to mark him off from all those who were guilty of the sin of compliance. But he did not comply. He was a protestant in the true meaning of the word. Neither the dictates of Old Light or New Light Presbyterianism would enslave his reason or warp the promptings of his heart.

He would seek the company of men like John Rankine and lads like Davie Sillar—open-hearted honest folks caring nothing for rank or privilege or possessions; caring only for honest worth whether clad in rags or clothed in good broadcloth.

Having come to the decision that henceforth he would assert himself and claim his true birthright amongst the sons of men and the daughters of women, he raised himself from the springy turf and went striding down the brae to where the others were busy in the peat bog.

TARBOLTON DANCING

Time was beginning to sour the temper of William Burns. No matter how hard he worked or how skilfully he planned, success did not seem to fall to his lot.

Lochlea was not a failure. Indeed he was making ends meet and managing to save a little against the rainy days he felt would inevitably descend upon him.

But Lochlea was far from being the success he had hoped for. There were many long years ahead of him before the place would really begin to pay. If only he could lay his hands on more capital in order that he might better sweeten the soil and extend the acres of cultivation. But the use of capital was not for him who had no security other than his own labour to offer.

All this tended to sour William Burns and exacerbate his already overstrained nervous system.

Even had his temper not been so irritated, he would still have opposed Robert's suggestion that he attend the dancing school at Tarbolton. True, his opposition might have been less unreasonably posed; but he would have opposed nevertheless.

To Robert, feeling the sap of life rising in him and feeling the need for human companionship after the years of friendlessness on Mount Oliphant, this opposition of his father's seemed wholly unreasonable. He could not understand his father's fears, nor could his father explain his fears to him.

William loved his son—loved him above all others. But long ago, in the harvest field with Nelly Kilpatrick, he had realised that his son was highly sexed: that girls inflamed him. Now he feared any activity that would lead Robin into an association with sex-conscious women.

And what was dancing but an association of the sexes based on reciprocal sexual attraction? They certainly did not join together in dancing because they were repelled from each other.

So when Robin, after supper one evening, suggested he was

going to join the new dancing school at Tarbolton, his father answered him briefly and sternly.

"I forbid you to go near any dancing school."

"But why?"

Agnes looked coldly at him.

"Your father has spoken, Robin."

"Yes ... I know. But surely I can be given a reason?"

"There's nae need for your father to give reasons."

Robin was silent for a moment. He hadn't expected to meet with such a blank and bewildering refusal.

"They're all going. Davie Sillar, Willie MacGavin ... Annie Rankine. None of them work any harder than I do—maybe few of them as hard. My manners need a brush. At Mount Oliphant we saw nothing. Here it's different. Even if we had to live like hermits at Mount Oliphant, is there any reason why we should do so here?"

Gilbert and Nancy looked at him askance. This was a new way for Robin to talk. Something would happen now.

Agnes looked at him strangely.

"Robin! I dinna ken what's come over you. There's Gilbert—*he* doesna want to go near ony dancing——"

"Am I to be judged forever by what Gilbert does and what Gilbert doesna do?"

William turned his head from the fire towards Robin where he stood defiantly in the middle of the kitchen.

"I am not going to bandy arguments with you. I am ashamed of the way you have spoken to your mother. You never stay a night in the house. Maybe you are getting too proud for our simple way of life. But the way of life here is the Lord's way; and I'll have it no other. If you go near this dancing school, you will go in absolute defiance of my command."

"I will not go if you can show me good reason why I should not go. But unless——"

"Are not my commands good enough reason for you?"

"... no: I want reasons!"

"Then go your ways! But remember: you are disobeying your father. Remember that. And remember I'll have no fornicators darkening my door."

"I am no fornicator."

"No: not yet . . . not yet. But you're setting your foot on the road that will lead you there."

Robin looked straight into his father's face—a face almost contorted with rage. He had never seen him so angry. But anger was mounting in him too. Fornicating! He would throw that back in his father's teeth.

He held his father's eyes, burning with anger in their sunken sockets, till he turned his head away. Not one of his brothers or sisters looked at him. They sat with bowed heads.

Robin lifted his bonnet from the chair and went out into the darkness.

He had burned his boats now. He had begun by defying his father. Well: his father had been more than unreasonable; he had been unjust. He had lost his temper. He was doing that quite a lot now: flying into a tantrum whenever he was crossed—or imagined he was crossed. Well: he had shown them he wasn't going to have his life laid down for him every hour of the day. When he did a day's work and did it well, he was entitled to spend a few hours of the evening in relaxation or in company.

Never spent a night at home, did he not! Well, what kind of a home was it? What pleasure was there for him in the house of an evening? Gilbert was nineteen: Nancy was seventeen. Bell was fifteen and Willie was twelve. John was coming nine or ten and Isabel would be coming eight. And all of them crowded into the kitchen. He was supposed to crowd in amongst them—and enjoy himself! It would be more like the thing if Gibby and Nancy came to the dancing with him. Nancy would like it. Aye: and Gibby too—if only he would get up and shake himself.

Anyway: hadn't he a right to see life and enjoy a few hours of freedom while he was young and had the chance? He needed to mix with young men and women of his own age and learn how to conduct himself in mixed company. He was no better than an uncivilised clod not to be able to dance at his age.

Fornicating! His father was becoming impossible. That hurt though. Maybe. . . Well: damn it: what if he did want to know . . . and experience. . . But not fornicating—that was unjust and cruel. There might have been Fisher Megs in Kirkoswald: there were none in Tarbolton.

But there were sweet lassies and bonnie lassies, and they weren't all proud Tibbies. Just honest country lassies fond of a laugh and a kiss and a cuddle—as they should be. Aye: and all after the day's drudgery—after they had earned their right to play and enjoy an hour's pleasant daffing.

How would he ever write poetry— But what was the use! He would never get anywhere reading and writing poetry. He would have to live it first—better still, live it all the time. Life didn't last very long—not the short life that was lived between the short hours of working and sleeping.

Davie Sillar was waiting for him at the road end.

"That you, Davie?"

"Aye. . . You managed, Robin?"

"What was to hinder me? Oh, I had words with my father. But—I'm here, Davie; and that's all that matters. Are we picking up Willie MacGavin?"

"If you like, Robin. Are we going to see some o' the lassies?"

"Aye . . . but let's see if we can collect Sandy Brown and Watty Mitchell. It'll be best if we get together some of the lads we know before we go in."

"Are you feeling nervous, Robin?"

"Me? No: I'm no' nervous. But I'd rather wait till after the lesson."

"Are you going to see Betsy up the road?"

"No: I don't want to be late. No . . . I'll wait and see who's there."

"Getting tired o' Betsy?"

"Oh—I was never very set on Betsy."

"Annie Rankine'll be there."

"Phew! I hope I don't get her for a reel."

"By God, Rob, Annie would oxter you home."

"If she gave you a hug she'd break your ribs."

"And if you gave her one she might break your neck."

"D'you think so?"

"I wouldna like to risk it. Would you?"

"I don't know, Davie. There's something about Annie. Aye . . . I wouldna mind finding out what she was like . . ."

They went on into Tarbolton together discussing their intimate problems intimately with each other. Davie was by nature cautious and maybe cunning. But in Robin's company he felt bolder and more sure of himself. Robin drew something out of him that, by himself, he would rather have suppressed.

Davie tried his hand on a set of verses just as he tried his hand at a tune on the fiddle—merely to amuse himself. Davie was a gentle amateur with a mild artistic bent. Robin made him feel that poetry and music were important—even more important in a way than being in love with the lassies. Davie had always liked poetry and music; but never till he had fallen in with Robert Burns had he thought they could be important.

Robin, delighted to meet a pleasant lad bred to the plough stilts like himself and son of a tenant farmer and sharing his intellectual and artistic interests, saw in Davie a greater gift and a greater promise than really existed. The ram-stam impetuosity of his questing mind could not stop to note that Davie was only too often reflecting his own image and echoing his own thoughts.

The dancing lessons had been timed with an eye to the waxing and waning of the moon. She was the country folks' lantern to light their way along the dirty cart-tracks and over paths across the boggy moors. But the moon was not yet up. Great drifts of black-bellied clouds scudded across the sky, though there was but little wind below. It was unlikely there would be rain before morning.

Willie MacGavin, Sandy Brown and Watty Mitchell were gathered round the embers of the smiddy fire when Robin and Dave came forward.

After a round of salutations Robin said:

"Well, lads: this is the night we learn to foot it neatly. I hope you're all feeling in grand trim."

Willie the smith's son said:

"Foot it neatly! I hope your feet are clean, Rab? You dance wi' the bare hoofs at Anra MacAslan's school."

Sandy Brown, the apprentice wheelwright, added:

"You only get the pumps on when it's the ball."

"To hell!" cried Watty, who was learning the dyke building. "I don't know when I washed my feet last. I'd better give them a plouter in the trough."

He sat down on the anvil and cast off his shoon.

"I think I'll give mine a plouter along with you, Watty. If it doesn't clean them it'll cool them off."

In no time they were all splashing their feet in the stone trough.

"Here's a piece o' bag," said Willie. "This'll scour the kell off them."

While they were splashing and rubbing and laughing a cadenza of girlish laughter came fluting down the village street.

"That's Peggy Dunlop," cried Watty. "I'd know her pipe anywhere. Here's the bag, Robin: I'm finished."

While they hurriedly pulled on their stockings and thrust their feet into their shoon, there was another flutter of laughter.

"Where the hell did I put my other stocking?" cried Watty. "That's Mysie Graham wi' Peggy."

"Whether is it Mysie or Peggy for the hame-gaun?"

"I'm not particular, Rab. You can have your pick: I'll take the leavings."

"No," said Davie. "You're wrong. Robin's for Annie Rankine."

"By God, Rab! You'll need a tight girth on your saddle

if you ettle to ride the Rankine mare. Boy, if she was shod she'd kick the lights out of you."

"Quiet now: here they come. Never a word."

They withdrew into the shadow away from the fire. When the girls were abreast of the smiddy door, Watty let out an ungodly agonised howl.

"The whole bloody village will be out now!" muttered Willie.

"Wha's that?" cried one of the girls.

They had stopped dead in their tracks. Then the voice of Annie Rankine cut sharply across the silence.

"It's only one o' thae daft Tarbolton colts gettin' shod for the dance. Come on!"

Robin stepped out of the smiddy.

"Good evening, ladies! I trust my coltish friend——"

"That's Robert Burns," cried Annie. "Awa' wi' you, man!"

Mysie and Peggy giggled. The others emerged from the smiddy and gathered round.

"You'll have to show a clean pair o' heels the night, Annie, or you'll no' get dancing."

"You must have been scrubbing yours for a week then, Mr. Mitchell."

"One up for you, Annie. You're the boy for them."

"I'm the boy for you too, Willie MacGavin."

"May we have the pleasure of escorting you——"

"Oh, you shut up, Robert Burns. You're a grand speechifier——"

Willie MacGavin and Watty Mitchell had made their way to the sides of Peggy Dunlop and Mysie Graham.

"Come on up the street," said Willie. "Rab can argue it out with Annie."

So Robin and Annie fell behind. Annie was very sensitive to her robust proportions: it had become second nature with her to be on the defensive. Now that Robin was alone with her he felt drawn towards her—yet he was nervous.

"We were only joking, Annie."

"Oh, I can take a joke."

"Take one and give one?"

"I can look after myself."

"I never heard any suggestion to the contrary, Annie. But I wouldna like to quarrel about it."

"You can quarrel if you like: it's the one odds to me. I came here to dance."

"So did I, Annie. But it would be nice to be friends about it. I've always been hoping to get up to see your father."

"You ken the road, don't you?"

"Yes: I ken the road. I admire your father, Annie."

"He'll be set up about that."

Robin laughed softly.

"I surrender, Annie: I surrender."

"I think you've a mighty conceit o' yourself, Robert Burns."

"Is that a bad thing?"

"No' if you've got anything to be conceited about."

"You don't think I've got anything?"

"I'm not interested."

"You're a poor liar, Annie."

"Compliments are flying high the nicht."

"You're worth a dozen o' thae gigglin' Tarbolton hizzies, Annie. And damn fine you know it. You've an honest tongue in you and that goes wi' an honest heart. And you've got good looks and charm in plenty. Only—you think I'm no' serious: you think I'm only repeating fine words. Well: time will show, Annie. All I ask from you is that you give me your friendship till I prove my sincerity to you."

Annie had no rejoinder ready at the tip of her sharp tongue. She had never been spoken to like this. She didn't know that a young man could speak like this—or any man for that matter, young or old. Compliments she had known, crude joking she had known—more than enough. But never before had a young man called her a liar in a way that sounded like a compliment; never before had a young man—obviously attracted—asked for nothing but her friendship.

There did not seem to be any reason to doubt the deep calm sincerity of this Robert Burns of whom her father spoke in such terms of admiration and respect.

And yet Annie was not sure of herself. This Robert Burns wrote poetry. Poetry, her father said, that made Saunders Tait look like a spavined spaewife and Davie Sillar a prattling schoolboy.

Maybe. She knew nothing about poetry other than what she had got at Tarbolton school—and from the rag-picker rhymes of old Tait. But somehow she had gotten the notion that poets were kittle cattle and not to be trusted. Maybe this Robert Burns who was but his father's ploughman at Lochlea —and an incomer to the district and a poor one at that by all accounts—was less to be trusted for all his fine words than any other lad.

He'd been turned down at the Bennals. But that hadn't stopped him from making up to other lassies in the parish— swanking about on the Sabbath day too—quite the dandy with his fancy plaid and buckles to his shoon.

Oh . . . she didn't know. If he could be trusted . . . she would show the other lassies. But if he was playing with her . . . she'd show him something more than a sharp tongue.

Maybe it was just as well that her father, who had business in the village, would be waiting to take her home.

Robin was discomfited by her long silence.

"You—don't believe me, Annie. You—don't want my friendship?"

"Don't be so quick, Mr.——"

"Not Mister——"

"Robert then."

"Robert if you must, Annie: Robin if you will."

"Och, you'd wile the bird off the bush. I'm not going to call you anything or I'll call you whatever I like. Seeing I'm a liar it winna matter."

"Right then, Annie. But you know you're not that kind

of a liar. But I'm glad we're going to be friends. Here's the others waiting for us. . ."

He found her hand in the dark and gave it a sudden, impulsive squeeze. Annie did not resist.

Anra MacAslan, having taken his shilling fee at the door and memorised each face as they filed past him, mounted the wood-block at the far-end of the barn and viewed the throng of young people.

A temporary plank seat went up each side of the barn. The beaten earth floor had been freshly swept with a heather broom. Four tallow candle lights gave illumination from the iron lanterns hung from the roof-bauks.

It was a pleasant and warm-hearted scene: groups of lads and lassies standing about the barn laughing and joking; the lads in their hoddin-grey homespuns, coarse knitted stockings and cobbled shoon; the lassies in their short-kilted gowns of homespun, nearly all of them with a plaid shawl homespun or hand-knitted. None with stockings, but all with rough shoon. And all with bare arms from the elbows. Most were sun-tanned and weather-beaten: some of their forearms were a mass of reddish brown freckles: some had a thick down of black hair.

Anra was a small wiry fellow in his middle forties: his reddish beard was beginning to show streaks of grey. Because he was almost totally bald, he never removed his blue bonnet: folks said he slept in it.

"Now, if you're all ready we'll begin," said Anra. "First I've a few rules I would like you to remember. And when I say rules I mean rules. Your fathers and your mithers lippen on me to conduct my dancing class in the maist respectable manner. Therefore there's to be no horseplay of ony kind. Onybody the worse o' drink will be putten out—immediately. Now that's a rule canna be broken. There's to be no quarrelling among each other. This is a dancing school and no' a school for houghmagandie. The lassies will sit on the right side o' the barn and the lads on the left hand. Partners will be chosen and sets made up strictly in rotation, depending on how the dance works out. Now then: if you've brocht a lass here and some other lad gets intil a set with her, that'll just be the way things run out. So I'll hae nae fechtin' ower that. Now, when it turns out that it comes your turn to link up wi' a lass, you'll remember first of all that you're a gentleman—or that you're learning to be gentlemen. Now it may turn out that your partner for the moment happens to be a lass that you're in love with or a lass that after a manner you dislike. Now—and this is most important—whatever your feelings to the lassie may be you'll show no feelings of a personal kind at all; you'll neither show familiarity nor yet will you show contempt. You'll show what's called breeding. You'll show your partner at all times and under all circumstances a proper and genteel respect. That holds for every one o' you lads and lassies.

"Just another thing. You'll dance on your bare feet. That saves a lot o' trouble—and it kicks up less stour. When it comes round to the ball, of course, that'll be different. You'll have your dancing pumps then. I'll tak' orders for them at ony time—three shillings a pair and cheap at the money.

"Now for the lessons. Take up your positions, ladies and gentlemen. Ladies to the right: gentlemen to the left.

"Now: the first essential I want you to get is this. In all dancing you maun learn to hold yourself erect: head up, shoulders square—square, I said—no' hunched up round your lugs—back and down. No' too stiff. Now: hands on your haunches—both hands—thumbs to the back. Your back—where your spine is—or where it should be. Your haunches—feel your haunch bane in the lisk of your thumb and forefinger—like this! That's better. Now then: heads up, eyes front. And don't look at your feet—even though you washed them just afore you came out. Never look at your feet—look as if you were looking at your partner's forehead."

Anra jumped down from the block and came to the centre of the floor.

"Now: here's the first lesson. Two steps with your right foot to the right: like this. Then two steps with your left foot to the left: like this. Now the turn—the full turn—right—like this: left like this: right like this: left like this. Now the same again . . . now the full turn. There you are: back exactly where you started. Same for both ladies and gentlemen. Simple and easy.

"Now I'll play the measure to it and do the steps at the same time. Watch me closely."

Anra tucked his fiddle under his chin and scraped the gut. Every eye was glued to his feet and every foot tapped the beat of the measure.

"Now get your bare feet and get ready."

Anra returned the fiddle to a sharper pitch and finished up with a flourishing cadenza to show them that he could play the fiddle as well as dance. Then he took his stance on the wooden block.

"Ready now—into position! Hands on the haunches. Thumbs to the back. Now you maun make up your minds where your backs are. The opposite frae your bellies. That's better. Oh, you're learning—you're learning. Now do you all know your left foot frae your right foot? Oh, you needna snigger. Some o' you don't know your backs frae your fronts —or your thumbs frae your fingers. Everybody hold out their right leg. The right leg. That's the leg furthest away from your heart—or where your heart should be. Have you quite made up your minds now? All right then. Now that's the foot you start with. After I count three. . . Ready. One—two—three!"

It needed great patience and a great flow of gentle sarcasm to make a successful dancing teacher; but Anra MacAslan was successful.

"Step out you, Mr.——?"

"Robert Burns."

"Take a step forward, Mr. Burns."

"And you, Mr. Sillar, and Mr. MacGavin and Mr. Orr. Now the ladies. Eh—you, Madam——?"

"Alison Begbie."

"Alison Begbie? Thank you, Miss Begbie: take a step forward please. And you Miss Brown and Miss Cumming—and Miss Douglas."

"Now, if you ladies and gentlemen will do the steps again, will the rest of you watch carefully and by next night you'll be doing just as well as them: aye, and maybe better—I hope. Ready then. One—two—three!"

Robin was pleased at having been among those chosen to show the others the steps. The rhythm of the music was in his blood and, though he had not realised it before, he had been born to dance.

He squared his shoulders, though this cost him some little effort, for his frame had been moulded to the plough stance. He held his head erect and was conscious of a flush of excitement and exaltation on his face.

But he did not fix his eyes across the barn floor on his partner's forehead. His smouldering gaze sought her eyes. They were clear honest eyes—maybe a bit cold and a bit austere; but they were intelligent and not unkindly. They met his gaze without any sign of recognition or emotion.

Without letting his eyes roam over her face and figure, he could see that she was finely moulded with a long slow curve to her bare legs; and her skin was milk-white against the berry-brown of her companions'.

Just how he was unable to say; but Alison Begbie seemed different from all the other girls to whom he had been attracted. She was finer in the grain with a peculiar chaste quality about her. He imagined her conversation would be at once of a more intellectual quality and of an altogether superior tone to the girls he had courted—Anne Ronald of the Bennals not excepted.

As he approached her in the measure of the dance and

looked straight into her clear eyes, he felt he must know this girl in a very different way from Annie Rankine—or any other girl.

Indeed he began to imagine so many rare qualities in Alison that before the fiddle had stopped playing he had convinced himself he was her enslaved admirer.

Apart from the intense concentrated look in his eyes and the now faint smouldering behind them, he betrayed nothing of his emotion. Annie Rankine, watching him closely from her seat against the barn wall, thought him cool, unresponsive and remarkably self-possessed. Not for a moment did she guess that he was thinking so intensely about Miss Begbie. And yet a flicker of jealousy stirred in Annie's magnificent bosom. If she could only be sure he was not joking with her? How she would show the other girls if she could walk out with Robert Burns as her lover—as her betrothed.

Alison, for her part, was well aware that this Robert Burns, who was beginning to cut such a figure between the Sabbath sermons, had his eye on her in a way that betokened more than casual interest. Nor was she averse to allowing this interest to develop to the point of conversation. His appearance was attractive, his countenance comely. But what of his mode of address? She had heard that he was but the ploughboy son of a poor tenant farmer of a rather poor farm.

Alison was not impressed with this background. She was housekeeper to a neighbouring bonnet laird with some pretention to gentility; and she was due to marry above the station of the likes of Robert Burns.

But Robert managed to see her part of the road home.

Instinctively he spoke his best Murdoch English which was far beyond anything that Alison had expected. Indeed it made her feel somewhat ill-at-ease, since she was hard put to remember enough phrases from her school books to bandy in conversation.

"I am sensible, madam, that my introduction to you may appear forced——"

"Forced, Mr. Burns? Indeed, sir, I saw nothing to suspect its propriety."

"Indeed, madam, and that is so. But I assure you I would have been cast down had I not been able to comply with the niceties of the matter. I am aware that they are not as highly regarded by our farmers and artisans as they deserve—— But I knew, madam, from the moment you addressed yourself to the measure to-night that the honour of your acquaintance could be won by no off-hand approach."

"I must say, sir, you speak very fair to the book."

"I am by way of being a bookish man, madam—nor yet was I dragged up at the tail of a labouring ox—— But since you have done me the honour—an honour which I assure you I will ever cherish and respect—may I crave from you the honour of your further acquaintance—always, of course, at your best convenience?"

"I'm afraid, sir, I hardly ken what you mean. I do not give my acquaintance lightly——"

"Indeed, madam, were it otherwise I should not be so bold in courting the honour. As to my intention: I ask no more than that I may accompany you for a stroll of a fine Sunday between sermons—or that I may even commence trade with you in the epistolary way."

Alison took a few moments to think over her reply. In the bright moonlight she could see her friends waiting for her at the ditch slap. It would be better if she took her leave of him now. This Robert Burns was beyond her immediate measure. But he was a very presentable youth, though formal to the point of priggish boredom.

"My friends are waiting for me—I must ask you not to trouble yourself further, Mr. Burns. It has been very kind of you to accompany me this far."

"But we will meet again?"

"Yes. . . I think so."

"Then I bid you a very good night, Miss Alison, if you will

pardon the familiarity. I have been signally honoured by your company——"

Robert Burns bowed very low and rather grandly.

But Alison had no stomach for palaver in sight of her friends who did not share her genteel conceits.

She made a very stiff and very slight curtsey.

"Good night to you, Mr. Burns."

Until he met up with Davie Sillar, Robin remained in his grand mood.

Alison was a princess among the Tarbolton charmers. Such manners, such command of herself. Here was no rustic to be courted with passion. Here was a goddess to be won with quality of intellect. But to win her? What a prize lay there! Riches to which none of the Tarbolton lads dare aspire.

All that was worst in the Anglicised teaching of John Murdoch was rekindled in his mind. All that was most formal, pedantic and artificial in the writing of the Wits of Queen Anne's reign began to form on his tongue.

He began to wish he could win free from the bondage of toil at Lochlea; win free from the emotional toils of his family; win enough freedom for himself to set himself up in a house of his own and think about taking a girl such as Alison Begbie to wife. But not as spouse in the vulgar sense—a marriage rather of like minds soaring above the clods of all mundane and passionate trivialities. A marriage, indeed, free from the flesh with all its urgent panting thought-destroying immediacies.

But here was Davie Sillar waiting at the tryst.

"Well, Robin—how did it go?"

"You don't refer to Alison Begbie, Davie?"

"Damn fine I do! I never thought you had a notion that airt?"

"If we are to remain friends, Davie, I must ask you to make no ribald references to Alison Begbie. I am assured there is no more estimable young lady in the parish."

"What's come over you, man? Estimable? She's damn

proud o' her gentility, if that's what you mean. You won't find me wasting a night's sleep over Alison Begbie—I thought you got enough from Annie Ronald?"

"We'll not discuss the matter any further, Davie. Don't misunderstand me. I value your friendship too much. I'll tell you what I would tell no other living soul. I place a higher value on Miss Begbie's friendship—note that I say no more than friendship—than I have ever done on any other member of the sex. But what worries me, Davie, is that I may never aspire to win more than that. Indeed, I daren't hope for more. Do you understand me?"

"In a way, Robin: in a way. And in a way I don't. But you can lippen on me no' to say a word about you and Alison to the rest o' the lads—though I canna prevent folks talking: you know that as well as me."

"That's all I ask, Davie. Just leave Miss Begbie out o' the picture an' we'll get on bravely."

"——here, before I forget. John Rankine was looking for you. I didn't say where you were: I didn't like the look in Annie's eye."

"John Rankine, eh? Davie: we'll need to go up to Adamhill some night—thegither."

"Oh, it's you John Rankine's after—no' me. He's taken a fancy to you, Robin—and he's a bad man to get the wrong side o'."

"Oh, I'll no' get the wrong side o' Adamhill. Only I don't want him to think I'm after Annie."

"And I don't want him to get the notion I am."

"But still—— Damnit, I'll need to push up the brae, Dave. William Burns will be waiting up for me wi' his brows drawn like a gathering storm."

They parted good friends. But Davie thought Robin was becoming much too deep for his understanding. Alison Begbie —a stuck-up haughty bitch if ever there was one—had turned his head and damn near turned the sense inside it. Damnit, he had ranted enough about the Ronalds of the Bennals not to know she was but another of the same. Well, if he got another slap in the face there he would only be getting what he was asking for. Miss Begbie forsooth! Huh! if she had a sark on her back and another in the wash-tub she was lucky. At least the Ronalds had enough groats to fill a girnel: Alison Begbie would be fortunate if she could buy herself a new set of ribbons for Machlin Races. But—there was no telling Robin anything once he'd set his mind on a thing.

And the high-flown way Robin would sometimes be talking! Clean ridiculous for a ploughman, even if his education was above the ordinary, and even if he was a bit of a poet. A man shouldn't forget his mother tongue. Robin was too often inclined to forget his. But when he was in one of his merry moods, then the mother tongue fairly birled on his tongue the way this damned polite English never did.

But again, reflected Davie, Robin maybe was not altogether to blame. His mother was as broad Ayrshire as the best; but his father had an English all of his own—proper enough but mixed, he supposed, with the twang and idiom of the North-east coast.

Ah well: they had had a grand night's fun and dancing: so what the odds? To-morrow would bring hard work and plenty.

For all those who had nothing but their labour to sell there was always plenty of work to do; and hard work was as general in the parish of Tarbolton as it was throughout the Lowlands of Scotland.

Yet conditions had improved since William Burns had been forced to leave Clochnahill.

Patrick Sillar, the father of Davie and farmer of Spittleside, liked to hear William Burns, on one of his visits to the spence-ingle, talk about his wide experiences.

"Well, Lochlea," he said to William one night after they had discussed the improvements that were being effected with the aid of David MacLure, "you'll hae seen big changes in your day frae one end o' the country to the other? For mysel', I've never managed to stir a foot outside o' Kyle, Cunninghame or Carrick."

"Yes, Patrick: I have seen great changes—but I must say they have been for the betterment of the countryside. There's nothing like the droves o' beggars and destitute bodies there used to be."

"Beggars! Man, they used to be the plague o' the parish—especially the cripples and the bed-ridden gangrels. You'd get one laid at your door every other day. True, man: there's no' near the poverty there was."

"There's no doubt that the new improvements in working the land have worked a great change. The old run-rig was a verra wasteful husbandry—except in the verra best of soils. Mind you: I'm not sure that in levelling down the rigs and filling up the draining bawks we're doing the right thing?"

"Aye, man?"

"It's my own notion that the top soil's the best soil—and in using it to level up the bawks we're leaving the rigs verra bare."

"Maybe you're richt, Lochlea. I got gey scanty corn frae the brow o' my rigs after I'd levelled them down—until I limed them weel. But d'you no' think the better seed we're using now has been a God-send?"

"There's no comparison. Thae old grey oats gave a poor crop. Then there was no grass for winter fodder for the cattle beasts. How we got through some of the hard winters was due to the providence of the Almighty and not to anything man was able to do for himself."

"I suppose you're richt, man. Min' ye: the Lord's hand lay gey heavy on us hereabouts. The bellman had a throng time o't ringing out them the Lord had called away. . . But you think our children can look forward to better times?"

"They're softer than our generation, Patrick—and there's a spirit of levity about I don't like to see. As things prosper I see a greater greed for money. Indeed, Patrick, the greed for money's greater than the fear of the Lord wi' the gentry nowadays. Ony industry a man puts on the land, the landlords and their rascally factors plan to rob you of by way of an increase in your rent."

"You're richt there, Lochlea. You soon ken that if you're in the market for a few acres the now."

"Nor are they doing right by the small men whenever their tack is up. Out they go if they can't meet the increase."

"Out they go any the ways o't. For they're nearly all looking for bigger farms. More and more they're running the twa-three bits o' tacks thegither and letting them out to their richer friends."

"And that shouldna be, Patrick. That's clean against the Book. I'll grant you there are lazy indolent cotters. Aye—but the man who is willing to work and can work should never be handicapped and held down for want of cash to pay iniquitous rents. For say what you like, the earth is the Lord's; and the lairds have it only on trust—and it's a trust they are abusing sorely."

Patrick Sillar was an older man than William Burns; but

he was much younger than him in experience of the world. He saw he had touched a sore spot with his neighbour who was evidently having a hard struggle to keep his end up. But he said nothing. William Burns was a strange man, upright but headstrong: a good enough friend and one to be relied on at all times—but a devilish bad enemy and one not to forgive an offence easily.

Patrick himself was more easy-going in temperament. He made shift to change the drift of their talk.

"I see thae laddies of ours run thegither gey brawly, Lochlea. He's got a byornar head on his young shoulders has Robin—and Gilbert's no' far ahint him. They do great credit to the education you got them."

The words were balm to William Burns.

"I did my best for them, Patrick. That's no more than a father's duty."

"Withouten doubt. I did the best I could by my laddies; and I must say it's stood by them."

"The grace of God and a good education and there should be no fear of them."

"Aye; but I'm thinking your Robin's gotten something more than education could give him. Man, he's got a rare tongue for a crack. I like whiles to way-lay him here when he's in for Davie. Man, he's got a'bodies i' the parish preened down to a nicety. And he'll argue about onything under the sun. As for theology: man, he could put auld Patie Woodrow that's a doctor o' divinity through his catechism; and a' else forbye. I misdoubt nor he got a' that weight o' lear at the school. But then, Lochlea, your own learning's long been the talk o' them that ken you?"

"I'm but a poor scholar, Patrick. But such as my poor talents were, I did not seek to bury them. Had I got half the chance my laddies have gotten, I wouldn't be bogged in Lochlea to-day."

"Well . . . it's no' for me to advise a better educated man nor myself; but if I were you, Lochlea, I'd see about giving

Robin something else to his hand than guiding the plough. What about the flax-dressing now? That's a coming trade; and since he's doing so bravely with the cropping o't, what's to ail him at the dressing?"

"Well . . . there's something in what you say, Patrick. Spinning's a great industry. Linen is coming along in a way I little thought of. You'll hear the clack of looms in every house in Tarbolton as you pass down the street. If we could dress the flax for the weavers it would be a good speculation and a certain stand-by in bad weather. I misdoubt that Robert has the notion for it."

"Aye . . . of course it's no' a pleasant trade the heckling. And it's particular sore on them that suffer frae a consumption o' the lungs. . . But here's the laddies coming. . . Weel, lads: where hae the pair o' you been stravaiging to the night?"

"Oh: just down wi' the lads at Tarbolton."

Davie nodded to William Burns.

"Gran' evening, sir."

"It is a gran' evening, David. You're keeping in good health?"

"Yes, Mr. Burns, thank you. I'm in fair good fettle the now."

"Well, Patrick: Robin and me will be pushing across to Lochlea."

"It's early yet, man. You can't go withouten you taste a sup o' the wife's sowens. And I ken Robin here's particular fond o' a supper o' sowens. Come up to the fire here, laddie, and have a seat. That's better. Your father and me were just cracking about auld times and how much better off you young deils are nowadays, what wi' one thing and another."

"Things could be worse, Mr. Sillar."

"But no' much, eh? Aye: things could be worse, Robin. There's Davie: he spends more time scraping away at his fiddle than he does working in the fields."

"Now, faither, the truth . . ."

"I wonder if they never got time to scrape a fiddle in the auld days?"

"Some did, Robin: some did. Oh—the auld days had their good times too—eh, Lochlea?"

"Well, Patrick, speaking for myself, I never knew them. Maybe I was unfortunate. Fortune never seemed to favour the Burns folk in the North. Of course the Rebellions—— Well, that's an auld sang as the saying goes."

"Aye: we escaped the worst effect o' that disaster hereabouts. Still, d'you think the Union's been such a good thing?"

"It has given us peace—and we needed peace."

"Aye; but we've lost a lot too, mind you. There's a pickle o' wealth gan south o' the Border since seventeen an' seven. A lot o' the gentry would rather spend their money about Lunnon than Killie or Auld Ayr. It must cost a hantle o' Geordies to keep them lodged and set-up in Lunnon. . . You're no' saying much, Robin?"

But Robin did not like to express himself freely in his father's presence.

"Bad cess to the lot o' them's what I say, Mr. Sillar. And bad cess to them that sold Scotland's independence. I don't hold with the Auld Stewarts; but I hold still less with the German lairdies."

William Burns stirred uneasily. "Politics never advanced a man as far as I could see, except those that had the favour of people in power. Many a man has ruined his prospects by being overbold in expressing thoughts he could never put into action."

"Aye . . . I've known them that could get into a blazing wrath about a mere question of this or that when, as you say, Lochlea, it didn't really matter a docken what his opinions were, since they were just opinions and nothing more. Man, an opinion can be the very devil. . ."

"But if a man has no opinions how can he ever come to act?"

William Burns's face clouded for a moment. "If a man

does his duty to God—and his neighbours—there is no need for him to act in any other way."

Robert wished he had never spoken. It was always the same now. If he spoke his mind, his father was sure to contradict him or censure him by implication. The days were over when they could converse amiably as father and son, as instructor and pupil. Ah well: he would remember his teeth were in front of his tongue where his father was concerned.

Patrick Sillar guessed something of the relationship between William and his son.

"Come on, Davie my boy: get your fiddle and give Mr. Burns a tune—and tell your mother we're ready for the sowens whenever she is. Oh no—you maun taste the wife's sowens. She'd be affronted if you didna, Mr. Burns—and I'll take no refusal myself. Aye, it's a good step across to Lochlea. . . Man, Robin, I had Sawney Tait here the other day doing a bit job for me—damned, Sawney's steeks are getting fully longer: aye, he's making them a guid twa thumb breadths now. Aye . . . what was I saying? Oh aye . . . Davie and you seem to have gotten Sawney's birss up? You'd better watch your step, the pair o' you. Sawney can run up a poem quicker nor a pair o' breeks. Aye, and some o' his verses can be gey nasty—he has a good-gaun cloot-clippin' tongue in him, has Sawney. You don't know Tait the tailor, do you, Lochlea?"

"I know the man when I see him. Beyond passing the time of day with him, I know nothing about the man."

"Maybe just as well, Lochlea. Mind you: Sawney's a weel-thocht o' man about Tarbolton. He used to be baillie o' Tarbolton at one time. Born about the Borders somewhere—Innerleithen way I've heard him say. Oh aye: and he's no' down to his last groat is Sawney. Devil the bit. At one time he owned four or five houses in Tarbolton. . . Of course, when you're a baillie things come your gate whiles. . ."

"He's got the wame for a baillie even if he hasn't got the brain for a poet."

"Maybe, Robert, maybe; but Davie and you are making a

mistake if you think Sawney hasna got a good long head on him."

"I can't be bothered wi' him," said Davie. "You would think to hear him talk that young folks ken nothing. Because he was a sodger once and travelled over half the country, he thinks he knows everything——"

"Oh, well: come on wi' your tune then. But if auld Sawney blisters you wi' a scalding verse or twa, dinna blame me."

Davie winked at Robert and tucked the fiddle under his chin. Ben in the kitchen the sowen coggies clattered on the table.

BROTHERS

"Sit down, Gilbert: we'll have a rest. I'm not so able as I was . . . and the beasts could do with a rest too."

Gilbert turned the plough on its side and took a seat beside his father at the end of the rig. He was worried to see how much his father had failed and was failing.

"You're no' feeling very well, father?"

"It's nothing, Gilbert—nothing but age creeping on me. Aye . . . there's a lot of work to be done here on Lochlea and I'm afeared I'll not live to reap the harvest."

"Oh—you'll live, father. Things are bound to get easier. Only you're trying to do overmuch. You'll need to take things easier in the pace. Robin and me can do a bit more."

"Aye. . . You've worked well, Gilbert."

"So has Robin! I often think back on Mount Oliphant. Robin worked like a slave there. And he works hard here."

"Aye . . . but Robin's mind is not on his work, Gilbert: his heart doesn't lie to it the way it should if he is to succeed in life."

"I sometimes think you're . . . a bit hard on Robin: he has great gifts."

"Hard? I wouldna like to think I had been over hard on your brother, Gilbert. I've always tried to do what was right by both of you—aye, all of you. I ken Robin has gifts. He would have made a grand scholar if I had been able to give him the education. But I couldna, Gilbert. I'm trying to make a good farmer out of him—for he'll have his bite and sup to win for the rest of his days . . ."

"I know, father . . . I know. And Robin knows that too. Only he doesna always show what he feels."

"Gilbert! Would you like to go to this dancing school at Tarbolton?"

"Not if you're still against it."

"Never mind that. Would you like to go with your brother?"

"I would, father. I see no harm in it."

"Verra well then. Take Nance with you. I can depend on you, Gilbert."

"You can depend on all of us, father. Surely you know that?"

"Aye . . . that's been a great comfort to your mither and me. But temptation lies waiting in queer places, Gilbert. Especially where folks are pleasure-bent. I've seen the world and I know something of its wickedness and its temptations. But if you must dance, then you must. What's denied you the one road you'll seek for another gate."

"But surely, father, there's nothing sinful in dancing—proper dancing?"

"We'll see, Gilbert, we'll see. Davie Sillar seems an honest upright lad?"

"I like Davie . . . 'twas me first got to know him. . . I introduced Robin to him."

But that was always how things worked out, thought Gilbert. He was popular enough till folks met Robin: then he had to take a back seat.

"So . . . you like Davie Sillar? He's fond of music: maybe I missed something there."

"I like music—Scots music. I like to hear Davie playing the strathspeys and jigs and reels—and the old songs too."

"Ah, your mither used to be a grand singer of our old songs, Gilbert. When she was younger she sang like the thrush."

"I remember. She doesna sing so often now. . ."

"No . . . your mither had the song crushed on her. We've had a struggle, Gilbert, ever since we were born . . . your mither and me. Nothing but slavery all our days and no sign of it ending this side of the grave."

"No . . . no . . ."

"I can speak to you, Gilbert. I feel in my bones that my days are not long for this earth."

"You'll need to take a good rest—then you'll feel a lot better. Maybe you should take a week in your bed. They say Doctor MacKenzie in Machlin's a skilled man in medicine. Maybe——"

"No: no need for any doctors. Oh, I'm no' finished yet. But maybe I'll content myself taking the darg a bit lighter on the load."

It wasn't altogether that William Burns was feeling sorry for himself. He was genuinely feeling his years and he knew his strength was fast ebbing. Bitterness for the moment was gone from him. It its place came a wistful sadness, a quiet Presbyterian sorrow, surging with acceptance and resignation.

He raised his head and gazed round the uplands of Tarbolton, watched the smoke rising from the small farm houses cluttered about the hollows of the land. The humps of hills were bare and uninteresting, and there was bogland everywhere. The pity that he had never been able to win a farm in good carse land that would have turned kindly to the plough and received the seed with a sweet fertility. But for him and his like it had to be the uplands, boggy and sour and full of boulders, with only bog-hay and peat-moss as a gift from nature. Not much of a gift at that, since neither could be won home without much toil.

Ah well . . . he had done his best. There was no good in setting his face against the pleasures of this new generation. And the presence at the dancing school of Gilbert and Agnes would help to restrain Robin if, as he feared, restraint would be needed.

That night Gilbert followed Robin out of the house.
"Robin?"
"Aye?"
"Could I have a word wi' you?"

"Surely . . . I've never refused to be spoken to, have I?"

"Maybe you think I'm against you. But I'm not."

"Well?"

"Are you going down to Tarbolton?"

"Aye . . ."

"I'll walk down to the road-end with you."

"All right. There's still some freedom left in the country, Gibby. What's on your mind?"

"Nancy and I are coming to the dancing next night."

"What?"

"Our father spoke to me the day—asked if I wanted to go with you. You don't mind?"

"Mind? No: I don't mind. He didn't think *you* would turn out a fornicator?"

"Robin: our father's failing. He had to give up this afternoon when we were ploughing on the high park—and he was only guiding. He said that his days weren't long——"

"Have you not noticed before this he was failing?"

"Aye . . . but I didn't like to say, Robin. Hell! It would break your heart to see the way he's hashed and slaved—all his days."

"Aye . . . I've thought about it—often and often. Maybe I've wept bitter tears about it afore now, Gibby. And when you look at him you see what the pair of us are coming to. Damnation, Gilbert: you know the kind o' life he's led. Nose to the grindstone all the time. Never easing up. Never able to relax and lie back and look about him—or listen to the lark. Into Ayr or Machlin or Tarbolton—there and back. Never stop to take a drink and spend an hour blethering wi' a cronie round the tavern fire. . . I met him in Patrick Sillar's the other night: he'd been over to see that new grass seed. But he wouldn't relax: itching to get away all the time. Ill-at-ease when Davie was playing the fiddle. Hardly spoke a word to me all the way home—other than to suggest that I might take up the heckling trade. Damnation! are you and me to end up like that? You can if you like, Gibby; but not me. I'll have

some taste of life now when I can enjoy its flavour. And
when I'm done I'll have something to think back on. I had
all the slavery I ever want at Mount Oliphant. Gibby! if you'd
only shake yourself and see what's before you! Realise before
it's too late that you're only young once and that only for a
damned wee while. Aye . . . come to the dancing. Don't let
anything or anybody crush your spirit. And if you see a lass
you fancy—meet her in the gloaming and enjoy an hour's
daffing. That's what the lassies are for. They enjoy it. And
it's time Nancy had her fling: time she got kissed and cuddled
and rolled down the brae. There's a lot of fun and pleasure wi'
the lassies without houghmagandie. But that's what our
father doesna realise. When he sees a lad and lass daffing
about the braes or cuddling in the barn, he thinks on houghmagandie right away. But please yourself, Gibby my lad.
You'll please yourself anyway. But I've made my resolutions
—and I'm sticking to them."

"There's a lot in what you say, Robin. Only—I don't want
to hurt our parents . . . I don't want to cause any upset or
ill-feeling——"

"And do you think I do?"

"No, I don't think that. Man, how could I? I know you
wouldna harm a mouse. But you have your own way of doing
things, Robin. Sometimes, maybe, you don't think just how
you're doing them. I mean . . . I wish I had your spirit . . ."

"What's different about my spirit? You mind yon first
years on Mount Oliphant? D'you mind how the summer's
days were long and sunny and the birds never seemed to stop
singing and the oats grew yellow on the rigs? Aye . . . d'you
mind how we played about the grassy banks of the burn?"

"And we paddled in the burn and the water was like
ice?"

"You mind that, Gibby?"

"Aye . . . I mind . . . there's no' much I hae forgotten."

"That's what I'm coming to. You've forgotten how to
live. You were a bright lad then, Gibby—there was aey a

gurgle o' laughter in your throat and the imp o' mischief danced in your eyes. But the laughter was damn soon drowned in that seeping bog. Your guts were knocked out on the Mount, Gibby."

"No: it was your guts that were trachled, Robin: I know that now if I didn't always know it."

"Maybe you're right. Maybe. . . But it didn't crush my spirit. For a while the flame burned low: it damn near went out—several times."

"I know . . ."

"No: you don't know—nobody'll ever know. I get goose-pimples when I think back on it yet——"

"I didn't understand—then."

"Ah well—that's behind me now. But you lost something on the Mount—lost your zest for life. Hell: I don't blame you. I didn't understand then either. Sometimes I could have smashed your face in, Gilbert—other times I could have wept for you. Aye . . . and maybe I did; and for myself too."

"We misunderstood each other. But I've tried to make up for that since, Robin. I've always stuck up for you—when you weren't there."

"Right. I don't want to quarrel, Gibby—and I don't want to leave you out. Only: I go my own way. If you want to come part of the way with me you're welcome. But by God, Gilbert, don't ever preach to me if we are to be friends! Don't even preach with your eyes."

"I didn't know I did that, Robin. I don't mean to."

"Well: I'm warning you. I can do my own preaching—sometimes I think I've overdone that in the past. No preaching, Gilbert. Now I'll tell you about a project I have in mind, so that you won't think I'm merely concerned with having a good time wi' the lassies. Indeed, Gilbert, I have my eye on a fair charmer—and if I can win her I'll marry and settle down to be a good industrious husband—and father."

"Do I know her?"

"Well, you do—and you don't. I didn't mean to tell anybody. But I'll let you share the secret wi' Davie Sillar. Tell me what you think of my choice—Alison Begbie."

"Alison Begbie? She's—— I've never spoken to her, Robin: I know her by sight and I've heard some talk about her."

"Never mind that. She's—what? You were going to say something. Damn it, Gibby, speak up!"

"I was going to say that she didn't strike me as being your choice of a lass—I mean the kind of a lass you would fall in love with—but then, I don't know her."

"I see. Do you think I've got some special kind o' lass?"

"You usually go after the one kind, Robin: you know that."

"No: I don't know that. Do you think Annie Rankine would be my type?"

"I'll speak honestly?"

"For God's sake don't speak any other way wi' me."

"No: I don't think Annie Rankine's your type—but she's a damned sight more your type than Alison Begbie is. But I've told you I don't know her. Annie, if you won't misunderstand me, is a larger edition of your choice of a lass."

"Damnit, folk know more about me than I do myself."

"You know what I mean?"

"No, I don't, Gibby. Alison's different from any girl I've ever known. She's finer, better mannered, better educated—she's got brains, Gibby. Intellect. Breeding. But brains, Gibby! That's what you don't find around Tarbolton."

"Maybe . . . what about . . . affection?"

"Oh, damn you! You don't think about cuddling and kissing brains, Gibby—or breeding. Alison's no peasant lass —or farmer's daughter used to mucking in the graipe—or humphing cow-sharn out to the parks."

"Maybe. . . But why shouldn't you want to put your arms round her? She's flesh and blood, isn't she?"

"Well: she's not a marble statue. You don't understand, Gilbert. I'm finished with flesh and blood love—I'm finished with the fleshy lusts. To hell: a man should have brains as well as—— But I'll be offending you with my coarse talk."

"You'll no' offend me. I'm damned if I see anything coarse about a plain, honest statement. Alison must be having a genteel effect on you. And is this the project you were going to tell me about—marrying Alison?"

"No: that's a secret and see you keep your meikle thumb on it. I'll say no more about it."

"It's safe wi' me, Robin."

"It had better be. No: I've another project. I'm thinking about forming a debating society."

"A debating society—what for?"

"What the hell d'you think? To play quoits?"

"Aye . . . but——?"

"To debate, of course. To brighten up our brains and brush up our manners so that we can talk about—oh, ony damned thing in the universe."

"I would like that."

"Of course you would. We're not just clods of earth—and never were. There are good lads in Tarbolton that meet in the smiddy. Lads wi' brains and ideas. None of them fools. I'm going to suggest that we get thegither and see if we can get a place to meet for our debates. Oh, and it won't be just debates. We'll make it a club—a bachelors' club. A select club, with rules, regulations and office-bearers—and a modest subscription. Come in wi' me, Gilbert—you'll be a good example. You've got a head on you—and a good tongue. You're a clever chiel, Gibby—but you hide your light under a bushel——"

"No: you're the one with the gifts, Robin. And sometimes you forget them. There's nobody in Ayrshire at your age can come anywhere near you——"

"Well . . . we've got a good conceit o' oursel's, Gibby. Together we'll let them see that William Burns of Lochlea didn't father a couple o' gowks."

They parted at the road-end where they had stood talking

till they were chilled. Walking home himself, Gilbert experienced a queer ecstasy of elation. What a brother to have! What a lad when he opened up and spoke just what was in his mind. Gilbert was elated they had bridged the gulf that had so long separated them from exchanging their inmost thoughts.

And he was elated to think how he had tried earlier in the day to defend Robin in the presence of his father. Elated perhaps most of all because Robin had praised him—genuinely, with that generous warmth of his that held nothing back. No doubt about it: Robin was definitely the first lad in the parish. His father would be proud of him yet—they would all be proud of him. Even their mother—but did his mother really have any inkling of the world of Robin's mind—of his ideals and his aspirations?

Gilbert was fond of his mother. He understood her: or thought he did. And he was sure his mother did not understand Robin. Maybe she would never understand him. But he was sure that one day she would realise that at least there were other folks who understood Robin and appreciated him.

And maybe he wasn't so daft about Alison Begbie. If Robin was taking a new bent then she might be the wife for him.

Gilbert was in the mood of hero-worship. He would give Robin the benefit of the doubt over Miss Begbie. But if he had done any real courting of her then he had been more than usually secretive about it.

When Gilbert entered the kitchen of Lochlea, his mother looked at him sharply. She was certain he had been courting some girl. She knew that look—on others.

"And where were you galavanting tae the nicht, son?"

"I was just down to the Tarbolton road-end wi' Robin."

"An wha' did ye fa' in wi'?"

"Nobody, mother."

"Naebody—dinna tell me that, Gilbert."

"Naebody, mither. Not a living soul."

"An' where's your brither stravaigin' tae?"

"Oh—just to see the Tarbolton lads."

"An' the Tarbolton hizzies?"

"No . . . Robin's turned his back on them."

"Huh! There's some parritch in the pat for ye—and a drap o' soor cream i' the coggie. Tak' your meat while you can."

"No . . . I'm no' hungry. I think I'll go up to the loft and have a read in my bed."

"Reading'll no' stick to your ribs like a good bowl o' parritch."

"What are you thinking of reading now, Gilbert?"

William Burns dropped the set of harness from his tired hands. The thought of a good book stimulated his tired mind.

"I don't right know," said Gilbert, honestly enough. "I might try Allan Ramsay. . . I've a notion for poetry. Not prose. There's something about poetry . . ."

"Read us something," cried Nancy.

The rest of the children took up the chorus.

"Aye," said William. "Read us a verse or two, Gilbert. I never cared much for it; but to-night. . . Aye, read us a verse. . . I once stood in Allan Ramsay's shop in the Luckenbooths of Edinburgh—the same Allan Ramsay. That was a long while ago. . ."

"Robert will write better verses than Allan Ramsay!"

"Will he?"

Mrs. Burns looked up from her knitting.

"Much good will it do him! A song that folks can sing—there's something to be said for that. Not that folk'll pay you money for making a sang——"

"But mother: who wants money for writing poetry?"

"I'm no' talking about writing poetry. I'm talking aboot a guid sang."

"Robert will make good sangs too."

"He'll no' do much at onything—galavanting the way he's doing."

"Let's have your reading, Gilbert."

Nancy said: "Are there any ballads?"

Gilbert looked through Allan's pages but he did not light on anything that gave expression to his mood. He wanted something that would uplift him, transport him from Lochlea into the world that Robert had opened up to him. Unlike Robert, Gilbert needed to be led, sustained and encouraged.

BACHELORS' CLUB

Robert no sooner propounded the idea of a debating club to his comrades in and around Tarbolton than the idea was seized upon and translated into action.

They arranged to get Jock Richards' back room. Jock gave them the use of the room free of charge when they agreed to purchase at least one refreshment each during the session. Jock reckoned it was a good bargain, since he would secure their custom as individuals at other times.

Of course there were many discussions round the smiddy fire in the evenings before they held their first meeting. They argued about the name. Though Robert was keen to have it as The Tarbolton Debating Society, Willie MacGavin won with the more homely Tarbolton Bachelors' Club.

They didn't want any married men coming to their debates, since they aimed to discuss many topics that would not be suitable for married men—and to discuss them in a way married men wouldn't like.

The drawing up of the rules gave rise to more discussion than any other item. Their commandments were a bit high-flown and prolix, but they were all of them in a high-flown prolix state of mind. Robert let himself rip when it came to the framing of the tenth and last commandment. It was approved with unanimity and general acclamation.

"Every man proper for a member of this society must have a frank, honest, open heart; above anything dirty or mean; and must be a professed lover of one or more of the female sex. No haughty, self-conceited person, who looks upon himself as superior to the rest of the club, and especially no mean-spirited, worldly mortal, whose only will is to heap up money, shall upon any pretence whatever be admitted. In short, the proper

person for this society is a cheerful, honest-hearted lad, who,
if he has a friend that is true, and a mistress that is kind, and
as much wealth as genteelly to make both ends meet, is just as
happy as this world can make him."

That would settle any doubts, thought Robin, when he
wrote it out. But it raised as many doubts as it settled. It was
indeed the final challenge of the ten points of their manifesto,
and when news of it came to the ears of Saunders Tait, he was
ready to spit blood.

Saunders was in all things naturally inclined to reaction;
and his keen-scented reactionary nose didn't take long to sniff
out the challenging note of class against class, especially the
setting of the artisans and peasants over against the great ones
of the land, the gentry and the rich merchants, whose cultural
and economic flunky Saunders had always been proud to
proclaim himself.

In every line of their manifesto, in which Saunders was
certain he sniffed the rebel from Lochlea, he saw challenge and
contempt. And as he himself was beyond the age of active
physical participation in the pleasures of the flesh, he was
particularly incensed with the references to the female sex.
Unorthodoxy in religious belief was bad enough. But to set
up the standard of libertinism in Tarbolton was an outrage;
a much worse outrage indeed than casting aspersions on the
gentles.

Had Saunders been present at the first meeting of the club,
he would probably have taken a stroke.

Robert was elected president, and the event was duly
recorded in the minute book by Willie MacGavin under the
date 11th November, 1780.

After the constitution had been discussed and approved,
Robert got up to open the first debate, the subject of which
bore the grandiloquent title: "Whether is a young man of the
lower ranks of life likeliest to be happy who has got a good
education, and his mind well informed, or who has just the
education and information of those around him?"

The subject had been set by Robert, and it was very much to his mind.

After some preliminary and rather pedantic observes, he got heated up and forgot his carefully prepared notes.

"But why should peasants and artisans be content merely to labour and sleep and have no thoughts beyond shelter and food and their masters' interests? How can they be happy in such a position? For what is the position? It is surely the position allied to that of brute creation, or more correctly that part of brute creation man has domesticated for his own ends and to lighten his labours. The man in the position I have described is equal to the domestic labouring animal. I have not heard anyone hold to the view that the brute beast, groaning under its burden, is in a state of happiness.

"But we know that man was not created to be a beast of burden, though many of them are compelled through no fault of their own to labour worse than any beast.

"We have scriptural authority, whatever Dr. Patrick Woodrow may proclaim to the contrary, that man was created in God's image. And we have the authority of the Westminster Catechism that man's chief end is not to labour for narrow brutal existence, but to glorify God and enjoy Him forever.

"If man is to raise himself to his full stature and enjoy the full benefits of creation, then he can only do so by raising himself above the level of the dull and narrow life he finds all around him.

"And how can he do this unless he improves his mind by education? But his education must be broad and embrace the whole field of knowledge. He must know something of history —the history of mankind of all races and of all climes, as well as the history of his own country. He must know something of geography—of religion, of philosophy, of language.

"But the more fields of knowledge the mind reaps, the greater will be the happiness of the individual—especially the individual belonging to the humbler walks of life.

"For then he will not be concerned with wealth of riches

or fine acres of land, or having servants answering to his beck and call. He will not be concerned with property or cash or the mean cent per cent of merchant cunning. . .

"But everything else will interest him. The sun, the moon and all the stars. . . He will notice a reed blown by the wind and learn much from the spectacle. . . All this and much more. He will find enjoyment in browsing over the speculations of the philosophers, of men who have revealed the mystery and wonder of creation; of poets and dreamers. . . Music will fire his blood or soothe his breast and every manly virtue will exalt his mind. . ."

When Robin sat down there was a burst of applause. Immediately he became self-conscious and wondered what he had said and how he had said it. Perspiration beaded his forehead.

Gilbert, who had taken the chair while Robin was speaking, now rose and intimated that William MacGavin would take the opposite view.

Willie needed some applause to encourage him, and he got it—generously.

"I was to have taken the opposite view in this debate, but Robert has left me little to say. I always knew he had a great gift for words, but I never knew that he had such a gift of eloquence.

"You'll need to excuse me—and bear with me while I read my notes—for the purpose of this debate.

"Now why should a lad of the lower ranks of life improve his mind beyond that of his fellows? Only, I submit, if by doing so he can improve his lot in life.

"Mere improvement of his mind will not make a man any happier. May we not say that it will tend to make him unhappy? Assuredly it will make him discontented with his lot; and how can a discontented man be happy?

"But if a man is honest and works diligently and applies himself to his tasks, he will be content; and contentment I hold to be the basis of all human happiness here below.

"If he maintains an easy, familiar intercourse with his fellow-creatures, partaking in the common tasks and common hardships, partaking equally with their good fortune and their bad fortune, sharing with them the simple pleasures and enjoyments that fall to their lot—then he will be of them and as one of them. I hold that by doing so he will find more happiness than in withdrawing himself from their society, rude and uncultivated though it may be to the learned college-bred persons, in order to improve his mind and so widen the gulf between himself and his fellow-creatures. For surely as he withdraws from them, they will despise him and think him vain and foolish. . .

"Moreover—and I think this is verra important—he will require to shun the company of the females of his circle. And since he will not have the wealth or pedigree to court the company of more elegant dames in a better station of life, he will end the most miserable creature in the universe, and one much to be pitied."

Willie got his round of applause too—even though he had read his notes in a flat monotone.

But Robin had fired his comrades, and in the general debate that followed, most were in favour of Robin's thesis.

When Jock Richards came through with the drinks, they were all in a merry mood. The Club was a success. It was the best night they had ever had.

"It's a lot better nor dancing wi' the Tarbolton hizzies," said Willie.

"Here!" cried Robin, "no slighting remarks must be made about the lassies—bless them! If man does not live by bread alone, neither does he live by brain alone—else we'd better a' be gelded afore we leave the school."

"Hear, hear, Robin. Let wha like hae the brains as long as we hae the ballocks."

They had each a gill of good Kilbagie and a generous measure of Jock's own brew of ale.

By the time the drink had warmed the cockles of their hearts, they had forgotten the improvement of their minds as a high duty, and were enjoying the comradeship of the bottle.

And then Watty Mitchell, who had been visiting the rear of Jock's howff, came in with the news that Saunders Tait was listening—or appeared to be listening—at the door of their room.

"Fetch him ben here!" cried Hughie Reid, "and Rab'll give him a dribbin'. Give us yon sang ye made on him, Rab."

"Here ye are, Hughie:

> "Ae day as death cam' tae the toon
> An' clachan o' Tarbolton,
> His bloody heuk held high aboon
> An' mounted weel a colt on.
> He lookit up, syne lookit doon
> For ony word o' Saunders,
> But Tait the Tailor was awa'
> Colleaguing on his daunders——"

Just then Saunders, the ale caup in his hand, burst into the room.

"That'll dae ye, Rab Burns—that'll dae ye! You're an imp o' hell to mak' a sang like that on a man that could be your father——"

"To hell!" cried Tammy Wright. "Shut the door, ye auld lecher, an' hae a drink."

"No, you don't!" spoke Willie MacGavin. "Out ye go, Saunders. This room's reserved for the Tarbolton Bachelors' Club and, though ye may be a bachelor, Saunders——"

"Bachelor my——"

"Haud on, Hughie——"

"Ye damned pups!" roared Saunders. "Ye damned whelps o' hell. But mind ye, Rab Burns, I'll be even wi' ye. Ye'll no' mak' a sang on Saunders Tait an' get aff scot free. I'll sang ye!"

"G'wa' wi' ye—prick the louse and jag the flea!"

"Hey, Sawney! I hear John Rankine o' Adamhill was complaining ye mak' yer steeks ower lang. He said the last pair o' breeks ye made for him were that lang steekit he didna need . . ."

The lads roared with laughter and Saunders spat through his yellow teeth.

But Jock Richards came on the scene and oxtered Saunders out of the room.

Robert rose and chapped his wooden bicker on the table.

"Well, lads: we've had a gran' nicht. But don't let's overdo it. We've had a good debate, a gran' crack and a good drink. I'll ask you to be upstan'in' till we sing a verse o' Guid-nicht and joy be wi' ye a'."

EPISTOLARY LOVE

June was a grand month in the year of eighty-one. Robert found his eye lifting beyond the bare hillocks and the swelling ground to the white-washed clouds in the intensely blue sky. The swallows skimmed the quickly drying mill-pond that lay in a reedy hollow below the steading; the cuckoo called from the branch of a gnarled thorn—hidden in the greenery; the landrail craiked incessantly from the bog hay; the lark from its viewless flutterings fluted its endless trills and burbled the beauty of its sun-drenched theme.

The herd laddies, keeping the cattle from the growing crops, sang and whistled or chased the red sodger bees or the peacock butterflies.

The young queys bellowed with mounting urgency for the bull; and young foals frisked in the sunshine.

The fowls, thin and scraggy, strayed far from the midden-head. A clocking hen sat snugly on her still undiscovered nest in a bed of nettles behind the stackyard.

Robert noted every aspect of the scene—noted it unconsciously. The incredible freshness of the virgin green was over all the earth and all the earth was fecund. The sickly sweet smell of the thorn blossom with its curious almond tang worked like a drug on his senses. . .

But deep within himself he was uneasy and fretful. His courtship with Alison Begbie had not prospered. He had courted her honourably and with unnatural restraint. Maybe Gilbert was right: she was not his kind of woman. But why? If he didn't love Alison—if she didn't love him—if he had failed to make her understand how much he loved her—why? He wanted Alison. Wanted her not only because she was different from all the girls he had ever known—he wanted her because of her clear-cut quality of intellect. She was not

163

emotional: he knew that. But emotion was not a good foun-
dation for a permanent basis on which to build affection.
Alison was not passionate: he was sure she was not passionate.
Passion was the twin aspect of emotion—and as unstable.

But Alison had brains and she had all the qualities that
have their origin in the reasoning faculty: manners; elegant
conversation; the judicial weighing of the pros and cons of
any matter; the cool balance of judgment that brakes the
headlong rush and ram-stam of ungovernable impetuosity; the
character of intellectual awareness and sensitivity.

Alison had these qualities and these he wanted in his life
companion.

Robert did not for a moment doubt his estimate of Alison:
he did not know how much he was fooling himself. He did
not know that though Alison had no heart, it was possible she
had no brains either. He did not know he was confusing the
character of intellect with the sharp instinctive cunning of a
calculating woman determined to let no emotion of love affect
adversely the prospects of her worldly success.

Alison was indeed flattered by the attention of Robert
Burns: she was, in her chilly way, somewhat touched by it.
But she feared it: feared that his quiet selfless ardour might
enter into the core of her ego and consume it.

Robert Burns was distinguished far and beyond any man
of any class Alison Begbie had come within the prospect of
knowing. But he was the poor son of a poor tenant-farmer;
and the best he had to offer her was no better than the best
offer of a labouring hind in Kyle, Cunninghame or Carrick.

Alison had won to the position of a superior domestic in
the household of the gentry. She did not know any alternative
other than to reject the rather frightening address of Robert
Burns. Frightening, since she knew from personal contact that
his advances were not born of impertinence or ignorant
boldness.

Alison looked over his letters once again before she

determined to submit them, page by page, to the candle flame.

She straightened out the folds and turned the sheet towards the light. Some passages she whispered to herself.

"What you may think of this letter when you see the name that subscribes it I cannot know . . . . . . as my heart means no offence but on the contrary is rather too warmly interested in your favour, for that reason I hope you will forgive me when I tell you that I most sincerely and affectionately love you. . . I am perfectly certain you have too much goodness and humanity to allow an honest man to languish in suspense only because he loves you too well, but I am certain that, in such a state of anxiety as I myself at present feel, an absolute denial would be a more preferable state. . ."

Alison put the edge of the first love letter she had ever received, and the first love letter Robert Burns had ever written, to the flame of the candle and waited till it had burned to grey ash in the iron saucer of the candlestick.

She picked up the second letter.

"I verily believe, my dear Alison, that the pure genuine feelings of love are as rare in the world as the pure genuine principles of virtue and piety. The sordid earth-worm may profess to love a woman's person, whilst in reality his affection is centred in her pocket; and the slavish drudge may go a-wooing as he goes to the horse-market to choose one who is stout and firm. . . I disdain their dirty, puny ideas. . ."

Poor Robert: marriage would be a sore disappointment to him. The second letter was burned even as the first had been.

"People may talk of flames and raptures as long as they please; and a warm fancy, with a flow of youthful spirits, may make them feel something . . . but sure I am the nobler faculties of the mind, with kindred feelings of the heart, can only be the foundation of friendship, and it has always been my opinion that the married life was only friendship in a more exalted degree. . .

"I know were I to speak in such a style to many a girl who thinks herself possessed of no small share of sense, she would think it ridiculous—but the language of the heart, my dear Alison, is the only courtship I shall ever use to you . . .

"I know your good nature will excuse what your good sense may see amiss."

How foolish even the wisest of men can be, thought Alison, as the third letter was held to the flame.

There was one sentence in the fourth letter that gave her a momentary qualm.

"There is something so mean and unmanly in the arts of dissimulation and falsehood, that I am surprised they can be acted by any one in so noble, so generous a passion, as virtuous love."

But by the time she had read the fourth love letter Alison Begbie felt sick and depressed. She could not be sure she was doing right—right in the only sense she knew: in her own best interests. Somewhere she had a prompting that life should be more just—or at least less harsh in its demands. Given a chance, it might be possible that Robert Burns would know greatness. But she had to choose; and she had to reject. Robert Burns was not a lad to be trifled with even though he might be deceived; and to have trifled with him longer would have risked her reputation for unblemished virtue and superior attainments.

Alison rose, snuffed the candle and, opening the attic window of her barely-furnished room, cast the charred grey fragments of the letters to the night breeze that blew softly across from the banks of the Cessnock. As she did so, a barn-owl hunting mice for its young and disturbed by the movement at the attic window, gave a great screech and launched itself silently into the night.

Alison withdrew hurriedly and went down the narrow wooden stair to the kitchen to get her candle re-lit. She shivered and she knew fear.

She feared she had led him to believe she would become his lover. But what could she do? She had known poverty. She had no desire to live a life of poverty with a poor ploughman slaving on a poor soil—eating the bread of miserable days and hungry bairns. He might talk all night and write all day; but she knew he would father children as long as children could be fathered. . .

The fear remained. For despite all his queer ideas, Robert Burns was irresistibly attractive. In this as in almost all other aspects—the possession of worldly goods alone excepted—Alison felt he was above and beyond all other men. This was the knowledge that lay at the base of her fear. She was woman enough and had intelligence enough to realise she might know regret to the end of her days.

VISIT TO ADAMHILL

From the heat of the June sun, Robert found shelter beneath the kindly shade of a stunted oak-tree. He had been cleaning out a ditch and had found the labour oppressive in the broiling noon-day heat. His spirit was heavy: he was depressed.

From his pocket he produced a letter and read it over line by line. It was a letter from Alison Begbie rejecting his advances. It was a short letter intimating curtly that she saw no point in continuing the correspondence.

The letter had been like a deep knife wound to him. In the coldness of its formality there was evidence of bluntness of feeling. This evidence troubled and depressed him.

He realised now that he had set Alison Begbie on much too high a pedestal. But had she accepted him he would have made every effort to maintain her on that pedestal. Her refusal he had feared, even while he had hoped against that possibility. . .

Hadn't she been pleased to walk out with him along the banks of the Cessnock? And to walk and talk with him between the Sabbath sessions of Patrick Woodrow at Tarbolton Kirk?

She had never said she would accept him as a suitor: nor had they ever discussed the possibility of matrimony. But she had not spurned his advances. She had listened to talk of love. They had engaged in lovers' talk even though such talk had always been circumspect. He had kissed her; and though the kisses had been few and had little of passion in them, she had never refused. . .

After a bout of melancholy, Robert was forced to the conclusion that Alison had rejected him because of his poverty and his lack of social position. He hadn't been good enough for the Cessnock housekeeper. . .

Still, it was hard to believe that a girl of such splendid

intellect could be so mean and calculating. But—that was how the world was; and there was no good of driving himself into a mood of despair. He had had his lesson—and he would take the lesson to heart. Never again would he set a woman on a pedestal no matter what he might think of her. Yet he wouldn't let Miss Begbie think he was disillusioned with her—or with her kind.

He took out the letter he had written in reply to her note of refusal. He was quite certain there was nobody in the West of Scotland who could have written letters like those he had penned to Alison Begbie.

For a moment he began to wonder if he had been more in love with the idea of writing love letters to Alison than he had been in love with her for her own qualities. Then he remembered that night of the first dancing lesson at Tarbolton; and then he knew he had been in love, not so much with Alison Begbie as with the image she had created in his mind. She had had all the qualities of the kind of woman to whom his intellect responded—all the outward signs of having these qualities. What her real qualities were he would never know, because he would never really break down the outward calm of her reserve—nor had he ever been interested in so doing. All this he now realised as he sat under the gnarled oak-tree, shaded from the heat of the June sun.

But however he might try to rationalise his feelings on the matter, there still remained the stab—the refusal—the blow to his pride.

Damn them! He would take the track across the moor to Adamhill and see John Rankine. He would tell him he wanted his name put forward to the brethren of the Lodge in Tarbolton.

So he stuffed the letter back in his pocket and made off over the low hill that lay between the farm of Lochlea and Adamhill. It was a grand day and the ditching could wait—it would certainly be waiting for him when he returned.

Adamhill was one of the finest farms for miles around. The

land was rich and fertile and John Rankine knew how to get the best out of it. But Rankine had capital enough to develop his land and add to his stock as he thought fit. His farm buildings were considered substantial for the third quarter of the century.

Robert had never visited Adamhill, though he had passed close to it many times. Yet Rankine had never tired of inviting him to his fireside. . .

John Rankine saw him come over the hill. He set off down the edge of the park to meet him.

"Damnit, Rab," he saluted him when they met, "is this you coming to Adamhill at long last?"

"Aye . . . I suppose it is, John."

"Well, you're welcome, lad. It's a grand day for coming over the hill. An' what ails you?"

"Ails me?"

"Aye . . . ails you. There's a worried look on ye, Rab. Ye havena couped one o' thae Tarbolton queans?"

"No; but maybe one o' them's couped me!"

"Damn the fear!"

"I was thinking o' joining the Masons, John—if you would put my name forward?"

"I'll do that. Damnit, it'll be a grand day when I see you through your Third Degree. Well . . . you couldn't do better than join the Craft, Robin, and I've no doubt but that you'll grace the chair yet. You were made for the Craft—or I've sore misjudged the way you lay out your principles."

"Principles are important——"

"Aye . . . but there's more in the Craft than principles. Principles'll no' fill your belly when it's empty."

"Aye . . . and if you have principles your stomach's never likely to be overfull."

"Well. . . You're no' likely to suffer from the gout, I'll grant you that. But . . . you've got to make some provision against falling on evil days, as the Craws would say. That's where the Craft can help a lad like you, not overblessed with a rowth o' the world's gear. It'll insure you against want and against want o' all kinds."

"I was speaking to John Wilson in Tarbolton about that."

"John's our secretary and no' a bad lad—lang luggit a bit —but he's got to earn his living as much by his wits as onything else."

"I agree that lads like me could do with all the safeguards against poverty and want we can get. I've no desire to join the Masons just for the mystery of it."

"And the greatest mystery about Masonry, Robin, is that there's no mystery about it. Oh, there's bits o' secrets and bits o' mystic ploys; but they're nothing—mere ritual . . . some flummery to dress up some plain truths. But come you on up to the house and have a drink."

"No . . . let's sit here for a bit, John—if you don't mind. There's some things I'd like your advice on."

"Certainly, Robin. No', mind you, that my advice is worth much——"

"There's no other man's advice I would sooner act on, John."

"That's a nice compliment, Robin. Fire ahead, lad: I'm listening."

"When I said that maybe I had been jilted I was speaking the truth. You know Alison Begbie?"

"——over at Cessnock House?"

"That's her. I courted her—seriously—too seriously."

"A damn sight too seriously. She's too cauldrife a bitch to clap into the marriage bed. You surprise me, Robin. What's come over you?"

"God knows. I thought she had brains—and intelligence— but if she had she had no heart to balance them. I think it was my poverty that told against me."

"Wi' Alison Begbie I've no doubt. Brains? Brains are all right—in the head. But you don't marry a woman for her head. Oh—a bit of good kintra sense, yes. But brains—that's a man's province. A woman wi' brains can be a menace—

especially to a man's peace o' mind. No, no: you marry a woman for her good broad back and her good broad hips. Beware o' thae narrow-hipped hizzies: I've never kenned them do ocht but turn out a barren lot o' ill-tongued bitches and thowless jads. Tight i' the leg, broad i' the beam and well scrieved i' the back and the breast. You canna do better nor that."

"The way you would choose a beast?"

"When you choose a beast do you ettle to bed wi' it? Hae sense, man! No: that's the physical side o' the business. You've got to love the lass. So you've got to see that she's got the right kind o' affection. And the seat o' affection's in the heart —no' the head."

"There's plenty choose them as they would a mare."

"Aye: and breed them the same way. But that's no' the airt you ettle to travel. And Alison Begbie jilted you? Weel, that's a God's blessing. You'd never hae written another verse gin you had yoked wi' her in the matrimonial plough."

"I've written little enough verse as it is."

"It'll come. It'll come when you fa' in wi' the right lass."

"I don't know. I'm finished wi' the lassies."

"Damn the bit. You're at a bad age, Robin. Just what age are you?"

"I was twenty-one in January."

"Aye . . . a bad age. The world's opening afore you. You don't know what road to turn and many o' them look gey inviting. And you're no' like other lads, Robin. You're a poet. And you'll be a great poet yet. Now there's nothing queerer than a great poet: life maun ever be a mighty maze o' conflicting turns for him. He'll want to travel a' roads at the one time, tak' every turn to right and left, and yet head straight on. That's what you want to do, Robin. Marry Alison Begbie, play the fiddle, learn to dance, form a Bachelors' Club, study a' kinds of books, improve your farming, experiment wi' flax— and join the Masons! Weel, Robin: you can't do everything. Some things you can dae: many things you maun dae—but *everything*—you canna. Now: you want my advice. Well, who am I to advise a poet? Still, I'm a bit o' a poet myself and my own sister's married on one John Lapraik—you'll need to foregather with Auld John some day: he's at Muirkirk. But that's another story, Robin. . . My advice is just this. You'll never do onything weel till you fa' in wi' the right hizzie—and marry her and father bairns on her. But she maun be the right lass. Your difficulty will be deciding which is the right lass. That much I can tell you. You'll maybe think you've gotten her. Then you'll find out too late that she's no' the right one at the hinderend. Sae: go easy. Don't be in a hurry. Try them out. Put them to the test. For the Alison Begbie that refused you, there'll be fifty to fa' at your feet—aye, and go behin' the bush wi' you. But it's one thing going behin' the bush wi' a lass however willing—and damnt they're a' willing—and quite another thing going to the manse wi' her or compearing afore the Craws at the Kirk Session. Sae: tak' your time and see that you're certain afore ye harness yoursel' to the yoke. As for being certain—you'll know that right enough when the time comes: your heart'll tell you. It was your brain that was battering you into a passion about Alison Begbie—and now your brain's telling you you have had a damned narrow squeak. You follow me?"

"Aye . . . I follow you, John. Only too well I follow you. And I know you're right. But I'm only at the beginning of my knowing."

"And bide there a wee, Robin: bide there a wee. It'll a' come to you. Come to you in great shafts o' light. By God it'll come to you as it has seldom come to any man. That'll be your cross, Robin; but, by the holy, it'll be your crowning glory as well."

"Why do you believe in me, John—in my poetry, I mean?"

"I believed in you the first time I saw you—and heard you speak. When I heard you read yon first lines on the Ronalds o' the Bennals I was confirmed in my belief. John Rankine's no' bloody eediot when it comes to sizing up a man. I've sized up too damned many in my day to make any mistake about you. To hell, man: what way do you think I've been so anxious to have you at my ingle side? I can hae the pick o' the parish in my spence ony time I choose. There's no' an ingle-cheek in the countryside I canna visit, frae the humblest clay biggin tae Montgomery himsel' at Coilsfield. But laddie as you are, I'd rather hae a crack wi' you at my ain ingle-cheek than any o' the damned dirt o' gentry frae Maidenkirk to John o' Groats, wi' the General Assembly o' the Kirk o' Scotland thrown in for good measure——"

"You're not afraid to turn my head——"

"Turn your head! No: I want you to hold your head up! Haud your head up. Haud it heigh—for Lord God Almighty— an' I use His name wi' a' reverence—there's no' another head like it in Scotland. Damn you, Rab: hae I to catechise you like Patie Woodrow or Daddie Auld? Gather yourself together, Robin. Coorie in ower the marrow o' yoursel' and husband your forces. . . Laddie: the world's afore you . . . an' the world's yours . . . aye, tae its hindmaist secret . . . the world o' men an' the world o' women, an' a' the ways o' them. God, laddie, but you've got me roused. I ken what's in you and I ken what can come out o' you, for I ken what was in mysel'— locked in mysel'—and I never got the key—could never unlock mysel'. That's something about John Rankine not another soul on this earth has an inklin' o'. And when I hear you, Rab, I hear what I might hae been mysel'. And . . . weel, I might as weel mak' a clean breast o't now when I'm at it. I've courted you, Rab, even as a lad courts a lass. Courted your company, courted your conversation. . . Aye, I've baited the trap wi' my ain dochter Annie. Dinna hang your head, Rab. Annie's no' for you. Richt then. Let it be. But you dinna ken Annie —yet. You'll come round tae Annie yet and she'll come round to you. She's John Rankine's lassie, dinna forget that. But if she never touches you, Rab, it'll mak' nae differ atween us. And now I've confessed a' to you, laddie: me that could be your father. But we'll no' come over this again. What I've

said 's buried atween us—let it lie there. And now come up
to the house and slocken your craig, for by God, boy, I've talked
myself dry: my wame's like a bowster o' c'aff. I'll no' feel
richt till I've ca'd down twa-three chopins o' the wife's ale—
an' ye couldna lip a better brew i' the Baillerie."

After they had refreshed themselves with the good wife of
Adamhill's well-brewed ale, and provided themselves with
some ballast in the form of cake and cheese, they walked over
the rising ground, lazy with the ripening heat of the sun,
towards Lochlea.

They had talked and better talked; but mostly it had been
John Rankine who had talked. Now it was Robert who talked
quietly and earnestly. Despite the elation he had experienced
when listening to the rough eloquence of Adamhill, there were
still many problems to which he wanted answer.

"You know: I'm no fool in the sense that I'm subject to
flattery. I know you had no notion of flattering me. I know
my worth—or at least I know something of my powers. I know
I could write poetry—but I don't know where to start. I lack
an aim, an ambition, a purpose. Easy enough to say what I
should do—but difficult to be sure of the first steps. First I
must make shape to secure some kind of independence for
myself. If I had security against hunger and want, then how
easy would be the road. . .

"But the road isn't easy, John. There seems to be no
alternative but to go to Irvine and tackle the heckling trade. . .
To be honest, I don't want to go: my heart doesna lie to it.
But I see nothing for me at Lochlea—nothing that will give me
a modest independence.

"And there's my father. You know something of his worth;
and his integrity and his honesty have never been questioned.
Yes: he has a temper; he's headstrong; and when he's crossed,
unjustly crossed, he would fight through the flames of hell
rather than submit. I can see him running into trouble with
MacLure. And if he falls foul of MacLure he will only be
worsted in the end, for MacLure, justice or no justice, has

money and power on his side. We fell foul of Fergusson's factor after the provost died—we lost in the end—paid a price in starvation and slavery that no human beings should have been asked to pay. . . Is the same going to happen again here at Lochlea? Don't think I intend to leave my family in the lurch. If I leave them it will be to ease the strain at Lochlea—and with the hope I will be able to bring in some hard cash. . .

"I once crossed my father . . . went to the dancing at Tarbolton against his wishes . . . I think I was right . . . but he has never been the same to me. It's difficult to talk about it, John . . . damned difficult. I have a regard for my father I can't put into words. . . My mother: there's little sentiment about my mother. She's changed greatly since I first remember her at Alloway and the first years at Mount Oliphant. God's everlasting curse on that place, John. It killed something in my mother, sucked the song and the sentiment out of her. It calloused her hands; but it calloused her spirit too. She used to sing, John, sing like the lintwhite and the mavis. Any singing that's in me I got from her for my father never had the sough of a song in him: I've never known him tap his toe to the lilt of a tune. . . Maybe both my father and my mother are disappointed in me—for different reasons. As for the rest of the family. There's Gilbert. Gilbert's a fine lad: I've high hopes of him yet; he's strong where I'm weak and foolish; but he's weak—as yet—where I'm strong. Gilbert bows his head in resignation where I would make a fight.

"My sisters? They're good lassies and have good hands and heads on them. No doubt they'll make good honest wives to good honest men. But . . . they're my sisters, John, and I pine for other company.

"Nobody knows how the shadow of my father hangs over our house. How different when I go over to Davie Sillar. Patrick Sillar is not fit to buckle my father's brogans. But there's laughter in Patrick. And the Presbyterian bile hasn't turned sour in his stomach. . .

"John, I must get away from Lochlea. Sometimes a choking

feeling comes over me . . . then I've just got to get out into
the fresh air . . . away across the parks . . . or walk the roads
in the dark . . . often by my lone, for sometimes I canna bear
the sound of a human voice even when my heart's breaking
to talk to someone who might understand.

"That's the hell of my life: drifting. Drifting from day
to day and dreaming away my nights. Dancing, debating,
reading and reading, working hour upon hour . . . but never
really settled, never sure, never setting a course and keeping
to it. . . A purpose, an aim, an ambition . . . a plan of life and
myself as part of that plan. But if I go to Irvine that'll be part
of a plan, something definite, something from which there
won't be any turning back. For I'll be my own master—or as
much my own master as I can ever hope to be. And at least
I'll have no eyes looking at me when I sit down to my bite
and my sup, trying to read my thoughts and showing disapproval in advance of what they cannot know and can't ever
know. . ."

The tilt of the earth entered the twilight of the day and
the slow sweep of its turning gathered the gloaming along
the blur of its distant edge. The low hills softened and sank
down to rest in the haze of the long day's heat. The sun had
gone down in a far hosanna of gold and purple chords muted
against the dove grey that curtains the tired eye against the
glimpses of eternity.

And now the white smudge of a moth fluttered in the coarse
grass; a sudden snipe riccochetted from its early rest; maukin
and mappy swivelled an ear and drummed a warning on the
velvet nibbled turf; across the dew-drenched earth came the
slow cry of the herd-boy gathering the cattle beasts to the
closure; and though a lone peewit battered itself into an
erratic frenzy against hidden danger and an owl screamed from
the topmost branch of a stunted oak, yet the hushed breath of
the evening smoothed and caressed every sound back into the
silence. . .

They had sat on a knowe facing the dying west; and

eventually the silence had claimed them too. Robin's voice had hushed to a whisper before he had finished all he wanted to say to John Rankine.

But he felt he had said all he could to John Rankine and the farmer felt he had heard all that was necessary for him to hear—and to understand. He could not follow Robin in all the turns and twists, all the subtle undertones of his thinking and his feeling.

And there was also a limit to the sympathy and under- standing John Rankine could draw from the wells of his being. Not that his heart or his head were in any danger of hardening against him. He felt indeed so drained of sympathetic response that he was in danger of becoming melancholy.

So they rose and the farmer put his hand on Robin's shoulder.

"Robin lad: ye maun do as things'll do with ye. Think about all I've said to you, but mind that in the hinderend a man must gang his ain gate. And there's nobody can travel the road for you. When it comes to advising you about the road you maun gang—weel, I'm afeared, Robin, I would need to be God Almighty Himself afore I could venture to advise you. . .

"Oh, I'll be seeing you soon again. And I'll see that you go forward to the Lodge without delay. . .

"And guid-nicht tae you, lad. And take care o' yoursel'. I'm hoping to hae your company at Adamhill mony a nicht, Irvine or no Irvine. And, damn ye, if we dinna make our laughter shake the rafters o' Adamhill, then my name's no' John Rankine."

ST. DAVID'S LODGE

In the darkness there were many strange voices and many strange words were spoken. When the light was restored to his eyes, he was aware of the glittering points against his flesh, aware of the flashing downwards thrust of the blades. The steel seemed to flash and flicker in the light cast from the tallow candles.

Robin was afraid and he trembled. But a hand was stretched out from behind and it caressed his damp head. From the hand flowed a sense of protection and of love and strength: he knew it was the hand of a friend.

Then came the sound of a voice whispering courage, bidding him have no fear. He knew the hand and the voice were John Rankine's. He ceased to tremble and all his fears vanished. He ceased to be conscious of the cold dampness seeping through his flesh from the cold dampness of the earthen floor.

The labour of the Lodge having passed, Robin was relieved when refreshments were brought in and normal good fellow-ship again prevailed.

John Rankine passed him a full coggie of Manson's strong ale and bade him drink up.

"Get that down into your wame, Robin: you're bound to have a gey empty feeling there. I know, laddie: I know. We all came the same gate. It'll a' come back to you—and whatever you've gathered, you'll put something to it yoursel': something you'll maybe give back to the brethren here years afterhand. You're on the road now. And Robin lad: you did well. Keep your head high. You've nothing to be ashamed of."

Gilbert was carting away the peat cuttings Robert was taking from the ditch-side to spread on the bare high ground. He paused for a moment at the ditch.

"So you're for Irvine at long last?"

"Aye. I see no other way, Gibby."

"No . . . I suppose there's no other way."

"I'm afeared no. . ."

"Glad to go?"

"In a way. . . I've got to go sometime. It'll be easier this time o' year."

"I'll miss you, Robin."

"Damn the fear. . . You'll get running the place the way you want. You'll be in charge. And you'll be able to bring the laddies to heel. You're aey telling me I let them off far too easy."

"Maybe you do. But I'll miss you: we'll all miss you."

"Aye . . . I'll miss the old place. Miss the lads at Tarbolton: miss John Rankine."

"You get on wi' John Rankine."

"Gibby! John's a remarkable man. I'm proud to claim his friendship—and he could be my father. John looks rough and he speaks rough; but his heart's the pure metal. And he's got a head. There's more solid wisdom in John Rankine's head than there is in the collected brains o' the Presbytery o' Ayr. Keep the right side o' him, Gibby."

"I don't mean a thing to John Rankine. It's you has all the gifts, Robin. Everybody knows that."

"Gifts, Gibby! And what the hell good are they to me bogged in a ditch?"

"Your heart's no' in farming, Robin?"

"Is yours?"

"It'll have to be: there's no other road for me."

"But is your heart in it?"

"No' in Lochlea. If we had better soil . . ."

"That's the hell o't, Gibby. We'll never have richer soil. We could never pay the rent. Rent: that's what matters: that's what counts. Rent's the curse o' Scotland. Rent's the cause o' misery, poverty and ignorance. Aye, and the source o' the gentry's wealth. MacLure sits snug in Ayr wi' nae mair education than enables him to sign his name to a deed-bill and cast up a column o' figures in his ledger, while I've got to howk in a bog ditch to improve his land. . . Aye: the earth is the Lord's, says Patrick Woodrow. But you don't pay the rent till the Lord . . .

Maybe I'll show you a verse or two I've licked thegither on that theme—The Prophet and God's Complaint."

"I get feared when you write in that strain, Robin: it'll do you no good. It'll only get the gentry's backs up against you."

"Damn them: and what if it does?"

"You canna fight the gentry."

"No? Well . . . I'll maybe blister their hides another way."

It was a dull cold day, as only summer days can be cold and dull. There was nothing to relieve the monotony of the scene. Gilbert was depressed. He did not know where Robert got his spirit and the burning fire of his defiance.

To-morrow Robin would depart from them. Maybe he would not come back again. Gilbert feared that. He would be lonely without Robin, even though he had often denied him his company, even though he had often gone into one of his gloomy taciturn moods and refused to exchange words with him.

But the happy memories outweighed the withdrawn moods —especially since they had come to Lochlea. Now there would be no one to talk to in bed at nights before dropping off to sleep. His younger brother William would never be able to fill the gap Robin would leave.

Well . . . there was nothing else for it. He would need to bow the neck, as always, to the yoke of circumstance.

Gilbert took the rein in his hand and led the pony across the slope of the hill.

Robin leaned on his spade and watched him go. He was a good lad Gilbert. Damned, he was sorry to part company with him. A long-suffering lad: too long suffering. Not enough fight in him. But too good for Lochlea. There wasn't a finer, more industrious, more level-headed, sensible fellow in the West. And Gilbert was waiting behind to take on the extra burden of work while he went to Irvine. . .

Robin thrust his spade with savage energy into the boggy peat. To hell: it wasn't he who had created the injustice in the world. And did anybody think he was going for a holiday?

Part Four

IRVINE INTERLUDE

MEN AS MERCHANTS

THE SEAPORT of Irvine was the largest town in the West and one of the finest and busiest ports in Scotland; but the days of its prosperity were beginning to wane.

As Robert Burns entered it on the Machlin fly, in the sultry heat of a July day, there was nothing to indicate that Irvine had topped the brae of its prosperity; nor could the most observant and nimble-witted oldest inhabitant have noted that the grade was downhill.

Difficult to gauge the economic pulse of such a mixty-maxty motley of a town. A good broad High Street, at least as far as the Tolbooth, and good substantial stone-built houses flanking either side of it. Parts of the street in good repair, though on a wet day (and there were more wet days than dry in Irvine) the street was a muddy channel of glaur, gitters and nasty pot-holes: a menace to man and beast.

In summer, a couple of days' sunshine would dry the road into a fine dust: then the wind would swirl up in gusty breaths from the sea and send clouds of dust and horse-dung through the town.

A stirring thriving town with plenty of mean shacks in its narrow vennels; many foul and filthy backlands opening out from the closes in the High Street, festering in the shade of a four-storey tenement building or sheltering, clarty and cosy, from the winter blasts and the interminable blattering of long rain from the sea.

Plenty of eating, drinking and whoring. Plenty of money to be made in a quiet steady way. And yet Irvine went cannily to the Kirk and sat, for the most part, under the canny care and unobtrusive zeal of the Reverend James Richmond. There were dissenters of various kinds and a few hundred of them sat under the Relief minister, the Reverend Hugh Whyte, a hysterical maniac suffering from a variety of ecclesiastical delusions. But, for the main, Irvine sat snugly, if not over zealously, under the shadow of the Presbytery.

Such a rough through-other place, fidging and clawing its trade-sweaty oxters, was bound to be an attraction to beggars. So there was a flotsam and jetsam of scamps, scoundrels, ne'er-do-wells and all manner of itinerant whores, whore-mongers and riff-raffery.

The crumbs and tit-bits from the creeshie tables of the merchants, tradesmen and prosperous mechanics fattened more than did the bannocks and peas-brose of the hungry townships of the West. Bannocks and peas-brose were luxuries in other towns. In Irvine the crumbs and tit-bits were substantial as pig-brock.

As the Machlin fly ambled along the main street, Robert, from his vantage seat beside the driver, noted many interesting aspects of the town and its diversified inhabitants. He did not and could not note the full significance of what he saw; but significant flashes registered on the film of his mind—to be later developed in the brooding dark-room of recollection.

He noted the parish minister hurrying along with his shuffling ill-shod feet, a parcel hugged under his left arm, his right hand clutching a thorn stick, poking tentatively and erratically at the uneven ground.

The Reverend Jamie, suddenly conscious of the rattling wheels on a boulder-paved stretch of the roadway, gave a hasty upward glance from under his three-cornered hat (brown dusted in its folds) and momentarily caught the black smouldering eye of Robert Burns; noted the deeply tanned visage and the round heavy shoulders.

But the flash was as the momentary flash of a dragonfly's wing against the glint of August sunshine. Besides, Jamie's mind was preoccupied and wholly absorbed with a great task to which he had been setting his hand for some months.

At the corner of the High Street and the Manse Road he almost collided with the burly provost, Charles Hamilton, who, in his capacity as Customs collector, was returning from a visit to the wharf-side.

"You're in the deevil o' a hurry, minister."

"Ah—it's yourself, provost. Yes: I am in a—er—hurry."

The minister was conscious of the questing glance the provost gave the parcel under his left oxter.

"Just been down to Willie Templeton's for a supply o' paper —the best quality rag, I may say—for my statistical account of the parish. Oh aye—and three goose quills: my own are rather to the soft side for the making o' a fair copy."

"I see. There'll be a fair pickle o' clerking in your account, James."

"Byornar, provost: byornar. Oh, it's a labour: a maist onerous labour. It's my hope that the editor, John Sinclair, an' his friends in Embro will be taken up wi' it."

"They'll just hae tae, man. Certes, you've done a power o' snooking and nosing about the burgh, plaguing this one and that wi' your questions."

"You were maist helpful yourself, provost. Indeed, in my covering letter I purpose mentioning to Mr. Sinclair just how much his Account will be beholden to you."

"Aye . . . aye. . . Oh, it was nothing. No more than my duty as provost."

"If a' bodies had done their duty like you, provost, my task would have been considerably lightened."

"Well . . . that's another way o' looking at things, minister, as the auld wife said—— Ahem! Yes. Aye. Well . . . now. Ye'll hae your Account drafted out now?"

"Yes . . . a fair good draft."

"Aye. . . Ye'll be ettling to let me have a keek ower it afore ye send it off to the Capital. Aye . . . it's warm work the day peching down to the wharves. . ."

"Yes, indeed. Ahem! Maybe, provost, you would step into the Manse and refresh yourself wi' a bicker o' Mrs. Richmond's home brew: it's in grand shape, I promise you."

"Weel, I'll no' shake my pow to that, minister. I'll say this for your guidwife: she can aey put down a guid caup o' ale."

"Thank you, provost, thank you. I have also a droppie o' French brandy——"

"Honestly come by?"

"A present, provost, a present. But from an honest source——"

"Mention nae names, minister: I've nae desire to see the Cloth mixed up wi' official business. Aye . . . and maybe you could read me ower some o' your notes while we were refreshing ourselves? I'm verra anxious, baith in my private and official capacity, to see what ye hae done for the burgh. The royal burgh, Jamie: the royal burgh. Man, it's no' every day ye hae the honour o' writing up an account o' a royal burgh."

The Reverend James had a comfortable manse down on the bank of the river—looking across to the thatched hovels of Fullarton sprawling untidily along the low-lying southern bank.

The manse was built on to the gable-end of the kirk and was a rambling house with a storey and an attic and a pillared porch over the front door facing the river with a fine view, beyond the thin spirals of Fullarton lum reek, of the hills of Arran.

Mr. Richmond hastened indoors for the refreshments, leaving the provost, at his own wish, to take the air on the wooden seat outside. While Mrs. Richmond busied herself with the ale, unwrapped a sweating cheese, and shuffled a handful of meal cakes on to a wooden platter, her husband gathered together his notes and swallowed a hasty mouthful of contraband brandy.

The burly provost sat beside him on the bench doing full justice to the cakes and cheese, and partaking of the ale and the brandy as inclination moved him. Mr. Richmond, his thin grey hair wisping across his thin forehead in the slight breeze, began to intone his notes.

"Irvine, or, according to its ancient orthography, Irwine——"

"No' sae ancient, minister: no sae ancient. Damnit, there's plenty auld folk i' the town say nought else but Irrrwin."

"Yes . . . well . . . but the more modern——"

"Oh aye: Irvine nowadays: I'm no' objecting to that: it's the ancient bit aboot your orthography I'm objecting to."

"I'll make a note of that, provost—a mental note. Or——"

"No, no: carry on, minister. I'll no' interrupt ye again."

"Thank you, provost, thank you. There are quite a few notes. . . Well . . . now. Irvine . . . stands on a rising ground, of a sandy soil, to the north of the River Irvine, and about half-a-mile distant from the harbour. It is dry and well aired, has one broad street running through it from the south-east to north-west. On the south side of the river, but connected with the town by a stone bridge, there is a row of houses on each side of the road leading to the harbour; these are mostly of one storey, with finished garrets, and occupied chiefly by seafaring people. On part of the great road leading to Ayr, which intersects the street, nigh to the bridge, are the same kind of buildings. Most of these buildings have been erected forty or fifty years before, and are on the increase. Irvine is a royal burgh in the Baillery of Cunninghame and shire of Ayr. It appears from the records of the burgh, that Alexander II granted a charter to the burgesses of Irvine, confirming some other royal grants. No mention is made of their other charters, which are many. From one granted by Robert II it appears that the burgesses of Irvine were in possession of the whole barony of Cunninghame and Largs. The magistrates of Irvine do not now enjoy so extensive a jurisdiction. On the quay are several store-houses, coal-yards, and an inn or public house, which, by a singular feu has the exclusive privilege of selling ale and spirits there. A fly goes regularly from this to Glasgow, by Kilwinning, Dalry, Beith, and Paisley, three times every week. A stage-coach runs from this to Greenock twice in the week, and continues to be well employed. Four roads lead to and from town: Ayr, Greenock, Kilmarnock, and Glasgow roads. They are all kept in tolerable repair by the statute labour, which is converted into money, and paid to the trustees. Three shillings sterling are paid by every householder in the town for that purpose, which, in many instances, is a very hard and oppressive tax, especially on sailors' widows, left with numerous families, and often in poor circumstances. This is an evil which calls for redress. Besides the statute money there are tolls nigh to the town on the Stewarton, Kilmarnock and Ayr roads.

"Manufactures, as yet, are not carried on here to any extent. The young men, in general, are sailors, or go abroad to the West Indies and America as store-keepers, and planters. Many from this place have gone to the East Indies; some in the mercantile line, others in the physical seafaring and military, and have returned with large fortunes. Many of our young men are also employed as sailors and shipmasters from the Clyde. There are three master shipbuilders, a tan work, a rope work, and a bleach-field. There is one whisky still, which consumes about 950 bolls of malt yearly. There is one small brewery, most of the ale being brewed by retailers themselves. Many private families brew their own beer; and the practice of brewing strong ale has been much revived. There are a great many grocers, and small huckster shops, and four or five hardware shops. There are some weavers of muslins and silk gauze. About three years ago, a company of manufacturers in Glasgow set on foot a tambour-work here, and have now about seventy girls employed, who earn from 1s. 3d. to 2s. per week. Last year a spinny Jenny was erected, which employs about eighty hands. Coals always form chief article of export. About 24,000 tons of coal are exported annually. Considerable quantities of woollen carpets, and carpetins, muslins, and stuffs of silk, lawns, gauzes and linen called Kentings are exported to Ireland. The chief articles of import are hemp, iron, Memel and Norway wood, ship timber from Wales, raw hides, skins, and grains from Ireland. 10,000 quarters of grain have sometimes been imported from Ireland in one year.

"Perhaps in no seaport town of the same extent are the

inhabitants more sober and industrious. They are social and cheerful, but seldom riotous; it being very unusual for any persons to be seen upon the street after twelve o'clock at night. The people in general are in easy circumstances, many of them are wealthy, and all of them remarkably hospitable. They are happy in each other's society, and entertain frequently and well. Their entertainments are more substantial than showy; though in this, on occasions, they are by no means defective. As a proof of their moderation and good conduct, there has not for many years been an instance of bankruptcy among them, one or two incomers only excepted. They are humane and generous, though these qualities may not, in every instance, be exerted with necessary prudence; and this perhaps is one reason of the streets being so much infested with vagrant poor. In other instances their liberality has been well directed.

" There are in Irvine two public schools, and several private ones. Before our connection with America was dissolved, many young men from that country and the West Indies were sent here for their education. The rector's salary is £18 per annum; his perquisites arise from births and marriages. The English teacher's salary is £10; his perquisites arise from testimonials, and his salary as session-clerk. There is one minister only, but he has an assistant.

"There is also a relief meeting-house, with about 240 followers. The town-house stands nearly in the middle of the street, but the street at that place is so wide that the building is not an encumbrance. In the ground floor is the town clerk's office, with a room for the meetings of the Council. The rest is let as shops.

"In the town are two banks: Old Paisley Bank, and Ayr Bank.

"There is only one fair worth notice—it is called the ' Marymass Fair,' which begins on the third Monday of August, and continues the whole week.

"The bridge over the Irvine, being the road to the quay and to Ayr, was rebuilt in 1748, and consists of four semicircular arches. It is too narrow for two carriages to pass each other.

"Principal commodities are linen, cloth, horses, wood, etc.

"Meal and flesh markets are near the Council-house."

When the Reverend James had finished and was pouring himself a drink of ale, the provost mopped the sweat from his brosey face with a large square of scarlet silk (as French and as contraband as the brandy). Then he snapped open his snuff mull and shook out a liberal dose on to the back of his sandy-haired, bap-contoured paw, and snuffed it into the great sandy-haired cavern of either nostril with ostentatious but very evident pleasure.

"Aye, man: that's a fairish account o' the burgh. I'll no' say that I haud wi' it in every particular. You're fully strong wi' that observe anent the taxes: fully strong, James. An' there's a fair hantle o' hemp heckling goin' on i' the burgh the now and the farmers are putting down mair ground under flax. . . An' I don't know that it's essential to point out that the New Brig is sae damned infernal narrow. Another thing, James: food's cheap and wages are good in the burgh. Eggs fourpence a dozen and cheese fourpence a pound——"

"Mrs. Richmond has paid fivepence the pound."

"Aye: for a cream cheese—or a yowe cheese. Good fresh butter sevenpence to a shilling the pound according till the season. Ye can hae hen-bree twa-three days i' the week on a fivepenny fowl or a guid fat roasting bird for saxpence. I've clapped the best o' twa o' them into my wame for my supper mony a time. And what's wrang wi' a bullock steak at saxpence, or a breast o' lamb for fivepence-ha'penny the pound? That should give the Embro folk something to lick their lanthorn-jawed chops ower.

"Now wages: hired by the day a man'll get a shilling and saxpence for his darg."

"Aye . . . but if his wife's at the spinning she'll barely get that for a whole week's darg."

"And will ye tell me where she'll get ony mair?"

"It's hard on widow women."

"Damned, Jamie, life's meant to be hard on the unfortunate. Ye canna run the world on an almous dish; and even if I am the provost and have aey been to the forefront extolling the virtues o' the toon, I never hinted that the Royal Burgh o' Irvine was the Kingdom o' Heaven—yet."

The provost opened his snuff mull with a vicious snap and glared at the downcast eyelids of the Reverend Jamie through his own bulging bloodshot eyes.

But though the mixture of brandy, ale, cheese and cake was disturbing the metabolism of the provost's vast and paunchy innards, he had no sooner inhaled the snuff than he belched offensively and, thus relieved, found his usual good nature flowing harmoniously along its accustomed channels.

"Mind ye, minister: ye've no' to tak' ony offence at my strictures. Ye've written a dunnerin' good report and if you'll work on it a bit mair I'll warrant it'll pass muster wi' the best. And now I'll need to be peching on up the road to my office for I've a feck o' work afore me yet and it's haudin' on for suppertime. Sae guid evening to ye, James; and tell your guid wife that her brew has sharpened my auld guts against a grand supper."

The minister bade him good-bye very civilly for the provost was a power in the burgh and a man to keep the right side of at all times. He envied the provost his zest for life and his capacity for eating and drinking. But as he watched him stumping down the road, he thought that black silk stockings would have sat better on his own shanks than on the burly and bowed stumps of the provost of Irvine.

As he gathered up his papers he recalled that Charles Hamilton had never sported silk till he became the Customs collector; and only since then had he sent his son, John, to college with the view to studying medicine. Aye . . . maybe he should have put in a note about that—and not only for Mr. John Sinclair's edification.

PEACOCK AND PEAHEN

Robert had met Alexander Peacock when he was on one of his visits to Machlin. Together with his father they had discussed the business side of their projected partnership.

He hadn't liked him then—even though he did claim to be his mother's half-brother. Now that he was sitting down to a meal with Peacock and his wife, he liked the woman even less. She was a thin shrew with a clout-clipping tongue. Her address and her manners were those of a dirty slut and she looked as if she hadn't washed in years.

They were a middle-aged couple—and childless. They worked hard and drank hard in turns. When they weren't snarling at each other they were sulky and moody.

Sarah Peacock disliked Robert from the moment she clapped eyes on him: her dislike increased the moment he opened his mouth. What the hen's feet did he think he was? The ploughman son of a small farmer in the backlands, the wilds beyond Machlin. Giving himself the independent airs and graces of a gentleman and speaking like a young minister just new let out of the college. Well: if he was to learn the heckling they would need to break the pie crust off him. . .

Peacock, on the other hand, had no great like or dislike to Robert. The premium had come in handy. But he was looking to the work Robert would do. If he was any way quick in the uptake—and he seemed a smart enough lad—he might be able to take the burden of the heckling off him and leave him the more free to concentrate on the contraband trade: there was a pretty penny to be made at that—and easily turned.

Alexander Peacock had developed a thirst for French brandy and as a consequence had developed a distaste for what was known as honest work and honest living.

But Peacock thought Robert Burns was many kinds of a

194

fool and a great gomeril for having anything to do with heckling. He was puzzled by the way he spoke; but then he had been puzzled by the way his father spoke, and decided, without interesting himself any further in the business, that it was a peculiarity native to the North country.

Peacock was a stringy foxy-faced individual with a thin untidy brown mouser straggling across his pendulent upper lip. He spoke in small cutting phrases and was not given to conversation.

The Peacock house in the Glasgow Vennel that led off the High Street was mean and dirty, ill-lit, ill-ventilated and low thatched. The thatch was badly rotted, infested with rats and stank with a mouldy rat-sour stench.

Across from the house, on the Smiddy Green, was the heckling shop, a low-roofed but and ben like the living house, but more recently thatched and, as yet, comparatively free from rats.

Peacock helped Robert to take over his corded chest to the shop which, he explained shortly, would constitute his living quarters.

Though he disliked the place heartily, Robert was glad he was not living with the Peacocks. Yet he doubted if he would be able to live for long in the heckling shop. If the Peacock's house stank, the shop stank with a very different but equally offensive stink. Principally it was the stink of the flax. It was an oily sickly smell; and it was all-pervading. Bundles of flax lay in one end of the building in various stages of preparation, some lay on the drying racks in front of the fire, some lay ready for use on the long heckling benches; and everywhere, like a gossamer dust, lay the oose and fluff of the heckled flax, scutched and heckled and combed to a fine wool all ready for carding and spinning by the weavers. In the middle of the floor was a deep rotting vat, additional to the ones outside, for rotting down the flax in the first stages of its preparation.

In the far corner was a crude stall that Willie Gowans, the coal merchant, had rented for his horse. In the other corner was a crude bed made with sundry pieces of driftwood and covered with grey blankets as coarse and matted as they were dirty.

"You'll be richt enough in here," said Peacock; "and the beast here helps to warm the place on the cauld nichts. If you want a drink, you'll find Maggie Lapper's doon the Vennel as guid's goin'. An' if you'll tak' my advice—and you'd better tak' my advice—keep clear o' the waterside: the tavern there— well, it's no' for the likes o' you. We start at six in the morning. You'll get your breakfast the back o' nine i' the Tolbooth knock. When we're busy I've seen us work on till nine at nicht —but we're no' often as busy as that. An'—eh—the wife doesna like nicht-hawks—she expects you bedded by ten at the outside. If I'm no' aboot in the mornings, don't let that haud ye back. I trust you're no' bothered wi' your nose, Mr. Burns. The Vennel folks are touchy. If you hear ony ongauns in the nicht, dinna fash yoursel': keep to your bed gin you dinna want folk to get a bad opinion o' you—— I wouldna like that. Here——"

Peacock deftly fished out a flat bottle from the tail of his frieze coat.

Robert scarcely wet his lips with the brandy and handed back the bottle.

Peacock took a full swig.

"I think you and me understand each other, Mr. Burns?"

"I think we do, Mr. Peacock," said Robert, finding his voice at last.

They shook hands and, without another word, Peacock turned swiftly and went out the door.

He had spoken more that first night than he was to speak during the next six months. And Robert was to be grateful for his taciturnity.

THE GLASGOW VENNEL

July passed in working and sleeping. It turned wet and cold. But Robert was indifferent to the weather. He was sick and tired by night. Sometimes he went down the Vennel to Maggie Lapper's house and drank a measure of tippenny; sometimes he flung himself down on the bed and fell asleep only to waken in the night sick with a dizzy headache and pained and aching wrists, strained from the unaccustomed fatigue of the heckling gear.

By the beginning of September he was beginning to find himself and beginning to make a few acquaintances.

The provost's son, John, was on his summer vacation from the college of medicine in Glasgow. Sometimes of an evening he would drop into Maggie Lapper's (the provost's house was at the corner of the High Street and the Vennel). He was a friendly lad but a year or two older than Robert. He was interested in literature. He knew something of the poets and he was soon pleasantly surprised, not to say astounded, when the heavy glum face and the dull pained eye of the Ayrshire ploughman-turned-heckler suddenly became animated and the smouldering eyes flashed with unexpected fire.

"You should pay a visit to old Willie Templeton," he counselled one night, conscious that Robert was far better read than himself. "You'll get all the new ballads and pasquinades there. I'll have a word wi' Willie if you like."

"You're very kind, Mr. Hamilton."

"A trifle, sir, a trifle. And you needna worry about payment. Willie's got a keen sense o' literature and he'll be more than glad to hae a crack wi' a lad as well versed in the poets as you. Damned, sir, I misdoubt but Willie seldom gets a crack wi' onybody hereabouts in the literary way."

"I should have thought in a town of this size there would be many folks deeply interested in books?"

"Ah, you know little of Irvine, my friend. In Irvine folk are interested in making money, in eating as much as they can and drinking as much as they can—and doing as little work as they can. Now thinking is work. Damned hard work if you have to think against your inclination. Books demand thought and the reading o' them puts nothing in the pocket. So—— What d'you expect? The book the Irvine merchants like best is not the Good Book either. Oh no. The book they treasure above all others is their counting-house ledger."

"Centum per centum. They're mostly figures—and figures speak for themselves."

"True enough, Mr. Burns—and the words are golden. Aha! That's worthy of another bicker o' Maggie's brew. Drink up, Mr. Burns. My worthy father's the provost of this royal burgh and I must say he doesna stint his son. Ony time you're short o' the price o' a drink, sir, do me the honour to mention my name to Maggie and she'll put the bawbees on the sclate."

"Sir: I never was blessed with much of this world's gear or cash; but I'm no sponger. When I canna pay for my drink, a drop of well water will taste as sweet."

"You're a man o' independent spirit, Mr. Burns. I admire you the more for it. Though believe me, you can be too independent if you want to prosper in this wicked world. But see you now: come round some night and meet my father. You'll like him—and he'll like you. And he's always willing to help a young lad to make his way in life. He's fond of an argument on politics or religion. And on a winter's nicht when he's drawn up to the fire wi' the luntin pipe in his gab and a half mutchkin of good whisky warming his wame— you'll find him as good company as you'll get this side o' the Border."

"I would be honoured to meet your father, Mr. Hamilton.

I have heard nothing but the most estimable reports of him since I came to Irvine."

"Look you, Mr. Burns: Provost Charles Hamilton is a man of very sterling worth and ability. He works hard for the burgh—even if he doesn't forget himself. I'd like to hear any man say a word against him in my hearing."

"That's a manly sentiment, Mr. Hamilton. I'll be pleased to make your father's acquaintance. I have for some time made it my practice to catch the manners living as they rise, as Pope says in his Essay on Man—the First Epistle if I remember aright —and for this alone it would be fine honour to meet with a living provost and the provost of such a town. But don't mistake me, sir; it is not my intention to study your worthy father as I would study Taylor on Original Sin. No, no: it is not my intention to put into practice an impertinent anatomy, if I may borrow a metaphor from the medical schools——"

"Damn you, Burns: you've mistaken your trade. You should have studied for the chair o' metaphysics and logic. But to hell, man, wi' a' this learned jaw: we're too young to be courting the grey-beard professors. Drink up. Youth's a stuff will not endure as your poetic friend Shakespeare has it."

"Ah Shakespeare! It isn't easy to enter into the world of Shakespeare. There's a great jungle of thought there."

"There's a bigger jungle o' thought in that head o' yours. You can read too much, my learned friend. Books can constipate the mind."

"Ah, but they can give wings to the spirit. And I don't have much time on my hands for reading. What books I could read had I only leisure."

"But surely life is more important than literature?"

"But what kind of life? Do you think that the life of some drudging slave or some dissipated squire is more important than Milton's Paradise Lost or the works of Pope? Life, yes. But we'll never know what life can be like till we've studied the best of man's mind and spirit. And how are we to do that if we never lift our eyes from the task or take the bowl from our lips?"

"Well, for me, Mr. Burns, I'm prepared to take life as it comes. And I hae nae intention o' being miserable as long as I can get my hands on a big bellied bottle. We don't live that long and the flesh is subject to many divers diseases. And we'll be a hell o' a lang time dead. So here's health, Robert—if I may be so familiar. Health and happiness—and to hell wi' dull care!"

"Aye, to hell wi' dull care, John. I'm with you there. And if we're goin' to hae a drink, let's hae a drink. I've naebody to speak tae but that auld mare o' Willie Gowans—and by God, sir, she's dull enough. You could jot down her lear wi' the wrang end o' a goose quill on your thumb nail. . . Often at hame I thought it would be fine by my lane—there's a big family of us—but no: man wasn't made to live alone."

"There's plenty o' lassies in Irvine, Robert. A' shapes and sizes. Plenty for the nod and mair for the plack. You know, Robert, there's more whoring done in Irvine than in any other town outside o' Embro."

"I'm not interested in whoring, John."

"Well, keep that way; for the foul disorder is not a thing you want to trifle wi'. But, damnit, there's honest lassies in Irvine too. A fine upstanding lad like you has no need to run after whores."

"I prefer the company of men."

"The devil you do! Man: you need the lassies: life would be a savourless business without them. As long as you don't go and lose your heart to one o' them: it can be the devil's own birkie then. I'll tell you—have you read The Man of Feeling of Henry MacKenzie? All right. I'll loan it to you. I don't hold wi' much o' it. But you'll like it."

"I've heard a lot about Henry MacKenzie and The Man of Feeling. I like the title."

"Oh, you'll like it. I just thought on it the now. But for guidsake, Robert, drink up: the ale's gettin' sweeter. The mair you drink the mair you want to drink. That's the great thing wi' the nappy. You can go on till you fa' down."

"I like it better when I can stand up. I've no stomach for a lot of drink. A gey wee drap oils the cogs o' my brain—and that's just fine."

"But man, Robert, when you're bitchfu' you don't gie a groat for god or devil, prince or prelate—or the provost o' Irvine. 'John,' says the provost to me ae nicht when I staggered hame properly bitchified—that's a good word, Robert—'Man,' says he, 'haud up yer heid and don't go stottering ben the hoose there like a sick calf. And damnit, sir, when ye canna, hae the sense to lie doon and sleep it aff. Once you've waukened i' the gutter twa-three times ye'll learn to haud your drink!' An' he's right, Robert: he's right. You try it and see if it doesna work."

"It's easier to hold drink than hold your thoughts. You've never been drunk wi' thinking, John? Well . . . I have. That drunk I didna ken where I was walking, whether it was raining or shining, whether it was nicht or day——"

"That's the first stage o' the horrors, Robert. Auld Nick sitting on the bed rail girnin' at you; pickin' his teeth with a roasting iron; great brutes o' teeth like a bluidy tiger's. As you say, you don't know day frae nicht for time's grilling on the hob o' hell."

"Come on, John. It's time to tak' the road. Auld Nick'll be lying in bed waiting for you if you don't."

"I'm no' drunk—yet, Robert."

"No' yet. But by the time you get won round to the High Street you'll be shaping that way."

"Right then, Robert. If you say so, that's good enough for me. But I'm for a half mutchkin wi' me for through the nicht. That's when I do my thinking; and, by certes, the thoughts are no' pleasant. Man, there's some foul and filthy diseases i' the world. If you want to hae a sample o' the horrors when you're dead sober, mak' a few visits wi' a Glasgow doctor. There's folk living and dying and begetting their kind in midden-holes and cesspool-cellars you wadna coup pig-dung into. I wouldna practice medicine in Glasgow no' for a' the tobacco leaf in the West Indies."

"There are foul dirty holes in Irvine too, John; and if they're worse in Glasgow they maun be damn bad. There are plenty o' stinkin' hovels o' houses in the country—but at least the air about them is fresh. I haven't smelt fresh air since I came here."

"I never thought o' that, Robert. You coming straight frae the plough-stilts in Tarbolton. Aye: there's stinks and stenches in the Glasgow Vennel—but nothing to what's doun at the River. But Glesca! Man, Robert: I've seen mountains of human excrement twenty to thirty feet high an' fifty feet long in some o' the back courts, wi' just a narrow path round them to let you intae some o' the closes . . . and in the summer heat I've seen clouds o' flies on them that would hae blacked out the sun. And that's the honest God's truth, should I be struck dead where I sit. Man, the doctors there a' carry a powerful smelling salt in the head o' their canes; and if they didna haud it till their noses when they were visiting some o' thae places they would boak up lights, liver and ga'. Aye; and the maist astonishing bit about the whole show is that the human manure brings mair siller to the factor nor the rents."

"I think I'll go back to the plough, John. How the hell folk can be content to live like that I don't know. I'd sooner cut my throat."

"An' yet folks wonder whiles that doctors tak' heavy tae the drink! I've known them that drank laudanum."

"I've no doubt. But come on up the road, John, for you've had enough for ae nicht."

"Aye . . . I'll come, Robert. I was getting light-headed a wee while back; but I've talked mysel' sober. I'm ready. I can tak' a long lie i' the morning but you've to get up for work."

When they reached the provost's house at the corner of the High Street, John Hamilton asked Robert to wait for a moment.

He returned with a slim volume.

"There's The Man of Feeling for you, Robert.   Laugh and the world laughs wi' you: weep and you weep with Harley— Mr. Harley—and if you can discover what his Christian name was I'll thank you to hear what it is. Guid nicht, Robert—and joy be with you."

THE MAN OF FEELING

For three nights Robert sat on his bed and read the master-piece of Henry MacKenzie, Scotland's Man of Letters. Every one since 1771 who cared anything for literature had read or was reading *The Man of Feeling*: many who cared nothing for letters were doing likewise, their curiosity excited by the talk the novel had aroused.

Feeling, or sensibility as it was sometimes more correctly termed, was in the air. Mr. Harley, the hero of Mr. MacKenzie's book, had much feeling—indeed he was nothing but feeling, pure and undefiled.

He had little or no money. True, there was a small matter of some £250 (per annum) of unearned income. But on such a miserable pittance he could not be expected to support and sustain much feeling.

So, early in the book, Robert found him setting off for London with the hope of securing (by much display of feeling and a touch of jobbery and corruption) a suitable means of adding to his income.

The genuineness of Mr. Harley's feeling was in no essential part to be doubted. He could part with a shilling to a poor beggar if the beggar gave any evidence of feeling: or, more economically, Mr. Harley could shed a solitary tear—"one tear and no more."

But though he could perform this feat with no apparent difficulty, he could also rise to more copious flows. When he did not " burst into tears" he "kissed off tears as they flowed, and wept between every kiss."

Robert was moved, deeply moved. Here was a man who wept for the sorrow and suffering of others; wept for the cruelty and injustice of the world of men; wept when innocence was soiled by guilt; when virtue went down to defeat before violence and justice was blinded and bruised by the machinations of brute force. . .

And here too was a vital and important fact, the significance of which could in no way be slurred over. This fact did not matter to the comfortable readers of Mr. MacKenzie, who could weep tears or dry them away with equal indifference. It mattered supremely to Robert Burns.

For here it was admitted that there was injustice in human society; that there was one law for the rich and only the law of blind chance for the poor; that where wealth accumulated men decayed. More subtly, but more poignantly, it was clearly stated that for the man of feeling, the man with a keen and delicately-balanced sense of the moral law (about which his father had written so admirably in his religious *Manual*), the world was little better than a slaughter-house for sensitivity—and a kirk-yard for ideals.

Never before had Robert read a book that so clearly illustrated the essential condition of society. Never before had he read in print of how the dice were so shamefully loaded against the poor. He could do no other than accept this picture of life for the picture corresponded, in emotional effect, with life as he had hitherto known and experienced it. Well he knew that Mr. Harley had only touched the fringe of life and a very genteel fringe at that. The significant fact was that Mr. Harley, where he touched life, touched it with feeling and with a sensibility that was on the side of the angels.

It was not, however, till the third night that Robert wholly warmed to Mr. Harley and his creator Mr. MacKenzie.

Towards the end of Harley's sketchy adventures, the occasion presented itself when, more in sorrow than in anger (but most certainly without the shedding of any tears), he declared himself without equivocation on the subject of empire building.

"I have a proper regard for the prosperity of my country: every native of it appropriates to himself some share of the power, or the fame, which, as a nation, it acquires, but I cannot throw off the man so much as to rejoice at our conquests in India. You tell me of immense territories subject to the English: I cannot think of their possessions without being led to inquire by what right they possess them. They came there as traders, bartering the commodities they brought for others which their purchasers could spare; and however great their profits were, they were then equitable. But what title have the subjects of another kingdom to establish an empire in India, to give laws to a country where the inhabitants received them on terms of friendly commerce? You say they are happier under our regulations than the tyranny of their own petty princes. I must doubt it, from the conduct of those by whom these regulations have been made. They have drained the treasuries of Nabobs, who must fill them by oppressing the industry of their subjects. Nor is this to be wondered at, when we consider the motive upon which those gentlemen do not deny their going to India. The fame of conquest, barbarous as that motive is, is but a secondary consideration: there are certain stations in wealth to which the warriors of the East aspire. It is there, indeed, where the wishes of their friends assign them eminence, where the question of their country is pointed at their return. When shall I see a commander return from India in the pride of honourable poverty? You describe the victories they have gained; they are sullied by the cause in which they fought: you enumerate the spoils of those victories; they are covered with the blood of the vanquished.

"Could you tell me of some conqueror giving peace and happiness to the conquered? did he accept the gifts of their princes to use them for the comfort of those whose fathers, sons, or husbands, fell in battle? did he use this power to gain security and freedom to the regions of oppression and slavery? did he endear the British name by examples of generosity which the most barbarous or most depraved are rarely able to resist? did he return with the consciousness of duty discharged to his country, and humanity to his fellow-creatures? did he return with no lace on his coat, no slaves in his retinue, no chariot at his door, and no burgundy at his table?—these were laurels which princes might envy—which an honest man would not condemn!"

When Robert had finished reading this passage he had to put the book down and go out. Here was sensibility with social fervour to it! Here were words that scalded as no tears could scald. Here was truth that came as a flaming sword.

Now indeed was Mr. Henry MacKenzie the first of novelists even though he should be one of the six attorneys in the Court of Exchequer and a rapidly ascending star in the literary, social and political firmament of the one-time capital of Scotland. Indeed anything might be forgiven Henry MacKenzie for having given Mr. Harley the opportunity of declaiming on the politics of colonisation and nascent imperialism—and the moral rights of man.

THE SOW OF FEELING

"Henry MacKenzie," said Robert to John Hamilton when they were seated in the far corner of Maggie Lapper's spence, "is undoubtedly the first of our novelists."

"I hope to God he's no' the last, Robert. But I knew you'd like the flavour o' him. I knew that from the moment I met you. Not, mind you, that I think you're an eaten and spewed drink o' pig-wash like Mr. Harley——"

"You can think of him like that?"

"That's how I think of him, Robert. And that's how you'll think o' him once you've met some o' his kidney. But I understand you. Fine I understand you. Mr. Harley's got the right kind of feeling in him—even if he's got it in the wrong place. Naturally you think Henry MacKenzie must have the right feelings too?"

"And why should we doubt that?"

"Oh—I don't know for sure, Robert. All I know is that it doesna work out that way—or Henry MacKenzie wouldn't live like a gentleman in Edinburgh—and London. You'll never find Henry MacKenzie sitting drinking in a tavern wi' the riff-raff o' the town."

"And why should he? I wouldn't sit drinking wi' the riff-raff o' the town."

"No. . . But then, Robert, you'd be riff-raff to Henry MacKenzie—for all your scholarship. If Mr. MacKenzie cares to wear his heart on his sleeve and weep crocodile tears for the edification o' a cat-gutted public—that's Henry MacKenzie's way o' trade. But don't you try to beg a bawbee frae him on the strength o' that. I haven't a tithe o' your lear, Robert. I come off a coarse-fibred folk and there's damned little poetry in us, and I could never hope to have your delicate fine-fingered approach to life. Not that the Hamiltons are clods or wanting in a warm-hearted philosophy. But I've seen more o' life in the better grades o' society than you have, Robert; and I'm not taken in wi' their fine manners and their genteel gab. And don't you be taken in. You've got something they havena got; and don't forget that. A yellow Geordie's a better friend than one o' that tribe o' gentry: ask the provost gin you get on the crack wi' him: he's seen more o' them than I have."

"Thanks, John: at least you've got honesty and an honest way of expressing yourself. I think you're right about the gentles. Maybe I know more about the worse side of them than you give me credit for. But I beg leave to reserve my judgment on Henry MacKenzie. A man would need to be a howling hypocrite to write like that and not mean every word o' it. Oh! I grant you MacKenzie hasn't put his quill to the real evils o' this world: but he's pointed to the seat of all virtue. And that's something, John; and he's done it a damn sight better than Beattie or Shenstone or Thomson. Aye, or any writer I have yet read. Maybe MacKenzie doesn't fully realise the significance of all he's done ... maybe. I'm damned certain that his readers in the fashionable world see little of the real working o' his mind. But that doesn't belittle his achievement any—rather it enhances it. But however that may be, John, I've learned a lot from him and I'm grateful to you for having introduced me to his work. The first chance I get I'll be down to Templeton's shop to order a copy. I'll have The Man of Feeling for a companion from now on."

"All right, Robert ... I canna follow you along that road —though I think I catch the drift o' your meaning. But before you make up your mind, hae a read o' Bob Fergusson's satire The Sow of Feeling."

"It sounds like blasphemy to me."

"It sounded worse to Henry MacKenzie. But I've a notion if I meet you ten years—or maybe ten months—frae now you'll be more in sympathy with puir Bob Fergusson than ever you were wi' Henry MacKenzie."

"I don't think so, John. But then I've never come across any pieces of Fergusson's."

"You havena! Well then, Robert, I say this and I'll make a prophecy! You've mair in common with Fergusson than you have wi' ony other writer I know. And you'll live to tell *me* that, whatever you tell to other folk. Now for Godsake let's hae another drink. I've enjoyed your company here, Robert. I'm off tae Glesca at the end o' the week and I'll no' be back till Ne'erday. But I hope we'll aey be frien's whatever happens."

"I'll give you my hand on that, John. I don't know what I would have done without your company—and your kindness."

"Come on then, boy: we'll drown our sorrows in the nappy."

"My, my," said Maggie Lapper to herself as she let them out into the quiet street in the quiet of the soft summer's dusk. "My, my, but thae laddies are happy: they havena a care i' the warld."

And she stood at the narrow door of her tavern and watched them oxter each other down the Vennel.

THIRD DEGREE

There wasn't much time for reading. Soon after the provost's son returned, the new flax crop was to hand and with it, according to Peacock, a desperate need to fulfil overdue orders.

Robert worked hard. Peacock had to admit to his wife that Burns might be a born idiot but that there wasn't a lazy bone in his body; that he worked harder when left alone than when supervised and that he had picked up even some of the finer points of the scutching and dressing and that, all in all, his work was a credit to any heckling shop in the burgh. This had the effect of mollifying to some extent Mrs. Peacock's rank prejudice against Robert (more and more she felt that he was contemptuous of her presence and that this contempt was so cold as to be almost maddeningly impersonal). But, conscious that she had fed him like a dog, she tried to make amends. As Peacock said: "He'll maybe learn sense quicker than would be healthy for us. Considering how much we're making out o' his work, it's a damned bad plan to grudge him his bite and sup—seeing it doesn't cost us a bluidy plack."

Sometimes Robert did not converse with any one for a week on end—except to exchange a few words with Willie Gowans, the coal merchant, when he came for and brought back his old mare. Not that Willie had much to say. Business was poor and he had great difficulty in making ends meet. What his connection with Peacock was, Robert was never able to find out. But beneath Gowan's surly servility to Peacock, Robert saw that he both feared and hated him.

One morning a note was delivered to him from John Wilson, secretary to the Tarbolton Lodge, intimating that the third degree would be conferred on the first of October.

His heart leapt at the thought of going back to Tarbolton,

to meeting again with Davie Sillar, Willie MacGavin and the other lads of the Bachelors' Club. And just as fine, though on a new level, would it be to meet with John Rankine, John Wilson and the brethren of the Lodge. It would be good too to see the family at Lochlea—especially Gilbert.

He spoke to Peacock. Peacock said he couldn't be spared. But Peacock was a brother Mason, and when he heard of Robert's errand he felt he could not well refuse—that if Burns established Masonic connections in Irvine it wouldn't be politic for it ever to be said that he had stood in a brother's way in the important matter of the third degree. In the end it was agreed that Robert could go for the ceremony, provided he borrowed a horse and was back at his bench early the following morning.

So in due course Robert went to Tarbolton and met some of his old friends, though they were fewer than he had hoped.

When John Rankine saw him he said: "Good God, Rab: are you fearing your ordeal, or is that bluidy hecklin' gettin' the better o' your health? Or are you no' gettin' your meat?"

Rankine was troubled about his appearance: he looked far from well—and far from his usual buoyant self.

And Davie Sillar said: "How is it going, Robin?" And Robin told him it was almost beyond bearing, but that if anybody, especially about Lochlea, was to ask he was to tell them different.

Gilbert said, fiercely and bitterly, and in a tone unusual for him: "Give it up, Robin: give it up and come back home. Throw your damned gear in the fire and let Peacock keep his bluidy premium. What's a better position in life if you're left with no health to enjoy it? You were never meant to be shut up in a bluidy hecklin' shop. God knows, it's slavery enough at Lochlea; but at least you're breathing fresh air and you get a good sup and bite—and a clean bed to lie down in."

But Robin said simply and without any show of emotion: "I've put my hand to the heckling, Gilbert: I'll see it through. It could be worse. I'm getting to know a lot of things about myself I never knew before. There's profit in that."

"Damn little profit gin you ruin your health."

"My health was ruined at the start, Gibby: I never had your constitution."

"Well . . . I can't do more than warn you, Robin. You know best. Leastways anything I could say wouldn't make ony difference. Are you coming home for the night?"

"I'll look in wi' you. I've got to get back to-night. I borrowed a horse: it's a clear night. And when are you joining the craft?"

"I've been speaking to John Wilson."

"You could do worse, Gibby. God, but I'm tired!"

Gilbert hung his head and kicked at a stone in the ground. He said nothing.

He was now fully initiated into the brotherhood of Masons and he had in his pocket an introduction to the Irvine Lodge of St. Andrew. He would go round some night and meet the brethren—by all accounts there were some good fellows there.

If only he felt better. There was something working on him, though what it was he could not say. He felt he was working towards a fever of some kind.

He wasn't a week back from Tarbolton when the fever laid him low. Peacock tried to give him advice but Robert spurned it.

"Let me be, man: I'm not going to die yet. Just let me be and I'll be all right."

Peacock went away. Later, his wife came in with a hot gruel. But she could get little response from him.

The gruel lay on the floor by his bedside and the rats ate it in the quiet of the night.

He was in the fever of pleurisy and the fever raged violently. All Robert knew was that he was very ill indeed.

After a while Peacock became alarmed. He was certain Burns was going to die and that very soon unless something was done. But he didn't know what to do. He wasn't going to be at the expense of getting a doctor—even if a doctor would be able to do any good. But he could not afford to have him dying on his hands. He wrote to William Burns at Lochlea and told him that his son was gravely ill.

Immediately he received the news, William saddled a pony, filled a saddle bag with some food and rode steadily into Irvine.

He was much distressed when he saw how low his son was; and he was no less disturbed at the filthy poverty of his surroundings.

Robin lay exhausted on the pillow, his face pale and hollowed.

"Robin, lad," said his father, easing himself gently on to the bed, "this is a sad way to find you. Could you not have got word to me sooner? I'll see Peacock about that after. How long have ye been lying like this?"

"I don't know, father. I've lost all count of the days—aye, or the weeks. What date is it?"

"It's the eleventh of November, Robin."

"Your birthday! I hope you'll be spared to us for many a birthday yet, father."

"I'm no' what I was; but I'll need to hold on for a while yet. Now tell me, lad, have you no real notion o' how long ye have been lying here?"

"Three weeks."

"The Lord have mercy on us!"

"But I'm bye the worst. I'll mend now if I could get a bite o' food and get my legs under me."

"I hope so, Robin: I hope so. But you'll need to get out of a place like this. Had I known you were bedding in a place hardly fit for beasts—aye, hardly fit for rats——"

"Willie Gowans's old mare has been good company. I could say what I like to her and she never answered back."

"Ah, Robin lad: you're far from well. Have ye broken fast yet?"

Robin shook his head.

"The Lord bless us and keep us. What kind o' folk are the Peacocks to treat ony lad like this? What would you have a notion of? I've cheese and bannocks and a poke of freshly ground meal. Maybe a thin gruel o' parritch? No? Maybe an egg beaten up intil some hot milk? Ah: you'll need something to tempt your belly and build up your strength."

"There's no' a sup o' fresh hen bree?"

"Hen bree? The verra thing. Your mother drew an old cock's neck this morning and your sister Agnes cleaned and plucked it for you. But no—that'll be too long i' the pat,

Robin. I'll see it goes on without ony delay. The egg and the milk will be quickest."

Robin nodded—anything to avoid argument with his father. What a father! He had never seen him more concerned, more anxious, never so filled with that quiet gentle-flowing solicitation. And yet never had he seen him look so pale and ill and drawn, so near the grave. . .

He lay unmoving while his father stepped over to the Peacocks.

Mrs. Peacock knew she had met her match the moment she set eyes on William Burns. Never before had she trembled at the sight of any man: she found herself, to her inward consternation, trembling at the sight of the Lochlea farmer.

William knew the value of silence. In one cold merciless glance he summed up the character of Mrs. Peacock. He would not bandy words with such a woman. He would cut her to the bone with his contempt.

Not that he gave any thought to this: the searching glance, the result and the resolution followed in a swift intuitive sequence. He was much too concerned with his son to waste time in thought or words.

"I would like some fresh milk heated for an egg. I have the eggs."

"I'll do that, Mr. Burns: this very minute. D'ye think the lad's bye the worst o' his fever?"

"Here's an auld cock: ye might make a drop o' hen bree."

"Hen bree? Surely, Mr. Burns. A grand thing coming out o' a fever, hen bree."

"Mr. Peacock's not about?"

"No . . . he's . . . doing a bit business in the town. But he shouldna be lang."

"I'll want to see him whenever he comes in. Is there such a thing as clean bed clothes?"

"You're not suggesting, Mr. Burns——"

"I'm suggesting nothing, woman."

"I'll see what can be done."

"Verra well. I'll take this milk over."

Robin sipped at the egg and milk. He had no relish for it. But he had not the heart to refuse his father. He had watched him beat the egg and pour in the milk with a care no woman could have equalled.

"This'll soon put me to rights. I'm sorry, father, to have brought you down."

"I should have been here long afore this, Robin. Robin lad, you've your Maker to thank that you've pulled through this fever."

"Aye . . ."

"You never forget your prayers?"

"No . . . I never forget."

"I didn't think you would. It's a cruel world, this world here below. The only mercy you're likely to be shown is His mercy. Always put your trust in Him, Robin: never in men. Aye: it's a cruel world, Robin: the wicked may seem to flourish but they're cut down in the end. . . Are you feeling liker yourself now?"

"I'm fine, father—weak a bit—but fine. But—your coming here will give me all the strength I'll need."

"There's one thing. You'll need to get another lodging."

"Aye . . ."

"Just as soon as you're fit to move. Do you ken of ony likely place?"

"I . . . might get a room down the Vennel."

"What kind of room?"

"I'm not certain. There's a Mrs. MacCutchin—I heard she had a room. But the money——"

"Direct me to her and I'll speir her price and look the place over."

"Let me see . . . nine doors down on your right hand."

"MacCutchin?"

"I could ready my own bite——"

"We'll see, we'll see. Now dinna fret yourself. I'll no' be long till I'm back."

Nor was he. William had to be back in Lochlea before nightfall. There was no moon and it was a treacherous road on a black blustering night. But he was determined to see his son settled before he left.

When he returned, Robin saw relief in his grey countenance.

"Aye . . . ye could do worse, Robin. She's a decent homely body Mrs. MacCutchin. A widow woman. She'll take a shilling a week. It's a lot of money. But if ye can make your own bite you'll win through. I'll send you what we can spare from Lochlea. You're set on seeing this heckling through?"

"I . . . what else is there for it? I set my feet this gate and I carry on. It'll no' take me long to master this trade . . . and we'll need the money it will bring us."

"You think there's a future in it, Robin—for yourself, lad?"

"Aye . . . it'll help us all out."

"I hope sae, Robin, I hope sae. We'll need all the help we can get. MacLure's pressing me hard . . . hard. I never got things the easy road . . . never. But MacLure is bent on ruining me completely. He'll not rest content till he has me rouped and cried at the kirk door. And why? Because he's put his money a bad road and he wants to squeeze the blood out o' me. You know how we've slaved to make a better bit out o' Lochlea? Drained it, limed it, levelled down the auld rigs and filled up the bawks atween? Drained the Loch itself, cut off the moss from the soil, bigged dykes. . . And all that to go for nothing. Nothing's to come off the rent for all that—labour and toil that no money could pay for. Oh—it wasna that at the beginning. You'll get full credit, generous credit, Mr. Burns, for all your improvements. But now that he feels the grip of his ruinous investments—and am I to be held responsible for the failure of the Douglas & Herron bank; am I to be held responsible for the war with America . . .? And now that the blackguard's feeling the pinch, he presses me. Aye, and threatens me in the utmaist rigour of the law. Jail, Robin: that's what he threatens me with. Aye, and he'll turn every stone to see me there. . . If only I saw you better, lad, and on the road to setting yourself up in a steady way of employment, maybe I could fight MacLure with a better heart. But this hungry ruin that's aey settling on me. . . We pay a hard price for our immortality, Robin; and maybe it's just as well we have no foreknowledge of His inscrutable plans. But . . . with His help I'll fight MacLure though I die a cadger's death in the sheugh at the hinderend. Never bend the knee to injustice, Robin. Man's justice is not His; and the things that are Caesar's maun be resisted with the things that are Caesar's. . ."

William Burns poured out his thought to his son. Robert lay, hearing not so much the purport of his words as their saddening sough. For it was now clearer than ever that his father was fighting back against overwhelming odds from the lip of the grave.

But it did William good to empty himself to his son. Too long he had repressed himself: locked the resentment of his spirit within him. By the time he had finished talking the hen bree was ready. He shared a coggie with Robin, bade him good-bye and rode back to Lochlea. Feeling much comforted, he imagined he had left his son in the same restful state.

But Robert was cast into the depths. Hungry ruin! So after all their struggles at Lochlea a malignant fate was to rob them of their just reward! Was the blood of the Burns folk cursed at its source, and, if so, what had been their sin?

Then he heard the solemn pedantic voice of John Murdoch reciting from Arthur Masson's *Reader* the lines of Addison:

> " When by the dreadful tempest borne
>   High on the broken wave:
>   They know thou art not slow to hear
>   Nor impotent to save."

High, yes; but always the wave had to break below the crest. Not slow to hear, no; but slow in response. Not impotent to save, but withholding salvation nevertheless. And why? Was salvation to be granted in the next world? Why?

There was no answer; and Robert knew there would never be any answer. Not in this world. And even as he reasoned the wave broke and he sank down into the trough of melancholy. . . He was but a Harley in a world of suffering and hardship, destined to suffer always and so pass unrequited to early and unlamented death. And his sufferings would be more intense than Harley's for he had not even Harley's means and wealth to avert the necessity of toiling for his daily bread. Alison Begbie must have seen the curse of sensibility written upon his forehead. If death must come now, then he must needs prepare himself against its coming. He would leave a melancholy verse or two to mark the occasion. A dirge or lament to winter and the early winter of his days; or a prayer on the approach of death. . . A verse or two such as the gentle Harley, had he been a ploughman, would not have been ashamed to have left to the supercilious eye of an unfeeling world. . .

Robert mended slowly. Indeed he showed little improvement until he quit the foul-smelling heckling shop and moved down the Vennel to Mrs. MacCutchin's room.

Here he made shift to provide himself with some creature comfort. It was pleasant when the wet wind howled and shrieked down the Vennel to sit baking in front of an honest fire and sup gruel steaming hot from the red coals.

But the poison of his pleurisy had debilitated him. His nerves were threadbare with anxiety, lack of sleep and undernourishment. His damaged heart was dangerously strained. He had been very near to death: its shadow had lain with him in solitude too long. In this condition it was easy for his mind to become a stagnant pool of melancholy vapours. In this mental habitat the little fishes of Henry MacKenzie's *Feeling* luxuriated.

The truth was that the fushionless Harley was beginning to fester in his mind. He had travelled a long way since he had first come under the spell of Allan Ramsay's *Tea-Table Miscellany* with *The Bush Aboon Traquair* and *Doon the Burn, Davie.*

A long way he had travelled since he had written his song to Nelly Kilpatrick in his own adolescent Allanesque. Pope with his astringent wit and social criticism had given his mind an edge, tempered the blade of his own native humour. But Shenstone had sickled it over and Thomson had Anglicised it beyond recognition. All had forced him from his true bent; but now MacKenzie and pleurisy had polluted the pure well of his fancy.

Morbid in his thoughts and dangerously at the mercy of self-pity, Robert dragged himself up the Vennel to the heckling. He was but the physical shadow of the man who had come into Irvine and who had caught the eye of the Reverend James Richmond: mentally he was but the shade of the man who had harangued the Tarbolton bachelors with burning eloquence.

But, though slowly, he did mend. The quality of his nervous energy was such that it needed but little of it to trickle back into the reservoirs of his being to regenerate him. But the trickle was beginning, drop by drop.

THE SAILOR WITH BLUE EYES

Robin wrote a pious letter to his father for the approaching New Year's day. He subscribed his name and added, by way of anti-climax, for the pangs of hunger were coming over him—"My meal is nearly out, but I am going to borrow till I get more."

He read over the letter: it pleased his mood and he knew it would please his father. He hadn't put that quotation from *The Man of Feeling* about the bustle of the busy and the flutter of the gay in quotation marks: his father would not care to learn that he had been wasting any time on the trash of novels.

After he had sealed the letter Robert felt much relieved. Ah well: that was that. He would spend the Ne'erday in Irvine.

But somehow the taste of the epistle was sour on his stomach. He took his blue bonnet from the nail behind the door and went in search of human company.

"Aye, aye, sir," said the sailor. "I was the only man saved from the good ship Isabel—— After the pirates had landed me, naked and empty, upon the wild Connaught coast, I made my way home—due to the kindness of the Irish, sir: due to the kindness of the Irish. The Irish are a kind and generous race: aye, give me an Irishman to a Scotsman any day for wit and worth and a bold generous temper. A lousy sailor; but the finest son-of-a-bitch ashore. . .

"Well . . . here I was back in the auld toon and here I am yet, Richard Brown, master mariner, looking out for an owner. Oho: don't cast off your bow ropes yet! I could get an owner any day of the week—including the Seventh Day. But I've sailed foreign too long not to know every splice o' the ropes.

I want a good ship and a good crew. A good clean ship with a good clean bottom. A clean bottom, sir: essential in a ship and desirable in a woman. Your barnacle-bottomed bitches drag along as if they were trailing their guts on the bed of the ocean. And when a pirate comes upon you——"

A woman came up from behind and tipped the master mariner's hat forward on his head.

"Who the hell—— Ah! Jean Glover! Good-even to you, madam. Come sit down—by my worthy friend here—and give grace and charm to our social hour. Mr. Robert Burns, madam. Sir: Mistress Jean Glover of that ilk. Jean: I was just telling Mr. Burns here how essential to a good ship is a clean bottom. I don't know that he understood me aright: for in these matters he is but an ignorant land-lubber. But I warrant *you* don't misunderstand me?"

"Captain Brown, you're maybe a good sailor. Maybe ye ken a' aboot ships. But you ken damn little aboot women. I see by your friend's blushes that he thinks the same as me. Am I richt, sir?"

"I'm afraid you must forgive my friend: we have been drinking."

"Damn you, sir. I'll have no one apologise for me. You see, Jean: Captain Dick always brings luck to his friends. Here's my friend here, Jean: he doesn't know you. And damn me: he's something of a poet—and a thundering good fellow. Just recovering from a malignant squinancy, Jean: a proper bitch o' a fever. Well enough now to benefit from your charms, my dear. But come! Your pleasure, madam."

"You're a hell o' a man, skipper. See if there's a decent brandy i' the hoose."

"The same sweet sonsy Jean! I'll sample it myself, lass: now be good to Mr. Burns."

When he was gone, Jean Glover looked Robert straight in the eyes.

"You're a stranger hereabouts, Mr. Burns. But there's Ayrshire in your tongue for a' that."

"You must not pay any attention to what Brown says, madam."

"Jean—jist Jean Glover. You don't know the captain well?"

"Indeed, we only met the other night."

"I jaloused as much. Are you for staying here long, Robert?"

"Another six months maybe."

"Oh! we maun get acquaint, Robert. Don't you worry about Richard Brown. He has a fancy for me——"

"I don't blame him."

"Don't jump to conclusions. You've gotten a fancy for me yourself."

"Madam, I——"

"Dinna blush, laddie. Maybe I'm yours gin you want me: I've been watching the pair o' ye."

"You mean?"

"The captain said you were a poet. Poets are no' sae blate. I'm a bit o' a poetess mysel'."

"You write poetry?"

"Sangs . . . aye, and sing them."

"In heaven's name, madam: who, what are you?"

"Me? Jean Glover: a honest enough lass, gin ye know her."

"I would like to know you, Jean."

"Weel then: what's to ail you?"

"I—I don't know. I've never met a lass like you before."

"I ken that fine. You've never kenned ony lass."

"You're wrong there."

"No: I'm no' wrang. I've kenned mair than one lad like you—but not at your age."

"And what age do you think I am?"

"You might be coming thirty—let me see. You don't know enough o' the warld to be thirty. Twenty-seven?"

"Twenty-three!"

"You were born in '59 like myself! Aye, you're old for your years, Robert, in some ways. Am I going hame wi' ye?"

"Home—wi' me?"

"Dinna be affronted, lad. Jean Glover doesna give her affections for money."

"You mean——?"

"Here's the sailor——"

Richard Brown came back with the brandy.

"Here's your brandy, lass. And rare good stuff. I was round the back o' the house for a breath o' the caller air. Well, Mr. Burns, and what think you o' my Jean?"

"Your——"

"Never mind him, Robert. He's——"

"Oho: you're at the Robert stage. You don't let the grass grow under your feet, Jean: I'll say that for you."

"Weel: you never saw grass growing on a busy street, captain?"

"You rogue. Well . . . am I seeing you hame, Jean?"

"No' the nicht, captain."

"Mr. Burns doing the honours?"

"Why not come down to my room in the Glasgow Vennel —both of you. Maybe you'd sing for us . . . Jean?"

"Two's company, Mr. Burns," said the captain.

"Since you are friends of each other cannot you both be friends of mine?" replied Robert

"Well, damn you, Burns: you speak fair and like a gentleman. What d'you say, Jean?"

"Thank you, Robert."

"Right then!" cried Brown and slapped the table. "We'll take down a bottle o' the landlord's best."

Robin leaned across Mrs. MacCutchin's deal table.

"Sing to me, Jean. Sing! Your voice melts the marrow in a man's bones."

"Ye're a beggar, Robert Burns. Ye can do mair to me wi' your eyes than ony other man ever did wi' his love-making. Is it only my voice that melts you?"

"I'm no beast, Jean."

"No: you're no beast. I knew that the moment I clapped eyes on ye. Oh, ye're a daft beggar, Rab: hae ye no' a kiss for me yet?"

"Sing and I'll kiss you—kissing that'll drive ye crazed."

"Why did you bring that drunken skipper?" She nodded to Brown who was lying asleep in front of the fire.

"Jean! I've never lain wi' a lass—yet. But by God! if I kiss you I'll lie wi' you and the de'il can count the reckoning."

"Brown'll no' waukin . . ."

"No! I canna, Jean . . . not here."

"I canna sing either, Rab. God! ye ken little o' women."

"Mair nor ye think!"

"You don't know me."

"I don't, Jean. But I don't want to know anything about you that you wouldn't like me to know. That song ye sang afore Brown went down: it's not your own?"

"Why no'? I travel the roads, Rab."

"By yourself?"

"Sometimes . . . I hae a partner in my tramping. I suppose you'd say he was my husband."

"Husband?"

"Aye . . . we're married in the only way we know. But . . . dinna mistake us, Rab. It's only a handy kind o' arrangement atween us. We entertain and sing round the taverns——"

"But your dress: you don't look like a strolling-lass?"

"Oh, I'm at hame for the winter wi' my auld mither. I live the life I do frae choice, Robert. I canna be shut in in the simmer. It's in my blood. My mither used to say I was an ill-blooded hizzie . . . but she kens better now. . . Rab, I shouldna hae drunk that brandy . . . I'm telling you things I shouldna . . . things I never told to ony man. If you winna kiss me I maun talk to ye. Ye'll see me again, Rab—when he's no' wi' us?"

"Where's your husband?"

"He's no' jealous: we're no' in love. He's away wi' another lass to Glesca for a month or twa. He can make a shilling there an' be ready for me gin the spring. . . I canna thole this place . . . but my auld mither needs me on the long black nichts——"

"I'll see ye again, Jean. God lass: I've been at death's door this last month back.   Lying doon in Peacock's heckling shop——"

"He's an ill scart o' hell—he's in the contraband—a receiver —an' a dirty blackmailing beggar—watch your step wi' him, Rab."

"I thought as much. . . Lying in that stinkin' hole, Jean . . . I thought an' better thought. . . Maybe, Jean, you've gotten the right way o' living . . . better than ony way in ony book."

"Maybe. . . We all die a cadger's death in the end." She cupped her breasts in her hands. "My flesh is bonnie flesh, Robert—bonnier than ony sang. But the sangs live on and soon enough my flesh will be shrivelled and wrinkled like my mither's. There'll be sangs when you and me are happed i' the grave, Rab. I kent that lang afore I kent what a man was like. I kent that frae the day I could look at my mither sleeping and her stretched at my side. . . No: I don't give myself freely, Rab. The feck o' men are beasts where a lass is con- cerned. But it's nae sin when ye loe a body, a clean decent body that's no twisted in his soul."

"Soul, Jean?"

"Ye think I havena a soul?"

"The soul can wither tae, Jean."

"If you let it. But dinna tell me the Black Craws o' the Kirk have gotten their nebs in you?"

"I'm a Christian, Jean—or I try to be."

"If you'd been that kind o' a Christian you wadna have sat there and filled your eyes wi' me. I ken your Christians, Robert; and you're no' one o' them. Give me another sup o' the brandy, laddie, and I'll away hame to my auld mither. You're a big soft-hearted lump, Robert Burns: you shouldna worry your head about things like the soul for that'll set you on to worrying about salvation; and you'll end up a drunken sot or a black-hearted lecher wi' a bastard bairn in every parish; and a' the young lassies'll tak' till the ditch when they see you on the road. . . You're the first lad that ever refused me, Robert Burns. . . My bloom must be fading. . . The brandy, laddie, the brandy: you'd drive ony lass to drink. Has no lass about your side o' the country ever told you about your eyes? You should have been a lassie, Rab—you'd have had a' the lads in your parish running about foaming at the bit and nickering like stallions—or roaring like bulls. . ."

The candle spluttered and went out. The firelight filled the room with a warm glow. The sailor breathed softly on the floor.

"Oh Robert, Robert . . . put your arm round me, laddie, and let me sleep . . . the drink's got the better o' me. Robert . . ."

She rose unsteadily and came towards him. He rose and caught her in his arms. She was conscious of the strength that flowed in him . . .

When Richard Brown woke from his drunken sleep he found Robert Burns sleeping on the top of the bed. There was no sign of Jean Glover. He lifted the brandy bottle from the table: it was empty. He went over to the bed.

"Wake up there. Wake up!"

Robert woke slowly. He had finished the brandy after Jean had gone.

"It's you, Richard! What time is it?"

"Time? The hell wi' time!"

"It's morning! How are you feeling, Richard?"

"Hungry as a hawk. You've nothing to drink?"

"Water?"

"To hell! Come down to Maggie Lapper's—she'll ready us a bite."

Robert pulled on his brogans.

"I didn't mean to finish that brandy, Richard. I should have left it for you."

"Maybe no, Robert. You would need it after Jean Glover left——"

"What d'you mean?"

"How did you enjoy her? You're a lucky beggar, Robert. I drank myself to sleep: to give you your chance——"

"I didn't need any chance. Jean slept off her drink on the bed there and then went home to her mother."

"Aye?"

"You don't think I took advantage of her, Richard?"

"You don't think I'm a bloody gowk, do you?"

"Richard! If we're to be friends, you must understand I don't tell lies."

"You mean to say——"

"I tell you Jean went as she came so far as I am concerned."

"If she did, you've seen the last o' her."

"I don't think so."

"Damn you, Robert, you don't mean to stand and tell me that you let her go?"

"Why shouldn't she go when she wanted?"

"She's a whore, man. What d'you think she came here for?"

"She's no whore."

"She's no *common* whore; but she's a whore just the same. Aye . . . and when her mind's set on't, she'd out-whore a' the whores o' Babylon."

"Whore or no' whore: I love her."

"Love her? Are you clean mad? Damn you, Robert: you're a simple gowk. She would tell you she loved you. You're a tarry—— Come down to Maggie Lapper's till I talk sense into that daft head o' yours. You're like an innocent babe in a den o' thieves. Love! God Almighty——"

"You'd better go yourself."

"Now, now, Robert. You took the wind out o' my sails. You've been reading some trash of a novel. You didn't tell Jean you loved her?"

"You love her yourself, don't you?"

"Me? What in God's name put that daft idea into your

addled pate? *Me* love a woman! Robert! You mustn't go falling in love wi' women—that's the damndest mistake you could ever make. Here! Have you ever had a lass?"

"In your sense—no!"

"That's it! By certes, Robert, I nearly slipped up there. You're a virgin. *That's* what Jean Glover saw in you. That lass kens her trade. I'll need to talk to you like a brother. You're no' fit to be goin' about loose, man. My God! to think that but for meeting wi' me you might have taken home a whore to your father's sacred roof-tree. I'll talk to Jean Glover——"

"You'll not talk to her."

"I'll skelp the pretty doup off her."

"Richard: I don't want to quarrel with you over this; but don't think I'm a fool. I know what Jean Glover is better than you do. If I wanted to marry her, and she would marry me, neither you nor the Session nor the Presbytery nor the Synod would stop me. By heaven! don't cross me too sore. I'm no saint; but I'm not in the habit of trading in illicit love——"

"*Illicit* love? To hell: a' love's legal. What d'you think women were made for? Illicit love, my granny's mutch. It's every woman's job to get her man: granted. Oh, and they get them: there's plenty damned silly sheep i' the warld. But a man wi' ony glimmer o' sense acts different. Women are there to be enjoyed—without the legal chains o' holy matrimony shackling you. That's only common sense. I've told Jean Glover I loved her; but she's mair sense nor believe me. But I've told plenty that hadn't the sense o' Jean Glover. Of course you tell a woman you love her: she expects that. If she believes you that's you safe through the harbour lichts. But you watch your course after that—unless you want to compeare afore the session."

"You would deceive an honest lass?"

"Robert, Robert. For the love o' God give yoursel' a kick on the backside and waken up your brains! If a lass is daft enough to let you there afore the priest ties the knot—that's

her look-out. She kens fine the game she's playing as well as
you. She's gambling as well as you; and the stakes are even.
Listen: gin you were a lass would you wait till the knot was
tied?"

"It would be different if I loved the lad."

Richard Brown groaned.

"There you go again wi' this damned gowk's gabble o' love.
D'you mean to tell me you *believe* in love?"

"I do!"

"Well, by the Lord Harry, you're in for a rude awakenin'.
You'll get your hair combed yet—wi' a broomstick! You're no'
haverin' through the dregs o' brandy? Man, Burns, you've
got me feared. Me thinking you had the best head on you for
a man o' your years I'd ever fallen in wi'! I just damnwell
canna believe my own ears."

"So you think I'm nothing but a gowk? I won't deceive
you, captain: you've seen more of the world than I have.
You've known illicit love. That's something I've never known
and never wish to know. That makes me a gowk, does it? I
think you can know women without knowing illicit love—and
I don't mean holding their hands either, gowk as I am. There's
a border line for any man of moral sense. Maybe that's what
makes me a gowk—moral sense. If so, I don't mind. Would
there were more gowks in the world: there would be fewer
unhappy and unfortunate women."

"They'd be damned sour ones."

"I doubt it. There can't be any happiness in illicit love. A
betrayed woman's bound to turn sour: sour in her sorrow and
sour in her hatred of the falseness of men."

"To hell, Burns, to hell . . . damn your preaching! You're
no' in the pulpit. I threw all that rotten bilge overboard long
ago. In fact I never poisoned my stomach wi' it at the beginning. Oh, it's all right for novels—but it doesn't work in
everyday life; and damn right too. Folks are flesh and blood:
no' texts and sermons. What's moral sense but a set o' blinkers
for a blin' cuddy? And you're no' a blin' cuddy . . . you're a

man and you're something o' a poet. Keep your moral sense
for high days and holidays and for parading on the poop deck
o' the Presbytery for a' the crew o' the kirk to see ye: there's
sense in that. But the lassies, man! They were made for love.
The saftest bed that 'er I got was the bellies o' the lassies. . .
Aye: every damn time. Illicit love! Some bog-spavined gelded
Craw started that talk. It would make a dog laugh. And to
think that you had Jean Glover within your grasp—and you
let her go! Man, man. . . You talk about being a poet! Oh, I
don't mean any offence, Burns. Only—— Oh come on down
to Maggie Lapper's: I'd vomit werena my guts hingin' empty
on my ribs and my mouth like the bottom o' a parrot's cage.
Dinna get downcast: we shouldna argue about women on an
empty stomach or first thing i' a winter's morn. To-nicht's
Hogmanay—that's something to cheer you up. Come on, come
on . . . you can make a fresh start in the New Year. D'you
hear me?"

"You've lain wi' many women, Richard?"

"Hundreds—and slept and ate the better for it. And you'll
do likewie gin you learn sense."

Richard Brown was a sailor, a magnificent figure of a man,
with a strong clean-cut face and frank honest navy-blue yes.
He was but a few years senior to Robert. Despite his terrible
talk about love, Robert could not help thinking that Richard
Brown was something of a hero. Somehow he had never met
a man who looked and spoke the part with more genuine
conviction. And there was no evil in his laughter. . .

But to make love, carnally, to a lass and boast about it—
he didn't like that. It shocked him. Not the carnality: the
boasting. A lad might be tempted and might fall; but he
would repent his fall and hide his shame. Otherwise he was
but a beast and wanting in those moral and religious principles
that raised man above the level of brute creation. Many men
were brutes in their love-making. Yet lust ought not to be
dignified with the sacred name of love.

Robert sat on the end of the table looking down at his worn

shoes. Jean Glover was no woman betrayed. Jean was no prostitute. Jean was life with the red rhythm of a song bubbling on the red lips of her loving.

Now he was feeling better than he had felt since coming to Irvine. He would go down to Maggie Lapper's and enjoy a bite and relish more of the invigorating company and conversation of Richard Brown.

ANOTHER JEAN

Robert should have been working in the heckling shop rather than eating and drinking and talking and reciting poetry in Maggie Lapper's ale-house. But Maggie was good to them and all morning they had the comfort of the ingle neuk to themselves.

That morning ripened the friendship begun so casually in the Tobacco Tavern at the wharfside but a few days before. They exchanged life stories; and Brown's had been as unfortunate as Burns's. And though Brown was the elder by a few years he recognised in his friend a maturity far beyond his own.

When they had got behind the philosophical and ethical façade of initial conversation, they found they were both passionately fond of the lassies. They agreed that for the future they would join forces both at kirk and market and in their courting expeditions.

Richard promised to meet him in the evening at the Tobacco Tavern; but only for a short time. He had promised to bring in the New Year at the house of an influential merchant who had a pull with certain of the ship owners. . .

In the afternoon Robert worked at the heckling; but his spirit wasn't in it and he felt weak and tired. Peacock seemed to be absent: he had avoided him since that day his father had visited him.

It was bitterly cold. Darkness came early and with it snow. Robert didn't light the lamp. He went home to Mrs. MacCutchin's.

His room was in the attic and a narrow wooden stair at the back of the house gave access to it.

Mrs. MacCutchin, her plaid hooded over her head—she was

carrying a pail of slops—interrupted him at the bottom of the stair.

"A cauld nicht, Mr. Burns."

"It's a' that, Mrs. MacCutchin."

"Ye'd company last nicht?"

"I had."

"I keep a respectable hoose, Mr. Burns."

"I never doubted it, Mrs. MacCutchin. I wouldn't have brought respectable folks here if I had."

"Aye . . . weel . . . folks talk, Mr. Burns."

"They do, Mrs. MacCutchin—especially when they've nothing to talk about."

He left her at that and went up the stair. He lit the fire; but it was dour to burn.

To hell with them! He tidied himself and went down to the Tobacco Tavern and secured a seat by the blazing fire.

For a time he listened to a couple of well-to-do strangers discussing the American war, the one blaming North and the other blaming General Cornwallis, the first countering with a devastating attack on General Clinton.

With the heat of the fire and the drowse of conversation he fell asleep only to be wakened sometime later by Provost Charles Hamilton.

"Sleeping already, Mr. Burns? Wake up, sir. Or are you ettling to bring in the New Year with the dawn?"

Robert was instantly awake.

"It's yourself, provost."

"You're feeling better now, Robert, after your ill turn? Man, I only heard the other day you had been badly. Here you are, Jean! Come forward, lass—here's the verra beau to see you home."

In the glow of the light her hair had the burnished sheen of ripening barley; her eyes had the delicate blue of the harebell; her lips were full curved, sensuous and astonishingly red. She was tall, well bosomed, and walked with a long lithe leg.

Robert surveyed her in a glance; and in that glance his heart missed a beat.

"You know Jean Gardner, Mr. Burns? Come right forward, lassie, and get acquainted with Mr. Burns here."

"I am honoured, madam——"

"There you are, Jean: that's the manners they have about Tarbolton parish. Ah, but I thought you'd kenned our Jean, Robert! Sit down, lass, and we'll have a mouthful o' wine. Aye . . . I met Jean coming down wi' a roast for the landlord— you'll be taking something back for your father? You ken Willie Gardner round at the Seagate, Robert—the best flesher i' the burgh? I've a wee bittie o' business wi' the landlord myself. But Robert here will convoy you home, Jean. A dirty nicht—and wi' thae drunk sailors i' the toon a lass like you is the better o' an escort."

"It's verra kind o' Mr. Burns; but maybe I'm taking him out o' his way?"

"Not in the least, madam. I shall be more than honoured to conduct you round to the Seagate."

"You're verra kind, Mr. Burns."

"Ah, Robert's a well-mannered lad. And a poet, Jean— damned, a good one too. I was expecting John doon frae Glesca, Robert; but it seems he canna manage the length. Busy folk in Glesca—and damned unhealthy."

"Your news is good for all that, sir?"

"Oh, John doesna say much: he'll have a lass there, like as no'. But you'll no' meet in wi' bonnier lassies than we have i' the burgh, Robert—what's ailing Willie wi' the wine— Are you writing a bit verse or twa back and forward like the now? Wait till I see what's keeping that gomeral wi' the wine. You'll excuse me, the baith o' you?"

Jean placed her quaich on the table.

"If it's no' impertinent, Mr. Burns, micht I speir your business in Irvine?"

"I'm learning the heckling trade with a view to working my own flax."

"You grow your own flax?"

"Well . . . my brother and I work a few acres. . . You're not in a hurry for home?"

"Oh, I can't stay, Mr. Burns."

"Tuts—it's Hogmanay! A lonely bachelor seldom has an opportunity to converse with—such beauty."

"Mr. Burns!"

"I'm sincere, Miss Jean . . . I beg of you the opportunity for a deeper acquaintance."

"You're a friend of the provost?"

"I have that honour. But believe me to speak the sober truth when I say that I would be prouder still to be able to say I was your friend."

"I'll need to be getting home."

"You have a suitor?"

"You're fishing, Mr. Burns."

"And you've caught the hook, Miss Jean. Come! another cup of wine. Oh, you can't refuse me. It's an innocent drink."

"It's verra nice."

"I suspect our good friend the provost is something of a judge of a fine wine—and may I add—of a fine woman."

"They say he's verra big with the lassies, Mr. Burns. I suppose, seeing you're a poet, you'll ken a lot o' them yourself?"

"Now you're fishing!"

"Och—you're all the same: you say what you think pleases."

"Do you blame us for that?"

"Och, I wish men would talk sense."

"Sense? Miss Gardner! You rob me of any capacity I may have for talking sense—save such sense as I've been talking. I'm told this is a private room: only those who have the landlord's favour are allowed ben. At any moment now we may have company. I must see you again—soon."

"I bide at the Seagate: you can see me there. And why *must* you see me, Mr. Burns?"

"You know why!"

"Indeed and I don't."

"Do you want me to tell you?"

"No . . ."

"You will see me?"

"No . . ."

"Where do you sit in the Kirk?"

"We're of the Relief Kirk."

"Ah! I must worship there of a Sabbath."

"You're no' afraid o' hell-fire and damnation, Mr. Burns?"

"I'm more afraid of your disfavour, Jean . . ."

"I must be getting home: my mother'll kill me."

"It's Hogmanay. . ."

"You don't know my mother."

"I intend to have that privilege soon. To-night—I shall hand you over to her. I have the provost's instructions."

"You're a verra determined man, Mr. Burns."

"Robert."

"Och, come on home."

"Robert!"

"G'way. . . I hardly know you!"

"Robert!"

"All right . . . Robert."

"And you know me fine."

"Indeed and I don't. I think you're a wild man. I don't know that I'm safe to go home wi' you."

But Jean Gardner allowed Robert to see her home. She was taken with him. He excited her almost as much as she excited him. When he put his arm round her they were both trembling with the intense, almost unbearable physical thrill that the mere touch of each gave to other.

Ordinarily she would not have allowed him the liberty of putting his arm round her waist. But the night was wild and in the black blizzard of swirling snow she needed the support of his strong arm.

They didn't speak all the way to the Seagate. Words would have compelled the admission of consciousness and Jean did not want the meaning of words imposed on her physical awareness. And Robert, though he was prone to make love in a torrent of words, knew when words lost their power of meaning.

Already he was in a love fever. All day he had haunted himself with the vision of Jean Glover. He had gone to the Tobacco Tavern even though she had told him she would not be there. And now here he was with his arm round a vastly different but even more seductive Jean. Last night he had been certain he was in love with Jean Glover: to-night he was equally certain he was madly in love with Jean Gardner.

But the delicious present was too precious for any philosophic moralising. Indeed his head was not involved in any conscious way. His emotions were aflood: his senses were aquiver; and his flesh was a riot of passionate stimulation.

THE FIRE IN THE VENNEL

Jean had promised to see him again. William Gardner had received him very civilly and told him that any friend of the provost's was more than welcome to the hospitality of his home. Even Mrs. Gardner had beamed on him and had insisted that he sampled her own brew of ale. She had given him a sample of her fancy baking to take home: hech, Mr. Burns, but the sands are running out o' the auld year's gless. . .

And there Jean had stood in the bein warm kitchen, her back to the great fire roaring in the wide fireplace, her berry-ripe lips open on a smile and her eyes glimmering with lights of unapprehended ecstasy, an egg-shell tint of blue to the whites and the pupils flooded with a deep lilac. He thought her simple dress of blue linen vastly became her.

He had not dared to overstay his welcome. He was afraid, moreover, that Mrs. Gardner would sense something of his newly-born passion for her daughter.

When he came out into the night he found the blizzard much abated, though it was still snowing.

He decided he would call in on the Peacocks' as much to relieve the tension of his feelings as by way of paying a Hogmanay duty call.

The Peacocks were glad to see him: they had no visitors as yet.

". . . I just looked in to pay my respects."

"Aye . . . come your ways in, Robert . . . you've gotten ower your bad turn?"

"I'm fine."

"Hae a drink, man: ale or whisky?"

"Ale, by your leave, Mr. Peacock: I've little stomach for Kilbagie."

"You're wrong, Robert, there. Man, a drop o' Kilbagie

240

steams the vapours out of you. Pour out a strong ale, wife.
Aye . . . I've had a throng time o't, Robert. Aye . . . business
you ken, business . . . bits o' things back and forward. I'm
working up a wee bit trade wi' Ireland . . . takes me down
aboot the wharf a bit. I hear you were down there about the
Tobacco Tavern? Richard Brown, a harum-scarum laddie
Dick. . . Aye, and Jean Glover. You'd be the better o' watching
your step there, Robert. She's a fell hizzie, Jean."

"You've been well informed——"

"No offence, Robert. Man, Irvine's a gossiping place. You
canna change your sark i' your ain hoose but a'body kens.
They clash aboot ony damned thing—especially if there's
a bit scandal going—and there's aey that. Come on, wife:
you're no' doing the honours. Fill up Robert's stoup there.
It's a guid ale that—a special brew frae a wife i' the burgh
here. . ."

Peacock's foxy eyes were glazed with drink, his thin cruel
lips were moist and loose. Peacock wondered how much Burns
knew about his activities. He had decided to keep the right
side of him, butter him up if necessary until he found out.
Either Brown or the Glover hizzie might let something
drop. . .

A mate from a ship in the port came knocking at the
door. He had business with Peacock; but he was out for an
evening's drinking as well. He was a bluff Fifer with a merry
laugh.

But the mate soon grew tired of the ale and he did not
appear to relish the Kilbagie.

"Hae ye nae a bo'le of guid French brandy, man?"

"Brandy?"

"Awa' tae hell—oot wi't."

"Wife! Oot tae the shop."

"Where?"

"The rettin' tank, damn ye, and dinna speir sae mony
questions."

Mrs. Peacock swayed out the door.

"I keep a bottle oot-bye, Robert—it's guid for the gripes. It was honest come by . . ."

The mate gave Robert a hard look.

"We're a' honest fowk here."

"Aye, aye. . . Robert here's learning the trade wi' me. An honest lad, Robert."

"You've a fell honest eye i' your head, Mr. Burns. You're gey and canny wi' your drink."

"Oh, Robert's right enough, Mr. Stein. He's just coming round after a bad bout wi' the fever."

"Whatna fever?"

"Just a bad chill i' the lungs."

"I dinna like fevers. There's some bad beggars abroad."

Mrs. Peacock came back with a large bottle of brandy folded in her plaid.

"Bar the door!" commanded Peacock.

The mate fished a large corkscrew from his jacket pocket.

"See's it, wife: I'll draw it."

"Clean quaichs, wife: it disna do tae spoil the flavour."

The mate tossed a full measure of the burning brandy down his throat.

"Damned, that's grand. That's the drink, Mr. Burns, 'll burn the fever oot o' you. Clash a coggie ben your sour guts, Peacock, ye foxy-faced auld beggar ye! That's better'n glauber salts for scouring the dirty water out o' yer bilges. C'mon, Mr. Burns: tip your coggie—or spew your auld year kail."

There came a sudden hammering on the door. Drunk though he was, Peacock stiffened.

"Clap that bottle i'the kist!"

He went swiftly to the door.

"Who is't?"

"Come oot, come oot. Your shop's on fire."

Peacock wrenched at the bar of the door.

They could do nothing. The inside of the heckling shop was

crackling like a fire of whin sticks. The sodden thatched roof, weighted with snow, was beginning to sag. Any moment now the roof-timbers would burn through and the house would collapse.

Already a crowd was gathering. Small boys were yelling with delight and throwing snowballs through the flame-spitting windows.

"God be thankit for that fa' o' snow!" said someone in the crowd. "Thae sparks would hae set the Vennel on fire. Hoo did it happen?"

No one knew how it had happened.

Robert and Peacock guessed and guessed rightly. But Mrs. Peacock, who had left the candle burning on the bare heckling board, could not remember. She could only cast a furtive agonised glance at her husband's bloodshot eyes and whimper: "It wisna me, Alexander: it wisna me."

An onlooker said to his neighbour:

"An' only last week I met Willie Gowans takin' his auld mare till the knackers."

Robert Burns stood back from the crowd and watched the fire till the roof collapsed and sent a shower of sparks into the night.

He watched without emotion. He knew it was the end of his heckling days; and he was not sorry. But the loss it signified in hard cash numbed him. Here he was standing in the snow waiting for the New Year and he hadn't a sixpence in his pocket. Well . . . let it burn. He had never had any luck. The damned star of his fortune was cursed in its course. Always when he had been getting on top of things along came a malignant fate to knock him down again.

Peacock came up to him and said:

"God! this is terrible, Robert: it's worse nor terrible. Don't you worry, Robert: just keep your mouth shut. I'll see you get peyed for the loss o' your gear. You keep your mouth shut: naebody kens what was burned in there. Aye . . . an' they talk aboot a guid new year! You'd better slip awa' hame, Robert, afore folk start asking questions."

"Aye . . . maybe you're right. As for what's destroyed—I can only speak for my own gear. I'll see you in the morning."

Robert turned on his heel and trudged down the Vennel. Folk spoke to him in commiseration from their doorways. But his head was down and he was in a black dwam: he didn't hear them.

"I was just noting down some impressions in my diary, Jean."

Jean Glover warmed her hands by the fire.

"Aye . . . so you take down more nor auld sangs, Rab?"

"I like to catch manners living as they rise, Jean."

"For instance?"

"Oh, nothing much. I was merely recording here how I am left not worth a sixpence after that wretched fire in the Vennel."

"What's Peacock giving you for the loss o' your gear?"

"The damned scoundrel had the impertinence to offer me three pounds. But I'll not take a penny less than five."

"And what are your plans now?"

"Plans? I'll bide on here for a while and see what turns up. Richard Brown says I wouldna make a sailor. And to tell the truth I don't think I would. Strange, but I have little affection for the sea: it has some queer kind of obscure terror for me. I find it best to withdraw my mind from it——"

"You're wise, Rab. You'd never mak' a sailor——"

"God kens what I'll mak', Jean. Peacock was wanting me to go into partnership wi' him in a shop in Montgomerie-Boyd's Close . . . but I'm finished wi' heckling."

"Dae you expect to gae back to the plough?"

"Maybe; but I'm no' thinking about that yet, Jean. Damnit we've got to live sometime. I've learned a lot in Irvine—seen a lot; and there's more to learn and see yet before I think of resuming the plough. . . And I want to hear more of your songs, Jean."

"O'er the Muir Amang the Heather is the only one o' mine worth onything, Rab."

"You ken, Jean, when you first sang that to me I was com-

245

pletely captivated—apart altogether from the sweet rusticity o' its theme. You're a real poetess, Jean."

"Me? Na, na, Rab. Yae sang doesna mak' a poetess. And you ken fine I hae nae education. There's nae book-learning aboot me."

"And are you the worse for that? Damn the fear. Learning would only put your mind in a cage, Jean. You must be free to sing like the lark."

Jean crouched over the fire. She knew him now, knew that she would need to wait till he had talked himself out. She didn't mind waiting: she enjoyed the talk.

Robin sat at his papers at the end of the table and watched Jean's profile low against the glow of the fire.

She dressed well. Her fondness for colour set off her beauty to greater advantage. God! but she had beauty—a wild, weather-tanned, sun-browned beauty; a beauty that didn't belong to the vennels and closes of Irvine; a beauty that belonged to the banks and the braes, the green dusty loanings, the rigs of yellow corn and the windy heights by the shore. A roving beauty free as the birds were free, wild as the deer and as tender as the wind that shakes the barley. . .

Most folks about Irvine thought Jean was mad and a whore into the bargain. Robin knew she was neither. Singular she was undoubtedly; but a lass of great moral courage, unusual strength of mind and something of a poetess.

"She's as bonnie a bawd as I've seen," Provost Hamilton had said to him one evening in his parlour. "But bonnie as ye never find a married woman or a virtuous maid bonnie. But bawd or no', ye'll no' pick her up and lay her down for a gowpen o' groats. Na, na: Jean Glover's a byornar bawd—let the town say what it likes."

That had been the provost's summing, and Robert, remembering it now, admitted that it was shrewd even though it was rough in its justice.

Why was it, thought Robert, that women like Jean Glover and men like Charles Hamilton appealed to him? Hamilton was certainly a man of first worth. He had enjoyed many nights in his company—and not only because he was a fellow-member of the Lodge Saint Andrew. . .

Strange too that he was so friendly with men so much his senior—men like Hamilton and John Rankine and William Muir of Tarbolton Mill. Was it because they had about them the salty tang of the essential Scottish virtues—kind hearts, rough tongues and honest, direct minds?

But apart from the provost and Willie Templeton the book-seller, there weren't many men with whom he was on really intimate terms—at least not among the older men. Richard Brown was a boon companion; and John Hamilton's friend-ship had been all too brief.

On the whole he didn't warm to the Irvine men or the Irvine women. He thought of them working about their filthy vennels and closes; he saw them taking the air in the broad High Street; he saw them of a Sabbath morning sitting under the Reverend James Richmond—their chins sunk in fat rolls, their pig's eyes half agleam with animal cunning. . . The women as fat and greasy as their blubbery-lipped husbands. . . True there were some thin scraggy fellows; but, like the scraggy women, they had the leanness and the viciousness of wolf-dogs. . .

Jean Glover, from the ingle-neuk, saw that Robert was drowsed in a dwam of dreaming. She began to undress.

Robert ran the crook of his forefinger round the back of Jean Glover's ear.

"I love you, Jean, even though I know I shouldn't."

"No: you just like me, Rab."

"Maybe you're a bitch—but I love you."

"I'm no' a bitch. And I'm no' a whore—if that's what you're thinkin'."

"You've lain wi' other men?"

"Aye . . ."

"Just as you're lying wi' me?"

"No. . . No. . . Sleep, laddie, sleep. . . You're different frae a' the rest. You're soft and tender, Robin: gentle . . . and as smooth as silk. . . But you've the secret strength o' a lion in your lovin'. That's how a lass likes to be loved, Robin. But she's seldom loved that way. I could lie wi' you here till the world cam' tae its end."

"You like me as a lover, Jean? You know you're the first?"

"Fine, laddie . . . and that's what I'll treasure. I'll keep myself for you, Robin, and only for you—till you grow tired o' me."

"I'll no' grow tired o' you, Jean."

"Aye, you'll grow tired o' me. A man like you will never be faithful to the one lass. She's no' born—the lass that could haud you."

"You don't know me——"

"No . . . but I know bits o' you better than you know yourself. I ken a' aboot Jean Gardner."

"What's to know about Jean Gardner?"

"Nothing . . . yet! You're in love wi' her!"

"How did you know?"

"Robin, my love, dinna deceive yoursel'. There's nae end to the women you could love. You've kissed and cuddled wi' many already."

"You think I'm a libertine?"

"You use too mony lang words, Rab——"

"You think I'm a fornicator? In my mind: in my intention?"

"Fornication's an ugly word: leave it tae the ministers and the elders. Ye ken fine when ye cuddled the kimmers in Tarbolton ye wished ye could have straiked them down the way ye do me?"

"Honest, Jean: I did—and I didn't. You don't believe me. I've had the chance: many a time. But something aey held me back. The moral sense, Jean: something you know nothing about. If I'd done anything I would have married the lass."

"You'll no' can marry them a', Rab. What are you going to do then?"

"D'you think I'm going on like this? You're daft, lass. I had to *know*, Jean. And it had to be you. You're like a man in this . . . you can talk about it. I never knew a lass that would talk about it. There's only one Jean Glover in the West. I don't feel I've wronged you."

"I suppose you maun talk: that's part o' you. But dinna talk about sin, Robert. There's no rights and wrongs . . . just dae what your heart tells you and you canna go wrong.

"If you want the dirty rotten beggars o' this world, Rab, seek out the wise, prudent, canny ones. The same wi' the women. You never met in wi' a kind, soft-hearted bitch, did you? Na: they've a' got hearts o' flint. I ken them. Too weel do I ken them—baith men and women. You micht easily have learned frae a bitch, Robin, and gotten yourself into a queer feck o' bother and heartbreak. You ken I'll no' trouble you. You ken I'll no' come shouting your name in the street—or seekin' ye out to shame ye in the tavern—or laying ony complaint afore the session . . ."

"Aye: I know that, Jean. For all those things do I love you. An' though I couldna marry you, lass, I'll aey have a spot in my heart for you. And now enough o' our talking o' the whys and the wherefores! The nicht's wearin' on and the landlady stirs early in the morning and, Jean lass——"

But Jean had already found his lips with hers and put an end to talking. Robin ran his hand down her bare back to her buttocks. Jean went limp and sobbed in her ecstasy.

And Robert was certain that neither in this life nor in the life to come would there be any experience capable of overtopping the delirious delight of the love of a lad and a lass.

Not in the wide rolling lands of Tarbolton parish, folding many a green bed to their quiet bosoms, was Robert Burns initiated into the fullest rites of love; not with Alison Begbie nor Annie Rankine nor Anne Ronald, nor Mysie Graham nor Lizzie Dodds nor Nancy Fleming nor Peggy Borland; but on a chaff bed in an attic room in the Glasgow Vennel, Irvine—and with a light of skirts who was no stranger to but something of an artist in the most urgent, the most sacred (and hence the most often degraded) of all human rites.

And though Robert hid Jean Glover deep below the speaking level of his memory (as he was to hide many another) he often lit a candle for remembrance where no one could see it burn.

Richard Brown knew the difference in him. He said:

"So you went through wi' it, Robin! Jean Glover or Jean Gardner? Or them baith? No: don't tell—if you don't want to. But I hope we'll hear no more blethers about illicit love."

"Well, Richard, I don't know for certain. I must still hold to morality: or drift. I know that the marriage sheets do not sanctify all that goes on between them. I know that when you take a woman willingly and she knows what you are taking her for there can be no sin. But to betray a lass—that I can never forgive, Richard. As you say—and as I well know—it may be a fashionable failing; but that's no' the gate I learned my creed."

"Damn it, Robin, you must aey be moralising—you think too much."

"You can be happy enough thinking."

"I suppose you can—you can onyway. For me: give me the pint stoup and give me the sonsy willing lass and you can take your morality and your preaching to hell."

"The trouble wi' me, Richard, is that when I'm in love wi' a lass, thoughts boil up in me and a terrible itch comes over me to be at the scribbling of my verses. That's how it affects me. When I'm not in love then I've no desire to write and little desire to think—other than melancholy thoughts. You mind yon Sabbath day we took a turn out to Lord Eglinton's woods? I read you some of my verses then?"

"Yes . . . I do, Robin."

"You thought they were good enough for a magazine?"

"And I still think so. I wasn't thinking to turn your head."

"No. . . But did you ever see The Weekly Magazine or Edinburgh Amusement?"

"I never did."

"I saw some back-dated copies in Willie Templeton's. There are poems there by a lad Robert Fergusson. I'll read you some o' them. Fergusson can write. I'm just a scribbler."

"And who is this Robert Fergusson?"

"Now you ask me! This is no world for a poet, Richard. He was the sweetest singer Scotland ever had: there will never be a sweeter."

"That's a big claim."

"Not so big when you know Bob Fergusson. He died about nine years ago. Twenty-four years old. A year or so older than myself. Died in the madhouse. And they let him die there. He was but a poor scrivener to the lawyers though he'd gotten a fair schooling at the university at Saint Andrews. But lack of this world's gear put an end to learning, so he had to come back to Edinburgh to hack at the copying work. I don't know the full story yet. But I'll sift it out.

"My abiding and everlasting curse on the gentry o' Edinburgh! It wasn't madness that killed Fergusson: it was poverty, starvation and neglect. That kills ony man; but it kills a poet quicker. And yet, Richard, one night's money from an Edinburgh gaming table would have set him up, fed him and clad him and freed him from the clerk's desk. But the gentry don't care for poetry—unless it flatters them. Hell's blackest curse on them. . .

"But you know, Richard, if you were to ask me what I like best—a fine lass or a fine poem, I think I would say the poem."

"That's plain gowk-talk, Rab."

"No, no! A fine lass is easy come by: not so easy a fine poem. The lass withers: a poem may bloom down the centuries. A good song will outlast the mountains."

"Ah, you're a queer beggar, Rab. You maun be a poet. Yet the poets were aey fond o' the lassies. What's your pretty Fergusson to say about them?"

"Not so much: he was too young and maybe too poor to have much experience of the lassies. But there's more to life than the lassies—God bless them for all that."

"What is it you really want in life, Robin?"

"Little enough—at the hinder-end. Time to read, time to talk, time to think, time to make love and time to scribble away. Before I read Fergusson, I had thought of giving up my scribbling. All my writing lacked aim and purpose. I was but copying the English poets though I hadn't forgotten auld Allan, or Hamilton o' Gilbertfield, or Semple o' Beltrees or any of our auld sweet singers. I was for modelling myself on Pope and Shenstone—grand poets, Richard—and Thomson and Beattie—Scots poets who write in the English. But Fergusson's changed all that. Aye . . . Fergie's showed me what can be done with our guid auld mither tongue. Man, Richard, there's nothing our Scots tongue canna get round: there's mair pith and sense and richness and red blood to it than the English. You have to think out the English; but the Scots comes sweet to the tongue, dripping off it like honey. Aye . . . I've found my purpose now. I'll write Scots verses and sing Scots themes. There's mair than enough in Scottish history and Scottish character for ony poet. If only I could get a swatch o' security to get down to the job. If I wasn't aey worried about my damned future. You see: I maun work. I've idled away my time since I got that money for my heckling gear from Peacock. I've been hoping that I wouldn't need to go back to Lochlea——

"Farm work's hard brutal work, Richard. It never ends and you seldom see onything for your labour. I've slaved since I was a bit o' a laddie. . . This is the only kind of a holiday I've ever known, Richard. I went to Kirkoswald once to a noted school there to learn the dialling and mensuration—that was something of a holiday. There was a lass there, Richard: Peggy Thomson! The nights I had wi' Peggy. . . Oh, innocent . . . and maybe better that way. Now . . . ? Damnit, I've aey been after some lass or other. Mind you: I never missed the other thing. Oh, I was human—and the lassies were human. Maybe they thought I was backward. Yet we werena gowks. . . . I used to cuddle up with Peggy Thomson down the corn bawks—in the gloaming. They were sweet hours, Richard. . .

And now Bob Fergusson's shown me how I should write about them.

"But—I'm afeared, Richard, that I'll need to make my way back to Lochlea. I haven't told them yet about the fire. That'll be a disappointment to my father. What a man my father is! A pillar o' honest upright rectitude. Slaved all his days and now about to slave himself into the grave. And here's me, the eldest son, a damned prodigal, wasting away my time drinking and reading poetry and making love—— And yet—— I might as well confess it—— I could sit here wi' a pint stoup o' Maggie Lapper's tippenny talking till eternity came creeping in at the window wi' the dawn."

"And I could listen to you, Robin! Aye . . . it's been a grand privilege having your friendship this winter. For a' your daft notions, you've gotten a better head on you than onybody I've met—and it's no' drink that's making me say that. But you'll need to look out: sometimes you get too damned serious and then I canna follow you. Oh, I like guid talk. Still, Robin, you can take life too seriously. You love life the way you love the lassies—too damned seriously. Jowk and let the jaw gae by: that's as good a motto as ony. I suppose I'm no' a thinker. I maun aey be on the move. . . When you're a sailor you've got to be ready to weigh anchor and spread the sail cloth: you canna afford to let your roots get bedded onywhere. So you learn to take life the way you take the wind: as it comes.

"But hell, man! Lochlea's no' at the ends o' the earth. You'll come back to Irvine and look me up. What about Jean Gardner: you're going fully strong wi' that lass. And by the Lord, Rab, I don't blame you. Better no' bide too long away or I'll be tempted to kidnap her on you."

"You'll never kidnap Jean Gardner, Richard. Jean's a sweet lass."

"She's too bonnie to last long, Rab. Somebody'll snatch her up. Somebody wi' the yellow Geordies."

"I don't think so. Jean's got more character than that. Yet

what can I offer her? You see: everywhere I turn it's the same:
poverty bars every road.   You see men here in Irvine wi'
neither brains nor appearance nor ability of any kind, yet,
because they have money and can rake up something o' a
pedigree, they can lord it at kirk and market—and squint down
their nose at a poor poet. Sometimes I get bitter, Richard."

"Aye, and not without reason, Rab. Man: I don't know
how best to advise wi' you. I would take you to sea wi' me,
only you're a proper landlubber, bred in the bone——"

"I've no stomach for the sea."

"No: but a lad wi' your ability wi' the quill and your
education should be able to get some kind o' a clerking job."

"I've less stomach for that. I couldn't thole being tied to
the clerk's stool wi' my nose buried among dusty ledgers and
my eyes squinting up and down columns o' figures. Besides—
who would have me, a country ploughman?"

"Well, there's ae thing, Rab: you'll never mak' your fortune
atween the stilts o' a plough and you'll never mak' your fortune
writing poetry, so you'll need to think o' something."

"Think! I'm wearied thinking how to get out o' the bit.
But drink up, Richard. There'll be damned little drink for me
gin I was back at Lochlea."

UNDER THE PLAID

In no real sense did Robert woo Jean Glover: she wooed him. The relationship between them was one of love, pleasant, mutually advantageous and often enough wildly exhilarating. There was complete ease and complete acceptance between them. But, such being the lovers, the relationship could only be transitory. And though they stood to each other in a curious, almost unnatural state of equality, there was a profound sense in which Robert was the apprentice and Jean the mistress.

There are loves a man wishes to last no longer than a lover's embrace: there are loves he feels must outlast time— or see him to the grave.

Robert had always been on easy and familiar terms with the Tarbolton lassies; and yet to each one of them he made an individual and instinctive approach. With the minor exceptions of Anne Ronald and Alison Begbie this approach had never failed him—and in both cases he had failed through the blight of his poverty and prospects of worldly success.

With Jean Glover he knew to the narrowest limits where he stood. How different with Jean Gardner. Jean Gardner had to be wooed all the way all the time. Every meeting with her was a new experience. Thus he was ever on the tip-toe of expectancy. Here his experience with the Tarbolton girls (added to Jean Glover's practical tuition) stood him in good stead.

The early stages of his courtship with the flesher's daughter had been wonderfully intoxicating. He had to bring to bear on her all the arts of love-making before she would yield. But in the yielding what transports there had been; what delirium when he had her locked in his arms, his for the moment and for eternity.

For eternity? As always the hot urgency that was so vital a part of Robin's make-up could not wait for answer. Even in the transport of the individual moment he must have assurance for all the moments to come. But here Jean Gardner proved as elusive as she appeared ethereal.

They used to step out for an hour or two in the evenings and walk out along the Glasgow road in the dark. Sometimes they would take shelter in the lea of an old barn wall and Robin would wrap his plaid round her and clasp her to him in warmth and intimacy. . .

Jean would not venture to his lodging in the Glasgow Vennel; but otherwise she placed no restraint on his wooing. Virgin though she had been till she met Robert, she had not been innocent of lovers' kisses. But none of the young men she had known could make love like Robert; none had his tongue and his urgent flow of words; none had his quiet caressing strength; none roused in her such an unbearable tension of physical and spiritual emotion.

Jean was a nervously tensed girl, and though she did not appear to ail in any physical way yet she was by no means robust. She was capable of the most delicate responses. Her flesh was capable of a peculiar quivering quality and this evoked in Robert an equally sensitive response.

But she would not admit openly to Robert's courtship and she would not be seen with him in public. "We are of a different religion," she would say, adding that her father "would never understand."

Robert was hurt at this. His poverty and his long isolation at Mount Oliphant had heightened his sensitivity to anything in the nature of a slight or an affront.

He came near to quarrelling with Jean on the last night he saw her before he returned to Lochlea.

"Why won't you marry me, Jean?"

"I don't know, Robin. I couldna the now."

"You know we're as good as man and wife."

"Don't talk about it like that, Robin."

"Jean, Jean: I've got to talk. What's wrong with me when you won't own me in front of your father and mother—aye, or the world at large? Is there a something about me? Is there? You must answer me, lass."

"I canna, Robin. I don't know. I've nothing against you."

"Is it my poverty?"

She shook her head. She had not the heart to tell him that his seeming lack of gear, the seeming inconsequence of his economic position, was just the very reason why she could not mention his courtship to her parents. Not that this weighed greatly with herself. But there was an intense oddness about Robert that marked him off from other men. She could not put words on it; but it was because of this indescribable something that she hesitated to be seen with him in public. She felt in some obscure but intense way that if she did, then every woman they met would know they had been lovers—lovers to the extent they had been. She felt there was something about Robert, something in the intensity of his expression, that proclaimed the guilt of their love-making. Hypersensitive as she was, Jean could not bear to face such an ordeal. And as she could not translate this feeling into words, she had to remain dumb when Robert questioned her. Even had she been able to give tongue to her emotions it is doubtful if she would have risked offending her lover.

"Honestly, Robin, I care nothing for your poverty as you call it. Other folks might; but I wouldna. Robin . . . maybe we should never have gone thegither—no' the way we have: it's going to break baith our hearts."

"But if you'd only be sensible, Jean! You love me—what else matters? Father or mother—religion—— What does anything matter as long as we have each other? You know I'm going back home to Lochlea. . . I canna go and leave you like this. You know how I love you?"

"Aye . . . I know, Robin; and I love you."

"And yet you'll no' marry me?"

"There's plenty o' time."

"But I canna be running down from Lochlea every night to see you. I'll not manage the journey here and back as often as I would wish."

"But you will come and see me? I'll miss you, Robin."

"Jean, Jean: I just canna understand you. I canna see you're doing right by yourself to say nothing of me."

"Dinna let us quarrel, Robin. I'll need to be getting back hame. Kiss me ..."

He took her in his arms.

"This will maybe the last for a long time, Jean. Mind that I'll send you a letter."

"But you'll come and see me and I'll meet you on the Ayr road?"

"Aye ... whatever the odds I'll come and see you, Jean."

Whatever the odds? They were likely to be heavy. That would be the way his accursed fate would decree. He did not know that he would have been prepared to marry Jean Gardner immediately. He was little better than a beggar and beggars can marry only the beggars way. What rankled was that Jean would not admit she was prepared to marry him.

He was half afraid that once he was back at Lochlea someone else would take Jean up. She was too urgent in her loving to remain long without a lover.

But he had already overstayed himself in Irvine. He was at least six weeks overdue at Lochlea. . .

Aye, it would be terrible leaving Jean Gardner. But now Richard Brown was left for the Americas and Jean Glover was getting ready to tour the country. And the days were lengthening. Soon it would be impossible to walk out of Irvine in the darkness with Jean. . .

The nights when he would wrap her to him in his plaid against the wet winds and the darkness would be but a memory.

To-night the lapwings, back from their winter at the shore, tossing and crying as they were disturbed in the adjoining parks, reminded him with a bitter nostalgic minding, that the strength in his arms did not rightly belong to Jean Gardner but to the plough-stilts on Lochlea. Even now the peesweeps would be tossing there and calling plaintively across the high pastures.

Part Five

IN THE MIDST OF LIFE

REUNION

THE HOUSEHOLD at Lochlea had delayed their evening meal
so that they might share it with Robert. Gilbert had taken
down the lightest of the carts to Machlin to meet the fly and
bring him home with his kist. When William came in to
report the sight of them topping the hill in the early March
dusk he begged that he be allowed to go down the road to
meet them.

The family were greatly excited. Nancy and Bell were all
agog and had tidied themselves for the occasion. Robin had
been the first break in the family and they had missed him.
The sisters were devoted to him and were transported when he
read them something from a volume—especially poems or
ballads—and they were ever on the move to get him to read
some of his own poems. Sometimes when they were making
up the attic bed they would find a manuscript poem lying on
the old meal-kist lid that served him for a desk.

But any such readings had to be surreptitious. They dared
not mention to him that they had seen anything of his writing.
He would go into a towering rage if he discovered anybody
had been nosing into his books or papers.

But when they knew he was working at a poem they would
use all their wiles on him. It was easy to know when he had
finished a good verse, for then he did not need much coaxing
to read it over to them—especially if their mother was not
about.

Gilbert, Nancy and, to a lesser extent, Bell, had moments
when they wondered what had happened between Robin and
their mother.

Her attitude towards her first-born was critical. She rarely
put words on her criticism. Nancy could see, though Gilbert
couldn't, that their mother had a violent antipathy to Robin's

263

popularity with the lassies of the parish. Nancy knew her mother disapproved of any of the young men sending courier-blacklegs to the house to inquire after herself or Bell.

She was always pointing out the dangers of love-making to Nancy. Whenever a girl fell by the way, Mrs. Burns would point the moral and adorn the tale. While she might lash a lost woman with the tongue of her scorn, it was for the loose-living men—the whoremasters as she called them—that she reserved the most potent vials of her wrath.

But Nancy knew the girls in the parish and knew that Robin had a good name among them.

The word soon went round if a lad was overbold or was inclined to make dangerous advances. Nancy knew that at dance or party almost any girl would be glad if Robin took her up or made notice of her.

Nancy could not reason it out. She sensed the truth instinctively. Her mother was a strict Calvinist when it came to morals—especially the limited morality that governed the relationship of the sexes.

She remembered the story of her mother's first courtship. She had told her the story several times and always with a peculiar bitterness.

Long ago in Kirkoswald she had been plighted to a young man, a certain Willie Nelson. It had been a steady dull plodding kind of a courtship. In the fulness of time, when they would have enough money gathered they would get married. But eventually the tide of Willie Nelson's blood would not be stayed by the dykes of Presbyterian decorum. So he thrust a hasty and lusty leg upon a hot and lusty lass. . .

That had been the end of Agnes Broun's courtship with Willie Nelson. It would probably have been the end of all courtship had not William Burns happened along with his austere slate-edged uprightness. . .

Nancy knew that her mother had never known the daft daffing days of young womanhood. She knew her mother was right about the ways of men, and yet her sympathy flowed out to Robin who had so much of that same daft daffing shut down in him.

She loved her mother: she had worked with her in the house, in the byre and in the fields for fifteen years. She had teased, carded and spun with her. She had helped and nursed her when Willie, John and Isa had come. She knew something of what her mother had suffered and what she had endured. She was aware that her father was not quite as other men were —that if he was more steadfast in his righteousness he was also stubborn and sometimes dour; that there were difficult times when her mother had to humour him out of a temper trembling on the brink of violent action. She knew more than any other member of the household just how much its economy and its stability was due to the unceasing vigil and activity of her mother.

So she was bound to her mother by even stronger ties than those that usually bind a daughter to a mother. And yet there was that flaw in the perfect harmony of their relationship and understanding. Nancy loved Robin with an even deeper love than is usually found between an elder brother and a younger sister. It was not that Robin gave so much of his company to the house—not now—not since they had come to Lochlea.

What worried Nancy was the feeling that her mother did not have a normal affection for Robin. Gilbert was the favourite—far and away the favourite. Gilbert could do no wrong; the good that Robin did was passed over without comment.

There was nothing that Nancy could formulate in words— or perhaps she had not the courage to do so. She liked Gilbert almost as much as Robin. But there was a something Robin had that Gilbert hadn't—a quality, an aura she had known in no other being. And she was hurt and puzzled that there should exist this strained relationship between Robin and his mother, and, because of this, between Robin and every member of the household.

But maybe now that he was coming back after the long absence in Irvine things would be different. . .

But they all thought things would be different. William Burns had conveyed to Agnes his fear for Robin; and Agnes had felt deep sorrow at his illness and neglect. He was of her flesh and blood; he was her first born; even the thought of him was a catch at her heart. But oh, how sore the disappointment Robin had been to her. A dour child, he had been unresponsive to her mothering. Where Gilbert had a hug for her, Robin had only a queer look under his drawn brows.

And now that he had grown to be a man, she felt he had grown out of her influence—out of her consideration. He would never sit and confide in her: share his troubles and his problems the way Gilbert did.

Robin was a strange, strange laddie to be her laddie, with the warm smile for the stranger he never had for her.

But he'd been with the strangers now for a long time and he would know how they had neglected him. Maybe now he would appreciate the worth of a good home—and a father and mother to whom that home was everything on earth.

The thought that some scheming hizzie might have got her claws into him in Irvine flicked at her mind; but she shook her head and refused to let it fix there.

Dear, dear; but she would be glad to see him again, however things turned out.

There he was shaking hands with her. Bigger, stronger, looking healthier than ever he had been—yet shyer, more self-conscious.

Mrs. Burns said: "Aye . . . you've gotten ower that bad toyte ye had. Aye . . . you're looking brawly. Sit in then: we've kept the bite waiting on you."

And William Burns said: "I'm glad you're back with us again, Robin: I never felt happy about you in Irvine. I warrant you're glad to get back."

Nancy said: "Hallo. . . You're looking fine, Robin."

Bell said: "Hallo. . . I made you some crowdie—the kind you like."

And Nancy added: "I made the yowe cheese——"

Robin replied to all of them in turn and, his face flushed at the self-consciousness of the home-coming, he took his seat at the table.

They did not ask any questions at the table until William Burns had finished with his interrogation.

Immediately he had disposed of the more personal aspects of Robin's return (with some vital details about the burning of the heckling shop and his breaking-off relations with Peacock) he became avid for information of a general nature. He wanted to know what was the latest concerning the American War, as he was certain the port of Irvine would have all the latest information.

Robin told him what he had gathered and the old man shook his head. It was indeed a bad business and Scotland was sure to come out of it badly. He wasn't sure that he approved of his son's republican pro-American sympathies. Yes . . . there was something in what he said. . . Yes . . . it was difficult for the American settler. . . Yes, indeed, he knew something of the like kind of difficulties. But, it would be bad for Scotland since principles—though he was all for principles of the sound Christian variety—did not fill the bellies of the people. We were losing our trade with the American colonists—it would be a difficult time and we might never get back our trade again.

A declining export trade would send hardship and misery into every home in Scotland—especially along the Ayrshire coast. This, in turn, would depress farming—prices would fall on the selling market—wool: that wouldn't be worth the gathering presently.

Aye, William wound up, there were bad times coming for everybody, for folks were living in an evil and adulterous generation and they were openly turning their backs on the very essentials of Christian conduct and belief. Folks were turning away from God; and the lust after mammon was something terrible to see.

But William, though tired and gloomy (and he was depressed though Robin's return had for the moment lifted the depression), said nothing at all about the troubles that were gathering round him as a result of his embittered quarrelling with MacLure, his landlord. He would say something about this to Robin in due course; but it was not a subject to discuss before the family.

Then William excused himself. Since the pony was still harnessed he would drive across to the Tarbolton Mill: he had business to discuss with William Muir. No: it wasn't a dark night and the moon would be up against his homecoming. The beast knew the road better than he did himself.

"The best lan'ahin' I ever knew," said Robin.

"Well," said William straightening himself as best he could —"I wouldn't say now but you're right."

When he had gone the family gathered round the fireside and Robin occupied his father's elbow chair. He was plied with questions, and it touched him deeply to see how much they esteemed him. Indeed he had seldom known a prouder moment—even his mother smiled on him. And though she was busy concocting a plaister of herbs for a cow with an inflamed udder, she gave him her attention from time to time. And Isabel was almost at the point of protesting when she was taken out to the byre to assist her mother. Gilbert had gone out to see his father off . . .

Nancy and Bell wanted to know about Irvine and Bell added shyly that both Annie Rankine and Mysie Graham had been asking after his health.

And then it was Robin's turn to ask questions. He wanted to know from Willie how he was coming forward with his composition of the English language and what he was reading now.

"I'm reading the Fourfold State now, Robin—I'm nearly through wi' it."

"Old Boston, eh? It's heavy going, Willie—and it's not maybe the best theology nowadays. But it will set your teeth for tougher things. I mind when I first read Thomas Boston... But your writing?"

"I've done nothing but copying, Robin. I don't seem to have the knack of hitting on any idea of my own."

"Willie has worked hard all winter," said Nancy. "Gibby's been giving him an hour of the evening."

Bell said: "Did you no' bring anything frae Irvine to read to us?"

"Read? Are you still needing things read to you, Bell?"

"But you read different. It sounds different when you read."

John, who was leaning on the back of Robin's chair, said: "You've got a book in your pocket, Robin."

Robin turned round and looked with some concern at the pale-faced, burning-eyed boy.

"And how's wee Benjamin? Come round about here and sit down where you can get the heat of the fire. Are you thinking o' being my gaudsboy when I start the ploughing?"

John shook his head slowly and sadly.

"Oh, you'll need to make a start—and get some more colour in your cheeks."

But John, though he came round to the hearth, said nothing, but stared at his eldest brother with such an intense far-away look of melancholy that Robin could have stretched out his arm and taken him to him. He saw that John was far from well.

But even while he was speculating about John, Willie and the girls were clamouring for him to read.

This would have been the moment to read the *Farmer's Ingle*; but the precious Fergusson was lying safe in the bottom of his kist.

He fished out the volume from his pocket.

"What is it?" they cried.

He was in no way surprised at their interest and their

clamour. This thirst for reading aloud had always been a characteristic of the family. For a flash he recalled how Murdoch used to come up from Alloway to the Mount and read to them: sitting in this self-same elbow chair which his father always vacated for the distinguished visitor and welcome friend.

Robert opened the book. "Maybe you won't like it. I got it as a parting present from Mr. Templeton—the bookseller in Irvine. We used to have many a crack about books. He had a great head on him for the old ballads and out-of-the-way incidents concerning our own history—and the morals and manners of bye-gone days. . . The name, Bell? There's not much in the name: The Expedition of Humphrey Clinker—by our old friend Tobias Smollett."

"I know," put in Nancy: "he wrote Peregrine Pickle."

"Good for you, Nancy. I didn't know you'd read it."

"Oh . . . I didn't read it. I . . . I saw a part of it in the attic."

"Well, you've a good memory for names. Aye. Tobias Smollett: he's a grand writer with a grand sense o' the ridiculous. Aye . . . Smollett puts you in a fine humour. And by the by, Nancy, I never got round to reading Peregrine Pickle myself: that was the second part of the story you saw up above: I never laid my hands on the first part. . ."

He flicked over the thin grey pages.

"What will I read you? Would you like to hear about how the folks live away in London?"

Aye, they would like to hear about the Lunnon folks. They didn't want to raise any objections. He could read about the folks in Faucedyke for all they cared. Just to read to them—to hear his voice—was enough.

So he read to them about London and put all his art into the reading for he sensed how much this reading meant to them.

And between paragraphs he would lift an eye from the page and take in the happy, concentrated faces of his brothers and sisters.

Aye: it was good to be home again; good to see the bits of furniture and place his foot on the old hearthstone; good to be round a crowded ingle again, the centre of the circle of his own blood; good to hear the sound of his own voice in his father's house where every face and every article held a memory precious beyond all earthly value. . .

Only on his solemn promise to read more to them at the very first opportunity was he allowed to make his escape to Tarbolton with Gilbert.

They walked across the parks towards the clachan. It was keen frost; and there was a white moon in the deep indigoed sky.

Now that they were out and alone for the first time since he had returned, Gilbert was anxious for all the more private news of Robert's sojourn in Irvine.

"Did you come on any new books?"

"Aye: plenty. I'll give you Henry MacKenzie's Man o' Feeling. I read it after my illness and it gripped me. A grand novel, Gibby, with a grand sentiment. We'll talk about it after you've read it. But my greatest discovery was Robert Fergusson's Poems. By God, Gibby, Fergusson's a poet: never read anybody to compare with him. The volume's in my kist. . . . Wait till you get your eyes on it."

And there and then Robert launched himself into quotations from *The Farmer's Ingle*, *Auld Reekie*, *Leith Races* and something indeed of almost everything that Fergusson had written.

Gilbert was electrified. Here was poetry in the mither tongue that seemed to flow from the depths of Robert—it seemed he must have written it himself. When Robert paused for breath on the rise of ground beyond the Faucedyke steading he told him so.

"You're right there. Aye . . . I feel that the sough of Fergie's stuff comes right from my very midriff. That's the big thing, Gibby: I know now where I stand: now I know where I'm going—or where I can go. You've liked my verses up till now? But you've seen nothing. Bide a wee till I gather myself. I'll let you see something yet. I'll never top Fergie: I ken that fine: the man's no' born that'll top him; but I'll be up on the brow of the hill with him."

"Fine, Robin, fine: I thought that damned place was going to kill you."

"I'm no' so easy killed. Though mind you, Gibby: I was bad for a while: I'll never be nearer the abyss. Still . . . I jowked the Deil as I've done afore——"

"Take care, Robin. You know your constitution is not too robust."

"I'm fine."

"Aye, the now."

"Weel, the now's what matters. To-morrow? Jowk an' let the jaw gae by. Gibby! I've learned a lot while I was in Irvine. I learned something in Kirkoswald; I've learned a lot in Tarbolton; but Irvine put the coping stone on my learning. Oh, I'm no' finished learning—you never finish learning as long as there's breath in your body—but Irvine put on the coping stone for all that. I met in with a number of excellent fellows there. A young doctor—the provost's son: a sterling fine fellow. Aye; and his father the provost. The minister there, James Richmond: a knowledgeable clergyman—a good leavening of Willie Dalrymple in him—a different man altogether from Patie Woodrow on the hill yonder. . . I only went to the Lodge once. Not just the same as Tarbolton: not just so homely. A bit keener on the ritual—the formalities. Oh, I was one of the brethren all right. Good fellows; but they could stand being better acquainted with. There was a sailor there, a young captain by the name of Richard Brown. You'd have warmed to him, Gibby—when you got to know him. Didn't give a tinker's damn for man or beast. As for the lassies! He'd a way wi' him. He knew every quirk o' them—or nearly. . ."

"So you had time for the lassies, Robin?"

"At the hinder end, worse luck! Boy, but I have a charmer yonder!"

"Is this you under the spell again?"

"Again? Huh! I've only been playing myself here. I've a lass back there in Irvine: she's—— Well: don't be surprised if we're married some day."

"Another Alison Begbie?"

"No, sir: not another Alison Begbie. You never saw Peggy Thomson? This lass puts Peggy in the shade: puts the blankets right over her head."

"There's no curing o' you, Robin. You couldn't go from here to Machlin but you'd fall in with some lass."

"Maybe you're right, Gibby. And maybe you're wrong. Jean Gardner's her name: you'll no' match her in the West."

"Maybe she'll no' have you when it comes to the bit."

"She's had me, Gibby. And what an armful!"

"That was the coping stone?"

"Part o' it."

"Robin: you havena gone a' the road?"

"Every inch and bit of it."

"And you're no' frightened?"

"Frightened? Don't talk nonsense, man. . . What is there to be frightened about? It's done every day, isn't it?"

"By what kind o' folk?"

"All kinds: saints and sinners; and the middling feck o' folk in between."

"It's no' the gate we learned our creed, Robin. I'd be frightened if I were in your shoon."

"Gibby! I warned you once before never to lecture me. Don't you worry! I reasoned it all out for myself. I didn't take the bit atween my teeth and breenge at the slap."

"But you know a thing like this won't stop at Jean . . . what-d'you-call her?"

"Maybe it didn't begin wi' her! I'm not going to dispute wi' you, Gibby. You'll come to your senses in your own time. I'm telling you no more. And keep your thumb on what I have told you. Mind you: I don't regret having waited as long as I have. It was worth it. Only it had to come sometime. I haven't the money to get married. The hell! D'you expect to remain a celibate monk? I'm flesh and blood; and so are you."

"I know the difference between right and wrong—and so do you."

"Do you? I used to think I did. Now I'm not so sure. Oh aye: in some things. And don't think I'm defending libertinism or ony cheap come-easy, go-easy houghmagandie. Don't mistake me. But when you love a lass and she loves you—and mind you, I said love—what's the harm? Where's the sin? I can't see it, Gibby. And I'm damned if I'm going to look for sin where there's nought but the holiest o' rapture. So I'm going to marry Jean. Maybe not to-morrow, maybe not the day after; but as soon as I can and as soon as she'll have me."

"If that's the way o' it, Robin——"

"That's the way o' it, Gibby. I'll maybe need a bit of assistance from you to help me to win over to Irvine now and again."

"Oh well, Robin—— God knows; for I don't. But we need you here. You've come back in time. If you knew the way things stand here you wouldn't be thinking of marrying —or risking what you're risking. You can see how our father's shaping as well as I can."

"Hell, man, I know. I'm back. And I'll put my hand to the darg, don't worry."

"He's getting short in the grain and you canna blame him. I think he's wearing away. . ."

"Aye . . . he's wearing away fast, Gibby. My mother's getting gey sair bowed down too."

"She never stops slavin'. And you can't say Nancy or Bell hold back."

"I know."

"Willie does what he can. But I'm against driving the young ones too sore."

"So am I. When you've been made a bluidy horse the way I was——"

"I know, Robin . . . I'm aey telling him that—my mother too."

"Ah—that's past and done with. Only: it's no' happening to Willie."

"That means it's you and me."

"I know, I know. But what about this vulture MacLure?"

"Waiting on the carcase."

"We'll give him carcase, Gibby."

"I don't know, Robin. We've got to get quit of Lochlea. We'll be beaten down in the hinder end."

"Will we? Not as long as William Burns keeps above the ground. Maybe you don't mind what happened at the Mount after Provost Fergusson died? Press William Burns too sore and he'll commit murder. I'm not jesting. By God no. Still: that's not going to help us."

"We'll go over the place the morn and see what we think, Robin. I think we can do something."

Coming on the cluster of houses on the rising ground of Tarbolton, Robin was conscious of the snug way they crouched on the earth. They were so unlike the tenements of Irvine. He had never realised before how Tarbolton was a small and insignificant village: it was even smaller and more shilpit than Machlin. But most of the Machlin folks were strangers, while he knew every soul, more or less, in Tarbolton.

He was glad to meet the boys round the smiddy fire. Bob Ritchie, the wabster's son, was there with Hughie Reid, Willie MacGavin, Tam Wright, Sanny Brown and Watty Mitchell. Davie Sillar was not yet forward.

They gave Robin a hearty welcome. He was their natural leader and they had missed him. The Bachelors' Club hadn't been the same since his absence from its debates.

They were keen to fix the next meeting at which he could be present for they were sure he would have plenty to talk about, having absorbed all the news and views of Irvine.

None of the Tarbolton lads had the presence or the intellectual maturity of Richard Brown; but they were grand country lads and he had no difficulty in shining amongst them.

Some of the lads were waiting for the lassies coming along

so that they might slip after them and enjoy an hour's daffing in the dark, round by Willie's Mill or along the Ayr road.

But as soon as Davie Sillar and Jock Paterson came forward, Sanny Brown moved that they adjourn into Jock Richards' and pledge Robin's health in a session of ale.

"Ye'll hae a hizzie in Irvine, Rab?" said Willie MacGavin.

"Jist the yae hizzie? Damned, he'll hae a guid twa-three gin noo? Come on, Rab; tell us aboot the Irvine dames."

But Robin, though he told them many a droll story— mostly a bold embroidering of Captain Brown's stark outlines —was careful to tell them nothing concerning either of his Jeans.

Gilbert was much relieved at this. He marvelled at the change that came over Robin when in the company of his fellows. He seemed to grow in stature; his voice gathered into its timbre a rich and intriguing resonance; his wit— sometimes downright wicked—flashed fast and furious. The dusty bauks of Jock Richards' modest howff dirled to the gusty gales of laughter.

Saunders Tait, staggering from Manson's Inn to his garret with a full cargo of Tarbolton brew, heard the laughter and paused until he recognised the voice of his young rival in rhyme.

Bad cess to that brock! He had heard how he was quitting Irvine; but he hadn't expected him back in the village so soon. But if all he heard was true, Dawvit MacLure would soon settle all their hashes at Lochlea.

Saunders spat into Jock Richards' doorway and ambled on, cursing and muttering foully under his straggling yellow-white moustache.

The merriment inside the howff didn't last long. None of them had much money to spend and all of them were deter-mined to bed early. The session might have lasted longer had not Robin made move to have a private session with Davie Sillar.

He had much to tell his cronie, much to tell him about his

love-making, about his meeting with *The Man of Feeling* and the glorious verses of Auld Reekie's redoubtable (if unfortunate) Fergie.

He was determined to make a night of it. To-morrow he would be back to the plough. He had promised himself he would make a great effort to wipe off the shame of the unfortunate heckling adventure. He might not be back in Tarbolton for some weeks.

Ah, it was good to be back among the familiar friends, hearing the familiar voices and parrying the familiar thrusts. Here he was on his home ground breathing his native air. It was exhilarating: it was the rich wine of life itself.

But after his session with Davie Sillar Robin returned from the Spittleside road-end and went down by Willie's Mill where he had arranged to meet Gilbert.

Willie Muir was not abed when Robin called. Indeed Mrs. Muir was putting a bite on the table for Gilbert—at the place his father had not long vacated.

The Lochlea family and the miller were on the best of terms. The Muirs were good-natured and kind-hearted and Willie appreciated, as few of the Tarbolton folks did, the sterling virtues of William Burns. The Muirs were childless; and Mrs. Muir often declared that the Burns family was the finest she had ever known.

Robin, of course, was the favourite. Willie delighted in his conversation, and regretted he didn't have the opportunity of seeing more of him. He was given a hearty welcome and then plied with questions about Irvine.

"Your father was gey upset about that bad turn you had in Irvine, Robin. I've rarely seen him so concerned. By God, boy, you must ha' been bad."

"Well . . . God be thankit, you have every look o' having got ower it," said Mrs. Muir. "I don't think I've seen you looking better since you cam' to Lochlea."

"Ah, but you were richt to quat the hecklin', Rab. That wasna a trade for the likes o' you. Na, na: milling's a dusty job. But it's a good clean stour and no' yon stinkin' fluff an' oose that gets intil the lungs and clags up your tubes. To hell: I couldna abide yon stench. . . Na, na: you're better ahint the pleugh—even if there's no' the same siller intilt. Damnit, the pair o' you'll mak' guid fermers yet. The verra best. Your father never got a real chance wi' Lochlea—and yet he's improved it out o' a' recognition—especially in drainin' aff the auld mill dam. But the pair o' you'll reap the benefit. . . MacLure? Oh, a damned scoundrel—a cunning chiel o' a merchant—but a damned scoundrel for a' that. What's that, wife? Ken him? Fegs, I ken the same MacLure: you couldna lippen on his word frae here till the burn. Saunders Tait's a billie o' his. Tait does a feck o' snooking for the same boy in his travels. Y'ken: auld Saunders is gey ill-pleased wi you, Rab. Aye, I ken, wife: Saunders is nae mair a poet than I am; but you canna tell Tait that."

"Tuts!" cried Mrs. Muir in disgust, "he's just a dirty auld man wi' a dirty tongue in his head. How the likes o' him was ever a baillie in Tarbolton beats me: I wouldna let him ben the hoose."

"Agreed, agreed; but then Tait's seen better days. And mind you: he's a shrewd auld devil: Sawney kens how mony beans mak' five. What's that, Rab? Aye, he keeps a pet rat. Them that hae seen it tell me it has bite aboot wi' him at the table. Did you no' hear o' the fricht Maggie MacGavin got wi' it? Aye . . . she was up at Tait getting a pair o' Willie's breeks steekit when the rat, scared wi' her coming in, bolted up her claes—aye, an' Sawney efter it. You could hae heard the scraiches o' Maggie down here. Willie swore he'd gae up and redd the rat and Saunders tae. . .

"Well, Robin lad: I've enjoyed your crack. Aye, mind ye, Irvine's a'richt in its way; but there's nae place like Tarbolton. We doze awa' fine hereabouts; but we hae our fun back and forwards. And when are you giving us a look in again? Damned, ony time you're passing and the licht's still i' the window, dinna gae by withouten ye chap. And bring ower

thae verses you were talking about and let's hae a readin' o'
them. Now I'm lippenin' on you, Gibby, my lad, to see that
he does. We havena a brew like Manson's; but you can aey
get a coggie o' brose that'll stick to your ribs and dae you a
hantle sicht mair guid. . .

"Well: guid nicht, lads, guid nicht—and see it's no' sae
lang afore you're back."

"He's a hell o' a blether, Willie Muir," said Robin to Gilbert
on the way home; "but there's no' a kinder-hearted pair in
the parish."

"They're both genuine. Many a peck of peas he's slippit
in with the oats."

"Aye . . . and he knows the worth o' William Burns, bless
him. You know, Gibby: I've been down at the Mill with my
father and I've actually seen Willie make him laugh . . . aye,
and a good hearty laugh at that."

"I know. And the man that makes William Burns laugh
must have something byornar about him."

"Just honest good-nature, Gibby. There's not even the
tincture of evil about Willie—or his goodwife. Honest good-
nature, Gibby son: the rarest of human qualities—and I
wouldn't say it wasn't the best. Well . . . there's the moon
creeping ayont the Cumnock hills. It'll be a good day gin the
morrow dawns. And to think that this morning I was standing
in Willie Templeton's shop in the High Street of Irvine bidding
him good-bye! Well . . . it'll be the orra dudies the morn's
morn, Gibby. Then out wi' the pownies to the park. I'll work,
Gibby, as you've never seen me work. Farewell to idle fancies
and the idle hour. Work, Gibby: that's what's for us. We'll
win through yet, son: you and me: we'll show them."

"Where do you get the energy, Robin?"

"Energy? I could tear up the clods with my bare hands—
and pull a set o' new teethed harrows across the furs wi' my
own strength. Energy? Maybe I'm just glad to be back,
Gibby: like the prodigal son. I'm so damned grateful, Gibby,
I could greet and blubber like a big bairn."

Gilbert said nothing. He could only marvel—as he had marvelled many a time—how it was that they were brothers and of the same flesh and blood. And he trembled—as ofttimes he trembled—for the black chasm that would sometimes yawn between them and their thoughts. Sometimes Robin appeared, across the chasm, so strange and yet so wonderful that Gilbert wondered if anyone would ever understand him or gain any real glimmering of the strange greatness that lay in him, a greatness that would send a light flashing in his eyes—a light that seemed somehow holy in the queer ecstasy of its intensity.

The moon swung clear of cloud above and beyond the distant Cumnock hills and the sky throbbed with a dusting of stars and the planets pulsed like pebbles of burning gold. No wonder Robin seemed to walk with wings to his feet and carry with him the aura of a young god.

Annie Rankine remembered the first time Robert Burns had entered their spence at Adamhill. A square of Kilmarnock carpet covered the bare boards in the middle of the floor; but Robert had not thought to put his foot on it. She recalled exactly the careful almost deferential way he had walked round it.

Now he knew that a carpet was meant to be walked over—with clean shoon. But then nobody was so inconsiderate or ill-mannered as to walk into a spence with clarty brogans—unless he was a laird or some important gentleman.

Annie opened the door to his knock. They were no longer self-conscious with each other, though there was a natural shyness between them they both attempted to disguise.

"You've to go ben the spence, Rab."

"Right, Annie. And how are you the nicht?"

"Fine, Rab: never felt better."

"You could never feel ony other way, Annie——"

And then came John Rankine's thundering bass.

"Come your ways in, Rab, and dinna stan' there courtin' Annie. Right up to the fire. God, lad, but I'm glad to see you! A' your oats in?"

"Finished—aye."

"Annie! fill out a drink for Rab, damn ye—ye shouldna need telling. Man, Rab: I had a reverend gentleman here sin' I saw you last. And had we a ploy! He was partial to hot toddy. Damned partial. So I had the wee kettle there filled with neat spirit. And every time he watered his coggie—he watered her *up*. Man, you never saw a craw as blin' fu' as the Reverend Walter MacKillop o' the Boglands. Man, Rab, he was maist thoroughly bitchified: he couldna bite his thoomb.

I had him seein' Auld Nick at the bed-post girnin' and filin' his muckle lang teeth wi' a smith's rasp.

"'Dae ye no' see him, Mr. Rankine?' he yelped. 'He's come to rive me asunder.' 'Damn the fear,' says I: 'that's Black Ned frae the Bluidy Burn lookin' for a sup o' toddy.'

"'No, no: that's Satan himself: d'you no' see his cloven clits?'

"'Ah weel,' says I: 'that'll teach ye no' to lie wi' the servin' lass.'

"'That's no' the worst o' it,' says he. 'I gat the last twa wi' bairn and we put the blame on Daft Geordie—and I compeared them on the cutty stool myself.'—And damned but I wad hae gotten a' the details but the silly auld fool had to get the horrors. . . Ah—but I cured him o' that. I dragged him through the court and held his muckle head ablow the water in the horse trough: that settled his horrors."

John Rankine had more tales to tell, for he was always engaged in some ploy or other—especially a ploy at the expense of the clergy. But indeed he was famed in more than one parish for his wit and his practical jokes. Even the gentry feared him and took care to treat him with deference for John Rankine had an ever-ready tongue and he respected a man only for his innate worth.

To-night, however, Robin was anxious to get some information anent David MacLure. He waited until Adamhill had finished his tales.

"What d'you know of him, John?"

"Damn little to his credit, Rab. He's a foxy merchant, the same MacLure. Your father made a bad bargain wi' him—especially when he didna get it wrote out. No' that that would have made sic a difference. MacLure's weel-skilled jowking the clauses o' a contract."

"We're in bad hands?"

"Ye are, Rab. But I would put up a fecht. MacLure's no' in this himsel': there's other rogues in wi' him. An' he's deep in the clutches o' the Douglas and Heron Bank. Aye . . .

I wouldna wonder but MacLure's heading straight for bankruptcy himsel'."

"It looks as if he's for having the law on us—what that may mean I don't rightly know."

"Your father should see a good lawyer."

"What about Robert Aiken in Ayr?"

"Bob's no' a bad lawyer. But you should try somebody nearer hand. Gavin Hamilton in Machlin's a good man. Keep him in mind if ocht should gae wrang. Ach, but maybe it'll no' come to that. I doubt if MacLure will press on to the length o' the law. Oh aye: he'll threaten. . . But come on, damn you, Rab: drink up! Annie, see that Rab's coggie's kept fu': if you want him to gang courtin' wi' you you'll need to attend to him better."

"Rab doesna want to court me, faither; an' if he does he'll no' need you to tell him."

"That's well spoken, Annie."

"Oh aye; but don't you get ony notions: I'm particular who I let court me. I suppose you did a power o' courtin' when you were in Irvine?"

"Noo, noo, Annie: ye manna ask siccan questions. A man doesna like the backside spiered out o' his ongauns—especially wi' the lassies."

"You're a' the same—a wheen blackguards!"

"Awa' ben the hoose and keep your mither company!"

"I thocht I was to see till Rab's ale?"

"Weel then—clap your meikle dowp on the creepie there and get on wi' your knitting. Noo then, Rab: cast aside your cares. What verses hae ye been at now?"

"Well . . . I hae twa on my pet yowe."

"It wouldna be a pet ram, that's certain."

"Annie! Noo: I've warned ye. Aye . . . come on then."

"Well . . . I had her tethered on the ditch side where the grass is sweet—with her two lambs; and if she didna row the rope round her shank and coup herself into the ditch. You ken Hughie Wilson that herds for Faucedyke? He's an odd, glowrin', gapin' callan' no' just what he should be. Well, he came runnin' across to Gilbert and me where we were ploughing and told us the tale. Hughie was in a queer state, bawlin' an' bletherin' and bubblin': we could hardly make sense o' his havers. But Mailie was couped i' the ditch right enough and we just got her on time.

"Well . . . that's the story and now here's the verses I made on the occasion. I've called them The Death and Dying Words of Poor Mailie, the Author's Only Pet Yowe. An Unco Mournfu Tale."

When he had finished reading his tale, Annie had stopped her knitting. She thought it was uncanny that such a wonderful poem should have its roots in such a simple everyday incident. John Rankine was delighted.

"Damned, Rab, but ye hae the knack and no mistake. Damned but ye can hear the yowe speaking. Is there nae mair?"

"Well . . . there's Mailie's Elegy."

"Fill up, Annie. An Elegy, eh? Damned, this'll be even better!"

And when Robin had given justice to the Elegy, John was confirmed in his prophecy; but Annie said she preferred the Death and Dying Words.

"Ye'll need to pen aff a copy o' them baith, Rab. I'll learn them mysel'. Aye . . . man: I see you've been in the vein. Come on, lass. G'wa' ben and get some supper laid oot. We canna let the bard awa' on an empty stammik."

"There's some good hen-bree I could warm up, Robin?"

"Fine, Annie: I like nothing better."

"Tear aff the breast o' the fowl when you're at it, Annie. It'll be a tasty bite to follow wi' your bannocks, Rab."

"Och there's no need——"

"That'll dae. There's no' much I can give you, Rab; but we'll need to build the strength up in you to ca' on wi' the poems."

"Well, John, I missed you the while I was away."

"I missed you tae, Rab. But noo that Annie's awa' ben the hoose—how did you get on wi' the Irvine lassies?"

"At the hinderend o' my stay I fell in wi' twa. I ettle for to marry one of them yet."

"Aye, man?"

"But maybe she'll no' have me."

"Anither Alison Begbie?"

"No, no: nothing o' Alison Begbie about her. A sweet lass, John—and no holding back."

"And the other?"

"God, she was a warmer. An extraordinary woman, John, extraordinary. Thinking back on her, I can hardly believe it wasna a dream."

"And she didna haud back either?"

"She gave me my first, second and third degree—wi' full ritual and all the honours."

"The hell she did, Rab! God, you've been gaun your mile in Irvine."

"It had to come sometime, John."

"Aye: it's got to come sometime. Mind you, Rab, I aey had the notion you and Annie micht hae got thegither. I ken, I ken—you dinna need to get embarrassed wi' me. Maybe it's only the way I feel, but I dinna think this Irvine lass is the richt one yet."

"I canna see that."

"No. . . But if you were certain you'd hae a different way o' talkin' aboot her. Maybe I'm wrang. An' if you feel that way aboot her I hope I'm wrang. Somehow I canna see you married tae a toon hizzie. No' you. . ."

"If she's the right lass what does it matter?"

"Fegs it matters. If she canna milk and mak' butter and cheese it'll matter."

"Aye . . . but . . ."

"Oh, you canna hem an' haw aboot a matter like that, Rab. Damnit, you'll need to fa' in wi' a farmer's dochter or the thing's aglee frae the start."

"Maybe I'll never be a farmer—the way things are shaping."

"Aye: you'll be a farmer: an' a damn guid one. But you'll need to yoke wi' the richt mate."

"I wonder, John, I wonder. Sometimes I see my road clear enough. Then the mists o' uncertainty come down and I don't know where the hell I am. And that's the state I'm in now."

"Coorse, wi' this bother wi' MacLure and your father, I ken how you must be feeling. But we're no' worrying the nicht. I'll hae a word wi' Bob Aiken mysel' the first time I'm doon in Ayr. Dinna worry, lad: I'll put it sae's your father'll never ken. He's an independent man—you tak' after him there, Rab."

"I doubt it's the only thing I take after him."

"Sae come on ben and get some honest grub in your wame: a body's spirits droop towards the back-end o' the nicht unless they tighten up the wame wi' honest kitchen. . . Damned, Rab, but I warmed to your verses on your pet yowe: you can hear the brute talkin'. Aye: the verra accent. . ."

PRESSURE FROM MACLURE

There could be no doubt: Robin slaved with a new zest. For a time he won golden opinions for his application and industry: his mother continued to smile on him.

There was need to labour. Every day the dispute with MacLure grew fiercer. Soon there was no escaping the fact that he meant to prosecute William with the utmost rigour of the law.

The cause of the disputation was simple enough and did not require the assistance of any lawyer to unravel its pros and cons.

William had taken Lochlea on certain terms and at a certain rent. For improvements to the farm he was to be allowed certain deductions from the rent. But MacLure, finding himself between the tightening jaws of financial bankruptcy, did not choose to concede any improvements. He demanded his rent in full.

By September the dispute reached a crisis. It was referred to arbitration. James Grieve, owner of the nearby farm of Boghead, was to act for MacLure. Charles Norvell, gardener at Coilsfield House, was to act for William Burns. William Chalmers, the Ayr writer, drew up the necessary document in due legal form.

The dispute was now out of William's hands. He didn't like Boghead and Boghead didn't like him. Boghead would fight to the last ditch for MacLure's interests.

Charles Norvell, on the other hand, was a just and upright man, and William was sure he would allow no injustice to be visited on him. As he said to Agnes: "Charles Norvell's a God-fearing man; but neither MacLure nor Boghead have ocht o' the grace of God about them. I'm in safe hands."

But the family was worried, and William was worrying himself into the grave. If the decision went against him, it would mean ruination—stark, utter and irrevocable ruin. He would be thrown like a cadger on the roadside.

Boghead and Norvell met in Tarbolton in James Manson's howff. They met several times. But they could not agree. They went into the merits and the demerits of the dispute and always Charles Norvell sought for some basis of just agreement; but finally he had to admit that Boghead did not want to find any basis for agreement: rather did he seek every opportunity to aggravate the issues. Charles Norvell did not yet despair, however: and he felt that in the end he would wear out the evil in Boghead.

UPON A LAMMAS NIGHT

As the months wore on Robin began to relax. This was inevitable: no one could have kept up the gruelling pace he had set himself. He still managed to get a night at the Bachelors' Club and enjoy a modest night with the nappy. And between Dr. Patrick Woodrow's sermons he enjoyed a walk and a talk with Davie Sillar.

As Davie and he enjoyed that Sabbath walk they would meet with girls of the parish. It was then that Davie felt his deficiencies as a gallant. For David was shy and awkward with the lassies, though he enjoyed their company individually and was always hot for love-making.

But Robin was all-conquering. He became another man in their company. His talk flowed witty and brilliant; he flattered deftly and neatly; he could send the lassies into peals of merry laughter; and he could woo each and all of them with an audacity that depressed Davie.

Alone, Davie could make his own headway and good head-way it was—Davie had his own quiet way of getting round a lass in a quiet corner. But he could not shine in company. He lacked what Robin had in perfection—social flair.

Though he always managed to have a string or two to his bow in the parish (besides making an occasional dash into Irvine to see and enjoy his Jean), Robin kept up his acquaintance with John Rankine and Mr. and Mrs. Muir of the Mill.

And then one Lammas night when the corn rigs and the barley rigs gladdened the heart with their beauty and their promise of plenty, Robin made the journey across the fields to Adamhill to visit John Rankine, only to find that the farmer and his wife were absent on a visit to Craigie. But there was Annie to entertain him.

In a flash Robin realised that he hadn't come to see John. He had been drawn to his daughter.

He had lost his fear of Annie's overpowering physical presence. She had grown into a magnificent specimen of country womanhood. There was a glorious bloom to her cheeks; her eyes danced and sparkled; her body was a sweeping harmony of virile curves; her voice had the rich huskiness of allurement; her lips were full-swollen with the rich red wine of life; she moved with a soft panther tread, easing her weight imperceptibly to the ball of her naked foot causing her tight buttocks to alternate in a slow slanting roll. . .

The night was warm with the softness and warmth of lappered cream; a drowse of distant murmurings filled the air; the dusk came gently, almost imperceptibly, soothing and caressing, blurring the jagged edges of the day.

The old brown cock, with his harem puffed along the bauks, emitted weird but mellow sounds—a feather-muffled, neck-retracted chirrawak—from the dream of a yellow sun-baked dunghill and a flufftering harem that didn't run too fast: or didn't run at all.

The knock, with its weighted chains, folded its faded face against the shadowed wall—the consonants of its measure softened to diphthongs and its diphthongs mellowed to vowels.

The peats crumbled on the hearth and glowed with an ancient warmth. Auld baudrans, tired with her ablutions, coiled herself at Robin's feet.

Robin lay in Adamhill's comfortable chair, relaxed, in cushioned comfort, dreaming: apparently dozing. But through his long lashes he watched Annie as she trod the floor; moved through to the kitchen; stooped over the hearth; raised her arms to the top rack of the dresser; leaned across the table, placing a coggie here and a horn spoon there. . .

He watched her with slow satisfaction. What was the strange fascination about Annie that was about no other girl he had known? It wasn't a girlish quality though Annie was still a girl. There was nothing matronly about her; yet she had all the stature and easy confidence of a matron.

He had always been drawn to Annie—drawn by her blood—

the deep smooth-flowing tide of it. He had always been drawn to it even when he had subconsciously resisted the deep down-sucking of its magnetism.

The chemistry of their blood was flashing to contact across the stillness of the over-charged room. The air was impregnated with desire. The leap across the arc of reciprocal attraction was imminent.

Robin knew the signs. He opened his lips gently to breathe more freely. He noted how Annie ran her tongue across her bursting ripe lips; how she caressed her breasts with an almost imperceptible upwards movement as if she had suddenly become conscious of their fulness. . .

The tide of his passion rose steadily. He watched Annie closely, fascinated; compared her with the lassies he had known. Yet he could not reason about her for his reason told him that she was not the kind of lass who appealed to him; while his blood told him that she had an appeal more clamorous than any other.

His reason blurred. . . He saw Annie woven into a background of fragmentary images: the sweet thighs of Jean Glover; the scarlet lips and violet eyes of Jean Gardner; the urgent upthrust of Nancy Fleming's sharply contoured breasts; the marble-moulded hips of Mysie Graham (' the lusty buttock barred with azure vein '). . .

Yet the actuality of Annie disentangled itself, emerged from the floating images, imposed itself with overwhelming immediacy. Her presence was not gross; there was no out-thrusting violence of physical passion; the sense of her was deep-flowing and subtly interpenetrating; her strength was as the strength of the panther lying in quiet shimmering ripples beneath the tawny silken pelt. . .

Her hair, red-golden in the sunlight, was nut-brown in the soft shadowed spence. Jean Glover had been black, Jean Gardner flaxen. . . Maybe he liked the raven black for its intensity, for the vigour of the passion it promised. . . Yet how impossible Annie would have been with black hair. . .

She was in her twenty-first year: in the prime of her girlhood. She was still, despite much temptation, a maid—but without any naïveté; far from it: Annie knew as much as any ten matrons: she was John Rankine's daughter with the Rankine awareness and imagination. She was farm-lass around Adamhill—cow-wife, hen-wife, pig-wife. And she had known lovers and some of them she had loved, after a fashion. . .

But she had always hankered after Robert (as John Rankine sensed). Rab Burns was an enigma to her; but an intriguing enigma. In her heart she loved him. But she dreaded to show her love for the rebuff it might sustain. How often had she been abrupt with him for no other reason—when she saw his mind was elsewhere.

She knew he was a sincere lad; but only too often did a healthy mocking light dance in his great eyes (there was no escaping his eyes: they haunted her dreams); and she wasn't sure of herself, wasn't certain she had enough attraction for him. And yet—if it could only be. . .

How often had she debated within herself the meaning of that first night she had met him at the opening of the Tarbolton dancing school?

But to-night, as never before, Robert had a disturbing effect on her. The gathering inward tension was almost a physical agony: she could feel a tautness across her diaphragm; sometimes it gathered to a sense of sickness. Her movements became slower and slower. . .

The blood damned in her midrif; her limbs became heavy; her breasts tightened with a queer sense of fulness as if she might give suck to a child; she became conscious, alarmingly conscious of their weight and bulk; a nerve rippled and trembled along the inside of her thigh; occasionally her nostrils twitched and broadened under the adjustment of physical tensions. . .

She moved slowly towards the fire. Her flesh-smell was a challenge to Robin's nostrils. She bent down to place a fresh peat on the glowing embers. He caught and pulled her to him.

She was across his knees, her nape in the lurk of his left arm; their lips fused; the urgent right hand, deft and experienced, explored. . . The tension discharged in rippling spasms over her body. The cat fled the hearth rug as they slid down. . .

She sucked the air into her contracted lungs in urgent spasms; her bosom heaved. She thrust away from him and her strength was terrific.

"No' here, Rab . . . no' here. . . Let me go, you mad devil. Somewhere else. . ."

She freed herself and was out of the room in an instant.

He met up with her down by the rigs of barley and came quietly to her side.

It was a soft warm night and the gloaming lay deep in the hollows of the land. The light of the moon was showing behind the far-off hills.

He slipped his arm about her waist.

"God Almighty, but I love you, Annie."

"You devil, Rab. . . You've cast a spell on me."

"And what d'you think you've done to me, lass? D'you know where you're going?"

But fine she knew where she was going: she had visualised the spot too often, had thought out its safety. If she knew Rab aright, she could safely leave it to him to find it.

"There's a green bawk down here, Annie, wi' an auld oak at the rig-end. Do you know it?"

"You're a witch, Rab: you've been there afore now."

"No . . . but I often thought of you as I passed it by."

"Oh, you're a daft beggar Rab Burns—you've got me crazed."

His hand tightened round her waist. Words would not flow to his lips for he was almost demented with the passion that surged in him.

They sat down beneath the twisted oak-tree in the gloaming-green hollow of the bawk end. Corn on their right and barley on their left fringed the skyline above their heads.

Clumps of whin and broom and bramble grew along the short slope of the bawk. They were completely sheltered and hidden from view. . .

It was a spot Robin had looked upon with favour, and Annie had known of it for years—ever since she had seen her sister Peggy lying there one summer's night with her lover. She had never used it herself. Someday she felt she might be glad to know it was there waiting for her. . .

Annie was to remember this night; she was to sing about it when she was an old woman and no longer beautiful.

For the moment she was in a flux of sensation; the marrow of her bones was melting; her limbs were losing their heaviness. . . But sensation beyond sensation! Rab's arms were round her, their lips were together. . . She was his—and for the first time. Robert Burns: the lad her father lauded and whose friendship he valued beyond any others. The lad who sometimes sat alone with her father at the spence ingle immersed in the deepest conversation or laughing gaily and enjoying some uproarious joke; or reading some of his grand poems; or the show-piece of the company, dazzling her father's friends with the wit of his talk.

Robert Burns, the lad with the deep glowing eyes—or could she really think of his eyes in terms of words? Eyes that held her, brought a catch to her throat, tears to her eyes, a smile to her lips—and often that near-sick tension in her midriff . . . and the weakness trembling down her thighs.

Robert Burns who had remained till this rapturous night something of a puzzle; who carried with him a quality with which she could never take any liberty. . .

Now she had him as she had always wanted him. And how often had she feared she might never know him? How often had she dreaded that his approach might be wrong—and she would have to rebuff him? How often had she sworn to herself she would never give herself to him because he looked so differently at other girls?

She had him now and she would keep him: she would lock

her arms so that he would never escape. She would give herself to him so completely, so utterly, that he would never want another girl. She would give herself so that he would never forget her among the memory of all the women he had known —or would ever know. But all this was instinctive. Her arms went round him with passionate instinct. Her entire body embraced him in a series of involuntary convulsive spasms as if to draw him into the dark unconscious recess where life is born: the terrible maw of creation that forever destroys and disintegrates in order to recreate—so that the creative process shall be without end.

And Robin who had thought so consciously and sharply with Jean Glover, absorbing and noting every detail of the process, found himself completely absorbed by Annie Rankine. The embrace did not break till they were both utterly spent— till every atom of tension had flowed back into the quiescence of inactivity. . .

Robin lay at her side, his head resting on her bosom. She ran her fingers through his damp hair. She could feel the saliva trickling from his parted lips: she pressed his head gently to her breasts as she would the head of a child. . .

She had not known that love could be so overwhelming, so intense, so devastating to the emotions, so indescribably, bafflingly rich in sensation. . .

Robin sighed and sat up. There was a sudden coldness where his warm wet mouth had been. She sat up beside him and quickly buttoned up her bodice and shook back her hair.

She reached out and took his hand. It was hard and calloused with labour and his nails were split and broken. The hand was limp; yet she knew the tenderness it was capable of.

" You work hard, Rab?"

" Aye . . . I work hard, Annie. There's nothing else for it at Lochlea."

"John Rankine never worked as hard."

" Your father never needed . . ."

"Just because—he had the siller?"

"Because he had the siller—and was fortunate."

"But you'll no' aey hae tae work so hard?"

"Ah, what the hell does it matter, Annie? I'm here: you're here—that's what matters. There's the moon: it doesn't give a damn for you or me or ony other thing in the whole o' creation. I'm no' in the mood to question it, Annie. It's there —to bless us if we like to accept it that nocht else matters . . ."

He took her hand now and very gently prized open her fingers and appeared to examine her palm lines.

"Do you no' wish it could aey be this way, Rab?"

"Annie: I've never known an hour like this. This makes all the years of grubbing and moiling in the muck and glaur bearable. This is what life was made for, the chief end and purpose of life. Without this what signifies the life of man? Annie: I just canna put it in words—not here and now. But all the melancholy morbid humours that gather on me dissolve. And God, lass: if you knew how melancholy I get, how damnably depressed: aye . . . till I long for death to come and give me release. Aye: if it could always be like this. I weigh an hour like this in the scales o' my life and I find my life wanting. We've waited a while for this hour, Annie; but it has been mair nor worth the waiting."

"Rab! You know I would be good to you?"

"God lass: could you possibly be better to me?"

"Oh, but Rab: I want to be good to you a' the time . . . but I suppose it canna be?"

"Don't think on it, lass. Not here. Just accept what we have—and be thankful. The corn rigs there bowing to the breeze; the moon up yonder sailing through the nights o' eternity—there's nae thinking there, Annie."

"But I want you, Rab: I aey want you."

"And you've got me—to the last drop o' my blood."

"Rab?" She averted her head and her voice sounded im-personal—and lonely.

"Yes?"

"If . . . if onything happens you'll no' throw me aside? You'll no' deny me?"

He put his hand to her cheek and brought her head round.

"I would sooner deny the Holy Ghost—or my own mother that bore me."

They kissed on that, a tender pledging kiss. But even as they pledged their faith and trust in each other the flame of desire leapt and flickered between them. Nor was Annie fully conscious that already she was undoing the buttons on her bodice.

THE SONG IS BORN

The rain was lashing down; long lancing streams of it. The courtyard fell away from the dwelling-house at Lochlea, so the rain water ran down to the duck pond in hundreds of little streams.

It was as steady a fall of rain as Robin could remember: rhythmically steady. There was little wind; but an occasional squall would break up the long down-thrusting lances of rain and send the drops spattering across the boulder-paved court.

There was no possibility of work outside and there was little to be done inside. He took his fiddle and the sorely tattered copy of Craig's *Scots Tunes* he had bought second-hand with his second-hand fiddle.

He dashed across the open court to the stable and sat himself on the wooden corn kist, leaving the door open so that the grey daylight might reveal the music notes on the faded yellow-grey paper.

He tuned the fiddle and tuned it well. But it was a poor toned instrument. Though he was no fiddler (having sawed his way through a few rough lessons with Davie Sillar), his musical faculty was so deeply rooted in him (his every fibre was permeated with melody) that he drew from the inadequate instrument a richer and deeper response than was audible from the note vibrations.

He turned over the pages. *Corn Rigs*. Here was a grand old melody. He tucked the fiddle under his chin and worked his slow-moving, broken-nailed, toil-calloused fingers on the gut. The muscles of his bowing arm had been strained and stiffened by violent labour: he would never be able to draw a sweet bow with any dexterity across the strings.

But he essayed the tune and, taking it slowly, imposed a perfect timing on it.

Aye: it was a grand tune. It had been running in his head for days—with Allan Ramsay's words. But he didn't like Allan's words: they weren't good enough for such a grand melody.

The old ones were better. O corn rigs and rye rigs, O corn rigs is bonie; whare e'er ye meet a bonie lass, preen up her apron, Johnie. Aye: that was better; but still far from satisfactory.

He tried some other airs but came back to *Corn Rigs*. The tune refused to leave his mind.

Then the thoughts that had been running in his mind ever since that glorious night with Annie Rankine suddenly fused—words and melody.

He cast the fiddle from him—none too gently—and searched for the stump of pencil he always carried.

He began to write along the margin of the music sheet. He had no need for the fiddle now. The words would flow to no other than this music's measure.

And boy, boy! but the words were flowing sweetly. Far and away his best song yet; aye, and better nor Allan's effort. Wait though. Good so far—but he needed a finish—a grand finish—a verse to sum up the whole experience. And God! he'd gone through a life-time of experience with Annie that night. Had there ever been a night like it? He'd known some wonderful nights. Nights with some of the cronies—and the coggies lipping full! Aye, many a canty night he'd had with randy chiels when the nappy was in grand order. But the night with Annie far surpassed any night—or day—with the comrades.

Aye, damn it; and come to think of it: he'd been at his happiest when in the throes of creation—when ideas, images and a harmony of sounds were seeds fertilising in the brain: the process of thinking.

Just thinking: that was all. But when the thinking was right, when the ideas were blending and fusing so sweetly and effortlessly that the entire being was merged into a great dwam of thought—then by heaven was that not the perfection of living? Many a happy hour he'd had in that state.

And yet: which came first? Surely the experiences that gave rise to thought and the whole thinking process. Surely it was the experience that was vital—and primary.

Right then, right! The night with Annie was worth—for him—the whole of creation. For, by God, there was no escaping the fact: it was creation at its highest point—life soaring to the pinnacle point of experience, awareness.

Sure: that happy night was worth them a'—amang the rigs wi' Annie.

A shadow fell across the doorway.

There was Gilbert, hands in pockets, leaning on the jamb. He hadn't heard his step.

"What are you at now?" said Gilbert. His face was gloomy, his tone flat.

"I've written a song, Gibby. My best song."

"Aye?"

"What's wrong, man? It's a good morning to write a song. Damnit, there's no work can be done in that rain. I'm no' eating my bloody head off writing a song—am I?"

"I never said a word."

"Listen to this, Gibby." He picked up the fiddle. "You know Corn Rigs—or maybe you don't?"

"Oh, put down the fiddle, man. The noise you mak' on that is little short of infernal."

"And since when did your muckle lug begin to develop a taste for music? D'you ken Corn Rigs is Bonie?"

"*Are* bonie!"

"Come in out o' the light, you sour-faced beggar——"

"He'll be coming in here if you start playing."

"And what if he does? Is it an unforgivable sin to play the fiddle on a wet morning—aye, or a dry one?"

"Go ahead: I'm listening."

"That's better. I'm telling you, Gibby: it's no' every day I write my best song. Get the tune first."

To hell, thought Gilbert, I've never heard him playing so well. Damned near as good as Davie Sillar. There was that genuine old flavour about the air such as lingered in all the melodies Robin would ever be humming and whistling.

But it was a pity. Robin would never be able to play the fiddle: started too late: when his hand had got the set of the plough stilts. . . Still, it was a grand tune: already it had dispelled the gloom of the morning and had lifted the grey cloud from his own spirit.

"Well . . . what d'you think o't?"

"A good tune, Robin."

"You're right. Now listen to the verses."

"Did you write them this morning?"

"I did—but, truth to tell, Gibby, they've been forming in my head for days. Some of the words for years maybe. Listen now; and keep the sough o' the tune in your mind.

"It was upon a Lammas night, when corn rigs are bonie, beneath the moon's unclouded light, I held awa to Annie; the time flew by, wi' tentless heed; till, 'tween the late and early, wi' sma' persuasion she agreed to see me thro' the barley.

"Corn rigs, an' barley rigs, an' corn rigs are bonie: I'll ne'er forget that happy night, amang the rigs wi' Annie.

"The sky was blue, the wind was still, the moon was shining clearly; I set her down, wi' right good will, amang the rigs o' barley: I ken't her heart was a' my ain; I lov'd her most sincerely; I kiss'd her owre and owre again, amang the rigs o' barley.

"I lock'd her in my fond embrace; her heart was beating rarely: my blessings on that happy place, amang the rigs o' barley! But by the moon and stars so bright, that shone that hour so clearly! She aey shall bless that happy night amang the rigs o' barley.

"I hae been blythe wi' comrades dear; I hae been merry drinking; I hae been joyfu' gath'rin gear; I hae been happy thinking: but a' the pleasures e'er I saw, tho' three times doubl'd fairly—that happy night was worth them a', amang the rigs o' barley.

"Corn rigs, an' barley rigs, an' corn rigs are bonie: I'll ne'er forget that happy night, amang the rigs wi' Annie."

When he had finished he did not have to ask Gilbert how he liked it: acceptance had transformed his long face.

"Oh, that's your best, Robin. Far and away your best. That's inspiration if ever you were inspired. I'd give a lot to hear John Rankine sing that."

"Maybe you will, Gibby: maybe you will. D'you think he'll like it?"

"You know what he thinks o' Annie. But when did this happen?"

"Oh, about ten days ago . . ."

"Yon fine night you went up to Adamhill?"

"Aye. . . But I'm no' committed to her, Gibby."

"No? It sounds like it."

"Damnit, man: it's a song."

"I know. But maybe John Rankine'll no' tak' it that way. Nor Annie. . ."

"Annie's all right. She's one of the finest lassies I've ever known, Gibby: damned, she's the finest."

"But you're no' for yokin' wi' her?"

"Mind you: it's a gey queer business, Gibby. I like Annie and she likes me. Oh, she would marry me to-morrow—an' the backside sticking out o' my auld duds. And she'd make a good wife: none better. John Rankine—I've no doubt but he would set me up in a tidy farm. But—and there's the but, Gibby, that sticks like a burr in the mind: I just canna do it. Aye: I love Annie. Down in the corn bawk I loved her more than I've ever loved anybody or anything in this life. But marriage: that's a different thing. True, love and marriage gang thegither—or should. But there's some loves don't go wi' marriage—none the less love for all that—but, there you are, Gibby. And if there's one man in this world I think would understand that, that man's none other than John Rankine.

Damnit, I know Adamhill would like me for a good-son: he's told me that: he's done everything he could to bring Annie an' me thegither——"

"But what about the consequences—if any?"

"Of course, if she holds—that puts another snout on the sow's face; and I'll do what's right. Mind you, Gibby, that's the queer thing about Annie: a virgin, yes; and I could have had her years ago: clean daft about me although she would never show it; and yet Annie understands—just as well as her father. She wouldn't yoke wi' me unless the desire came frae me: unless there was a bairn in it."

"And what about Jean Gardner now?"

"Jean! I would have married Jean: I would marry her yet. There's something different about Jean. I don't know—— What the hell's the good trying to explain what just canna be explained?"

"Once you step out of the bounds of morality you can't explain anything, Robin."

"To hell wi' morality—and you too, Gibby."

"You know where all this'll end?"

"End? I've written a song: a good song: I know it's good. Isn't that end enough? You want a garland o' mouldy morality hung round it? Well: you're no' getting it. Patie Woodrow can supply the morality: Rab Burns will supply the songs."

"And Auld Nick'll supply the brimstane cooty."

"And Gilbert Burns will emulate Lazarus with quotations from the Westminster Catechism——"

William Burns appeared in the doorway.

"The Westminster Catechism?" His eye took in the fiddle and the music resting on the corn kist lid. "That's one thing you don't play on the fiddle. Now see here: is this a way to idle in the morning? Can you not find work to your hands?"

"We don't idle much——"

"We canna afford to idle any. Gilbert, you could have

made a start on teeth for the harrows. And you, Robert: you
ken the harness is in a sair state——"

"Half an hour'll see that right."

"Well . . . I don't like to see you idling away the morning.
It's a tempting of Providence seeing the way things are wi'
us——"

Gilbert turned quietly on his heel and went out into the
rain. Robin didn't look at his father: he knew that gaunt
accusing visage.

"Charles Norvell says he misdoubts nor Boghead ettles to
give ony kind of an honest verdict."

"Well . . . shouldn't we sell what we can in case the worst
happens? There's no point in leaving everything for the vultures to descend on us."

"And am I to be robbed of my own——"

"Nobody gets their own: you only get what other folks
allow you. There's little justice in the law: you should know
that. I would sell what we could afford. That would be using
the law to our own advantage—for once."

"Well . . . No: I'm in the right; and I'll take no steps
that would look as if I was in the wrong: a fine like thing it
would be if it got round the parish that I was selling off."

"It could be done quietly—and gradually. And we don't
need to drive our stirks to the one market."

Robert could see he was making some impression. But the
more William Burns realised the commonsense of the argument, the more stubbornly he resisted.

There was a patter of feet in the courtyard. William looked
out.

"There's that boy out in the rain again getting himself
soaked. John!"

He hunched his shoulders and went out into the rain.
John's lungs were delicate; but he would not take advice. . .

Robin patted the haunch of his favourite mare—a grey-
coated beast as docile as a pet lamb.

"Hup, lass: I've to see about your harness. It's just as well

for you you canna play the fiddle—or fash your thoomb wi'
the Catechism—or, by certes, lass, William Burns would give
you a moral currycombing that would tickle your theological
ribs. But maybe after all it's best to be dumb—and you can
think what you like."

The mare replied with a dry nicker and moved up in her
stall. A drooked hen with down-thrust tail cocked her head
in at the door and uncoiled a pathetically ludicrous chirrawak.

From somewhere behind the cart shed the voice of William
Burns could be heard scolding John.

Aye, thought Robert, that happy night was worth them a'
—among the rigs wi' Annie.

John Rankine examined the cow.

"It's had too big a feed o' bog hay: that's the maist that's wrang wi' it. She's gotten a belly o' sair guts." He cast a searching looks at Annie. "An' by the by, my lass: how's your own guts?"

Annie held his gaze and bristled.

"What d'you mean?"

"Wi' sma' persuasion she agreed to see me through the barley . . . damned sma' persuasion, I'll warrant."

"What pack o' lies has Rab Burns been telling you?"

"I hope I've been told no lies. You were down the oaktree-bawk wi' him?"

"Did Rab Burns tell you that?"

"Now, now, lass: don't get your birss up. Rab told me nothing. But, by God, lass, he's made a great sang on you."

"On me?"

"Well: I'm putting two and two thegither. I thocht that night you came in late and said you had only been down the hill wi' him that the pair o' you had been up to some byornar daffing. . . So I was wondering if I would need to be putting in a word wi' the howdie?"

"You'll need nae howdie for me—you can lippen on that. But maybe Rab Burns'll need a howdie by the time I'm finished wi' him."

"There you go. Haud on to him and dinna act like a silly bitch. Rab hasna been saying onything in your disfavour: you should ken that. He's put you intil a thundering good sang; and that's something you can weel be proud o'. Gin you play your hand richt, there's nae reason why you shouldna haud him—gin you want him."

Annie lifted her luggie and ran out of the byre. What had

happened? Was Rab Burns talking about that night? And
what kind of song had he made on her? She hoped it wasn't
anything like the kind of songs Saunders Tait made up about
the lassies. If it was, then she would never forgive him. But
no: no. . . Rab could never reveal what had happened. It
was unthinkable that he could ever be so callous. He was
every inch a poet: not a dirty rhymer like auld Tait.

Now that she knew she hadn't conceived to him she was
vastly relieved. She would be able to look him in the face:
aye, and any other body. And if it was a decent-like song he
had made on her, there was nothing to hinder her learning it
herself and singing it without shame. Why shouldn't she?
If Rab could make the song she could sing it. That would
prove the night had meant as much to her as it had to him.

But oh . . . Why was he so long in coming back to Adamhill?

A few days later Robin met with Annie as she was bringing
home the kye in the evening. The black cow had broken into
the corn and, with the aid of the herd laddie, she was trying
to round it up.

"Well, Annie; and how are you?"

"Oh fine, Rab. I never felt better. But what's this I've been
hearing about you? I thocht you might have let me hear the
first o' your new sang!"

"You've heard it?"

"You didna keep it to yoursel', did you?"

"Oh—you know what a song's like, Annie: it's meant to
be sung—isn't it?"

"No' a sang about me! And onyway: it depends on the
sang."

"I suppose it does. But you don't think I would make a
bad song on you, Annie? Did your father speak to you about
it?"

"You're fishing, Rab."

She was right. He looked past her across the rigs of yellow-
ing corn. . . He lowered his eyes and noted her strong broad

feet with the well-spaced toes. He let his gaze travel up her legs; noted the delicate golden hairs reflect the sunlight; noted how her legs were spattered with cow sharn. . .

He raised his eyes quickly and looked her full in the face. There was a quiet smile in her eyes; but he could not be certain that it was not sardonic.

"You're . . . all right, Annie?"

"Is that all that's worrying you, Rab? I'm all right: there's nothing to worry about."

"I'm glad to hear that, Annie: damned glad. Has your father said anything to you?"

"Did you tell him onything?"

"Who said I told him anything? He's the last man . . ."

"You must have told him something."

"Well . . . he knows we were down the bawk thegither that night; but nothing else—from me."

"Oh well. . . But are you no' coming up some nicht?"

"Aye . . . oh aye: I'll be up some nicht soon."

"You dinna care for me so much now, Rab?"

"I'll aey love you, Annie. How else could it be . . . you know that."

"Rab. . . It doesna matter: I'll need to get the kye hame."

"Aye: I suppose you will. . . If it's a good night I might be over at the tryst."

"If it's a good night?"

"I could read you my song."

Annie smiled and showed her strong white teeth.

"You're a daft beggar, Rab. You could get round onybody."

"As long as I get round you, Annie, I'll no' fash mysel' wi' the lave——"

"I'll need to go . . .

"Have you no' a kiss for me?"

"Well . . . just the one."

They embraced behind a screen of thornbush. Then Annie tore herself free and ran after the cows.

She was a fine lass, Annie; good-natured, kind-hearted

. . . and as strong as an ox. God, she was strong—and bound-lessly healthy.

So she was all right? That was the best news he had heard for a long time. . . No: Annie was fine for a night in the bawk or a night in the barn; but he just wouldn't like to marry her. But he didn't know why he wouldn't. A pity; for if ever he had had the chance to do well for himself and escape from the toil and slavery of Lochlea, that chance lay in marrying Annie Rankine.

He stood and watched her driving the cows up the long slope of the hill towards the steading. Whoever got her in marriage would get a wife in ten thousand.

THE MEN OF AYR

David MacLure had once been a small statured, barrel-bellied merchant with red chops and hard pig-like eyes.

He was still fat and he was still a merchant, though a financially embarrassed one. But his chops were no longer red and his eyes were inclined to water. His face was grey and the flesh flabby, his lips loose and blubbery. His teeth were badly decayed and his breath was foul. But then David MacLure was not a pleasant specimen of humanity. Neither were his partners, George MacCree, a youngish man of questionable antecedents, nor John Campbell of the Ayrshire clan who was a creature not above committing a murder by way of achieving his own shady ends. Campbell was an erstwhile physician of sorts who made money by any manner of speculation and who considered hard work as unprofitable and degrading to a man of intelligence who had a taste for the habits of the gentry.

They were all of them in a mild state of intoxication when James Grieve of Boghead came into Ayr to join them at Simson's howff.

Their speculations had gone agley. The war with America hadn't helped them and they had mortgaged most of their property to the Douglas and Heron Bank—and the Douglas and Heron Bank had gone to the wall . . . and no one knew how much they would be able to salvage: affairs were in a pretty mess and the lawyers were having the time of their lives.

But for many the situation was desperate in the extreme: MacLure and his partners were desperate. . .

MacLure was anxious to know how things were shaping at Tarbolton: he listened attentively to Boghead.

"So Norvell canna be made to listen to good common

sense ! You're sure you tried him wi' the sight o' good siller?"

"Aye . . . and got weel rounded on for my pains. No: he's like Burns in Lochlea: a damned narrow spawn o' theological bigotry. . . You canna reason wi' thae gentry."

"I see: birds o' a feather—thrawn, stiff-neckit beggars: I ken the breed. Weel . . . this means we'll be at the trouble and expense o' an oversman."

MacCree was impatient.

"And where the hell d'you think we'll pick on an oversman that'll see our end o' the business?"

"Weel: I've been sounding Norvell; and I don't think he'll raise ony objection to Sundrum."

"John Hamilton o' Sundrum?"

"Aye, he's a good man; and I think I could get him to see the sense o' a fair-like proposition."

"So you've had dealings wi' him, Dave?"

"Oh aye—I've had dealings wi' a'bodies back and forward, wet days and dry days. Them about Kyle, Cunninghame or Carrick that I havena had dealings wi' are of no account. You could get worse, Boghead: a damned sight worse. Sundrum's opinion'll carry weight. And we need a' the weight we can get—especially since we'll need to carry this in front o' the Sheriff."

"Willie Wallace?"

"Willie's no' the worst. He's had a flea in his muckle lug afore now. . . There's ways o' working the Sheriff."

"Weel," said Campbell, who was becoming impatient of MacLure's insufferable pomposity and air of owl-like wisdom, "we'll need to get this business settled. If this thrawn beggar in Lochlea's going to drag out the case—and he's no' doin' it on nothing: it's costing him money that should be coming our way—then we'll no' can bankrupt him afore the new year."

"If you ask me," said Boghead, "Burns is selling aff his stock against the possibility o' a roup."

"God's curse on the bastard!" roared MacCree. "If he does

then we'll a' be ruined completely." MacCree was white with rage.

Campbell said: "You've played wi' this long enough, Dave. It's time for action. I'd go up there to Lochlea and hamstring the bluidy stock myself."

"Steady now: steady wi' that kind o' talk—you'll hamstring us if you dinna mind your step. It's Burns we've got to hamstring."

"But how? You've been saying that for a long time now."

"And do you think you could conduct this business any better nor me? You're no' on the right side o' the law yet if it comes to that. If Burns had a good lawyer he could make things hot—and damned hot—for the lot o' us."

"Aiken! You dinna ca' him a good lawyer?"

"No. . . But Aiken's got his points—but no' on a case like this. Bob Aiken's nae fool. Don't get ony wrong notions intil your head about him."

"Ah, to hell wi' Aiken: we're no' getting forward in this business. We'll need to do something—something desperate."

"Aye: you're a desperate pair o' beggars, I must say. If the Bank gets its claws on you, you'll damned soon ken who's desperate. This business has got to be done wi' the full honours of the law—to keep doon ony chance o' suspicion. We can lose everything we've got—even yet: is that clear? We just canna risk ony slip on a thing like this. Now listen: we've got to get the right side o' John Hamilton o' Sundrum. He's the one man that matters now. Aye: we've got to get Burns sequestrated against ony possibility o' his selling-out his stock on us."

"And who's going to pay for all this? Lawyers cost a hantle o' siller—the bluidy horse-leeches!"

"A guid lawyer kens how things stand—and what side his bread's buttered on."

"Weel . . . I don't suppose there's much else I can do, Mr. MacLure?"

Boghead was a great raw brute of a man. His temper was

inclined to be surly at the best of times. He had done the work
MacLure had asked of him. Now he wanted the final settlement
of the money promised him.

MacLure put his hand in his pocket. Then he changed his
mind.

"You'll hae another drink, Boghead. . . There's another
wee bit job I think you could do for me. The Sheriff whiles
has a way o' getting to know things——"

"You're no' trying to threaten me——"

"Tits, tits, Boghead: you're in a public-house—no' on
your middenhead back in Tarbolton. You'll need to learn to
control your tongue in the company o' gentlemen, Mr. Grieve:
I don't think I like your tone."

But Boghead wasn't to be bluffed by David MacLure.
Besides, he had a good drink in him and was stirred to
aggression.

"When I do work for ony man I like to get paid for it;
and when I make a bargain wi' a man I like that man to stick
to the bargain."

MacCree said: "We've had enough o' this. If you don't
like the company, Boghead, you can take yourself to hell: we
don't need to take ony damned snash frae a muckle dung-
scailer like you."

"Steady!" cried MacLure. "Steady now. I'll do ony
ordering about that's to be done. But as a lesson to you, Mr.
Grieve, you'll get your siller when I find it convenient. You
understand?"

Boghead raised himself from the table slowly. He saw he
was in the hands of flint-hearted men who would stop at
nothing to gain their ends.

"I can understand richt enough . . . but I'll be back next
week. Maybe you and me'll manage to hae a word by our lane,
Mr. David MacLure. For by God, sir, it wouldna tak' much for
me to trail the guts out of thae cronies o' yours."

When he had gone, MacLure hastened to reassure his
companions.

"He's a muckle sumph o' a man, a damned stupid ill-natured clod. . . But he's done us a service—and he'll keep his mouth shut."

But both Campbell and MacCree began to see that David MacLure wasn't up to much, that he was but a small fry merchant for all his ill-gotten wealth. He talked too much—and drank too much. No doubt he was shrewd and cunning; but it would take more than these qualities to get them out of the hole they were in.

Yet there was nothing much they could do at the moment except drink. There was always the hope that the drink would help to blot out their worries and anxieties.

"Of coorse," said MacLure, "there's aey the chance that the Sheriff'll discover we had nae richt tae let that ground at Lochlea since, strictly speaking, it's mortgaged to the Bank."

"You mean Douglas and Heron's agents could claim the money we're claiming frae Burns?"

"That's about it."

"But God Almighty, man: d'you see where that can land us?"

"Fine. . . I wonder what the hell you think I'm sitting here drinking for and it the middle o' the afternoon? But allow me to see the road out."

"Are you ettling for to carry on wi' the sequestration?"

"Oh aye: we can aey go ahead wi' that and see how it works out."

"If we could roup him intil the ditch and lay our hands on the money, the Bank could rake hell for me."

"Maybe; but some o' us will need to stay behind ony the ways o't and face the music."

While they were snarling among themselves, Robert Aiken, the lawyer, and John Ballantine, the banker and Dean of Guild for the town, entered and took a seat in the opposite corner from MacLure and his partners.

Aiken, who was coming into his forty-third year, was a prosperous writer with a merry eye in a fat smiling face.

The Dean of Guild, who was four or five years his junior, was a very different type of man. He was slim, rather dandified in his dress (he wore black silk stockings and sported a yellow satin waistcoat elaborately braided) and seemed slightly conscious of his superior looks. Yet there was more than intelligence in his fine brown eyes: there was sympathy and understanding. But his understanding was judicial: he was in no way prodigal in his emotional responses.

"William Burns'll no' be long, John. It'll be worth your while to hear what's going on. He's bringing in his eldest laddie, Robert: a bit o' a poet frae what I hear."

"A rhymer, eh? I wouldna have thocht William Burns would have had a versifier in his family?"

"John, William Burns is the maist extraornar man I hae met wi' in the profession—aye, or outside it."

"Yes: he's a worthy man: a maist excellent type of Scot: his kind's dying out, Bob."

"God aye: mind you, the auld folks had character—there was my father now—Captain John Aiken——"

At that moment William Burns and his son came into the room, and Aiken broke off his sentence and rose to meet them.

"God!" cried MacLure, his grey gills turning white, "there's Burns frae Lochlea!"

"Who? That long lanky spindle-shankit beggar! He wouldna make a decent tram for a cart. Did you ever see such an ill-looking bundle o' rags and bones?"

"And to think," said Campbell, backing up MacCree, "that that bluidy mongrel cur is setting himsel' up to defy the likes o' us. I could break his back and throw him i' the ditch ony dark night."

"Aye," said MacLure, "that's William Burns. By God but he's failed since I made that bargain wi' him in this verra room six or seven years ago. You can say what you like, but he's no' long for this world—bad cess till him."

"Do you mean us to wait till he dies?"

"Thae threatened beggars live the longest."

"To hell: let's get out o' this," said MacLure, making for the door. The others followed him quickly.

Both Aiken and Ballantine were favourably impressed with William's eldest son. Aiken sensed a kindred spirit and Ballantine a kindred mind. Indeed, Ballantine was astounded at the quality of Robert's diction.

But William was grave and he appeared to be upset. Aiken saw he would have to devote the meeting to helping him with his problems. He listened gravely to all William had to say.

"Aye: just so. Well, William, I don't think you could do better than agree to John Hamilton of Sundrum. Hamilton's a man o' good report. Charles Norvell recommends him? Aye. You see, MacLure's desperate. He's getting deeper in the bog every day. If I ken Hamilton, he'll no' rush his report."

"Do I understand the position rightly, sir, in thinking that delay here is definitely in my father's favour?"

"You do, Mr. Robert."

"But I'm against ony more delay, Mr. Aiken. I've tholed this injustice long enough. How much longer am I to be held on the rack?"

"I know, William . . . it's a sair business. But you canna rush a business like this. The onus is on MacLure: no' on you. You've got to sit tight and let him spend the money on litigation. Of course we'll need to put this business on a proper footing. If we accept Hamilton then we'll need to put a Decreet Arbitral, as we ca' it, afore the Sheriff and get everything laid out in due legal form: there must be no loopholes——"

"If it must be, then I suppose I must just bear with it. But injustice, Mr. Aiken, is hard to thole."

Both Aiken and Ballantine were sorry for William Burns: their sympathy went deep in so far as their emotions were involved.

They did not regard David MacLure as a scoundrel: they took him to be a hard-headed business man who was merely trying to get the best of a bargain.

Ballantine, who had a much clearer and sharper intelligence, was not, of course, directly interested in William Burns's dispute. But Aiken, if he had not been so easy-going and sympathetic in his philosophy, might have troubled to scrutinise MacLure's credentials. He might have discovered that, since MacLure had mortgaged his Tarbolton holdings to the trustees of the failed Douglas and Heron Bank, he was no longer entitled to claim rent for Lochlea; and had the affairs of the Douglas and Heron Bank not been in such a muddle, this fact might have been revealed sooner than it was.

But Aiken felt that he had expended so much sympathy on William Burns that he could be excused the expenditure of his more professional services.

It was William Burns who was to suffer: it was William Burns who was to know the hellish inconvenience of the law's delay; it was William Burns who was to be made the battle-field for men's greed and ignorance and selfish sympathy.

"Aye," said Aiken, "it's a maist unfortunate business. Have another drink of ale, Mr. Burns. Of course—you might be able to come to some arrangement wi' MacLure——"

"You mean me to admit he's in the right?"

"Well: an arrangement might be come to—a mutual arrangement."

"No, no, Mr. Aiken: I'll never agree to ony such arrangement: it's a bad thing to make pacts with the devil's agents. I've had to earn my money ower sair to part with it unjustly. So you want me to agree to robbing my own self—and my family. If that's your advice——"

Ballantine interposed.

"No, Mr. Burns: I think our good friend Aiken only had in mind the saving of your money in legal expense—and in long and maybe weary months of worry and anxiety."

"I'm sorry if I've spoken sharply——"

"No' another word, Mr. Burns: drink up; and then we'll step down to my chambers and I'll take some particulars from you. We'll soon settle this business for you—aye; and to your satisfaction, sir—to your satisfaction. You agree, Ballantine?"

"I can only express an opinion. But you couldna do better, Mr. Burns, than leave your affairs in the hands of our friend. The law sometimes appears slow and cumbersome—but the layman usually comes to ruin when he makes the attempt to act on his own behalf."

But William, though a trifle mollified by this talk, did not show much hope. He rose rather slowly and went out with Aiken, who assured Robert and Ballantine that he would be back shortly.

And when they were gone, Ballantine turned to Robert and said:

"We are on your side, Robert. Bob Aiken's an able man and he has a high regard for your father. . ."

"I can see that, Mr. Ballantine; and I'm grateful for it. But you can see how deeply my father is affected by this vexatious dispute. Maybe it's only those of us who are of the family know what this has cost us in worry and anxiety. It's not easy to see a parent wronged the way my father has been wronged and keep a judicious calm, Mr. Ballantine."

"Worthy sentiments—and nobly expressed, Mr. Robert. And yet, what would you have your father do? Would you have him injudicious *and* troubled?"

"But must justice await on this damned fal-de-ral of legal flummery? Or is it only poor men who have to wait on the majesty of the law?"

"The law tries to be impartial."

"Tries? Aye; but I doubt if it were ever known to rack itself in the trying. Honestly, Mr. Ballantine; what chance do you think we have in this devilish business?"

"Well . . . I'll confess that I have gone over the outlines of the case with Aiken; but it isn't easy to size up all the points . . ."

"Good God, sir—if you'll pardon me—there's precious few points about it. MacLure's trying to best my father—and trying to wring blood out of us in the process. If you'd seen Lochlea when we entered upon it and saw it to-day; if you had any knowledge of the sweat and blood that's gone to enriching its poor soil you might realise how we feel."

"I'm not altogether blind, Mr. Robert. But you see there's machinery set up to deal with all such matters and both sides must be heard fairly and in fact. Now, I think your case is fair enough—more than fair. But then, what we've got to do is to prove your case *in* law and *at* law. Otherwise we'd be taking the law into our own hands—and you know where that would lead to."

"Maybe you're right, Mr. Ballantine. But if the law can't be reasonable and give justice in reason, then folk must just have recourse to their own stratagems."

"That's the poet speaking now, Robert: not the practical man of affairs."

"Oh, my affairs are of little enough account and not worth troubling the law about. But how comes it, sir, that you refer to me as a poet since I cannot pretend that my poor fame has reached the town of Ayr."

"Indeed, that's just what it has done. Not, mind you, that I am acquainted with any of your verses, Robert; but I hope to have that pleasure very soon."

"My verses, sir, are small matters concerning the affairs of the parish of Tarbolton. And though I grant them the merit of their rusticity and their worth to be bandied round the ingle-neuk of an evening, I cannot pretend that they are fit for the ears of the world."

"Commendably modest, Robert; but you arouse my curiosity. Indeed, you speak with a strange elegance. May I ask where you got your education?"

"From my father; and from the schooling of one, John Murdoch, in my childhood years."

"John Murdoch of the Academy here?"

"You knew him?"

"Yes: I knew him. He went South to London, I believe."

"My father had an unusual respect for him. My brother Gilbert and I owe him a great debt."

"You know why he left the town?"

"John Murdoch was ambitious——"

"You never heard of his quarrel with Mr. Dalrymple?"

"The Reverend William—we were of his parish till we moved into Tarbolton. I was christened by him. How Murdoch could have quarrelled with so worthy a man I am at a loss to understand."

"Murdoch, I'm afraid, got infected with atheistical beliefs——"

"I find that hard to believe, sir."

"Not so hard, Robert: I believe he had been to France at one time. . . But, any the ways of it, he consorted with certain disaffected elements in the town here and they made a set against Mr. Dalrymple and voiced some wild and blasphemous opinions concerning the worthy doctor's character, of which the accusation that he was a damned hypocrite was, perhaps, the mildest."

"I cannot understand how Murdoch, whom I knew to be a man of the staunchest principle and the most upright character, ever came to make such statements."

"Men change. Many a pious youth grows up into a manhood of blasphemy and debauchery. You have the image of Murdoch as he was in his youth. Aye . . . men change. Even the Reverend William is not the man he once was——"

"Have you ocht against him?"

"Well . . . that's not how I would put it. But he has become worldly, more puffed-up with his own importance than befits a clergyman. Nowadays William Dalrymple is a very proud man, Robert. Men change; they change with changing fortune."

"But surely a man, true to himself and true to his principles, does not easily change? I do not think my father has changed."

"No. . . There are exceptions, I agree. But then your

father is an exceptional man, Robert; I think you will join me here?"

"Aye . . . exceptional; and we see to what pass he has been brought!"

"Come, Robert, another caup of ale against your home-going. Things will turn out for the better, have no fear. And when next you come to Ayr, maybe you will honour me with a copy of your verses—for I am certain that they will have a flavour as unique as your powers of conversation. I am not given to flattery; but I have never before had the pleasure of listening to such finely-tempered talk. Aye . . . and in a slovenly, ill-mannered, careless-jawed world, good talk is something to be respected."

John Ballantine may have been something of a prig; intellectually he was head and shoulders above any man in Ayr. And his regard for Robert Burns, honest and generous though it was, was to know no diminution in the years that lay ahead.

As for Robin, the experience of talking to such a man as Ballantine, of meeting him on level terms of friendship, was as rich as it was satisfying. He was resolved that he would make a fair copy of his best verses and send them to him without delay.

THE GATHERING NIGHT

Black clouds of trouble and tribulation banked against William Burns and his family. His health failed to the point where he could do little or no work in the fields. All his life he had laboured to make ends meet, to provide his family with a higher standard of living than he himself had known. There had been periods during winter when he had endured on a basis of semi-starvation. The food he had eaten had never been very good and he had never been a healthy or a hearty eater. Long ago, at Clochnahill, he had been trained to subsist on the barest minimum of food. He had been inured to frugality. Even when there had been seasons of tolerable plenty at Lochlea he had been unable to enjoy them. Gluttony was a terrible wickedness. . .

Now there was the gnawing cancer of worry. The fear that he might be brought to ruin and end his days in a debtors' gaol worried him day and night. He had been browbeaten by factor and landlord, yet he had walked with a steady foot along the perilous edge of the abyss of poverty.

He had cause to worry: more cause than most. No more than lawyer Aiken did he know the truth about MacLure. But he did know he was liable to be sold up by MacLure and thrown destitute in the ditch-side.

Between hard work and incessant worry his health broke down. His lungs gave way first; for some time now he had had the hard bark of the phthisical victim.

He knew what his trouble was; but he would admit it neither to his wife nor to his family. The knowledge that his trouble was fatal, that his end was much nearer, added to his worry. Worry indeed fed on worry till there were times when he was almost crazed.

His temper, always brittle, now snapped at the slightest

strain. On wet days he sat about the fireside fretting, fuming and chafing at his enforced idleness. Sometimes he would potter about the out-houses trying to fill in his weary hours with useful work. Sometimes he would drag himself on to the breast of the hill and survey the work being done by Robert and Gilbert.

Sometimes he seemed pathetic and withdrawn into an ancient melancholy; sometimes he seemed so utterly worn out and tired that he was without interest and awareness: dead in his mind and in his body.

At other times he was so short-tempered and querulous that Agnes found it very hard to live with him.

Though he knew his end was come, William was not prepared to turn his face to the wall until he had won justice for himself and his family in his fight with MacLure. The flame of his anger at the cruel injustice of the world could burn with a violent flame. His wrath could still be terrible. He did not give himself over to the thought of death: he knew death was inevitable. It was only when the flame of his anger had died down that he gave the appearance of accepting death; that he seemed to have resigned himself to melancholy.

Robert and Gilbert were distressed to see the plight of their father. They could not hide the fact that he was dying from themselves or each other. And they were as worried as he was about the outcome of the dispute with MacLure. They could see the possibility of his death leaving them all in ruin and poverty. They were determined to save something from the apparently inescapable ruin. Their individual destinies and the destiny of the family depended upon that. What they could do was by no means clear. William Burns, ill though he was, was still head of the family: he still dominated the household and could not be ignored.

And so the winter of 1782 and the spring of 1783 passed in worry and gloom and hard work. The brothers felt the loss of their father's labour both in the barn and the fields.

Robert was to remember it as perhaps the bitterest year of

his life. There had been long bitter years in Mount Oliphant; there had been the bitter memory of Irvine; but now there was more than bitterness: there was searing anger that society could harbour such injustice. . .

There had never been such a year of brutal labour. He was no longer a boy: he was a fully adult man; but just as when a boy he had done a man's work, so now as a man he did two men's work. His frame already set to the plough now stiffened in that position. His height was five feet ten inches but he stooped an inch below that. But if his shoulders stooped, his body was thick and muscular.

He had the appearance of being strong. But the spells of rheumatic fever he had had at Mount Oliphant, the attacks of pneumonia and pleurisy he had suffered at Lochlea and Irvine, had undermined his constitution: his stomach was weak and his heart was flawed. The twin passions of sex and poetry raged in his heart and mind. . . No man was less suited to labour the way he had to labour; but the sense of duty he had learned from his parents could not be denied. Neither the love of poetry nor of life could lure him from what he conceived to be the path of his duty.

There were times when he revolted, times when he saddled a pony and rode into Irvine to see Jean Gardner, have a word with Provost Hamilton or enjoy a literary half-hour with Willie Templeton.

His affair with Jean did not prosper. More and more she fell under the sway of doctrinal fanaticism. A religious maniac in the shape of comely and pleasant Elspeth Buchan had entered the town and converted Mr. White of the Relief Church. Elspeth was sexually unbalanced: certainly unorthodox. She believed that if she lay on men and breathed into them she could impart unto them the Holy Ghost. Her belief was unshakable; and she enjoyed her work. There were men, and women too, who enjoyed being lain on and breathed into by the good-looking sonsy woman.

And Elspeth Buchan could preach: she preached against

social injustice and advocated the community of collective labour and the communion of saints. The world was coming to its end. Why should they marry and give in marriage when the Lord was about to come again among them and gather them to eternity?

It was a creed promising immediate salvation and, by linking sex with salvation, proved irresistible to many good people in Irvine.

With Jean, Robin attended a meeting or two of Elspeth Buchan's; but he was not the man to be influenced by such sexual mysticism: nor could one whose passions were so healthy find any attraction in a display of sex sublimated into so religious an ecstasy.

There came a time when Jean preferred the embraces of Elspeth to his own—by which time Jean was completely un-balanced. He tried to save her from her folly, tried to break the hold of Elspeth; but his visits to her were much too infrequent to enable him to compete against the holy mother. It was a blow to him, for he loved Jean deeply.

When at last the town rose in revolt against Elspeth and she and her flock (with the converted Mr. White) were turned out, Jean went with her.

Numbers followed. . . They left everything behind them: food on the table, cows in the byre, a girdle of cakes on the fire. . . They went as the call had found them and followed their holy mother, and headed south; headed south towards the new world; south to salvation; to world without end and holy saint Elspeth; hallelujah!

Maybe he would have worried much more had his worries at home not been so great. But Robin never again went back to Irvine; and he put the memory of Jean Gardner out of his conscious mind.

Sometimes Robin shut himself up in the barn and played on his fiddle. There were moments when he enjoyed the playing: enjoyed the lilt of the old tunes in his mind.

There were times when he went to the Bachelors' Club in Tarbolton; when he visited Willie Muir at the Mill, and John Rankine at Adamhill. . .

The months, though they were bitter and filled with hard work, were not without their moments of relaxation; but they were moments only.

And if he managed to see Annie Rankine or Nancy Fleming, he had no time to conduct any serious courtship.

He joined in occasional parties about the district, parties of young folks visiting each others' houses for a night's song and music-making.

He seized on such legitimate opportunities for diversion in order to preserve his sanity, in order to sustain his belief that despite everything life was worth living.

In the spring he got an award of £3 for a sample of lint seed saved for sowing from the previous year. The money was welcome and the Government award proved that he was not without ability as a flax grower; but Irvine had cured him of any notion of developing this side of his husbandry.

Inside the farm-house of Lochlea there was a general atmosphere of anxiety and gloom. Agnes was having a hard time with her husband; Nancy and Bell were having a hard time with their mother. They all worked hard, and Willie, now a strong youth, worked well in the fields with Robin and Gilbert.

But John continued to droop and pine. The lad was far from well though no one could say what ailed him.

Perhaps the work fell hardest on Nancy and Bell. They devoted themselves without stint to the house and the farm work. Apart from their visits to Tarbolton Kirk, they denied themselves any opportunity for social intercourse. They even refused the advances of the young men of the parish since they could not afford the time for courting. Toil hardened them and gave an unbending cast to their humour. Like Gilbert they tended to become over-serious and over-grim. . .

Robin spent as little time as he could round the fireside at Lochlea. When work was slack or when the weather prevented work outside, he would spend his time in the barn reading. Nothing ever prevented him from reading. He was a born writer: he had ever to be reading what others had written; his desire for knowledge was insatiable: the craving to know was always gnawing at him. As he was a poet his wonder was aroused by every manifestation of life. He was a prisoner to the soil of Lochlea so he had to find some means of escape. This escape, when it could not be found in company, had to be found in books.

He knew periods of elation: he was often in the bog of melancholy. Sometimes he knew health and abounding vigour: often he was sickly and ill. Sometimes, in his bouts of melancholy, he was apt to feed on self pity. . .

In May, the blow fell. MacLure got his Writ of Sequestration against them.

On the 17th day of the month, James Gordon, the Sheriff's officer, came to Lochlea to make an inventory of all the crops and implements on the farm.

William Burns could not be kept in his bed. He insisted in getting up and giving this servant of the law such a verbal assault as he had never had in the course of his unpleasant duties. When William returned to his bed he was completely exhausted.

Robin was consumed with anger. Gordon had with him as witnesses one Robert Doak, a servant of MacLure, and Jock Lees, the Tarbolton shoemaker.

Once Robin had been friendly with Lees: he had often

acted as Robin's blackfoot, as the lad who had made appoint-
ments with the lassies for him. And now, here he was going
round the farm with Gordon, witnessing all that Gordon did!
True, Jock did not feel too happy about his job; but it was a
job, and he needed the money. Yes, here was man's inhumanity
to man in all its naked cruelty.

Robin cursed them heartily from the depths of his being. . .

In the evening when anger had quietened down to grief,
he read over to his father the contents of the document Gordon
had served on him.

It was hard to read that the officers were " to sequestrate
and secure the stock and crops in the barn and barnyard, etc.
for payment of the current year's rent when due, or at least
till sufficient caution is found therefore, and also the said crop
in the barn and barnyard for payment of the year's rent
whereof it is the growth, or that security be found therefore,
as the said Deliverance, signed by the said William Wallace,
Esquire, advocate, Sheriff Depute of Ayrshire, bears . . ."

It was harder to read what the stock and crop amounted
to, as set forth in the Warrant.

"I, the said Officer, passed to the grounds of the lands of
Lochlea . . . and then and there I lawfully sequestrated and
secured four horses, two mares, two ploughs and plough gear,
one wheat stack, one half stack of corn, and a little hay, all
standing in the barn yard, four stacks of bear in the barn,
about three bolls of bear lying on the barn floor, two stacks
of corn in the barn, two small bags of peas in the barn, thirteen
cows, two calfs, one ewe, two lambs, fourteen bundles of shafe
lint, seven bundles of mill tow in the mill, five carts with gear
belonging to them lying in the shed, three cart wheels lying
in the shed, two cart wheels standing in the close, with an
iron axtree, two old ploughs, three long bodied carts in the
shed, two harrows on the land beside the house, a large parcel
of wheat straw in thatch sheaves, a large parcel of bear straw
in battles all in the barn yard, and a large parcel of corn straw
in battles in the shed, all to remain under sure Sequestration

for payment of the current year's rent when due, or at least till sufficient caution is found therefore, before and in presence of these witnesses, Robert Doak, Servant to David MacLure of Shawood, and John Lees, Shoemaker in Tarbolton."

The whole family gathered round the fireside were in tears before Robin had reached the end of the heart-breaking documents.

All except William Burns. He lay in bed propped up on the pillows; and his thin worn features were hard set like a stone axe.

They all thought the end had come upon them and the lassies cried bitterly.

When Robin had finished William said: "We have four days to give answer to this mockery of justice. You will take the pony to-morrow, Robin, and go into Ayr and consult with Mr. Aiken. I'm not dead yet, thank God; and before I go to my Maker, MacLure will be burning in hell."

"I'll go first thing in the morning," said Robin. "Maybe Gilbert and I could do worse than go over to Adamhill and have a word with John Rankine."

"Aye: if you think that will help you any with Mr. Aiken. If only I could have a word with our good friend John Tennant in Glenconner; but Glenconner's too far away."

"It's a clear night. Gibby and I could manage."

"No . . . the word I would be needing is with Auld Glen himself."

So Robin with Gilbert escaped from the grief of the house.

"We'll need to do something, Robin," Gilbert repeated again and again.

John Rankine was deeply sympathetic.

"You'll need to make the best of things, lads. This is no time to stand on ceremony. Look out for a bit place on the quiet and get as much of your stuff there as you can without anybody knowing. They'll be putting the drummer through Tarbolton on you: that will mean that nobody'll be able to buy your stock. . . . What's that, Robin lad? Aye, they'll cry you through the town . . . aye, and at the kirk door. Just as well your father canna be there to hear it or it would be the finish of him. Mind you: I didna think MacLure would go this length; but now that he has you had better be prepared for the worst. . ."

Going home with Gilbert, Robin said:

"Well, what do you think, Gibby?"

"I don't see any road out, Robin."

"What about looking for another farm?"

"And where would we look?"

"I'll see what I can do when I'm in Ayr to-morrow. There must be something to be got."

Bob Aiken said he would prepare the answers to the petition and lodge them with the sheriff. If only Hamilton of Sundrum would hurry up with his report. . . As for John Rankine's idea. . . Well, there might be something in it.

"Do you know Gavin Hamilton in Machlin? You do? Well, the last time I was speaking to Gavin he was looking for a likely tenant for his farm at Mossgiel. You know Mossgiel? Well, I understand it's a good farm. Gavin intended to use it as a summer place. He put it under a grieve so that he could go up there whenever he took the notion. He has got tired of it: so if he could get anybody to take the place off his hands. . . Of course Gavin wants to keep quiet about it— but don't ask me why. He is a cautious lad, Gavin Hamilton; but one of the best, Robin, one of the best. . . Aye, do you want me to give you a letter of introduction to him? You ken he's a Brother . . .?"

"I have seen him in the Lodge."

"Well: introduce yourself, Robin. Tell him I was speaking to you about Mossgiel: though don't go and open your mouth to any other body about it until you see Gavin Hamilton. As for MacLure: I'll attend to him; and tell your father not to worry too much, though, between ourselves, Robin, I dinna like the look o' things."

Shortly on the heels of MacLure's warrant came John Hamilton of Sundrum. Hamilton was a bonnet laird of the superior kind. Sundrum House was finely situated on the banks of the Coyle, some five miles away. He had examined all the documents of the dispute as they had been given to him by Charles Norvell and James Grieve; he had examined them very carefully and drawn certain conclusions. Now he wanted to see Lochlea for himself . . . wanted to go over the ground in detail.

He didn't say much; but when he had finished he had a final word with William Burns and gave him to understand that his findings might not be unfavourable. More than that he would not say. As much as this he would not have said had he not seen how ill William Burns was.

It was no more than a small grain of comfort. But William saw that Sundrum was an honest man. He had faith in his judgment.

The sounding of the drum through Tarbolton was a deep affront to all at Lochlea. Robert and Gilbert felt it keenly.

Old James Hoggart was the town crier and he rattled his drum through the village streets and cried the proclamation at the four ends of the village as well as the cross roads in the middle. It was a juicy bit of scandal to the villagers and the enemies of Lochlea. Though there were few openly rejoiced at the news, Saunders Tait was in his element. He went home to his garret and commenced a poem on the subject, beginning:

> "He sent the drum Tarbolton through
> That no one was to buy from you."

Saunders was delighted that the end was drawing near for Burns in Lochlea.

But the crying at the kirk door was the most humiliating of all. After the service there were many folks who came up to Robin and Gilbert and expressed their regret. But only those who were intimate with the family really believed that William Burns was wholly in the right, that he had the money to pay his due rent but was refusing to pay a penny more. They felt that honest William Burns had gone down under the strain of evil days, that he had failed in the struggle to make both ends meet.

Robin knew this and his anger boiled anew. He was too proud to protest innocence. Once a dog was given a bad name the bad name stuck to it. Yet he walked through the village with his head held high—even though his brows were drawn and his eyes smouldered. His sisters, on the other hand, drew their shawls close to their faces and with bowed heads went quickly past the houses and down the brae and over the bridge at Willie's Mill.

There were people who, hoping to make a bargain, were prepared to buy from Lochlea despite the ban of the proclamation. They were annoyed when their offers were rejected with contempt.

They were cried through the parish in May. On the 21st of June Robin wrote to his cousin in Montrose, James Burness (that was how they spelt their name in the North). James had written on behalf of his father to inquire after the health of his brother in Ayrshire. It gave Robin much satisfaction to reply since it gave him an opportunity to say much that was in his mind.

He read the letter over to Gilbert.

LOCHLEA,
21st *June*, 1783.

DEAR SIR,
My father received your favour of the 10th curt. and as he has been for some months very poorly in health, and is in his own opinion, and indeed in almost everybody else's, in a dying condition; he has only, with great difficulty, wrote a few farewell lines to each of his brothers-in-law; for this melancholy reason, I now hold the pen for

him to thank you for your kind letter, and to assure you, sir, that it shall not be my fault if my father's correspondence in the North die with him.

I shall only trouble you with a few particulars relative to the present wretched state of this country. Our markets are exceedingly high; oatmeal, eighteenpence per peck, and not to be got even at that price. We have indeed been pretty well supplied with quantities of white peas from England and elsewhere, but that resource is likely to fail us; and what will become of us then, particularly the very poorest sort, Heaven only knows.

This country, till of late, was flourishing incredibly in the manufactures of silk, lawn and carpet weaving, and we are still carrying a good deal in that way but much reduced from what it was. We had also a fine trade in the shoe way, but now entirely ruined, and hundreds driven to a starving condition on account of it.

Farming is also at a very low ebb with us. Our lands, generally speaking, are mountainous and barren; and our landholders, full of ideas of farming gathered from the English and the Lothians and other rich soils in Scotland, make no allowance for the odds of the quality of land and consequently stretch us much beyond what, in the event, we will be found able to pay.

We are also much at a loss for want of proper methods in our improvement of farming: necessity compels us to leave our old schemes; and few of us have opportunities of being well informed in new ones. In short, my dear sir, since the unfortunate beginning of this American war, and its as unfortunate conclusion, this country has been, and still is decaying very fast.

Even in higher life, a couple of our Ayrshire noblemen, and the major part of our knights and squires, are all insolvent. A miserable job of a Douglas, Heron & Company's Bank, which no doubt you have heard of, has undone numbers of them; and imitating English, and French, and other foreign luxuries and fopperies, has ruined as many more.

There is a great trade of smuggling carried on along our coasts, which, however destructive to the interests of the kingdom at large, certainly enriches this corner of it; but too often indeed at the expense of our morals; however, it enables individuals to make, at least for a time, a splendid appearance; but Fortune, as is usual with her when she is uncommonly lavish of her favours, is generally even with them at the last; and happy were it for numbers of them if she would leave them no worse than when she found them.

My mother sends you a small present of a cheese: 'tis but a very little one, as our last year's stock is sold off; but if you could fix on any correspondent in Edinburgh, or Glasgow, we would send you a proper one in the season. Mrs. Black promises to take the cheese under her care so far, and then to send it to you by the Stirling carrier.

I shall conclude this long letter with assuring you that I shall be very happy to hear from you or any of our friends in your country when opportunity serves.

My father sends you, probably for the last time in this world, his warmest wishes for your welfare and happiness; and mother and the rest of the family desire to enclose their kind compliments to you, Mrs. Burness, and the rest of your family, along with those, dear Sir, of

Your affectionate cousin,

"It's a good letter," said Gilbert; "and it gives a good account of the conditions of the country. Maybe things are not so good in the North either."

"Aye, we are all going to ruin . . . the whole damned country. If folks don't get this harvest gathered we'll all be finished. . . ."

THE MACHLIN DOCTOR

As their father's health did not mend, and as he began to have hæmorrhages, the need to have the opinion of a doctor could no longer be denied.

Robert rode into Machlin and left a message for Dr. John MacKenzie.

When MacKenzie called at Lochlea he found William Burns ill, but not so ill that he was prevented from telling him of his troubles.

MacKenzie was a young doctor—he was but a few years older than Robin—and he was sympathetic. Moreover, he was not very sure of himself. He could see that William Burns had a consumption of the lungs; but it was unusual to find a man over sixty so far gone. All the evidence pointed to the fact that William Burns should have been dead and in his grave long ago. What MacKenzie had to decide was how long his patient had to live: he knew there was little he could do for him.

MacKenzie looked round the kitchen. It was clean, tidy and comfortable. But for all that it was a poor room, telling of a hard bare poverty.

William had a grim tale to tell. But the tale, thought MacKenzie, was not nearly so remarkable as the man who told it. Here, surely, was a man of outstanding character and remarkable knowledge. . .

And as MacKenzie sat and listened, he found his gaze wandering to the young man who sat in the far corner of the room looking at him with dour burning eyes.

The conversation of the father and the eyes of the son gave him the feeling that he was up against something strange and somehow frightening. . .

After he had finished with William, MacKenzie asked Robin to step outside with him.

They went out through the close and turned up on to the hill above and to the rear of the house.

"You know your father's very ill, Mr. Burns?"

"I don't need a doctor to tell me that."

"No: of course you don't. But do you know that your father's dying?"

"Yes: I know."

"I see. . . Perhaps you know that there is very little I can do for him?"

"As God has given him up, I don't see that you can be held responsible for what you can't do."

"Naturally you are upset by your father's illness, Mr. Burns; but, at a time like this, I assure you that we are in God's hands and that though man may fail, He will not fail us."

"I hope you're right, sir: I am no theologian. I am but the poor son of a poor tenant father. I have long faced the fact that my father was dying; and I know that he would be better dead. Yes: I respect my father more than any man on earth; aye, or in heaven or hell. You heard what he said; and if he lives it may well be that he will die in a debtors' gaol."

"You may be the poor son of a poor farmer, Mr. Burns; but your speech knows no poverty; nor does your father's speech either. . . I am sorry, Mr. Burns, that there is little I can do, but I can and will, if you want me to, see that he has some ease and comfort in his last hours . . . yet how soon that may be is not in our hands. . . May I ask, Mr. Burns, how old you are?"

"I'm in my twenty-fifth year."

"I would have thought you older. I'm just coming thirty myself. And your brother Gilbert?"

"He is a year younger."

"I see. . . You have a big responsibility to face then when

the time comes. And I suppose if this wretched business with MacLure—— But I have no right to interfere with your private affairs. . ."

"Thank you, Doctor MacKenzie; but you have no need to respect a privacy that no longer exists. When you have been drummed through the parish and cried at the kirk door—and for a crime of which you are innocent—then you get used to the idea that you have no right to privacy. Damnit, sir, do you wonder that we are no longer fit company for ordinary folks, that we are apt to snarl like curs . . .? Forgive me, sir, for my rudeness to you. We should be grateful that you have come here to do what you can for my father. . . Here's Gilbert coming round the end of the house: I think it would be better if you had a word with him: he is not given to the storms of indignation that I am."

"Yes: I would like to have a word with your brother; and if there is anything I can do for you, for your family, I will do what I can."

"Thank you, sir: you are more than liberal in your sentiments. I wonder if you know Mr. Gavin Hamilton in Machlin —I mean, know him well?"

"Yes: Mr. Hamilton is a good friend of mine. Could I give him any message?"

"No: not at the moment. . . You do believe what my father told you about MacLure and the sequestration. . . I wouldn't like Mr. Hamilton to get the wrong impression of us."

"I see what you mean, Mr. Burns. I'll make a point of telling Mr. Hamilton how matters stand. And if there is any advice you want I can heartily recommend him to you. Mr. Hamilton is not called the poor man's friend for nothing. . ."

They parted on good terms. And MacKenzie was as good as his word for he made a point of telling Gavin Hamilton about the plight of the family in Lochlea.

THE POOR MAN'S FRIEND

Hamilton was a few years older than MacKenzie. He was in his thirty-third year, married and the father of a small family. He was a pleasant fellow, lazy, easy-going, good-natured—and with little respect for the Old Light theology of the kirk in Machlin or the authority of its pastor, the Reverend William Auld.

But though kindly and benevolent, Gavin Hamilton was also something of a social and intellectual snob. Gavin considered he was no small beer in Machlin.

MacKenzie, though he was drawn to Hamilton because they were both young and of professional standing, was more sincere in his sentiments though he was neither so glib nor so blunt with his tongue. And they were both of the new liberal trend in religion: vigorous New Light protagonists.

"Well, Gavin," said MacKenzie, "this young man seems to value your good opinion.

"Aye . . . so I believe, John. Bob Aiken was speaking to me about him the last time I was in Ayr. I might get rid of Mossgiel to him."

"He never mentioned anything of that to me, but maybe it was in the back of his mind. He is certainly a most remarkable lad. I may be mistaken, Gavin, but if that young man doesn't make some mark in the world I'll be surprised."

"I hear from Aiken that he writes poetry?"

"I wouldna be surprised. Poetry, eh? Now, that's just what he would write."

"Aiken read me some verses about a pet yowe o' his . . . I must say they were out of the common."

"We must get him down here some night for a crack. I'm much taken with him . . . and his brother."

"It's a pity they fell foul of MacLure."

"I believe that has more to do with the old man's illness than anything else."

"Well, we'll see. If the sons want Mossgiel I suppose they'll come when they are ready and not before. Keep your ears open, John, and let me know what you hear."

THE BONNIE MOORHEN

Work became heavier at Lochlea. The strain of nursing
William Burns began to tell on Agnes and Nancy and Bell.
Help had to be got. So they hired Elizabeth Paton from the
nearby farm of Largieside.

Betty proved a godsend. She was a good worker and a
cheery smiling lass. She soon became a general favourite with
the family.

Betty was no great beauty. But she had reached her twenty-
first birthday and what she lacked in beauty of facial feature
she more than made up in the perfection of her figure. Robin
was certain he had never known such a perfect figure in any
woman.

At first she was just a well-shaped, good-natured lass,
pleasant to look at and pleasant to work with. And then the
blood began to surge in Robin and he felt the longing to make
love to her. He wanted to sit and talk to her—discover her
inmost thoughts, plumb the depths of her emotional responses
—become familiar with all the strange facets of her personality, physical and spiritual.

It was easy for Robin to fall in love. It was as necessary
for him to love as to breathe. When he was not in love he was
unhappy and ill at ease. But he was not in love with Betty
as he had been in love with Jean Gardner—or Jean Glover.
His love for Betty was much the same as his love for Annie
Rankine or Nancy Fleming or certain of the Tarbolton lassies.

But it was a new love; and because it was new it was
unlike anything he had ever known.

There were times when he thought that his first night with
Jean Glover was the finest night he had ever spent with a
woman. But he had experienced a range and intensity of

emotion with Jean Gardner that added something to his experience with Jean Glover. But had any night with either compared with that night with Annie in the corn rig bawk? Or that night along the banks of the Fail Water with Nancy Fleming?

And what had those nights and those experiences done to him? They belonged to the past. But they had enriched his heart and his mind; given a greater depth to his already deep emotional range. They had given him a knowledge of life at its most revealing source—in the moments of its most vital fusing.

Yet his need for the society of men was no less clamant than his need for the society of women. There were times when he would have left all the women in the world to have enjoyed the company of men like John Rankine and Willie Muir; lads of his own age like Davie Sillar or Willie MacGavin—lads who filled the places of James MacCandlish, Thomas Orr and William Niven. Perhaps his social instincts were more highly developed than most. The fact was he needed the company of human beings: needed it as much as he needed food and drink, fresh air and sleep.

So it was natural for him to fall in love with Betty Paton; and it was natural that Betty should respond. She was young and healthy and in need of a lover. But a lover like Robert Burns. . . She was ready to be his lover for an hour or for eternity.

Before long they were exchanging lovers' glances. These were secret. Robin was careful to say nothing at the table. He knew that none of his family would understand or approve of any affection being shown between him and the serving lass. Certainly, his sisters, Nancy and Bell, would object. They were both proud of him and, for sisters, they loved him very deeply; and though there was no snobbery in them they considered themselves a cut or two above Betty. Betty had no formal education: she was a peasant with all the peasant's formal illiteracy. She could not write her name and she could

read only with the greatest difficulty. Her tongue was plain
and her dialect broad and strange. She had none of the refine-
ments that came from William Burns's schooling. But she
might well have been the natural daughter of Agnes Broun.
Mrs. Burns did not find her coarse: she warmed to Betty's
easygoing natural manners.

One day in the harvest field Betty was binding to Robin,
as Nelly Kilpatrick had done years before on Mount Oliphant.
It was a hot day. Robin paused for a moment in his labour and
turned round to see how his partner was getting on. The sun
was declining. Betty was working against the light.

She was thinly clad: she wore no more than a thin smock.
It was diaphanous against the sunlight.

Betty saw his look and her flesh quivered. She turned and
bent down to pick up her rope of twisted straws. Her smock,
in stooping, was half-way up her thigh. . .

Robin surveyed the field. They were far behind the others
and the bawk was close at hand. They could slip down into
its green shade unnoticed.

"It's warm, Betty: there is no good in killing ourselves.
We'll rest in the shade of the bawk here. . ."

Betty was tired. They had worked hard all day: they were
due a rest . . . and this was the first day she had been Robin's
mate. They might not be mates again.

She followed him down into the green bawk. Robin took
her in his arms.

"God, lass, but you make a sweet armful!"

"You think so, Robin?"

"Aye . . . and a lot more."

Her flesh was cool and damp with sweat. She quivered at
the caress of his toil-calloused hand: she flung her arms round
his neck and took him to her in a tight embrace. . .

Suddenly he tore himself free and sat bolt upright.

"God damn it!" he cried: "I might have known. Watch
yourself, Bess."

Along the edge of the bawk, hirpling with the aid of a stick, came the bent figure of William Burns.

"It's my father. Get in behind that thorn bush and hide. I'll go up and face him."

He could not be certain William had seen them, and he could not mend the guilt-conscious look he knew must show on his face.

William Burns looked curiously at his son.

"Aye . . . you've been working . . ."

"How do you feel the day? Do you think you should be up?"

"For all my time, Robin. . . Oh, I have felt worse. With the help of God I might get better yet. I just thought I would take a turn out to see what the rigs were looking like. Who's binding to you? The Paton lass?"

"Aye . . . she's down the bawk somewhere. . . I was just taking a minute myself: we've been working hard all day."

He found difficulty in looking his father straight in the face. He looked fragile and death-like in his pallor. Yet his eyes burned fiercely in their deep sunken sockets. The skin of his hands was curiously white and the veins were knotted in purple skeins. More like a claw, the hand trembled as it clutched the stick.

He said no more. But before he hirpled away he gave his son one of his peculiar looks. He had always had a peculiar way of looking with reproach—a look that was more terrible than any words could have been.

But Robin felt that this look came from the other side of the grave. It carried reproach; but there was pity and sadness behind the accusation.

Robin lowered his eyes and he felt the blood surge over his face and burn the tips of his ears.

Only when his father had gone some distance did he let his eyes follow him. He watched the bent figure and noted the long twisted shadow the sun cast from him across the yellow grain. That shadow had lain across his life. He thought of Nelly Kilpatrick and a harvest day at Mount Oliphant and how the shadow of his father had lain across that field.

He turned to the edge of the bawk and whistled on Betty. His father was bound to have seen them—or to have known they were down there together. . .

Well, what of it? He tossed his head as if to shake from his vision the sight of those burning accusing eyes.

Betty was apprehensive. She was anxious to know if William Burns had seen them.

"To hell!" cried Robin, " let's get on with the work. But if you're asked, I suppose you'll have the sense to deny that you were down there with me? We'll need to watch our step after this."

"Aye . . . I suppose we'll have to. Do you no' think your father's ower ill to be out . . .? You're no' angry wi' me, Robin . . .?"

"With you? No, I'm not angry with you, Betty. But I never seem to have any luck . . . and I have never been lucky where my father was concerned. . . Could you no' make an excuse to run over to Largieside the night?"

"I believe I could."

"Well . . . I could wait for you behind the second knowe."

And so Betty Paton came to fill the want in Robin's life. William did not say anything, but he watched them with a critical eye, and sometimes Robin found him looking in that sad accusing way that was so disquieting and so demoralising. . .

But he continued to watch his moves with Betty so that, for long enough, not even Gilbert had any inkling of the relationship between them.

"That's the position as Gibby and me see it, Nancy. I've had talks with Mr. Aiken and Mr. Ballantine in Ayr—Ballantine's taken a fancy to some o' my verses—and if things come to the worst we can aey enter a claim against William Burns."

"We canna do that. Oh, that would be an unheard of thing to do, Robin."

"No, no; the claim would mean that MacLure wouldn't be able to touch our wages. In the learned jargon o' the law we would become preferred creditors."

They were sitting in the byre talking over their problems. Gilbert was waiting his opportunity to bring in Bell, for they didn't want any one to think they were holding a meeting and their father lying so ill across the courtyard.

Soon Bell came skipping in from the rain with Gilbert close at her heels.

The sisters were worried, worn thin with work and worry. Unlike their brothers, they could see no way of escaping the threatening doom.

Robin and Gilbert may have had cause to feel they were overwrought and overburdened with responsibility. But their lives were varied and colourful compared to the confined existence of Nancy and Bell. They got no relaxation from their round of steading work and the nursing of their father. Their walk to and from the kirk at Tarbolton on a Sunday was all the variety and change of scene they ever got.

Nor had they much time or opportunity for speculation since nothing could be discussed in William's hearing. They could only worry as helpless women caught in a mesh of the world's weaving, the world of men and their strange inexplicable ways.

They were the drudges of Lochlea—patient, painstaking,

conscientious drudges doing all the dirty drudgery and the grinding darg of the domestic round.

So they knew instinctively that something extraordinary was afoot or they would never have been consulted.

"You know Mossgiel where the Tarbolton road joins the Kilmarnock road just above Machlin? Aye, well the Mossgiel nearest Machlin: there's three Mossgiels really. But Mossgiel's a tidy bit farm, and though it's smaller than Lochlea every acre of it could be put to good use. If we could get it at onything like a fair rent I think we should take it."

"But we canna do onything while he's lying there."

"We'll need to, Bell. There's no other way unless you're prepared to bed in the ditch. If we get rouped out o' here without a stick where d'you think we'll go?"

"Robin's speaking the God's truth," said Gilbert. "It would mean the splitting up o' the family—and service for every one o' us."

"But you ken he'll never agree to a plan like that, Gibby. He'll never agree: he still thinks he can beat MacLure."

"We'll beat MacLure and he'll never know. We must act quickly. Get a place, get it stocked as well as we can, how we can—and then jump when we see the blow falling. On the other hand, he canna be expected to last out the year. In that case, we move right away. And with our claim in for all our wages, we'll salvage something and MacLure can whistle for the balance."

"I'll agree to onything," said Nancy in desperation. "As long as we get oot o' this place, Robin, I carena what happens. Bell and me are about finished."

"Aye, we canna go on like this: it's a living death. Mither's worn to a shadow."

"We know, Bell. Gibby and me havena been idle."

"We should be grateful to Robin," said Gibby. "Robin's thought this out from every angle and talked it over wi' good friends in Ayr. I think it'll be our salvation."

"There's one thing: if we get Mossgiel we go into it

together—as a partnership. We'll sink everything into it and draw out a fair share. You lassies have your future to look to and you canna work for nothing. I'll be head o' the house then; but that's the only fair way I can see to make a success o' the venture. If you agree then my mither and the young ones will come in on a fair divide too. It's thè best we can do, lassies—though mind, we havena got Mossgiel yet."

"Oh, we agree, Robin; we agree. How d'you set about seeing if you can get Mossgiel?"

"I'll see Gavin Hamilton in Machlin. He's got the place leased from the Earl o' Loudon: now he's looking for a sub-let. Gavin Hamilton's an honest man: I see no reason to doubt we wouldna make an honest bargain with him. Only: not as much as a breath o' this to a living soul. That would ruin our project entirely."

"We'll leave it to you and Gibby: whatever you arrange we'll agree to. And I'll pray to the Lord every night that you may succeed, Robin."

When their sisters had gone, Robin said: "Damn it, Gibby, it's no' fair to the lassies. The place is killing them. They should be happy and fresh and singing—aye, and having lads to take them out or court them in the barn. They should be thinking about getting married."

"Have sense, man. How can they think of marriage at a time like this?"

"But this has gone on far too long. They've lost the bloom of youth and they've lost the light heart that goes wi' youth. They should be married. But the damned thing is they're not in a position to bring ony kind o' a dowry to a decent man— and they canna be expected to marry ony damned lout that takes a notion o' them."

"For God's sake, Robin, let us solve one problem at a time. Marriage isn't everything."

"Now that's where you're wrong, Gibby. Marriage means everything to a woman. Think what's to become o' them in later years—when they've lost every possible attraction to a decent man. There's no decent man in his right senses wants a withered and soured old maid. I tell you, if a lass doesna get married while the bloom's on her, she stands a damned poor chance when the bloom's off her."

"The bloom damn soon goes off them once they are married. There's no disgrace in being single."

"All right, Gibby. You're so cautious and prudent you'll never make a hasty marriage."

"I could have been married—if I'd liked. Aye: if I'd liked to leave you all in the lurch. Maybe I'm too strait-laced in my moral principles, as you're always suggesting, Robin. But they happen to be my principles and that's all that's about it."

"I'm sorry, Gibby: pay no attention to me. I suppose I blether whiles more than I should. Well . . . I suppose I'd better arrange to see Gavin Hamilton right away?"

"Right away, Robin. And mind that we're all behind you —every one of us."

Robin liked the look of Gavin Hamilton. He had a cool eye and a firm mouth. The tone of his voice was crisp and manly and it did not lack in authority. If he was a gentleman he was polite and kindly; and he had a fine sense of humour.

"I see no reason why you shouldn't have Mossgiel. True, we'll need to keep the matter dark until the dispute between MacLure and your father is settled. We dinna want the name of anything in the way of sharp practice. But you have every legal right to take Mossgiel. You are not your father, Mr. Burns—you are free to do what you like. And, of course, get the entire family entered against your father's estate as preferred creditors—since the family will be moving with you, they will need all the money they can lay their hands on. Yes . . . and if there are any bits of plenishing gear at Lochlea you think would help you in Mossgiel—well, you can be the judge of that. . . How would £90 do by way of rent for Mossgiel? Of course, you'll want to talk the matter over with your brother, since he'll be your partner. There's some good gear about Mossgiel: if you'd care to make a reasonable offer. . .

"You'll have a drink, Mr. Burns? This is the best Kilbagie: they can say what they like about Ferintosh: give me Kilbagie. Well: your best health and happiness; and may you find me as good a laird as I hope to find you a tenant. . ."

"So! and I hear you are something of a poet, Mr. Burns. I had the pleasure once of hearing Mr. Aiken in Ayr read some verses of yours: I was struck by them."

"I confess to having written verses **on occasions**, Mr. Hamilton. Maybe you feel that scribbling verses and farming don't go together?"

"No: I wouldn't say that."

"If once I was settled into Mossgiel, I'll write no more verses. I've had enough of poverty. . ."

"Commendable enough, Mr. Burns. It's a healthy instinct to have a fear of poverty. But I wouldn't make any promises about not writing poetry. I think you'll do well in Mossgiel; and once you get settled in you never know: you'll maybe write better poetry than ever you did. . . Are you acquaint with Mr. Auld who herds the faithful flock in Machlin?"

"I know of him."

"You'll get to know him better since you'll be sitting under him at Mossgiel. Mr. Auld is very stern on orthodoxy: a very stern man and a stickler for the letter of Kirk Law. I'm afraid I don't always see eye to eye with Daddy Auld. . . I take it you are not of the Auld Licht persuasion?"

"No: I am not of the Auld Licht party. I hope I take a common sense view of religion. . . I've heard Auld preach; and I don't think him a man of indifferent merit."

"So you have heard Daddy Auld?"

"Yes: a friend of mine near Tarbolton—Sillar of Spittle-side—perhaps you know his father?—we were wont to go abroad of a Sabbath to sample the preachers——"

"You didna go to hear the fornicators getting their catechism?"

"No . . . though I have heard many a tale from the stool of repentance."

"Oh, everybody likes to visit a kirk that has a good scandal for public rebuke. Maybe you have a taste for theology, Mr. Burns? Do you think we have some good herds in Ayrshire?"

"My first minister was William Dalrymple of Ayr; then Doctor Woodrow of Tarbolton—John MacMath, his assistant, is a good man—so is MacGill in Ayr. But there are few I haven't heard. John Russell——"

"Black Jock of Kilmarnock? Russell can thunder to some tune!"

"Moodie of Riccarton; Robert Duncan of Dundonald; William Peebles of the New Town; MacQuhae of St. Quivox;

Andrew Shaw of Craigie and David Shaw of Coylton. . .
There's other names escape me for the moment. But I think
it is best to hear as many as you can . . . and it helps to put
in the Sabbath'"

"Aye . . . well, that's one way of doing it. I'm afraid
they think me something of a back-slider; and maybe I am.
I don't mind Auld so much; but I just canna abide the Session.
You know that wee runt Willie Fisher? He goes about the
town snooking and prying on everybody. . . No: I'm afraid
Mr. Burns, I don't hold with the strict tenets of orthodoxy.
I like a man to have some freedom."

"I can join you there, Mr. Hamilton. I never had any time
for bigotry; and the more I see of the world the less I have
for it. Like you, I have a soft side to the man of independent
mind."

"Well spoken; well spoken indeed. I will need to arrange
some night so that we can have a crack with Doctor Mac-
Kenzie. By the way, Mr. Burns: when did you first come to
Lochlea?"

"Seventy-seven: about eight years ago come May."

"You're hardly an incomer either, Mr. Burns. And when
did your father's trouble with MacLure begin?"

"Three or four years ago: it's been dragging on for a long
time."

"Too long. And you're waiting now on John Hamilton of
Sundrum's report? Sundrum's an honest man: I dinna think
you'll have much to fear there."

"I hope you're right, sir. If folk would only realise what
this hanging on means to all of us—especially my father who
has lain at death's door this time back. . ."

"Aye . . . you must have had a wearing time. But
patience, Mr. Burns: the mills of God grind slowly."

"If I could be sure they were grinding——"

"Oh, they're grinding right enough: have no fear of that,
Mr. Burns. That's one of the things we can be sure about. I
believe everything works out for justice in the end. It may take

a time and a lot of patience may be needed; but sooner or later, Mr. Burns, justice is done and evil is punished."

"Even if justice came to-night it would be too late to bring consolation to my father."

"You don't know that, Mr. Burns: you canna know that. But I'm sure your father will die happy. And that's a greater thing than you know—or any of us know. An unhappy death-bed is a sobering, aye, a terrifying spectacle. I have witnessed many a sore death in my profession. Seen men struggling to settle their affairs in this world—and the pit o' hell lowing at their side. No: Mr. Burns, I wouldna despair: the wicked only seem to flourish like the green bay tree. And the discipline o' the kirk canna prevent Auld Nick from girning at you across the hob o' hell."

"You don't seriously maintain that there is a hell—in that literal sense, Mr. Hamilton?"

"No: not in the literal sense. But it's real enough to those who believe in it: verra real indeed. That's what troubles the Kirk Session in Machlin: they canna put the fear o' hell into me. Oh, they've threatened me with a' the flames and torments of the infernal regions. And what think you, Mr. Burns, is my crime? That I dug a few tatties on the Lord's day. Aye: Willie Fisher—Holy Willie as we know him here—saw my servant howking in the drill—and that was enough. Aye: they wanted me to compear on the matter. Then one charge borrowed another. I defied Daddy Auld to his face—and mind you, it's a strong face—so Auld has taken the case before the Presbytery in Ayr. Oh, they mean to have revenge, does the Machlin Session. However, I'm thinking I'll get Bob Aiken to defend me before the Presbytery: that'll make them sit up, Mr. Burns. Once Aiken gets wound up, believe me he makes a bonnie fechter. . .

"So you see, Mr. Burns, we all have our troubles. . . But if you decide to take Mossgiel I think you'll find Machlin interesting enough. Mind you, I'd rather bide here nor in Ayr, aye, or Kilmarnock."

"Yes, I must confess, Mr. Hamilton, that I've always had a hankering after Machlin. Of course, when we came here first and Tarbolton was our parish town, we though it a grand place; and I'll not dispute that I've had many a happy night in Tarbolton. But—I'm looking forward to Machlin, sir. It's handy to Mossgiel——"

"Yes, handy and convenient. And it can be a busy place with the north and south traffic gaun through it. And a good market, the best o' shops and merchants—and good howffs—the verra best, Mr. Burns. I'm sure that once your troubles blow by you'll be comfortably situated in Mossgiel."

"I can only pray we will be, sir, for we've had a long sore fight against superior odds. The dice, I'm afraid, have been loaded against us."

"Ach, you canna have bad luck all the time, Mr. Burns: your fortunes are sure to change. Just take your ease for a minute, Mr. Burns, and I'll look out an inventory I had made of Mossgiel: it'll maybe help you to make up your mind. Here, give me your glass till I top it up for you."

When Hamilton was gone Robin surveyed the room. It was a fine room in a fine house, even if it was adjacent to the kirkyard. Indeed, he reckoned it was the finest room he had ever been in.

The oaken furniture was heavy and expensive. There was a carpet on the floor and heavy curtains draped the bare stone walls. The whisky was contained in a fine stone jar, and it was drunk from glasses and not from wooden cups. Hamilton himself was elegantly put on. He sported a fine blue coat of English cloth, and his breeches were of the finest blue plush. His hair was powdered and tied in a blue silk bow. His silk cravat was cunningly knotted and a gold pin was thrust through it. A heavy gold ring with a curious seal adorned the third finger of his left hand.

Robin was conscious of the poor figure he cut. His hoddin grey coat and breeches—woven by his sisters; his thick-ribbed, coarsely knitted stockings and rough brogans felt altogether out of place in this elegant room. . .

And yet it was good to feel that this splendid fellow Gavin Hamilton did not judge a man by his clothes but was content to accept a man for the quality of his mind and spirit. It would be a fine thing to take Mossgiel even if it were only to have such a landlord.

Hamilton called him into the outer room that gave access to the Backcauseway, and introduced him to a young fellow who occupied a desk there.

"John Richmond, my clerk, Mr. Burns. You can leave a message with him any time you call and find me away from home. See that Mr. Burns is attended to, John, *whenever* he calls."

Robin smiled to the clerk. He thought it must be grand to work to such a gentleman as Gavin Hamilton.

"Here's the inventory, Mr. Burns. I hope you have good news soon. Let me have your decision about Mossgiel when you're ready: I'll be happy to see you any time—and your brother."

They shook hands warmly for there was warmth between them.

SUNDRUM'S DECISION

Bob Aiken, fat and physically lazy though he was, rode up from Ayr with the good news. John Hamilton of Sundrum had lodged his report with Sheriff William Wallace—and the report was in favour of William Burns.

Aiken sat in the elbow chair between the bed and the ingle and purred like a great cat.

"Wonderful, Mr. Burns, wonderful. Ah, but I never doubted the outcome for a minute. Aye, it's been a long time waiting. But worth the waiting, Mr. Burns, worth the waiting, sir. What's that, Mr. Burns? Oh, the money, yes. Weel, I wad hae spared you the fatigue o' listening to what is, after all, a lengthy and legal document; so I've prepared an abstract of the financial side o' the report and you'll see how it works out.

"First of all you're allowed five shillings in the pound for eight years' rent: that comes to the nice figure of £210 1s. 6d.; for liming you're allowed £86 13s. 4d.; for erecting dykes £18 10s. od.; for building houses £70 18s. 6d.; for grass seed £10; for coals for burning your limestone £36 6s. od. and then for sums paid in rent £111 8s. od.; making a total, sir, of £543 17s. 4d.

"That's a comfort, isn't it? And now for the contra. MacLure is allowed rent from November, 1776, till May, 1782, and this amounts to £715; for working thirty acres of limed land above half of the farm in the first year, £60, which makes a total of £775.

"Now, if you take the one from the other it means, Mr. Burns, that all you legally owe MacLure is just a matter of £231 2s. 8d.—about one third o' what he was claiming."

"God be praised!" sighed William Burns. "I knew He

would never allow me to be unjustly dealt with." He sank back on his pillow, nervously and physically exhausted.

Agnes rose from her seat where she had sat with folded hands on her lap and went over to the bed-side and mopped the sweat from his brow with a piece of cloth.

"Maybe you'll rest now, William. I dinna understand what it's a' aboot—but if you're content that's a' that matters."

William closed his eyes. "Thank ye, Agnes woman: my prayers have been answered. . ."

Agnes turned to Aiken. "Ye'll tak' a drink o' milk and a bannock, Mr. Aiken—and maybe a bit o' yowe cheese?"

"I will, Mrs. Burns, I will; and I thank you for your kindness. Now, Robert: what d'you think o' the settlement?"

Robin looked at Gilbert for a moment and saw that he approved.

"We are in your debt, Mr. Aitken, a debt we can never repay. Justice has been a long time in coming, but it has come; and we canna but be grateful."

"I understand how you feel. Aye, I understand full well. MacLure will be feeling a gey wee man in Ayr the day. But I think, with your permission, I'll convey in writing to John Hamilton your thanks in the matter. Sundrum's been a just man and done a thorough job o' work. Mind you: I never thought you would get such a grand decision. MacLure's been little less than a scoundrel in this business: nothing less than a thorough-paced scoundrel. . . Weel, I've business to talk over wi' Gavin Hamilton afore I get back to Ayr."

"You'll tell Mr. Hamilton how we've been upheld by the sheriff——"

"Certainly, Robert. Gavin will be glad to hear how you've come out. But then Gavin never did have much o' an opinion o' David MacLure. A shrewd man Gavin."

Gilbert said: "We canna be sequestrated now, Mr. Aiken?"

"Your father's been cleared entirely, Gilbert. Vindicated in the maist forthright way a man can be vindicated—vindicated at law. Once a thing's legal naebody can dispute it. As

I said to Robin there mony a time when he was getting anxious—ye canna hurry the law. But now you see how worthwhile the waiting's been."

"Do you mind if Gilbert and me ride into Machlin with you, Mr. Aiken? There are a few purchases we would like to make—and you could have our company?"

"Certainly, Robin: your company will be verra welcome. Saddle the ponies and I'll be ready."

Riding into Machlin Robin told Aiken how they had decided to sign the lease for Mossgiel.

"There's nothing to be gained in waiting. You see how it is with my father: he may go any day. Indeed this shock may prove fatal."

"Aye . . . your father's far gone, Robin—though I did my best to cheer him up. You couldna do better nor fix on Mossgiel. My business wi' Gavin will not delay me long and I'll tell him the good news so that he'll be ready for you."

"You are verra kind, Mr. Aiken: I don't know how we shall ever be able to repay you far less thank you."

"Ne'er fash yoursel', Rab. Man, it's a pleasure to dae honest folk an honest turn in this warld—and especially an honest man like William Burns. Aye . . . you've had a maist remarkable parent, Rab; maist remarkable. . ."

Robin and Gilbert came out of Gavin Hamilton's business room into the Backcauseway. They were in high spirits.

"Well, Gibby: that's you and me farmers on our own account now. Even though we don't get into Mossgiel till the spring, it's ours from November."

"Aye: it makes you feel different, Robin. Gives you an added sense of responsibility—as well as solid satisfaction."

"What about some liquid satisfaction? We'll cut through the Kirkyard here and see what John Dow has to offer us in the Whitefoord Arms."

"I don't mind, Robin. That was a good whisky Gavin Hamilton gave us to seal the bargain. Aye . . . I like the cut o' Gavin Hamilton. There's all the difference betwixt a gentleman like him and a scoundrel like MacLure."

"Of course there is. Ah, but MacLure'll no' find enough whisky in Ayr to drown his sorrows this day. Damnit, Gibby, we're passing rich compared with the way we thought things would turn out."

John Dow was busy with his ale when they entered, but he showed them into a back room.

"You'll be quiet ben here, gentlemen, if you want to crack and ease your shanks—and it'll give your pownies time to eat their bite."

When they were alone Robin raised his stoup. "Well, Gibby: here's to our success in our new venture—and the beggars' benison wi'it a'."

"And here's to William Burns, and may this glorious news bring him a new lease of life—and peace of mind to die happy."

"Amen to that, Gibby, amen. Here's to us, one and all—and may we prosper."

They were in high spirit. Their journey through the long black night of trial and tribulation was ended.

"Gibby: I think we're going to like Machlin better than we liked Tarbolton."

"Tarbolton's all right: we have had many a happy night there."

"Agreed, agreed; but there's more life in Machlin: you can see that without straining your eyes. There's more life here, Gibby; and it's a better life."

"I don't know: we have good friends in Tarbolton."

"Aye; and a lot of damned poor ones. There are plenty would be pleased to see us rouped out of Lochlea. But hold on, Gibby: we'll show them a thing or two when we get settled into Mossgiel. . ."

"Aye . . . but we'll have little time for Machlin when we are settled in Mossgiel: there'll be too much work to do."

"I suppose so. . . But there will need to be some time

. . . we can't be slaves all the time. . . Damnit, we've been slaves far too long. To hell with them, Gibby! You only live once. There's William Burns: never had a moment's pleasure in his life——"

"I wouldna say that. His idea of pleasure and yours differs: that's all."

"Oh: I don't think that's all: how the hell can you make out that he has had pleasure? Unless you count slavery pleasure?"

"If you havena got money you have to slave; and that's that! William Burns has had his moments of happiness . . . his own kind of happiness. You can get too bitter, Robin . . . you ken fine the majority of folk have to work all their days."

"Bitter? Sometimes I wonder, Gibby, if we're made o' the same flesh and blood?"

"You don't doubt that, do you?"

"Oh, not literally. . . But there are times when we both look at the same object; and you see it black and I see it white. How do you account for that?"

"I don't know; and I don't think we see things as differently as you make out. We aren't always looking at the same things."

"The main thing is that we have agreed to take on Mossgiel together and to make a job of it. And if I find I can do that best by taking a run down to Machlin of a night that'll be my business. . ."

"I hope you won't come here too often."

"There are lots of things I would like to see and do here. . . . But don't worry: I'll work. I've aey worked."

"Aye . . . except when you got more interested in a book or a ballad."

"You mean I let the horses take their own road through the parks? There was damn all in that. There are times when a horse knows its way better than ony human body. I might have had my nose in a book or a ballad when I was driving carts across the parks . . . but I never had my nose in a book when I was ploughing—had I?"

"It was a bad example to the younger ones."

"Oh, to hell, Gibby: you're becoming a bluidy Puritan. But here's John Richmond, Gavin Hamilton's clerk: I want to introduce you to him."

Richmond came over with his drink and, at Robin's invitation, sat down at their table.

"This is my brother Gilbert, Mr. Richmond. I would ask you to extend to him the same courtesy that you have extended to me."

"Certainly, Mr. Burns. I am honoured, Mr. Gilbert, to make your acquaintance."

Gilbert shook him by the hand and nodded. He was not sure that he liked John Richmond. His face was intelligent enough and his manners were beyond cavil. But there was something about him that seemed unstable—as if there was no real backbone to him.

Presently another young man came in and Richmond introduced him as James Smith.

Though short of stature and slight of build, Smith had a cheery red-complexioned face; and it was immediately obvious that he was lacking in guile and cunning.

"You'll join us, Mr. Smith?"

They talked about Machlin, its points of interest; they discussed the local people and passed some criticism on Daddy Auld.

Both Smith and Richmond were some four years younger than Robin. Though they were so much dissimilar in physical build, they were of the same age.

Gilbert could see that already they were looking up to Robin with respect and that Robin was drawing them out very skilfully.

And then Richmond said: "I have copies of your poem on your pet yowe, Mr. Burns. Mr. Hamilton gave me a set to copy and I took the liberty of making a copy for myself. . .

Indeed I have committed it to memory; and Jamie here has done the same."

"So my poor verses have come to Machlin before me?"

"Not poor, Mr. Burns. Indeed, we think them of particular excellence."

"You do?"

"Aye," said Jamie, who had not the English of his companion but who spoke in the broad Scots of Machlin, "I thocht they were real like the thing. You havena ony mair like them, have you?"

"Maybe, Jamie—I think we can dispense with formalities —I'll see what I have got copies of and let you know."

"Well, Mr.——"

"Robin, Robert, Rab: I acknowledge them all."

"Well . . . if you have any, Robert . . . it would be an honour——"

"Oh, damn the honour—— Mr. Hamilton didn't give you my Corn Rigs to copy, did he?"

"No . . ."

"And what's your business in Machlin, Jamie?"

"You see, I'm a step-bairn. After I lost my father my mother married James Lamie. I got her father's draper's shop —facing the Cross."

"Is your step-father Jamie Lamie the elder?"

"Aye . . . that's him. Lamie and Willie Fisher are Daddy Auld's chief disciples. You should hear Lamie laying down the gospel—according to Lamie. . ."

"I think we should be getting back to Lochlea, Robin. . ."

"Why? You're enjoying yourself?"

"I think I'll push on ahead."

"No: I'll come with you. Well, lads, I'll maybe have the opportunity of knowing you a lot better."

"I hope so, Mr. Burns. We've enjoyed your company——"

"Aye: it's no' often we get a chance o' meeting with a real poet."

"Damn the poet! We'll meet some other day and have a proper session."

Riding home, Gilbert did not say much; but he thought plenty. And he thought that Robin would need to be careful and watch his step with Machlin lads like Smith and Richmond. They were not like the lads of Tarbolton: Davie Sillar, Willie MacGavin. Without being able to give himself any explanation, he just did not feel easy about the promise of their future acquaintance with Robin—for Gilbert knew only too well how little it needed for Robin to be tempted into the easy social hour of the tavern.

THE HARD ROAD

But the hell-hounds that growl round the kennels of justice were not to be so easily placated as Robert Aiken had imagined.

No sooner had Sundrum's decision reached the public ear than William Burns was flabbergasted to find the number of claimants for the money he had thought was due to MacLure.

When John MacAdam of Craigengillan—who had a reputation for honesty—made claim to the money as the man having heritable security over Lochlea and the adjoining lands, William became so excited that Robin had to ride into Ayr and consult with Aiken.

He galloped into Ayr in a towering rage, handed over his steaming pony to the groom at Simson's Inn and stormed into Aiken's sanctum.

Aiken saw at a glance that something was amiss; but he was experienced enough to let Robin have his head.

"What manner of bluidy vultures run the law of this country, Mr. Aiken? If there's no such thing as justice then for heaven's sake tell me and let me go. Good God, sir, have I to stand idly by and watch a dying parent being murdered on his deathbed? Murdered, sir—as bluidy a crime as could be committed. Is it only when every penny has been robbed from us that the law will turn and tell us we can no longer hope for justice? As you have given me your advice and extended to me the hand of friendship, I beg of you to tell me the truth—hellish though that truth may be."

"Weel, sit doon, man, and dinna stand there wi' battle flashing in your eye. Tell me what's the matter and I'll tell you the truth—as far as I can."

"Here's a letter from Craigengillan. Is it truth or a pack o' bluidy lies?"

Aiken read the letter. He jerked himself to his feet.

"God damnit, Burns—this puts the fat in the fire."

"Whose fat? There's damned little fat left about Lochlea."

"But damnit, man, Craigengillan's a trustee of the Douglas and Heron Bank, and if I ken how mony beans mak' five MacLure's holdings are mortgaged to the Bank. It means MacLure's no legal right to a brown bawbee. By certes, Robin, and this makes a sow wi' a different snout. Here! We'll go round and hae a word wi' Ballantine: he's got a watching brief on this case as it were—and this'll gar him whistle."

"But Craigengillan's no' the only one that's claiming our money. We've heard talk o' others. The vultures are gathering, Mr. Aiken. Do they all want a pick at my poor father's bones?"

"Half the county'll be claiming this money yet. The Lord kens where MacLure's rights begin and end."

Ballantine ordered another drink. "There's nothing for it, Bob, but to take this matter before the Court of Session in Edinburgh and beg for a suspension of liability."

"That's exactly my own opinion, John: you've taken the words out o' my verra mouth. Apply for suspension—and then let them fight it out like a pack o' famished curs ower a marrow bone."

"And what does this mean by way of expense?"

"Nothing much, Robin. There's nae need to look sae glum, lad."

"I think we've friends in Edinburgh, Bob, who'll keep the expense down. I'll see what I can do if you wish."

"The verra thing, John."

"And what have I to tell my father?"

"Tell him MacLure won't get a penny once the Session grants the bill. That'll cheer him up."

"And meanwhile he'll just need to thole the worry and anxiety?"

Ballantine was sympathetic.

"Listen, Robin: nobody could have foreseen this development. The affairs of the country have been in a turmoil ever since the bank failed. All through the West here the best families have been plunged into ruination and misery. Folks dinna rightly know where they stand. But don't fret yourself: we'll see this thing through to the end—and in the end everything will turn out in your favour."

"You must forgive me if I've appeared ungrateful. But this has been a terrible shock to us all. Here I am just signed the lease for Mossgiel and I don't know if we'll ever have the money to stock it. In honest truth, gentlemen, I have little heart left to go back to Lochlea and face my family."

Despondency settled like a thunder cloud over Lochlea. The family waited anxiously for the cloud to disperse—or the storm to break.

Towards the end of the month a letter came from Aiken. It enclosed the verdict of the Session. "The Lord Ordinary, having considered this Bill: In respect that complainer has not specially stated before what Court he is sued at Craigengillan's instance nor has produced evidence of such actions nor has raised any multiple-poinding, refuses this Bill."

Aiken's covering letter sought to explain how the Edinburgh agent had merely slipped up on a technical point—a trifling matter of the correct legal phraseology and due form. . .

Robin and Gilbert slipped out from the weeping household. The world of nature seemed to be weeping in sympathy. A smir of late autumn rain hid the low hills around the steading. The breath of the summer's decay was thick in the damp air.

Their thin crops had been ingathered and safely stacked in the barn. But they had little heart for threshing. The heart of Lochlea had been destroyed on them. The wet bare rigs held no promise for another spring; and the thin pipe of the robin from the broken fence was lost in the grey melancholy, brave-hearted though its piping was.

The brothers moved slowly round to the shelter of the gable-end of the barn.

Gilbert was the first to break the silence.

"In God's name what's to happen to us now?"

"In God's name, aye. Man Gilbert, this is more than flesh and blood can bear. I don't know where to turn. And what's the good of turning? We're beaten every way we turn. Oh, I don't know, I don't know. . ."

"But you'll need to go to Ayr and consult wi' Aiken: you see what he says. It's just a technical slip. He's making another appeal."

"Have you any faith in them?"

"No: I canna say I have, Robin. But what can we do? Just wait till we're bankrupt and flung in the ditch?"

"The ditch? In some ways the ditch would be better: we'd know we could fall no lower! That's where they want to put us. We committed a grave sin when we aspired to raise our heads above the muck. Who were we to think we could be tenant farmers and earn an honest living on the soil? Soil, did I say? Wet bogs and stony braes! Gilbert: you can reason as you like: it's man's inhumanity to man that's at the root of most human misery and hardship. The dice are loaded: to him that hath—you know the rest."

Robin's young collie dog, Luath, licked the back of his hand where it hung by his side. In response he pulled gently at his ear.

"Even the dumb brute will show you more sympathy. God, Gilbert, but I'm weary o' all this."

Gilbert rubbed his hand across his face in a forlorn gesture.

"If you canna see a road out o' this, Robin, how are the rest o' us to see?"

"It's too late to ride into Ayr. But I'll go first thing in the morning. Not that it'll do a damned bit o' good, Gilbert; but it'll maybe ease my father's mind. However much we have to worry about, it doesn't take much imagination to realise something o' what he must be suffering. I may live to be eighty—which I verra much doubt—but that's something I'll never forget—nor forgive. Forgiveness is Mine, saith the Lord. I'll leave whatever forgiveness there's to be in His hands: I'll do the remembering. . . Fetch out my plaid like a good lad: I've a notion to walk over the hill."

"Can I come wi' you, Robin? I winna talk ony."

"All right, Gibby—fetch the plaids and come on. We've no heart for working and we canna sit in the house."

When Gilbert was gone for the plaids Robin patted Luath.

"Aye, boy. You ken fine what's wrong. But, rain or sorrow, you like fine to run across the braes. Weel: run till your tongue's hanging out, boy. Run while you're young and get the chance. . . And wave that gawcie tail o' yours abune your hurdies. You'll no' aey be young; but the hard road'll aey be a wheen o' miles afore you and though you run till you dee you'll never mak' the end o't."

"You're a sweet lass, Betty. I'm damned if I ken what I'd do without you."

"I couldna dae without you, Rab: you're guid tae me."

"I'm speaking the God's truth, Betty: I would need to have ta'en to the hills long ago if it hadna been for you."

"You mean wi' your poor father—an' a' this trouble wi' the lawyers? Aye: you've had a terrible time. D'you no' see ony licht yet?"

"Licht? Less licht than there is in the loft here."

"Och, something'll turn up. Cuddle doon, Rab, and tell me mair o' your verses."

They were lying together in the stable loft. It was the middle of December and the snow lay thick on the roads and drifted to great depths in the hollows of the land. It was a bad time for man and beast and for poor devils who had to travel.

The weather had immobilised the household. They had threshed all they could, battled their straw, repaired carts and gear and finished every odd job they could think of.

The lack of work added to all their difficulties. They were all worried and the women-folks were overworked even though the snow had brought some of them a temporary respite.

Inside the house the gloom and worry, the heartbreak and anxiety mounted in an atmosphere of agonising tension. Nerves were frayed and tempers brittle.

Night brought little ease to the situation. Agnes, partly undressed, lay down beside her dying husband; Willie and the ailing John shared a shakedown beyond the fire; Nancy and Bell, and Isa and Betty slept in the spence; Robin and Gilbert were more fortunate; they escaped to the small triangular loft, entered by way of a ladder from the gable-end.

And so Robin and Betty would meet in the stable loft, driven together by every circumstance and the mutual attraction of their blood.

Betty was indeed a sweet lass. If she had not the education of Robin's sisters, she was not lacking in lively intelligence. Her home at Largieside was a happy one and she had escaped the blighting effects of the Old Light theology. Neither her father nor her mother gave a snap of their honest thumbs for doctrine. They paid the minimum of outward respect to the kirk and lived as the day found them. And as Betty had no natural bent towards Puritanism and suffered from no physical or mental repressions, she was as free with her tongue as she was with the caresses of her finely proportioned body.

She knew almost as many of the old bawdy peasant songs as Robin; and she enjoyed many of them with an unself-conscious enjoyment.

Robin delighted in her unsophisticated, easy-going love and enjoyed the fresh naturalness of her reactions. And it was blessed relief to lie in the hay with her, kissing and cuddling, or saying his poems over to her, or talking quietly about his future hopes and ambitions.

Their companionship was innocent enough. Robin never really escaped from the presence of his dying father. That presence was a barrier at the end of their intimacy: an inviolate barrier as long as William Burns lived.

And so when Gilbert indicated that he knew their secret and added a mild and well-intentioned reproof, Robin rounded on him fiercely.

"By God, Gilbert, keep yourself to yourself and leave me alone. If you say a word to anybody I'll lay hands on you. Don't sit in judgment on me, neither you nor any other body. I'll answer for myself. I know when I'm doing right and when I'm doing wrong; and I don't need any advice from you. Don't sneak behind my back; and don't spy on me: that's something I canna thole. And mind: if you as much as make a move to take your spite out on Betty I'll see the reddest of you—brother or no brother."

Gilbert swallowed his chagrin and said nothing. He knew Robin too well to risk his wrath beyond the violence of his tongue.

But it did not make things any happier in the house; and there were nights when the estrangement between them made sleeping together an unnatural ordeal.

William's last days were pitiful. It was terrible to think that so emaciated a human being could yet live. The features were worn to the sharpness of a blunted axe, yet only in the sunken eye-sockets did life smoulder and burn. . .

William did not rage nor did he babble. Often enough he lamented the hardness and injustice of his days. Sometimes his mind wandered and he would talk of his boyhood at Clochnahill; of his father and his brothers and sisters. . . Sometimes he would rage at Agnes about some trifling matter and he would often speak sharply to Robin and Gilbert about their work on the farm . . . and there were periods when he mourned. He would talk to his wife in far away accents.

"We have travelled the sore road, Agnes, and the Lord has set His hand against us. He has seen fit to visit me as He visited Job . . . aye, but we mustn't complain. The Lord's will be done. I did my best and neither you nor me ever spared ourselves any. . . I mind when I first met you at Kirkoswald Fair: that was in '57 . . . aye, there was a bloom on your cheek then and your hair was golden. And I mind how I built the house at Alloway. We had happy times at Alloway— blinks of happiness atween the showers of trouble. . .

"Agnes: I set my heart on Robin: my heart's still set on him. But, lass, I worry for him. I can leave you all, for I ken you will fear the Lord and do what's right. But Robin . . . poor lad: he's gotten a wayward mind. . . And I misdoubt but he's troubled with the lusts of the flesh. Not that there's any real bad in him. . . It seems he's fated to be a rebel; but I fear he'll be a rebel against the Lord.

"Gilbert's your favourite, Agnes: I ken that. But Robin, if he would only put his trust in the Lord and keep to the paths of righteousness, would be a credit to you all. Robin has gifts from the Lord he kens nothing about. Great gifts. . . You say Betty Paton would make him a good wife. . . Maybe you're right, lass; and maybe it would be the best thing he could do to get married. Maybe the marriage bed would settle him . . . I don't know; but I doubt if Lizzie's the lass for him. . ."

So William talked to his wife when he was in quiet mood and his voice was a far away murmur of resignation.

But such moods were not frequent and it was not often that they had the kitchen to themselves. For long periods William lay with his eyes closed and, when he did not sleep, tried not to think. . . He tried to make his peace with life even as he imagined he had made his peace with God.

But it was beyond William Burns not to think. . .

Sometimes he lay and watched the spiders at work above his head on the rafters. Sometimes he would be content to watch the peat flames flicker across the rough sooty beams. The light might penetrate into the shadows above and catching a broken thatch straw gild it like a golden thread. He knew every crack in the rafters above his head; knew every axe mark; knew every crack in the walls. But nothing escaped his attention. He knew every wrinkle in his wife's face, so long had he studied her profile against the light of the fire; and Agnes's face was wrinkled more than her years justified. She was shockingly bowed. She did not walk so much as shuffle in a stooped position. Her tone was often querulous. She was in pitiful contrast to the woman who had stood on the beaten earthen floor at Alloway twenty-odd years ago. . .

There was nothing to be seen out the small window: the

panes were too small and the glass distorted. So he was compelled to turn his gaze inwards on the stuffy and over-familiar interior.

For the most part he lived for meal-times when his family were gathered round the table. The family were conscious of the eyes of their dying father and they felt—except the younger ones—ill at ease. Robin especially was uncomfortable. He occupied his father's seat at the head of the table and so faced the bed where he lay. And too often William's gaze lingered on Robert—who was thus driven to eat with lowered head and to rise from the table the moment his food was finished. He was driven to avoid his father's presence by every wile and stratagem he could muster. . .

And then William sank so low that he could no longer take an interest in the day-to-day, hour-to-hour happenings within the household. He lay sunk on the bed and was now so worn and emaciated that his form could scarcely be seen through the bed clothes.

At the beginning of February word came from Edinburgh that the Court of Session, with Lord Braxfield presiding, had given judgment in favour of William Burns.

All the years of his fighting had been justified; he was proved to be a just and upright man; MacLure and his associates (Paterson had fled the country and had been cried at the Pier of Leith) had been finally frustrated.

But the justification, the vindication, had come too late. When the decision was conveyed to him, William Burns groaned and turned his face to the wall.

There was a grain of comfort for Robin and Gilbert: they now knew where they stood; knew just to a penny how much hard cash they would be able to salvage. They knew what would go to the Douglas and Heron trusts: they knew what had gone and was going to the lawyers. As preferred creditors they would have their wages. And since their father could not live much longer—Doctor MacKenzie had said the end would be any day now—they could reckon on taking on Mossgiel with a bare minimum of cash—and no credit. They would have to build up the credit with their blood and bones: all of them.

Now that he was dying, it did not matter to William that he had won the long battle with MacLure: he was losing the longer battle with life.

In his sixty-third year, on the morning of the 13th of February, a bleak day of seeping rain, he died.

He knew his hour had come and the family, knowing too, were gathered in the kitchen. No one thought of work.

Agnes stood at the bedside attending to his needs, wiping his lips and drying the sweat from his brow.

Gilbert was by his mother; but Robin had retreated to the farthest corner of the room, and sat in the shadow, elbow on knee, head in hand. . .

William was normally conscious. He blessed the family, spoke a kindly word to each in turn, patted Isobel on the head and abjured her to walk steadfastly the path of salvation.

"I can leave you," he said, "having no fear but that you will walk uprightly in the fear of the Lord. . . Where's Robin?"

Robin sprang up and came to the bedside.

"I'm here, father."

William looked at him for a moment.

"I canna withhold my blessing from you, laddie—you least of all—and I'm leaving you wi' a sair responsibility. But I fear for you, laddie—you are gifted above the lave. . . Remember the Lord will expect more from you than from those less gifted. . . I fear for you, Robin, for I know the snares and temptations that await you on your journey through life. All I can do is to ask you to remember your Maker . . . and to . . . keep His commandments alway. . ."

Robin had a savage grip of the bed-rail. He was conscious of the sobbing in the room, conscious of the dying away of his father's voice.

God in Heaven have mercy on broken souls when it comes the hour to sunder from the broken body. He had a sudden vision of mankind struggling and toiling across the wilderness of time; and always when their trials and tribulations were sorest came the hope of the promised land, the promised land they never entered into; for always death came and gathered the generations to the dust. . .

The vision came in a flash against the inward eye for the outward eye was congested with bitter tears. He might have spoken to his father but his vocal chords were tautened beyond any conscious control.

William Burns sank back on the pillow and closed his eyes. Robin tore himself from the foot of the bed and turned to the small window where the grey daylight filtered into the room. The tears came burning and blinding to his eyes.

He could not watch his mother wipe the bloody froth from his father's lips. . . His instinct was to wrench open the door and escape to the hills. But he could not desert the room while there was breath in his father's body. . .

And then it was all over. William Burns lay there stiff and cold with the awful greyness of death on his hands and face.

The long stony journey from Clochnahill through the Scottish wilderness had ended in Lochlea; and his soul was now gone on a journey there was no knowing whence or whither.

They had waited so long on his dying they had thought that when death did come their grief would be blunted.

It was not so. Now that he lay there in the ghastly mould of death—and yet somehow child-like and infinitely pathetic —their grief was overwhelming.

But when the first engulfing waves had passed over, the two who showed least sign of sorrow were Robin and his mother.

THE LONG DARK NIGHT

The funeral arrangements had already been made: nothing remained but to call the mourners together.

William had no wish to be happed in Tarbolton clay. He had expressed a desire to be buried where he had known most happiness: Alloway. The first six or seven years there had been the happiest he had known.

So they slung the coffin on two long poles, with a pony fore and aft, and moved off after the Reverend John MacMath, Doctor Woodrow's assistant. had said a service in the court—the kitchen being much too small to accommodate the mourners.

They were a goodly company as they rode off with Robin and MacMath in the van. Gilbert followed with William Muir of the Mill. John Rankine was there, Willie Paton (Betty's father) from Largieside; Charles Norvell from Coilsfield and most of the neighbouring farmers.

Tennant, his old neighbour from the Mount Oliphant days, had sent his eldest son, James. There had ever been a warm friendship between the families. Auld Glenconnar thought very highly of William Burns; but he thought just as highly of Robert—and Gilbert.

It took four hours to make the journey for the roads were wet and boggy. And the company had to be refreshed. Every man had brought his own supply of whisky and some had a small cask of ale strapped to their saddles.

They went by Ayr and stopped at the Brigend Inn to have a coggie of Simson's mutton broth, a whang of cheese and some bannocks.

Here Aiken and Ballantine and other Ayr friends joined

them for the final stage of the journey so that they might be present at the kirk-yard service which was being conducted by William Dalrymple's assistant, Doctor MacGill.

One of William's last tasks when he had stayed in Alloway had been to repair the stone dyke round the grave-yard of the deserted Alloway Kirk.

It was a small grey building standing in a small grey kirk-yard sheltered by a group of bare stunted trees.

But for Robin and Gilbert the scene was rich with memories of childhood. Now they stood at the head and foot of their father's coffin beside the mound of freshly dug earth.

The rain had ceased for the moment; but the sky was grey and lowering. A whaup, flying in from the shore by the mouth of the Doon river, cried its short-long call and headed for the moorlands above Mount Oliphant. But beyond the distant clip-clop of a receding horseman there was no sound to disturb the solemn intoning of Doctor MacGill.

MacGill added a personal tribute. He had valued William Burns very highly: for over a quarter of a century he had been a member of the Auld Kirk in Ayr . . . now for a surety would the good and faithful servant enter into the kingdom prepared for him.

John MacMath, gaunt and nervous, added his testimony. William Burns, most upright and steadfast of men, had been with them in Tarbolton for eight years.

And then he was intoning in a harsh sepulchral voice: The wind bloweth over the green grass; it withereth. . . The Lord giveth and the Lord taketh away. . .

The rain came up in a bitter blinding shower from the sea. The mort cloth was withdrawn and the grave-digger hastened to hap the wet clay round the plain deal coffin. . .

They were shaking hands solemnly with Robin and Gilbert. Willie Muir of Tarbolton Mill was not ashamed to dash the big tears from his eyes with the back of his hand.

There was a tug at his sleeve and Robin turned to find John Tennant, the Alloway blacksmith.

"Aye, Robin lad, it's a sair time to find you. I had to come across and pay my last respects tae your father. Aye . . . I mind whan he cam' first tae Alloway. . . He was a lang time bed-ridden, they tell me? Aye, he's maybe better awa'; it's what we a' come tae in the end, laddie. . . God bless you, Robin: you've a gey heavy burden on you now. . ."

And after John Tennant came Jamie Young, hirpling with rheumatism, to offer his condolences and shake hands.

As he watched the company file out of the graveyard and gather on the roadside, Robin wondered at the respect his father had won in the hearts of the Ayrshire men.

Back they rode to Simson's. There they laid aside their crape ribboned hats and bonnets and talked more freely.

John MacMath drank liberally. . . He relieved himself of some conventional pieties and then, when the drink began to thaw out his emotions, he leaned across the table and said to Robin:

"This is for your own ear, Robert. Every time I officiate at a burial I feel envious o' the corpse. Aye: you may think that strange. However hard it may be to die, once you are dead all sorrow, all suffering is ended. And it's my own private opinion that you're beyond suffering forever and ever. . . . Amen. Not only beyond suffering but beyond *knowing*. Nothing can ever bring back consciousness. That's a great relief, Robert, a great relief. I'm afraid, I'm afraid, I canna believe—for myself—in personal immortality. Maybe I shock you; but I know you'll never come over my words. So I wouldna grieve for your father—he's best quit of it all."

"I suppose so. . . But if there is a hereafter I know he'll have nothing to fear."

"Nothing. . . Fear is with us while we live. It is only when we are living that evil can hurt us. Ah, Robert lad: I've pondered this many long gloomy hours—death, I'm convinced, is the great deliverer from all evil, from all pain and suffering."

Then the Reverend John MacMath, who was still a young man, took a great drink of neat spirit, grimaced, and lapsed into moody silence.

Robert went over to the table where Aiken and Ballantine were in conversation with John Rankine. He fished a sheet of paper from his pocket.

"I thought you might like to pass judgment on an epitaph I have drafted out for my father's stone when it is put up."

"Certainly, Robert," said Ballantine. "Read it over to us—if you feel equal to the occasion."

Robin sat down and read from the sheet:

"O ye whose cheek the tear of pity stains, draw near with pious rev'rence, and attend! Here lie the loving husband's dear remains, the tender father, and the gen'rous friend; the pitying heart that felt for human woe, the dauntless heart that fear'd no human pride; the friend of man—to vice alone a foe; for 'ev'n his failings lean'd to virtue's side.'"

Ballantine said: "I could think of nothing more fitting or more nobly expressed, Robert."

Aiken said: "Amen to that, John."

Rankine said: "That's the honest God's truth: every line o't; and that's more than can be said o' the feck o' sentiments that get chiselled on a headstane. I ken of no man in the West the wham befits it better."

Tennant said: "I would fain have a copy of that to take back to my father in Glenconnar. He would treasure it even as I would, Robin—you know that."

Robin handed him the single sheet. "It's no' likely I'll ever forget these lines."

They stopped for a last drink at Manson's in Tarbolton, though some, pleading the lateness of the hour, pushed on home.

In Manson's John Rankine said:

"Death is a final thing, Robin, and there's no argument

about it. It's the road we all go. Aye . . . and we never know the day. Some are cut down in their prime. Others, like your father, hae a long sair death. Aye . . . that's how it is. In the midst o' life there is death. But take it head for tail and what do you get? In the midst o' death there is life. . . In this case, you're the life, Robin. You're the head o' the house now, lad. And I know you'll put your best foot forward. And you're quit o' Lochlea. . . Mind you, I'll miss you and you over there in Mossgiel. But . . . you'll come and see me?"

"I'll come and see you, John."

"And you'll no' miss the Mill?" asked Willie Muir.

"You'd think we were going to the ends o' the earth. You'll be seeing me. Maybe not as much as in the past—at least not until we get settled. It's not going to be easy in Mossgiel. But we're all agreed to put our back into it. It's a joint concern. So good-bye to the nappy and good-bye to the Muse. The sober prose o' farming books'll be my reading diet from henceforth. I promised that to him who lies back there in Alloway kirk-yard; and I'll keep *that* promise."

"That's a hard promise, Robin."

"Aye . . . but it's a sensible one. You can turn men's minds with a poem; but you canna turn upland soil with one."

"Damned, for you, Robin, I misdoubt but there's ony other way. Dinna think to plough your gifts intil the ground."

Willie Muir said: "Your father, Robin, that's wi' his Maker now, was prouder o' your poetry than he was o' your ploughing—and he'd nae faut to find wi' that. Mony a time he's spoken in the Mill about your abilities. And you should hae seen the light in his eyes when he spoke o' you. 'That laddie o' mine,' he said to me ae nicht, 'if only I'd been able to give him a better schooling, would hae surprised the world. As it is, I misdoubt nor he'll be a credit to Scotland.' Now —that's his words. I canna see that your father meant you to give up the verses, Robin."

"Maybe no. God knows but I owe him everything—everything. From the earliest day I can mind on, he struggled to give me an education. He used to sit till he was bleary eyed spelling out the words to me when I was hardly above toddling across the floor o' that auld clay biggin' in Alloway that he bigged with his own two hands. I never knew him to spare himself in our well-being. Aye . . . and he'd struggle his way through mathematics wi' Gilbert an' me. Nothing was any bother: nothing could break his patience in those days. Strict—yes; but gentle. Quiet and gentle even as a woman couldna hae been quiet and gentle. Never raising his voice. And he worked himself—slaved himself—into the grave. And that MacLure—I don't want to swear to-day for he never let an oath pass his lips. Never. No matter what the provocation, no man ever heard a bad word on the lips of William Burns. You knew him better than onybody outside the family, Willie: you can vouch for that?"

"I can, Robin. I never heard an ill word on his lips."

"That's not to say he didn't have angry or bitter words. Aye; but no man had more cause for them—no man. And he was neither angry nor bitter till he was driven by cruelty and injustice far beyond breaking point. And that didn't start with MacLure and his crooked cronies either. It started away back in Mount Oliphant after Provost Fergusson died and his affairs got into the hands of a soulless lawyer."

"Aye . . . but did you ever ken o' a lawyer that wasn't soulless, Robin?"

"Well, there's Bob Aiken and Gavin Hamilton?"

"Ah, but they're no' that kind o' lawyer. You know the kind I mean. The kind that the gentry employ to hound honest folk into debtors' gaols and to manage their affairs while they go skiting ower the kintraside—or awa' tae Lunnon. Aye, or maybe abroad in foreign lands."

"Maybe you're right, John. If there's such a thing as justice—which I very much doubt—my father's all has gone amongst them that dispense it."

"Aye," said James Tennant, "but that's aey the way of things. Whenever you bring in the lawyers, the siller goes like snaw from a dyke. I've seen mony a family brought to ruin by going to law."

They talked over another ale. Death was much nearer to John Rankine and Willie Muir than it was to Robin or James Tennant. The older men were anxious to relieve themselves in conversation, to reassure themselves that they had nothing to fear.

But gradually talk wore thin and the party broke up. Robin said good-bye and rode home with James Tennant who, living some eight miles beyond in Glenconnar in the parish of Ochiltree, was staying the night with him.

James was some five years older than Robin but this made no difference to the warmth of their friendship. When Robin visited Glenconnar it was always James who rode back with him to the brow of the hill.

"Mind you, Robin, my father was gey disappointed that he wasna well enough to pay his last respects . . . he would have been proud of the company to-day. You'll need to try and win over to Glenconnar some fine Sabbath. I know it'll no' be easy for you and you settling into Mossgiel. But Auld Glen looks forward to your visits—but I don't need to tell you that."

"Aye—Auld Glen and William Burns belong to the old-style Scots—we'll no' see their like again. Don't think I place a small value on your father's friendship, James—or the friendship of your brothers and sisters. I've had many a happy day both at Laigh Corton and Glenconnar—and I hope to have many yet. It's only at a death, when you see folk gathered in a common bond round the open grave, that you realise what friendship means. Life would be damned dreich without it."

"You know if there's onything we can do for you to help you get settled down in Mossgiel you hae only to ask."

"Only to ask. . . Sometimes that's harder than you would think, Jamie."

"But you'll no' hold back for the asking——?"

"No. . . Mind you: it was little William Burns asked for in this world: gey little. If the Almighty could have looked on his suffering much longer, I couldna. There's a theological answer to that problem as you well know. But theology and life have a queer way o' girning at each other across the hob o' hell. . . It's easy to thunder from the pulpit from off the Big Black Book and drive out theological heresy with theological truth; but it's no' the thin sour wine o' theological doctrine that floods the human heart; nor are the bowels o' human compassion wrung wi' doctrinal diatribes. . . . And if William Burns is now gathered to Eternal Glory where's the sense in it?"

"You mauna think things like that, Rab——"

"Mauna? The Kirk and State can say mauna, Jamie. 'Deed, that's the feck o' their philosophy. But you can't say no to life. You can't deny the thoughts that come to you from the contradictions of our earthly experience. The life and death o' William Burns is but the owercome of ten thousand sangs. But however often I hear that chorus, I find no sense in it. Nor can I see that a gowpen o' gowd should daud doon the balance atween happiness and misery. . . And yet a mere handful o' siller—at the right time—would have saved William Burns's life and ensured his earthly salvation. And does that make sense?"

"It does not."

"And it makes a damned sight less sense to me than it does to you, Jamie. William Burns was a poor but honest tacksman in Lochlea to the good friends that gathered to see him decently happed away at Alloway—but William Burns was my father. . ."

As they dismounted at the Lochlea road-end they could see a light burning in the window. A great breath of wind gusting up from the sea soughed over the low thatched biggings near at hand: a dog raised its muzzle in the mirk and howled long and piteously at the night.

Head of the house now and weighted with great responsibilities, he thought how life at Lochlea had come to its final and irrevocable end.

The wind bloweth where it listeth. . . Aye: the wind that shakes the barley; and the naked tree. . . The wind that moans the fate of men and sighs the sorrows of the world.

The wind and the darkness and the piteous howling of dumb pain. . . And yet, as he tugged at the bridle and his wet feet slipped in the mire he knew that corn rigs and barley rigs would burgeon forth again; that the battle of life would be renewed; that love and laughter and hope and faith had not died in the world of men.

A man died and his friends bowed their heads in the sorrow of his passing; but, having passed, their heads were once more lifted up.

He bade James Tennant enter the house, called the howling dog to his heel and led the pownies to the stable where the cruisie light caressed the darkness.

"You're back," said Gilbert, sliding down from the corn kist and reaching out for a bridle. "It's queer; but that dog wouldn't stop howling till you came."

"Rub down the pownies, Gilbert: I'm ower tired. We're by wi' howling now. John Rankine has the right way o' things: in the midst of death there is life."

He bent down and stroked the long head of the collie. "God! but I'll sleep sound the night."

There was a soft movement. He raised his eyes. Betty Paton stood hesitant in the doorway.

"Mrs. Burns is asking for you, Rab."

"Verra well, Betty: I'm coming."

He placed a tired hand on her warm shoulder.

"I'm giving up my bed to our guest from Glenconnar: fetch across some blankets and shake them down in the loft here."

In the soft caressing light from the cruisie, life shimmered in the hazel glow of Betty's dark eyes.

"And get to bed, lass, and sleep. There's a new life waiting for us all against the dawning."

THE END